FICTION/RELATIONSHIPS: doomed or nonexistent

THE LOSERS' CLUB

"Retro-'90s" East Village Romance

The setting of *The Losers' Club* is New York City. And it tells the story of Martin Sierra, an unlucky writer addicted to the personals. Early he encounters Nikki, his dream woman, who remains unattainable romantically, yet who becomes his friend and confidant during his comic misadventures. Set amid the vibrant bars and clubs of the East Village during the mid '90s, this exhilarating novel is as much about a generation (we won't say "X") as it is about a specific time and place.

"Richard Perez is a clear-eyed chronicler of the New York club scene
and a compassionate observer of the lives lived in the carnival
at the center of the world.
He is a sociologist and a historian, telling the truth
about the way we live now. He's funny, honest, and compassionate.
We can only hope that The Losers' Club is but the first act
in Richard Perez's Human Comedy."

— **John Dufresne,**
Louisiana Power & Light, Love Warps the Mind a Little

The recipient of numerous writing awards, **Richard Perez** was managing editor at Angel Sun Press. He currently lives and writes in Galicia, Spain.

5½ x 8½ / 196 pages / Original Trade Paperback / 0-9713415-9-1 / 12.99

Breakthrough

Fiction Award

Acknowledgments:

A very special thanks to **Ron Kolm**
writer, poet, esteemed
East Village archivist—
for his editorial contributions
to the manuscript in progress.

The author would also
like to express
gratitude to **David Long**
for his
"writing intensive" and
his many, many
insightful suggestions
regarding the
The Losers' Club

Correspondence:
Ludlow Press
P.O. Box 2612 New York, NY 10009-9998
or
mailing@LudlowPress.Com

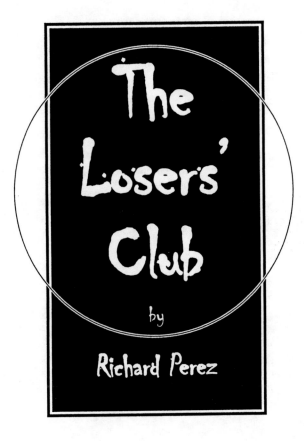

The Losers' Club

by

Richard Perez

Ludlow Press
New York
2003

For permission to reproduce selections from this book
write to:
Ludlow Press
P.O. Box 2612 New York, NY 10009-9998
LudlowPress.Com

<CIP data to follow>

The Losers' Club

AVE C

PIT

RID

A

E. 9TH E. 8TH ST

AVE B

C

S

Tompkins Square Park

E. 5TH

AVE A

East Village

1ST AVENUE

ST ST ST ST ST MARKS PLACE ST ST ST ST ST ST ST

2ND AVENUE

STON ST

13TH 12TH 11TH E. 10TH 7TH E. 7TH E. 6TH E. 5TH E. 4TH E. 3RD E. 2ND E. 1ST

3RD AVENUE

E. E. E. E. ST ST

EL

STUYVESANT ST

AVE

LAFAYETTE ST

FOURTH

ASTOR PL

M

OURTH

WAY

ST

PL ST

For Jane

A pretty face emerged from a pool of darkness.

"Disappointed? Sad? Need someone to talk to? A person who'll understand?" Her voice was soothing, her tone strangely sincere. "Believe me, I know how you feel."

She smiled. "Hi. I'm Sophia. And I'll be that special person, the one you've been looking for."

Her image doubled—split screen: "Reliable. Caring. Always waiting, always here..."

Now there were four identical faces within the frame (the chorus of voices beginning to warp): "Here, waiting ... just for you!"

Again the image divided: to eighths, then sixteenths. "So, tell me. Tell me. What are you waiting for?"

Again and again, it continued to splinter until her face was pixilated and remote, like a reflection caught inside the eye of an insect....

1.

Eyes flicking open, Martin Sierra tipped forward in his office swivel chair. At last, when he realized he could no longer postpone the inevitable—his time nearly done—he issued a long sigh, straightened up, and returned to scribbling on the latest creased manuscript: unfinished work from the previous morning.

Sure enough, hardly a minute later, he heard cursing outside the door as a key jammed in the lock.

"*WAA-AATCH-out!*" swelled the loud, unmistakable voice, finally bursting through.

Martin turned to see *who else* but—?"

"Chaz."

"*WHAT-CHA' doin'*, *bro?*" And, striding up, craning his neck, he caught a peek at what Martin was working on.

"*Revisions*," explained Martin, covering up.

"*Ha!* Revisions. Revisions, *my ass!* Beatin' off *again*, eh?"

"Yeah yeah. Ya got me. I'm so embarrassed," Martin said flatly.

"*Noooo*," he intoned, breaking into a broad imitation of their Japanese boss. "*Literature? Poetry? On the clock, no less!—Martin-san, that is no goood!*"

Martin opened the bottom drawer of his desk and tossed in the marked pages, lightly kicking the drawer shut. "Yeah yeah, I know. No good."

"Some people never learn." Chaz laughed again. Then, slamming down a folded copy of the day's *New York Post* in Martin's lap: "Now *that's* literature."

"Right."

"Any word from the gimp upstairs?"

"Haven't gone up."

Chaz stretched a bit, loudly smacked his belly through his gray NY Knicks sweatshirt, then sauntered back out through the door and into the warehouse to check on the arrival of new freight. Calling out: "*Late again?*"

Martin hung silent.

"'Won't get into that, *eh*?" His voice echoing.

Martin opened the drawer and neatly rearranged his pages of writing, which he then placed in a folder inside his knapsack.

A moment later, Chaz re-entered the office as if for the first time. "Looks like shit, so far. We got shit. Am I right?"

"Shit," concurred Martin. "When you're right, you're right."

2

Chaz finally removed his coat, a gray western-style duster. "There was something else I had to tell you." He scratched his head. "What *was it?*"

"Another phone call?"

"Shit, did I mention that?"

"What?"

"That *chick-pal* of yours—*Rikki*—called?"

"'Nikki?'"

"That's the one."

"When?"

"Yesterday. After you popped over to Customs."

A light blinked on Martin's phone, a Japanese woman's voice crying over the speaker: "Maaartee-san!"

"—Thanks for not telling me."

"Sorry. Them drugs, y'know."

"Maaartee-san!" the voice interrupted again. "New boss want to talk to you!"

"*New* boss." Martin sighed.

"You're in the shit now, my brother." Chaz smiled. "Listen, I'll ditty-bop upstairs."

"Put in a good word for me."

"Will do," he said, already out the door. "Right after I go— uh, y'know—*drop a brick.*"

2.

That evening, fresh from a Brooklyn-bound F train, Martin breezed up 6th Avenue to a run-down bodega where he could cop a cheap *forty*. "*¿Es todo?*" the clerk asked. Martin just wagged his head.

Sack in hand, Martin stepped outside to the sidewalk to take his first deep swig of the night—"*Ahhhh!*"—then headed south, aiming to lose himself on the ranging streets.

Meanwhile, along the way, swarms of yellow cab lights, the jazzy, unending flow of traffic: the bumping and pounding tires, the blaring horns.

He meandered—half-formed plans drifting in and out of his mind—until reaching W. Houston Street where he hooked a left, east, and headed down past Sullivan, Thompson, La Guardia Place….

Playing at *The Angelika*? One French, one Hong Kong midnight film with potential. *Keep it in mind.* He walked forward.

Now under the arched, blue-tinged streetlights, taking pulls of the bottle along the way, Martin realized he was heading up, past the looming presence and darkened facades of century-old cast-iron buildings on Broadway.

He thought about work, Chaz. "Shit, did I mention that?"

"What?"

"That *chick-pal* of yours—*Rikki*—called?"

"'Nikki?'"

Some club music off in the distance, until that open-windowed car *thump-thumped* by….

At last, tracking past a deranged beggar performing slow-motion karate moves, Martin took a final belt of the bottle and, on the corner of Astor Place, abruptly stuffed it into an overflowing city trashcan.

Just up the block was a new *Barnes and Noble*, and soon, ghost-like, he found himself penetrating it—floating past pyramid displays of new arrivals, the usual assortment of celebrity author and true-crime bestsellers—arriving at "no man's land": the meager poetry rack. Not a living soul in sight.

A volume of selected verse by Federico Garcia Lorca lay on the shelf. He opened it. *Bilingual.*

On page 275 was a section entitled, "Sonnets Of Dark Love."

He grew absorbed in the Spanish language text until a bespectacled hep-chick drifted into his field of vision. Urgently scanning the rack, she finally turned to him, "You work here?"

"Ah, no," he replied. "But maybe I can help you with something?"

She frowned, "Doubt that."

Martin frowned back. "If it's that book by Jewel," he said. "I think it's by the counter."

That did it. Face flushed, the girl looked at him narrowly, then huffed away.

Unsettled himself—his peace broken—Martin closed the book and returned it to the shelf. In the end, uneasy, he trailed past the restroom. Then, he found himself back on the street, feet hitting the pavement, now past the giant cube sculpture—a huge, cast-iron block tipped and suspended on end—and the young, mostly white, hip-hoppy skaters or "yo-boys" jerk-popping their boards and leaping over-turned city trashcans.

Past Cooper Union, Martin paused at the light. *What to do, what to do....*

St. Marks Place, in all its glory, lay just across the street.

His gaze drifted to the dark rock-'n'-roll bar, *The Continental*, up the block. Then he was sauntering up to the front of the club and a drove of people, the usual cluster of freaks and hooligans, loitering outside. A quick sweep of the eyes: scraggly hair, tattoos, motorcycle boots, dirty leather; sops, strays in black and gray, like Martin; some smoking roll-your-owns with a studied disregard, others talking at each other lackadaisically, eyes wearily averted.

Martin recognized some faces from "around" (other local bars and clubs), without knowing any names.

He scoped several attractive solitary females, but as usual, his own shyness prevented him from stepping up and popping a conversation.

He hung around awhile, eavesdropping a bit, trying hard not to look out of place.

At last, spying a lone, blue-eyed brunette, and fortified by a beer buzz, he sidled up to her. "Ey, what's up?" Indicating the club: "Who's on, tonight?"

She glared at him morosely and uttered, "*I* ain't your mother. See for *yourself!*"

Martin's face went blank.

"Yeah. Thanks, anyhow," he said.

The next moment, Martin-the-lady-killer was at the corner stationary payphone, plugging his other ear against the street noise. The phone rang twice before someone picked up.

"*Nikki?*"

"*Marty,*" replied the voice. "I was just thinking about you!"

His spirits were lifted. "No kidding?"

"No, I *was*," she insisted. "Where are you?"

"The East Village," he said. "By *The Continental.*"

"Oh yeah? Who's playing tonight?"

"Don't know yet, but I thought I'd check it out. Listen," he got straight to the point. "I didn't get the message that you called."

"That's okay."

"Whatcha' up to?"

"Huh?" she asked. "Why?"

6

"Well, I was just thinkin'—I mean, it crossed my mind— if you'd like to come down, maybe hang out?"

"You mean, *now?*" Sounding vaguely confused.

"Well, I mean ... sometime, tonight."

"Marty, really," she said quietly. "I wish I could. But, you know, those shows usually end so late."

"Uh-huh."

"And I have work, tomorrow."

"I know."

"Sorry," she said. "Can't."

Martin shouted over a passing ambulance: "Hey, it's good *somebody* cares enough about their job to wanna get to bed at a decent hour!"

She mumbled something sounding like: "I dunno."

"No," he forced a laugh. "I'm just saying: it's a *good* thing."

"Maybe this Saturday, Marty? Okay?"

"At the park?"

She laughed. "Of course. And don't get too smashed, tonight. I mean, try not to fall face down in the gutter this time."

Martin laughed. "Good one."

"*Hasta luego.*"

"Yeah. Bye, Nik." He hung up.

Within minutes, our man Martin found himself in the murky interior of the place, at the bar, ordering his second ice-cold one. "And make it a pint—*dark.*"

The counter person, a slender attractive redhead in her late twenties, glanced away and casually informed him: "No draft, tonight. Just bottles."

"A Red Stripe is fine."

Again eyes averted, the barkeep shook her head, murmuring something.

"Huh?" He leaned forward on his stool.

"We're out," she clearly imparted this time, leaning forward herself.

He looked at her. Then straight-faced: "How about a Bud Light?" *Jesus Christ.*

"Right," she said, suddenly chuckling over something else Martin didn't understand, then strutted away.

Just that kind of night. Come to think of it, *that kind of life....*

Martin was on his third—a Red Dog—when part of the first band—introduced as "Useless-Nameless"—took the stage, several of the male members, as was the latest trend, wearing ladies frocks.

"You *SUCK!*" screamed one drunken patron before they even got started.

"Keep it down, *ma,*" one member muttered into the microphone, cigarette dangling. "You *promised.*"

After five minutes of mistuning their instruments, amid a rising veil of cigarette smoke … the lead singer, a towering clown-faced transvestite—complete with emerald pre-styled wig and crown of thorns—took the stage, approaching the microphone, heels clopping, to an avalanche of whistles and catcalls.

"Pipe down, girls," he/she said calmly. "We can't all be the queen of the ball."

The transvestite turned to look at the members of the band. They seemed ready.

"This first little ditty," he/she grinned, "is a tune I wrote on the occasion of my first suicide attempt two years ago, right here in the loo of the famous *Continental Divide*."

"Better luck next time!" someone yowled.

He/she smirked. "Yeah. Maybe I'll take *you* with me."

Snickers, scattered applause.

"The name of this first song," he/she continued, "actually, it has two titles," turning back to acknowledge the female drummer with a nod, "'Loneliness Has Followed Me All My Life' or 'God's Lonely Woe-man.'"

Another lout contributed, "Yeah, *whatever!* Just *sing*, ya heifer!"

"*Sing*," he/she replied, "*right*." And then, with a wave of the arm, it began:

There was a clash of cymbals, followed by a surge of guitar fuzz inside a crackling electronic hum. Then, spitting and shrieking—*noize* music erupted from the PA.

"HA!"

One frenzied minute, then an unexpected halt: everyone froze—musicians, music, lead singer.

Suddenly the transvestite stood poised, smiling wickedly through a gauze of ascending smoke, gingerly cradling the microphone on its stand: a mutant Marilyn Monroe about to coyly sing "Happy Birthday" to the president.

"—FIVE SIX SEVEN EIGHT!" Another ferocious jolt and then a screeching sonic roar.

Reeling across the stage, the lead singer broke into a spastic war dance; distended guitar licks shredding and hacking, thrashing and wailing, flaring and surging with ecstatic life! The audience now electrified, hooting and howling: a pulsating roar sweeping through them.

"Crank it, *Ese!*" The lead guitarist went into full swing hunched over his lurching, shrieking instrument.

"—Rip it up!" And, here, contrapuntal to the relentless

doomsday drumming—plucking a thumping groove—the bass player stood with jackboots so wide apart that if someone had only tapped her back, she would have fallen flat on her forehead.

The strident, ragged-edged guitar riffs continued, churning and wrenching, throbbing and crunching ... now abruptly ascending, reverberating, wheeling steeply, onwards and up—rapturously!

Yet, at that point, closing his eyes, Martin couldn't help but think: *Where was she?* Really? Where was she, *right now?*...

3.

Later that night, outside his door, Martin dropped his keys for the second time. Despite his wooziness, he managed to locate the cylinder.

Inside his studio, he hovered unsteadily over the answering machine. No blinking light, nothing.

"Crap."

Clothes still on, eyes wide open, Martin lay on his stretched sofa bed, staring at the cracks along the ceiling.

Just then, if he listened closely enough, he could hear the squeaking bedsprings of the neighbors upstairs.

"It's so big!" He thought he heard someone say.

Shit...

He reached for the phone beside the sofa. Then, placing it on his chest, weighed his decision to use it.

Aaaah, why not.

"1," then, "900...." He could dial the number in the dark.

As always, the cheerful recorded message began: "Hello and thank you for calling—"

Martin stabbed another digit and the recording skipped forward: "Thank you. Please enter your four number extension."

He entered it.

"Now your five digit security code."

Martin did so. There followed an excruciatingly long pause.

"You have," the recorded operator informed him at last, "*zero* messages!... To continue or to browse other ads, please press—"

Click.

Again, the neighbors, upstairs: "*Ugh, ugh, ugh, ugh!...*"

The light still on, eyes hazy with sleep, Martin's attention drifted beyond the flood of sunlight, the wild flowers in bloom, hovering butterflies....

He made out a small figure—a boy—standing by a large pond, watching while other children his age laughed and played, taking turns easily skipping stones across the water.

Martin watched the boy try one: reach down, delicately pick up a piece of dry shale, feel it in his hand.

At last, he hurled it. Waiting for it to skip.

The stone splashed once—*plop!*

Sank.

4.

That Saturday, Martin met Nikki at a park not far from where she lived in untrendy northern Queens.

This park, "Oakland Lake," as it was known officially, consisted of a small, roughly peanut-shaped lake surrounded almost entirely by steep, sloping hills covered with tall, gangling trees. And it was *here*, this same place coincidentally, where years before Martin would skip from college—cut school—with the sole purpose of finding a comfortable tree stump or rock to sit on and spending some time alone. It was *here*, before ever knowing Nikki, where Martin would read and write and dream about his future, hoping for that day when he could at last, somehow, get his life "together." *Fulfill his promise.* Then, too, he had fabricated an elaborate fantasy in which he imagined himself an American expatriate living in the Paris of the 1920s—only he was living in his own country. He convinced himself he was destined for vast prosperity and fame.

Quite naturally, his *writing* would take him there.

Now, walking along the narrow path skirting the brambles, Nikki asked him for an update. Martin's face was a blank.

"—The *news*. Any luck with those magazines? Placing your work this week?"

Nikki wore white shorts that morning, her long chestnut hair loosely tied up in back so that a few long strands escaped, framing her lovely face.

"Any luck?" he finally answered back. "*Nah.* Just more of the same. Zip."

"And how about the other?"

Did she mean the ads?

She smiled, faintly nodded.

At last he confessed: "Even worse. If you can imagine."

Nikki seemed more disturbed by this than Martin. She tugged at him and sighed. "I wish I could set you up, Marty, I really do. Just, I can't think of anyone. And, you know, all of Mariella's friends are either attached or spoken for or"—frowning—"not exactly 'conducive' right now to a relationship. Least of all with any *guy*."

Martin stifled a big laugh.

"Really, Marty. I ask around all the time."

"I believe you, I believe you." Martin broke a smile. "And thanks." He bumped her affectionately. And she bumped him back, harder.

At that point a heavy-set female jogger appeared from the opposite direction. They stopped horsing around and trailed along the path.

"Listen," Nikki spoke up. "If it's any consolation, it's not easy for *anyone*. Despite what you may think."

Glad for this entrance, he asked, "So now that you've mentioned it—what's the score between you?"

"The 'score'?"

"Between you and Mariella." Martin laughed. "What are we talking about here?"

Nikki frowned, gazing down.

"I mean right now," Martin said. "Are we talking 'hiatus,' at this point?"

"If you can believe it," replied Nikki. "Only now she's proposing a 'reunion' date, too."

Martin asked, "And, if you get back together after that, and it still isn't working?"

"Guess."

"That's it, for good?"

She nodded. "That's what we've decided on. Once and for all."

They walked along the gently winding trail.

Martin blew a sigh.

"What's the matter?"

"It's depressing, that's all."

She turned to him. "What is?"

13

He shrugged. "Everything ... just seems so *temporary*."

Nikki bumped him again, laughing. "Lighten up, Marty. Things'll improve."

"You sure?"

Holding his gaze, she said, "Trust me."

Finally the path opened into a clearing. Martin and Nikki lingered there to look across the lake. A breeze was lightly ruffling the surface, and in the distance, geese and ducks spotted the water.

Impulsively, Martin reached down and grabbed a piece of dry shale.

Felt it tightly in his hand.

"Should I?"

"Go ahead," she grinned. "Tempt fate!"

It sailed. Splashed once.

Plop!

5.

JAPAN WORLD TRANSPORT (USA) INC.

[EXPORT]

As usual, the key jammed in the office door cylinder. *Shit.*

9:17, read the JAL wall clock.

Wasting no time after dumping his knapsack, Martin flicked on the copier machine, warming it up. Into his desk then, his bag—he withdrew a stack of badly creased poems and stories. Today, he needed to copy no less than a hundred forty-eight pages.

He was halfway done when he noticed the blinking red light on his telephone. Bouncing over, he hit "Intercom."

"Maartee-san," rang Tani's voice. "Boss want to see you!"

Martin snatched the receiver: *"Five minutes,* tell him! *Five minutes!"*

And with that, he went back to making copies, which he lovingly arranged in a new office folder—discreetly appropriated.

Five minutes later, Martin was seated at his desk (his precious copies stowed away) when he eyed the phone.

What's another minute…

Picking up the receiver, he dialed the usual number.

"Hello," began the cheerful pre-recorded voice, "and thank you for calling *The Voice Personals* line!"

Leaning back in his seat, Martin poked a digit, skipping ahead.

"Thank you," continued the message. "Please enter your four number extension."

He entered it.

"Now your five digit security code."

Martin did so. Waited. Was about to hang up, when:

"You have," said the recorded operator, *"one* new message!"

He stiffened in his chair.

"To hear your message," the operator reminded him, "please key *'eight'* on your touch-tone phone."

Martin keyed "8."

Finally: *Beep!* "Hiiii!" began a bright female voice. "My name is *Monserrat.* Really loved your ad. Thought it was the coolest. You sound *really* special. It's hard to meet someone who's, um, bright but not *mmm,* y' know, really *boring?* Um, I can see by your ad that you're interested in writing and books, the arts. Hmm, *well.* Me? I guess you can say I'm into film, right now. I'm *hot* on Italian movies.

Early Bertolucci, especially. Um, I went to Columbia University, received my M.A. in film studies two years ago. Currently I'm working toward my Ph.D. I'm twenty-six years old. An aerobics instructor in my spare time. Five foot four, a hundred and ten pounds. Long auburn hair; long and straight. Eyes, *mmm*, soft blue. My measurements since we're on the subject? Thirty-six, twenty-four, thirty-four." She giggled, pausing. "Oh, and as far as what I read? I'm very much into Gabriel Garcia Marquez and the South Americans. So? Let's talk. My number is—"

Martin flung aside some sheets to grab a pencil. To his distress, the receiver momentarily popped from his ear; he caught it against his arm and hastily drew it back up, barely cupping it in time for the last four digits: 1-0-9-2

He grimaced, jotting these down.

Her voice returned: "Again, my number—"

Martin brightened—ready—pencil poised.

At last: "1-*900* 555-1092."

His expression fell.

"Only *$2.95* a minute," she cooed. "Just a ten minute minimum!"

He sat there, the receiver plastered to his ear.

She went on sprightly: "You're over eighteen, *riiight?*..."

6.

That night in his neighborhood, Jackson Heights, Martin cruised for a parking space. He swept along 78th, past a cement courtyard and park, past the tightly parked cars lining both sides, until spotting a Ford Escort apparently ready to pull out. Easing alongside the car, he motioned to the driver inside. The woman, a stunning Korean with streaked hair, frowned and shook her head, *Nope.*

After stopping for a red light on 37th Avenue, Martin drove for a block-and-a-half until eyeing a Dodge Neon with its signal lights on. Smiling, he pulled up to the striking strawberry blonde inside, but this time before he could even make a gesture, she too resolutely shook her head, no.

Martin rolled on. And on. Twice around the block, he tried to approach yet another driver. This third woman, an attractive mulatta wearing afro-puffs and a red satin choker, tried to ignore him, until he lightly struck his horn. At which point, she too wearily conveyed this night's almost universal message: *No.*

7.

Much later, bag of chow mein in hand, Martin entered the lobby of his apartment building, stopping at his mailbox.

Anything? Hmm.

Bills, bills; then two padded business-size envelopes, each conveying Martin's name and address, in an exact, if all-too-familiar typewritten style.

He knew what they contained without opening them, but opened them anyway.

In the first envelope, along with his returned, badly creased work, was the standard rejection form (illegible from being copied *ad infinitum*); in the second he found ... nothing. Not even a small "no thank you" note. *But wait!* What's this?... Martin slowly unfolded the rumpled page in disbelief. Across the face of one of his best poems—was it? Could it be?—A smeared *mustard* stain!?..

"*Mutha'-fucks!*"

Inside his apartment, Martin immediately locked the

door, laid down his knapsack, unbuttoned his jacket.

That done, he sharply tore the rejection note and mustard-stained page in half—along with all the ruined copies of his work—and, crossing the room, flung them onto the stunning mountain of rejection letters rising in the far corner.

8.

"Just fuckin' wait!" Martin-the-martyr sat before his outmoded portable word-processor, printing out another stack of self-addressed envelopes. Preparing for his next assault.

Beyond the empty Chinese food containers, the fresh copies of his poems and stories—done that day at work—rested neatly in an open file folder on his sofa bed. On top was a fat roll of stamps.

One of the most important parts of the ritual of submitting work to small press publications and periodicals, was the necessary inclusion of the self-addressed stamped envelope with each manuscript. (Not including a SASE, it was said, would only serve to confirm one's ... "amateur" status.)

Of course, it usually followed that later—much later—it would be these *selfsame* envelopes that would return bearing the obligatory bad news.

And much of the humiliation, as Martin saw it, lay right there: it resulted not just from being rejected, but in having to provide your own envelope for it!

This time, no different than any other, Martin sealed crisp copies of his work in at least a dozen newly-addressed envelopes, hastily noting the submissions on a scrap record sheet.

Then he lunged for his denim jacket and was out the door.

"Watch it, now!" Slamming and re-slamming the mailbox lid, determined-Martin made sure *this* batch—beyond all others—was securely deposited.

His hope renewed, he next decided to treat himself to an ice-cold one and a copy of that week's *Voice*, his favorite Village tabloid. There was a seedy all-night bodega on the corner of 79th, where drunken derelicts would stumble in to buy cigarette "singles" for a quarter.

"Okay, let's see."

Back from his mission, expectant-Martin settled on the hardwood floor of his apartment, beside a half-emptied foaming forty-ounce, flipping backwards through the newspaper—past advertisements for 1-900 phone sex—to the personals. More specifically, "Men Seeking Women."

Running his finger down the column he made sure it was there.

Yep. Draining his beer, he had to laugh.

There it was: his one-monthly tease, his one guaranteed smile:

> *** CLOSEOUT SALE! ***
> SM, 26, 5'7, anti-hipster, into the Village, writing, the art life— seeks uncommon SF for long exhaustive talks, mutual support and, *well*....

9.

Paper rolled under his head, back on the hardwood, Martin studied the cracks along the ceiling, listening to the distant sounds of what he imagined was the number 7 train. Despite his efforts to fight it, he began to drift off.

One association led to another until at last, surfacing through a host of dim recollections, one memory took color and came into view. Growing at once brighter and clearer....

Again he was a boy. This time playing on a distant outcrop of rocks: a sandstone formation outside his parochial school.

Pulsing with energy, pretending to fly, he vaulted over chasms, jagged crevices—leapt carelessly from exposed boulder to rock. On this day, the sun blazed brightly.

Drenched in this light, Martin seemed blessed.

That is, till he heard a distant cry—a lonely woman's voice—drifting up, calling him. At which point, abruptly turning, he immediately lost his footing and plunged down a deep dark hollow, violently banging his head on the rocks below. Dark blood splattering across the stones.

Vaguely distressed and disoriented, Martin awoke to turn on the TV and open his pullout sofa bed. His beer was gone, and he felt too lazy to go out and buy another one. Instead, he ended up watching Wall Street Week in the hope it would serve to put him back to sleep.

Instead of the TV, though, his bleary eyes focused on a framed photograph on his bookshelf. Through the blue light, he could just barely make out her attractive, dark features.

His mother—then Martin's age—looked so much like him it was almost like looking into a mirror.

"¿Qué quieres de mi ahora, loca?" He asked her in Spanish.

The woman remained in the shadows, facing him, her dark eyes begging.

No reply.

10.

The Soft Descent

"Emptiness,"
she said.
"All emptiness
is open to me..."

The Sky Is Barren.
Dreams Are Useless.
Dissolution Rules.

Long ago, I dreamt
I fell through
the clouds...
I fell easily and
kept falling.
My arms extended,
my eyes open,
I descended
through the clouds
without a whisper,
without a sound
(as in a flickering
silent picture
show).

How well—
how well
and easily

I kept falling.

How often
since then
have I had this image
in my mind…
that
of my body
falling

without a whisper,
without a sound….

Some nights later, Martin was alone in his studio, trying to work out an old poem, when his thoughts strayed to days long past and memories of his departed *madrecita*.

—What recollections did he have of her?

A petite, fine-featured woman with dark curling hair—again Martin envisioned her in a familiar pose, lingering by the half-open shade of her bedroom window, staring out into the shadowy street.

Always this strange and tomb-like solitude: permanently shut away from the sun and the rest of the world.—*Why?*…

Once, while she stood by that window, Martin considered, in fantasy, sneaking up behind her and shoving her out. ("*¡Hala, vaca!*") Were it not for that rusted window guard, she might've fallen, too. Dropped down and down, in slow motion, five full stories, arms flailing, legs kicking wildly—her head smacking the sidewalk and splitting open like a ripe watermelon—brains and bitter sadness splattering for yards! Martin looking down at horrified bystanders, timidly waving a hand.

Other memories?

Not due to any sickness he could see, his mother's darkened form unable to get up from bed for days on end, her chest gently falling and rising, rising and falling. His mother sleeping more than anyone in the whole world.

Martin fixing his own breakfast, Martin walking himself to school, Martin pleading with her to take him to the big park, the one with the Indian caves, the quiet winding paths, the giant ball fields.

Rendered nearly powerless in the oppressive dark, his mother sometimes not bothering to answer the door when it rang or even pick up the phone. Stomping his feet, Martin flouncing into the next room to snap on the TV, turning up the volume. At last, she would cry out in a wrecked voice, "¡Bajalo!" But he would turn it up, losing himself in silly-happy dialogue and cartoon violence. "¡BA-JA-LO!" With that, the volume went even higher. Way up! In the end, staggering, she would burst into the room, eyes puffy, face incredulous: "¿Pero qué eres, IDIOTA!?.."

He recalled another time, years before, the two tranquilly reclined on her wide bed, taking an afternoon nap, facing each other, when Martin, suddenly bored, mischievously reached over and yanked down *hard* on her pajama bottom, his jaw dropping at the sight of her thick, hairy PUSSY!

"¡Cochino!"—and WHACK!—his mother slapping his face so hard his ears rang for a full fifteen minutes.

Other times? He remembered his mother without provocation, abruptly swinging—pelting him. Now, crumpled in a corner, open hands held up in surrender. *Thwack!* Martin seeing stars: a hot, tingling sensation on his skin where *mami* hit him. "AAAAAAAAAAAAAAHHH!.." he bawled, shivering. Then striking him again and again, suddenly ranting, "*¡Si no fuera por ti! ¡Si no fuera por ti!*" And with her bare foot, kicking him. Stubbing her big toe, somehow. "—*¡ Ayyy, Dios!*..." And as she did a hopping dance, her face screwed up in pain, Martin breaking into a laugh— a loud laugh—his cheeks still wet with tears.

Then, of course, there were the happy times. Her sadness ebbing, her mood lightened; his mother affectionate with him, suddenly warm and tender.

Together on the sagging bed, her softness against him, her skin milky: pleasant. Martin closed his eyes, floating back through time, feeling her light teasing fingers on the nape of his neck, softly along the back of his head, now stroking his hair gently, gently stroking him.

. Her face then pressed against his, her lips kissing him. *Smack!* Affectionately kissing him. *Smack! Smack!* Martin cringing. Her voice laughing; light laughter passing between them, cascading, ringing like bells.

The two embracing, squeezing each other a long time, in a firm hold on life, Martin slipping into a dream. Tight against her bosom, tight; hanging on, her heartbeat in his ear. Hearing her heartbeat then, he could not comprehend, could not imagine how it wouldn't last forever....

Then, recalling how his grandparents would show up to take him away.

As always, Martin at a loss.

In the end, the very end, amid the flashes of light and wide gaps in memory, the fierce bouts of anguish and pain, his grandfather arriving again, muttering—let in with his own key—this time to pack Martin's things: whatever remained. Martin frightened, confused: "*¿Qué haces? ¿Pero dónde está Mami? ¿Dónde está Mami?*"

In return, *nothing*. A widening silence, a crushing loneliness.

Sirens wailing in the distance, in the night ... his mother, *madrecita*, being taken away forever, away from that window, away from that bed, her shattered face receding, fading, amid a swirl of shadows, into memory, now as always. Amid a swirl of shadows, into the lonely night.

11.

They were at the corner of Second and Avenue A, where a film—*Beyond the Valley of the Dolls*—was being projected across the entire side of a building from the bar across the street.

Nikki asked him for an update.

"With the magazines?"

"With the new ad. Any luck?"

He shrugged.

"Maybe the ads work better for women?"

"There's that distinct possibility." They crossed the avenue, alphabet-bound. "I'm about ready to join one of those stupid dating services."

"I know someone who did that. Some gal from work."

He laughed. "Yeah? How'd it go?"

"Terrible."

Martin cracked up.

"She put up the money," Nikki went on. "And *zilch.*"

"Really?" he asked. "Which agency?"

"Can't remember. They advertise on TV, though. Late at night. One of those 'personal introduction' services."

"And she didn't meet anyone? Really?"

"Oh they set her up on a few dates."

"And?"

Nikki smirked. "Apparently anyone with money can get over on the 'screening process.'"

He laughed, again.

"Stick with the personals, Marty," she suggested. "At least, you have less to lose. And you may still get lucky."

"Lightning strikes when you least expect it, right?"

"That's right."

He turned to her. "And, after all, I met you."

Nikki smiled.

On the far side of Avenue B, they turned left and crossed the street.

Avenue B was considerably more run-down than Avenue A, nocturnal types here and there hawking brand names of heroin. The farther you went into the Alphabet, the shadier the neighborhood became, until parts of it—bombed-looking, rubble-strewn—began to resemble portions of the South Bronx.

Mercifully, at this hour, there were some revelers on the avenue, jetting to and from the performance space, *Collective Unconscious,* across the street or, beside that, the *Gas Station,* a converted Gulf station turned band venue, fenced in by rusting scrap-metal art.

Martin and Nikki safely arrived at the nondescript club

entrance where a toothless cretin was outside, strumming a monotonous tune on a homemade, three-string electric guitar. On the sidewalk was a childishly scrawled sign that read:

Show me a man
Whose not confused
And I'll show you
A moron.

"Ready?" Martin asked.

Nikki smiled. "Yep."

There was no line to wait on, of course—no velvet rope—so they went right in.

"Hold it," rasped a shadowy figure just inside.

After being patted down for weapons, Martin and Nikki followed a long dark hallway to the admissions window. Then they turned right and stepped through a short passage that led to a wide, dimly lit room, done in a garish Hong Kong motif of bright reds, yellows, and blues (Chinese lanterns hanging from the ceiling), the entire floor surrealistically carpeted in ankle-deep sand.

On the east wall flashed incongruous slide projections, and, as Martin and Nikki stepped deeper into the room, they noticed a lank-haired musician crouched over an electric violin, playing contrapuntally to the house ambience music—music filled with all sorts of warped industrial noises, like someone clanking on metal pipes and sawing wood.

As Martin and Nikki progressed to the back, they saw a booth where a tattooed, bald-headed woman was peddling so-called smart drugs, sold in glitter cups like fancy film containers. Beside these were offered certain "herbal treatments" and stimulants containing ephedrine or ma huang, "legal" drugs.

"Up for any?" Martin asked.

Nikki shrugged, pushing on.

Back upfront, full circle, a performance piece was in progress. A blank-faced blond in pearls and formal gown was doing an ultra-slow-motion dance to the warbling music, while another woman, manipulating a claw-like mirror, refracted shards of colored light in some vague commentary. The flashing slide images were mostly of holocaust victims piled lifelessly, like rag dolls.

Nikki tried to interpret it, "Society's indifference to human suffering?"

"Good guess."

Tired of treading sand, they found a couch. Beside them, piled high, were all sorts of gear and outmoded electronic equipment: EKG machines, scopes, TV monitors, emitting frequency waves and static. They tried to talk but the loud dissonant music made conversation difficult, so instead they settled for holding hands and exchanging amused looks.

Martin studied her face: Nikki never looked more angelic. She had large pale-green eyes, a faint cleft in her chin, and at the corner of her mouth, on the right, a perfect tiny mole, a beauty mark.

What's more, tonight she looked extra-luscious, dressed up in a pair of low-slung grape flairs and a cropped lemon T. At one point—for no reason other than she appeared to be happy—she impulsively reached over and embraced him. This, of course, led to a return squeeze on Martin's part, then to some playful fondling, finally to some light kissing: her skin, smelling faintly of lilacs, feeling petal-soft and warm to his lips.

Her body leaning against him, her breath soft in his ear, Nikki teased him a bit, rocking gently in his lap. Doped with affection, he took extra pleasure in supporting her weight, and in stroking and kissing her mouth and that faint sweet dot above her lip. Unable to resist, he slid his hands along her firm, slender body to warmly caress her lower back, hips, and thighs.

They necked and petted for what seemed close to an hour, the world around them falling off, until she pulled up and sleepily asked, "Maybe we should see what's downstairs?"

Wanting to nuzzle against her body forever, he whispered, "Maybe later?"

12.

When they languidly rose from the couch, still holding hands, they noticed the room had become considerably more crowded.

Near the entrance, a different performance piece was in progress. It featured a towering transvestite in an emerald wig, who Martin finally recognized from the band he'd seen at the Continental. *Useless-Nameless.*

Naked this time—except for being bound in Saran Wrap—eyebrows shaved, he/she was dreamily reciting poetry into a microphone without background music. "This one's called, 'Sophia's Recollection.'" He/she began: "*Last night / I dreamt / that you murdered me, / that while I slept / close to you, / you wedged a knife / into my chest, / until its icy-cold tip / pierced my heart. / I dreamt / that you held me tightly, then / kissed me, warmly, / as I coldly bled, / and all my life, / with all its dreams / and wishes, / poured away...."*

In the dim light Martin noticed the absence of genitalia. It dawned on him: he wasn't a transvestite, but a transsexual. *Post op*, at that. The transformation complete, "he" had become a "she."

Interesting...

"Let's go," Nikki urged, tugging at his sleeve.

13

Downstairs, in what resembled an underground bomb shelter, was the murkily-lit dance floor. The music playing in this cavernous refuge was pulsing house/techno.

After buying some bottled juice from the bar (the place being without a liquor license), Martin and Nikki found a lacquered bench to sit on and take in the slamming crowd. It was a freak scene: queens, kings, club kids, B-list models, downtown trendies, ravers (the more frenzied no doubt already high on x)—all grooving, going crazy. Heads wagging and bobbing, feet stomping, hips shimmying, asses shaking; glowing cigarettes dipping and rising in the dark. Through the yellow and red flashing lights and club smoke, as in a dream, Martin could just barely make out the outline of a few smiling girls dancing together topless. And through his heels, Martin could feel the relentless *boom!-boom!-boom!* of the jacked-up driving bass. Out of nowhere some inflamed queen appeared before them completely bare-assed, shaking his arms and legs in a kind of self-absorbed frenetic dance, then leaping back into the crush, and Martin and Nikki turned to each other and laughed.

Nikki nudged Martin. "Ready to dive in?"

"Let's!"

As always, Martin felt a bit self-conscious at first—and stiff—before being able to surrender completely to the enveloping rhythms: to convince himself that nobody here was watching, nobody gave a shit—*nobody*. It was time to get naked: *let it all hang out!*

Smiling, eyes closed to the world, losing herself in the wailing and swirling sounds, in the here and now, Nikki's own movements and dance steps were easily more relaxed and fluid, freshly sensual. And Martin derived almost as much pleasure from watching her as he did from dancing. *Priceless*, he thought, waves of excitement rising up his back. *Sweet heaven....*

14.

Martin and Nikki danced together virtually nonstop until 3:30 A.M., at which point the floor became too crowded and wild, and the both of them, exhausted but in good spirits, left the club. Enjoying the cool night air, holding hands, they walked up 2nd Street, past all the swarming night people: eccentrics, fashion victims, wild-ass kids (these mixed with assorted mental patients and homeless crackheads)—until reaching Avenue A, where they hailed a cab.

"West Fourth Street station," Martin announced to the driver, club music still throbbing in his ears.

He fell back into the seat next to Nikki. "So," he grinned. "Have a nice time?"

"Great," she said, eyes sparkling. "I really needed that!"

"You're not the only one!" Martin laughed.

In the next moment, they were affectionately touching, then, leaning against each other, playfully groping and kissing. Martin squeezed her sweaty body tightly, at one point French-kissing the nape of her neck.

"What are you *doing?*"

"*Tasting you,*" he said.

"Oh *really? Why?*"

"Why *not,*" Martin said. "Besides I may never get this opportunity again."

"You're *cracked,*" she laughed.

Martin whispered in her ear, "Are you *sure* you have to go to work, tomorrow?"

She smiled. Whispered back, "Yes."

That night, on the cab ride to the subway, he kept hoping to convince her otherwise.

15.

Hi.

I don't know what your name is, of course, so I'm not sure how I'm supposed to address this letter. I will say though that I just spotted your long detailed ad in the "write to me" segment of this week's *Voice Personals* and I was impressed enough by it to want to respond or send you, as you requested, "preferably a long, intimate and richly detailed letter." (I'll try to do my best.)

The truth is, I love writing letters but don't get much of a chance to do so these days since the few people I try to correspond with seem to take forever to write back - or instead just end up picking up the phone.

I was introduced to letter writing in high school, when the person I considered my best friend (who I was also in love with) - her name was Faith - would write me two, sometimes three letters a week and of course each time I felt compelled to write back. This, despite the fact that we saw each other every day, had lunch together, and after school often spent hours on the phone! Pretty funny, huh?

What made it even stranger was that we weren't even boyfriend and girlfriend! She was already involved with someone else when she met me. This may sound a bit dumb, I know - even masochistic on my part - but after a while I just couldn't help it. And, looking back on it these days, I still have to say it was one of the best times of my life, somehow. Innocent. Pure. I felt like a knight in one of those medieval romances. Until that point in my life I'd never felt so awake with love and so hopeful about the possibilities for the world. That first real intimacy was like being witness to the first glimmer of light at sunrise; it seemed to signal the dawn of my life. Anything seemed possible. God was everywhere!

Christ, should I start over? See, in letters, I often get carried away.

Hi, again.... How are you?

I think I forgot to introduce myself.

The name is Marty. My full name is Martin Sierra. - Nice to meet you!

A word or two about my ethnicity. I *am* American. Born and raised here. My mother, on the other hand, was from Spain. I use the past tense "was" because she's no longer around: she's gone - departed, as they say.

Anyway, not to worry, it happened a long time ago. She left me when I was a kid.

As for other specifics concerning my physical appearance (eye color, weight, height) please refer to the back of the photo I've included with this letter. It should all be there.

Yeah, it's true that I'm short, but I'd like to remind you that many historical figures were runts. Houdini was 5'1, Jean Paul Sartre was 5'3, Steve McQueen was 5'6 - and a good many assholes were even shorter! HA-HA.

I notice in your ad you say you're "into writing," which is cool - one more thing we have in common. Right now I have to say that my main focus is poetry, even though I also love novels and fully admire the strange individuals who write them. I also enjoy reading biographies - especially the beginning parts: the scrappy early years before an artist becomes "established."

Semi-autobiographical writers are great, too, especially if they have the guts to admit to horribly embarrassing, if not outright humiliating episodes from their own lives; this is a quality more rare among male writers, I think (since men - as *all* men - they are raised to be less honest about their thoughts and feelings, their shortcomings - even to themselves). To admit to failure is to admit to weakness, which is somehow unmasculine, as well as un-American. So, personally, I find myself less interested in being superficially "American" and in love with writers - the unconventional few - who feel that way, too.

Not to sound too self-righteous or smug, but I want nothing to do with false advertising. - What I want, in simple terms, is to make art and find myself: discover who I am. Right now my interest is poetry, but the method or the means hardly matters: the point is staying true. And I know I will continue to write, to search, in one form or another, until I'm permanently washed up, finished - buried.

I'll relate my greatest failure, so far. Bear with me.

Five years ago - unpublished then as I am now, and tired of waiting on my ass - I decided I would put out my own book of poems.

Not that I would go to any disgusting, rip-off "vanity press;" no - in the best fuck-it-I'll-do-it-myself tradition, I would start my own little imprint. And I went through all the steps: shopping around for the least expensive printer, providing the camera-ready pages and finished book design, obtaining the ISBN and copyright.

On the "business" side: renting a PO Box, obtain-

ing the proper business forms (and having them nota-
rized), acquiring a tax I.D. number under the
imprint's name. Opening the account. And printing and
posting flyers.

— Small potatoes, true, but it was a start! My
first little baby being a 114-page book entitled,
ironically enough, <u>Idealism and Early Wish-fulfill-
ment</u>.

... Well, it flopped. - Resoundingly.

It made all the noise of "one hand clapping," as
the Zen masters like to say. (It's okay, you can
laugh; I already have.)

As a last-ditch effort, I took up selling it in the
Village on the weekends. Right there on the street.
First, along Astor Place (in front of the big parking lot facing "the Cube"), then on St. Marks Place,
in front of the old *Deutsch Americanische* building,
site of the old St. Marks bookstore.

After about six months, I finally sold maybe sixty
copies. Then I called it quits.

In the end, I lost money. The whole experience
bruised my ego a bit. But, hey, that's life.

At least, I tried.

So, there you have it...

As a footnote to all of this, being a book peddler
put me more closely in touch with the Village than
ever before. Strange to say, it was the beginning of
my first real infatuation with the area. After being
on the street a while, I grew familiar with the other
street vendors, many who returned week after week.
Like them, I too became mostly invisible to the spec-
tacle of humanity passing by - as much a part of the
local landscape as the panhandlers, the pocked side-
walks, the graffiti. The East Village then was different than it is now. Darker. For a time, it was like
having this secret window at the bottom of the world.
And, while I was there, I learned to open my eyes and
take a good hard look.

These days when I'm down there I continue to keep
my eyes open. I try to experience all that I can. I

take in bands, performance art, bookstores - every-thing. I believe it's important to be a part of one's own time; and, for me, the Village is still happening.

Right, my boring digressions aside - and getting back to your ad - I'd love to pal with someone new, catch bands, go dancing, support off-beat shows. I don't care if it leads anywhere. I just want to know more people I can share life with. Enjoy it while I'm here.

Anyway, uh, if I haven't bored you stiff - and I probably have - drop me a line. Write or call. My num-ber is, 555-3468...

16.

Beep! "Hi, Martin. My name is Nikki. You don't know me, but you answered my personal ad, wrote me a nice let-ter. I'll leave you my phone number and maybe we can talk?..."

17.

Classical music wafted from Martin's cracked Toshiba clock radio.

He peeked at the clock: *7:20*

Maybe I'll just ... lie here. And, closing his eyes, drifted back to sleep, the music soon accommodated into the fluid context of his dreams:

... Again, he could taste her lips—
against his own,
feel them wet.
His arms,
like smooth vines,
like slender,
soft-bellied pythons
entwined

her body.
His hands,
like tendrils
apart from him,
reached gently
across her breasts,
between her legs.
His thirsting
hands....
Then,
from the roiling darkness,
blackest night,
like a fierce wind,
a face:

   —MAMA!

A moment later his alarm detonated, drilling tooth and bone.

18.

 At work, Chaz held up an inter-office memo.

"'Export Department,'" he read aloud, "'all staff must report to second floor each day to log in precise time of arrival. If any member of staff is late to report to the second floor, *reason* must be noted in appropriate 'remarks column' on time sheet, form triple A dash nine B ... also submitted on separate office-related form, A dash nine C—copy duplicated for own file—to supervisor for final approval and initialing.'"

"*Shit,*" said Martin.

"Check it: 'Lateness,' it says here 'will immediately be

deducted from OVERTIME pay—'"

"What the fuck! That ain't legal!"

Wagging his head, Chaz slapped the sheet on his desk.

"It's the fuckin' *new* guy," remarked Martin.

"Shit, bro," he snorted, picking up the memo again and waving it around. "I'll tell ya what *this* is. It's *pay back!*"

Martin looked at him.

"I'm sayin': payback for the 'big one'—*WWII!*" And with that, Chaz crumpled up the sheet and with one sure hand, shit-canned it.

In the next moment, Chaz entered the warehouse, and Martin couldn't resist the urge to dial a memorized number—starting, of course, with "*1-900....*"

He could dial the number left-handed. Eyes closed.

As always, the cheerful recorded message began: "Hello and thank you for calling the *Voice Personals*—"

Martin pushed another digit. "Thank you. Please enter your four number extension."

He entered it.

"Now your five digit security code."

Martin did so. There followed an agonizingly long pause.

Then from nowhere: "You have," said the recorded operator, "*one* new message!"

Martin straightened up, then pressed the digit that would make the system skip forward.

A young woman's embarrassed voice began: "*Hi*. This is *Lola*. Just flipping through the paper I saw your ad. Of course, I *saw* your ad.... What do I look like? How do I describe myself? Let's see—I *hate* this! Well, *all right*. I'm Uruguayan-American. Long dark hair with bangs. About five-*five*. Some people say, some people say I'm *ugly*—no, some people say I'm *okay-looking*—I don't know—*whatever*. Fuck 'beauty!'" She tittered nervously. "I'm into the *arts*, too. And the East Village. In fact I live there. With my *mom*, unfortunately. Uh, *okay*, let's see, I'm looking for someone—a 'decent' guy, I guess—to kinda hang out with, check out live shows . Crap like that." Chuckling, again. "I'm a painter, actually. I do canvasses. Even going to school for it. *Ooo*, wow, big deal, right? I know, I must sound like a real zero, a big loser. Still living at home and taking classes. Well, what can I say? I'm being honest. If you still wanna reach me after this—and *how* could you resist!—I'll give you my number...."

Grinning, Martin scratched down the digits.

The operator finally returned: "Press 'six' to replay the last message—"

Martin keyed "6."

"*Lola. Just flipping through the paper....*"

19.

The next night from his studio—in a fit of optimism—Martin tried the number.

On the third ring, someone picked up.

"Hello, can I speak to Lola?"

"You're from a collection agency?"

"No."

"Then, this is Lola."

Trying not to sound edgy, he started, "Hi. Hey, this is Marty? From the *Voice?*"

"Who?—*Oh*." It finally hit her.

"Do you like, have a minute or two?"

"What," she hesitated, sounding embarrassed. "You

mean, to *yak?* I have a minute. Or two."

And so they did. Taking their time. Martin commenting on the obvious weirdness of the situation, Lola remarking how hooking up through the ads was always freaky.

"You never know who you might meet, after all," she said.

"You're telling *me*," said Martin.

"A lot of whackos out there," she said.

"I know."

"You're not into dirty feet, are you?"

"What?"

"You know, one of those perverts."

"Huh?—*No.*"

"That's good. The last guy who called wanted to know if he could suck my toes. But only after I stepped in red clay."

Martin took a moment. "He was from an ad?"

"No. A collection agency, I think."

He asked her if she'd ever done this before.

"The personals?" She paused. "Does it matter?"

"No, no. Just curious."

Lola admitted, "I've done it before."

"Yeah?" he asked. "When was that? The last time?"

She paused, again, as if trying to remember. "'Bout … *three* weeks ago."

"Uh-huh," he said. "So, what happened?"

"You wanna know?"

Martin laughed. "Yeah."

"*Zip.*"

"Nothing?"

"Nope. And three weeks before *that*, I tried another one."

"Really?" Martin asked, "And how did *that* go?"

"Like crap."

"You met the person, at least?"

"Yeah, we met. A few times. Had a few 'dates.' Or whatever."

"Just didn't 'click'?"

She sighed. "Nope."

"So—here's an awkward question." He wasn't quite sure how to put it. Finally he asked straight out, "What are you looking for?"

"I don't know."

"I mean, why did you answer my ad?"

"Beats me. Why did you place it?"

"I dunno," Martin said, "I guess I'm looking for someone."

"So what are *you* looking for?"

He paused, then said, "This is gonna sound retarded, I mean, *dumb*, but … how can I say this without laughing—someone I can *talk to*, I guess. Go out with." He forced a laugh, then asked, "How about *you*?"

"What am I looking for?" She hardly had to think about it. "Same thing."

Clearing his throat, he felt safe to ask: "You're not seeing anyone? At the moment?"

"Nope."

"That's kinda interestin'," Martin said.

"Huh? *Why?*"

"I don't know. Being a *goof.*"

"Oh."

Martin cut to the chase: "Wanna get together, sometime? Meet?"

"In the East Village, right?"

"Right."

"*Maybe.*" Still considering it. Taking her time. Finally: "Yeah—it's a possibility. As long as it's in a public place."

Martin laughed.

"But let me say now," she said. "I can only hang out for a while. Like an hour. Max. I consider an hour my threshold with someone I don't know."

"Okay."

Lola confided, "There've been times when I got a little too 'invested' over the phone, only to find later it was totally *flat*—nothing happening at all."

"Sounds familiar," Martin said.

"Happened to you?"

"A few times."

"We shouldn't talk anymore then. We should just hang up."

"Right."

But they were on the line another fifteen minutes.

"I get to name the meeting place, right?" she asked finally.

"Sure."

"Okay," she said. She thought about it, then gave it.

"Got it," said Martin. "Meet you there."

20.

The following day at work, Martin asked Chaz if he could leave early.

"Why, bro?"

"When was the last time *you* got laid?"

"I'm married, kid. So the answer to that question is: 'Can't remember.'" Decent as always, Chaz laughed, "Yo— a *date*? Go for it. I'll cover for ya."

"*Muchacho*, I owe ya."

"Don't even mention it, *pendejo*."

21.

In front of *Kim's Video*, the meeting place, Martin checked his watch. *8:09*.

Shifting from one leg to the other, he was just starting to get antsy.

Long dark hair, he thought. Bangs. "About five-*five*...." The night prior she had comically alluded to her look as "'Bummy casual': torn black jeans and an m/c jacket with paint drips on the back. All my clothes have these little drips and drabs of paint on them," she said. "It's *embarrassing*."

So how did *he* look? He could just make out his own black jeans in the glass door. Indigo Panama shirt, black denim jacket, hair not sticking up too badly. He took a deep breath, tried to stand straight.

A slim, dark-haired woman with a beaded lip ring and faux leopard-skin jacket suddenly appeared before him, hesitating. Martin froze, eyes widening in anticipation. But then she seemed to recall where she was going and swept past him, into the store.

He stood around, trying to blend in, not look too concerned. Then it was twenty after.

What the fuck. He began to involuntarily rock on the balls of his feet.

Another woman stepped up now, half her head shorn, the other side dyed two shades of violet and aquamarine.

Martin looked at the pavement and sighed.

If she's not here the next time I check my watch, he decided. *I'm outahere'*...

Just then, from the crowd, a new woman appeared.

Approaching him directly, smiling, she spoke in a cheerful baby-doll voice: "Your name 'Marcus'?" She wore black leather, but the hair was off. Short and spiked, it was dyed platinum blonde with pink-red highlights. Out of her left cheek sprouted what seemed to be part of a corkscrew: a radical piercing of some kind.

"'*Marcus*'?" She repeated.

Martin looked at her. "Huh? No, 'Martin.'"

"'*MARTIN*'—*that's* it!"

Who *was* this woman?

Before he could even raise the question, she informed him: "I'm a friend."

He was even more confused now.

"A friend of Lola's," she explained. "She asked me to drop by to tell you she'd be a little late."

Martin looked at her.

"I just came down here to tell you that," she said.

"Right—I mean, *thanks*." Groping for something else to add, he nodded, "Sweet of you."

In fact, studying her face, he realized she was actually quite pretty: under all those post-punk accoutrements.

She said cheerfully, "*S'okay*, we try to help each other out."

"I like to hear that," Martin smiled. Then, uncharacteristically, he blurted out, "I feel like—I should buy you a *drink* or something."

She burst out laughing, hardly insulted. "You have a *date*, remember?"

"I know," he said.

"Maybe some other time," she grinned, now talking over her shoulder as she tipped away. "Maybe all three of us can get together."

"I'd like that."

"*See ya!*" She turned north on Avenue A.

Martin nodded and smiled. He felt invigorated, like some benevolent spirit had just swept over him.

Stepping out to the sidewalk, he followed her with his eyes until she vanished in the crowd.

A young derelict suddenly emerged from oncoming pedestrians, got in his face: "Spare some scratch?" He wore patchwork clothes, a rank squatter's smell, and, most impressively, a full-color eagle tattoo down the length of his face.

Before Martin realized what he was doing, he was digging in his pocket.

"Nice weather we're having," the guy said pleasantly upon receiving the coin.

And Martin had to agree, "Not bad."

The guy floated off and at that point Martin noticed the chalk drawing on the sidewalk directly beneath him. It was a tribal symbol of some kind, etched in black and gray in a deliberate primitive style, like a cave drawing.

"Pardon me!" emitted a petite goth girl, clutching a bouquet of barbed wire, mincing past.

Martin hadn't realized he was blocking the sidewalk. He wheeled around, back to the store—before nearly bumping into a raggedy-looking man, holding up an alarmingly large sidewinder, declaring: "For *sale!* For *sale!*"

Turning to watch the snake's forked tongue, Martin felt someone tap him on the shoulder.

He spun around nearly smashing into her.

"Martin?" She wore a leather jacket, torn denims, and had long black hair cut in bangs across her forehead—eyes dark and intense.

"Yeah?" He felt a pang of excitement.

"I'm Lola," she smiled. "Sorry I'm late."

Martin quickly mentioned that her friend had stopped by.

"Oh. She found you. Good."

Starting from the store, they cut right.

Martin found a pack of Juicy Fruit in his pocket and in his uneasiness pulled it out. He saw her looking at it. "Wanna piece?"

"Sure." She thrust out her hand.

Lola offered a simple explanation for her lateness: "I got caught ... baby-sitting."

"Baby-sitting?"

"Yeah. Twins.—Mina's, actually. That girl that was just here?"

Martin was chewing a wad of gum. "No kidding?"

"Yeah. She's a stripper on Broome Street. Afternoon shift."

"*Hmm.*" Hiding his surprise. "Must be rough."

"I'll say," said Lola matter-of-factly. "Tipping doesn't really happen till after dark."

They stood before a coffee house/bar.

Martin suggested it. "Cool with this place?"

"We're here," said Lola.

The popular hangout had a stylized, homemade sign on top that read, *Babyland.*

22.

Babyland was like the many bars and cafes in the East Village whose décor shared a similar kitsch/retro esthetic, the theme in this case varying slightly in that it also centered on "infantilization." Thus, aside from the insider irony of cheesy cardboard cut-outs of beatific nuclear families and wide-eyed freckled-faced boys dreaming of being astronauts, of floating egg creams and malted milk shakes, there was also, throughout the place, a multitude of stuffed animals and Fisher-Price toys and games and, amid other bits of mismatched furniture in the back, four extra-large cribs that diapered patrons could climb into.

The "café" part of the establishment was upfront by the door, and, seizing a window table, they soon ordered from the waitress, a sullen neo-punk. Then Lola excused herself to use the rest room.

When she returned it was all laid out on the table: a mango smoothie for Martin, licorice tea and black forest cake for her.

"Let me square it," she said. And removing a folded five-dollar bill from her jeans, slipped it to him.

"Too much," he said, pulling out five singles of his own and passing them back.

"You gave me *five*," she said, counting the bills. She withdrew a single and tossed the rest back.

"Thank you," he said flatly. "And *here's* your change." Sliding the same bills back.

"Hey, what gives here?"

"You wanna start a fist fight?" he countered.

"All right, all right," she said. "I'll get it next time." Then cracking a smile: "But I got my eye on you."

"I'll be careful."

Smiling, she asked, "Not one of those guys that gets weird when a woman pays, are you?"

"Nope. Just the opposite."

"Some guys get weird about it."

"Is that so?"

She nodded. "Their self-esteem's tied up with money."

"Not me," he smiled. "I'd be in trouble."

Martin watched her pick up her cake with her fingers and take a big, messy bite. He liked this.

"Hope your tea isn't cold," he said, distracted.

With her mouth full, she shrugged. She wiped the excess chocolate from her lips with her fingers and brought each finger to her mouth. Then she emptied four packets of sugar into her tea. Then some milk. "I like it sweet," she said.

He laughed. "No foolin'."

"Don't worry," she said, as if trying to read his mind. "I'm not on the needle or anything."

"That's reassuring!" he said.

"I know some people who are, though," she admitted, turning serious. "I mean, y'know, stone junkies. A pretty sad, pretty pathetic lot, if you ask me."

She sighed and went back to quietly devouring her cake.

Lola's face was narrow but attractive. She wore no make-up aside from simple eyeliner: a single pronounced line running along the edge of each upper eyelid, thinning outwards and up. Her eyes, beneath those even, neatly brushed bangs, were her most impressive feature. Not only were they large and penetrating, but they were *dark*—each iris nearly the color of the pupil—so that at once they appeared entirely black. Her gaze was mesmerizing.

"So," Martin asked. "You're an artist?"

Lola wiped her lips. "A painter. I hope to be an 'artist' someday. When I'm good enough. Anyway, I still have to get through art school."

"Hard?"

"No, not hard, but mostly a pain in the ass. I'm not a

'school' person."

"Meaning?"

"I hate following instructions. Hate being in a class, doing the same as everybody else. Hate being graded. It's all bullshit. This *herd* mentality. Anyway, I'm almost finished. This is my last semester. Hallelujah."

"Then what? What are you planning to do?"

She shrugged. Made an expression of helplessness. "Get a job, I guess. Paint on the side."

"You've worked before?"

She nodded, leaning forward to take a sip of tea. "Oh sure. Done lots of things. Most recently I had a job in a body-piercing shop on St. Marks."

He smiled. "Have any piercings yourself?"

"A few."

"How many?"

"None of your business."

Martin was enticed. "Tell me."

"No," she teased.

"C'mon. How many?"

"Five," she finally answered. "Not counting the ears."

"Five? Five separate piercings?"

"Yeah." She shyly took another bite of cake.

"Where?"

She laughed again. "Not telling."

"Why not?"

She shrugged. Took another nibble, looking away a bit flushed.

"I bet I could guess," Martin said.

"Yeah?"

He nodded. "I bet I could."

She grinned. "Fine. Go ahead. Guess."

"No piercings on your face. Except the ears. So I'm guessing the navel?"

"Uh-huh."

"Both breasts?"

"Maybe."

"*Hmm*, where else?"

Lola took a long swallow of tea, smiling faintly.

"The tongue?"

"Right."

"And ... and," Martin chuckled, "I guess that would leave one last area."

Eyes down, Lola smiled. "You guessed it."

"No kidding?"

"Yep." She laughed.

Martin teased her a bit. "And that doesn't cause ... any problems?"

She laughed. "Nope. Not usually."

"Not even during sex?"

Lola grinned. "That's ... not up for discussion, right now."

Martin was smiling. "Just curious."

Redirecting the discussion somewhat, Lola related, "Actually, I used to have another piercing. In my left eyebrow."

"Yeah?"

"My body rejected it."

"Huh?"

"Over time, the ring rose to the surface. Then popped out."

"Just fell out? For good?"

She leaned over, showed him the spot. "See? Don't even have a scar from it or anything."

Martin gently touched the corner of her eyebrow and

saw it was true. "That's funny."

She laughed. "Wish that would happen with other things in my life!"

23.

Their predetermined "hour" well over, Martin and Lola sauntered up Avenue A.

Along the way, she told him that her parents were divorced and that living at home was "a big mistake." She and her mom fought almost daily. "We hate each other, pretty much," said Lola. "She's a hard person to get along with. 'High strung,' you might say."

"What about you?" he asked.

"I take more after my dad, who's easy-going. But I think as I'm getting older, I'm getting more uptight. Or afraid."

"Happens, I guess."

"Maybe I'm starting to see I've got a real struggle ahead of me. My teachers put me down. They say my paintings are too dark. Too morbid. I say, they're just reflections of what I see, of this side of the world. Am I supposed to close my eyes to everything just because it offends a few people? A few *New Age* twits? What's the point, then? What's the point of making art?"

She turned to him. "Are you at all 'political'?"

"Not really."

Lola took it in stride. "I know I'm not a 'team player' but I feel the need, sometimes, to fuck shit up. Like the riots in Tompkins Park, remember that?"

"Heard about it."

"Five hundred cops in riot gear. With their badge numbers taped, clubbing the shit out of anyone in their way. And all for the sake of protecting what?" She sighed. "If

26.

The next day at work, Martin faced his computer.

```
Japantrack - Air Export Operations
MAIN OPERATIONAL ROUTINES
```

Among the tedious options were: "*Consolidation Mani-festing, The Shipper's Export Declaration, Direct Airline/ Masterbill Entry, Shipment Booking Entry, Housebill Entry & Update, Consolida-tion Pre-Scheduling....*"

"Yo, *Willy the Shake!*"

Martin snapped out of it, turning to Chaz where he sat at his desk.

The man was under a heap of papers, grinning. "Do me a solid, bro. Book the consol?"

"Right." The script was always the same:

MARTIN: Hello, I'd like to book space to Tokyo, please.

AIRLINE AGENT: Number of pieces and weight?

MARTIN: Two thousand pounds.

AGENT: Restricted cargo?

MARTIN: None.

AGENT: Company name?

He gave it.

AGENT: That'll be flight *KZ101*, departing from JFK at *0200* hours. Please have all freight and documentation in on time.

Etcetera, etcetera.

But this time, before Martin had offered the concluding line, his mind was elsewhere—in particular, on phoning Lola.

"So?"

"Can't hang out, tonight," said Lola. "I have school work."

"For an hour, then?" he suggested. "Like last time."

She considered it. "Maybe. I don't know."

"Think about it," Martin said.

"Okay. I will."

"Ring you, later?"

"Up to you."

27.

That night, precisely at 8:30, Lola met Martin at the *No Bar*, and together they grabbed some espresso and *flan* in the back.

The *No Bar* was a café in the tradition of an old European coffee house; a simple place with bare walls, unvarnished wood floors, and antique-looking tables and chairs. By the door, as Martin had entered, an intense chess game was in progress; others sat reading an anarchist sheet called *The Shadow*.

"Hardly anyone I know comes here," said Lola. Adding: "That's why I love it."

Lola looked as compelling as she had the first time, her dark bangs neatly lined, her hypnotic eyes made even larger by an expert smudge of eye shadow.

She was busy emptying six packets of sugar into her espresso, when Martin, trying to be polite, asked how things were at home.

"At home?"

"Yeah. How's your mom?"

"Terrible," Lola replied. "Grotesque. Like a character straight out of Hieronymus Bosch."

He tried to smile. "Still fighting?"

"Tooth and claw. From the moment we see each other. Deep down she's really pissed off."

"Pissed off at what?" Feeling obliged to ask.

"At life. For passing her by. At me—for still having *mine*." She dropped a spoon into her cup and stirred noisily.

"So why do you put up with it?" Martin took a sip of espresso, wincing.

Her eyes seemed to glaze over. "Huh?"

"Why don't you *leave*? Move out?"

"'Cause," she said. "'Cause she's my mother. And I ain't got *this*:" Frowning, she rubbed her thumb and forefinger together, indicating "moolah."

"Oh," Martin nodded.

A small haggard-looking woman with deep swaths under her eyes crept by their table after emerging from the bathroom. "By chance," she moaned, "did anyone here find twenty dollars?"

As Lola and Martin faced her, she went on, "I had twenty—*twenty dollars*—when I came in here. And now it's gone! Any of you find it?"

As Lola and Martin remained silent, she suddenly burst out sobbing: "Please, I'm poor. I *need* it!"

Right then Martin noticed the lesions along her face and neck, the pitted bruises on her arms.

"*Pul-leeze!*" she bawled out loud. "I *neeeed* it. I *need* it, *now*!"

At which point the manager appeared. "Hey! That's enough! That's enough shit! Get out!"

"Wha?" She turned around dismayed.

"Every night this week," he muttered to himself. Then facing her "—Out!"

Chastised, she immediately fell silent and exited the cafe.

"Sorry," he said to Martin and Lola and soon went back

to his post behind the counter, "Every night, *every night….*"

"Shit," Martin frowned, lowering his voice. "The fuck was *that?*"

"A bad case of the *dope flu,*" sighed Lola. "Christ, I'll be back."

28.

After Lola returned from the restroom, she edged back into her corner seat and murmured, "Where were we?"

Slouched in his chair, M. lied, "Can't remember."

"Oh yeah," she recalled then. "My *mother.*" She raised her cup and took a sip. Replacing it on the saucer, her expression changed. Grew soft. She said quietly, "*Perdóneme.*"

"Huh?" He looked up.

"Didn't mean to take it out on you. If that's what it seemed like."

"*Ah…*" Martin tried to wave it off.

"Well, I am *sorry.* Just that," she sighed, "when it comes to my mom, I have this thing. This *history.*"

"*Lots* of people have hang-ups when it comes to their parents. Believe me."

"I know, I know." She took a moment. "And maybe I shouldn't tell you this. You'll think I'm sick. But when I was little and my dad left me—that is, my mom and me—I got this *idea* that my mother wanted to murder me."

"Murder you?"

Lola nodded. "It was just this *feeling,* I don't know what else to call it."

Martin put down his cup. "So what did you do?"

"Well, I pretended *not* to notice."

"That your mom wanted to *murder* you?"

57

"Yeah." She bobbed her head up and down. "Then, more or less, I just stopped eating. So she couldn't poison me."

"You *stopped* eating?"

She nodded.

"And," Martin narrowed his eyes, "she didn't notice?"

Lola shrugged. "I was careful. Like, if my mom cooked me something—a hot dog, say?—I'd take one tiny bite, then hide the rest in my pocket."

He forced a dry laugh. "And then?"

"This went on and on. Till I felt too tired to go to school in the morning."

"I'll bet!"

"Then," she laughed. "I finally woke up at St. Vincent's."

Martin looked at her. "You did?"

She nodded. "Once there at the hospital, they didn't find anything, of course. They recommended a child psychologist, but my mom wouldn't hear of it. 'That's for crazy people! *Locos!*' she said."

"So—they sent you home?"

"Well, afterwards. Yeah. They didn't have a choice. And, of course, my mom started treating me nicer for a while. Because she was scared."

Lola sighed. "But let me tell you, once my dad left us, took off, we never trusted each other after that." She shook her head. "Never."

"Wow," Martin nodded slowly, frowning. "*Heavy.*"

At that point, the manager came by asking if there would be anything else. Martin casually asked for the check.

Lola looked uneasy. She took a moment to finish her espresso, then asked, "So ... what about you?"

"Me?"

"Yeah, *your* mom. Didn't you mention that she passed away?"

"I mentioned that?"

"On the phone," she said.

"Yeah. Long time ago. I was a kid."

"So who raised you?" she asked.

"Grandparents."

"In Queens?"

"Inwood. Manhattan. Up near the Bronx."

"I think I know where that is."

"Can hardly remember it, actually. Like I remember my parochial school. Remember these white rocks just across the street. Sandstone, I think. And I remember these great parks. This one *huge* park, nearby. With giant ball fields. And Indian caves. Beautiful." Martin leaned back. "I remember this one big rock that had a plaque on it, marking the exact spot where the Dutch supposedly bought Manhattan Island from the Indians. For twenty-four bucks."

"—Yeah right," said Lola. "Very generous of them, those Dutch."

"Well, somebody always gets fucked." Martin went on, "What else do I remember? I remember my mom, always sleeping. Being *depressed*. Only I didn't know why at the time. Or what it meant. To this day, I'm still trying to figure it out."

"Were you happy as a kid?"

"Happy?" He thought about it. "Nah."

"Me, neither," she said. "I remember wishing the whole world would end. I kept praying for those bombs from Russia."

Martin almost cracked up.

Lola continued, "I kept looking up at the sky at night. And saying, 'Where *are* those damn warheads, already?'" She laughed. "Seemed like such a waste to leave 'em, gathering cobwebs and dust."

"You were praying for *Armageddon?*"

"*Yup*. Now and then, I still do. For one last mondo-cosmic *ka-boom!*"

"Hey," Martin laughed, "I thought you were into social justice and all that? Politics."

"I am," she smiled. "That's what I mean."

"—Like that inscription outside of 7A?" Martin tossed in, "'*World Politics got you down? Try drinking.*'"

"Yeah. *Obliteration*—my point, exactly."

Martin chuckled, draining his cup.

"Hey," she suggested, "I have an idea. Why don't we get out of here? Go up to my place?"

It caught him unexpectedly. "But what about your mom?"

"She's out. Uptown, actually."

"And your school work and everything?"

"*Ah,*" she grinned. "Fuck *that.*"

29.

Lola's place—or the one she shared with her mother—was on the fifth floor of an old brick walkup on 13th Street. Up the rickety staircase just past the first floor lay a scruffy teenager, eyes rolled back in his head.

"That's just Steve," she said blandly. "He *lives* here."

"What's up with him?"

"Goofed up on *K*, probably."

Martin asked what that was.

She shrugged. "Oh, an *animal tranquilizer*...."

By the third floor, on the subject of drugs, Lola was telling Martin about her first boyfriend—some creep by the name of "Maze"—who, after their break-up, had become, as she put it, "a serious drug abuser."

"We were still speaking," she said. "Tried to stay friends, but it got hard. He started mainlining about four months after we stopped seeing each other. Till then, it was just some chipping. As a weekend thing." She turned to him. "Y'know, a little taste, now and then."

Mainlining? Chipping? "Right."

"So what'd he do for a living?" Martin asked.

"Not a whole lot," she replied. "He was kinda like a performance artist."

"Recited dramatic pieces 'n' stuff?"

"No." She sighed. "More like, he juggled on street corners. And sometimes panhandled."

"Oh."

"He was also in a band," she added wearily. "But they never really practiced."

"Uh-huh."

"Anyway, he's in prison now...."

Her apartment was a typical Lower East Side railroad flat, one ridiculously narrow space linked to the next. In the living room, Lola offered him a spot on the slip-covered couch. "Forgot I needed to pay a call," she said.

"Okay. Sure." He sat down, the plastic crackling beneath him.

"You can check out those dumb art books or whatever." She pointed at the stack by his feet, the kind of hefty hardcovers once sold by well-stocked book peddlers along the main drag of St. Marks. The top volume featured the work of the English painter Francis Bacon.

When Lola re-entered the room, Martin was still flipping pages.

"He had a habit of wearing fishnet stockings and garters under his pants," she casually imparted.

"Who?"

"Him. Francis Bacon. Helped him to relax."

Martin looked at a self-portrait of the painter's broad, wildly distorted face and tried to imagine it.

She went on, "I also read somewhere that he would gamble *to lose*. He wanted to lose."

Martin told her there was a French novelist like that. "Some old guy, what's his name?" Closing his eyes, he tried to remember. It finally came to him: "*Balzac.*"

"Guess when you think about it," Lola said, "not too many artists lead 'healthy' lives."

"Nope."

"Thought about this the other day," she continued, joining him on the couch, "that most artists probably need to maintain a certain level of 'dysfunction,' a certain amount of self-loathing. 'Cause why do it? Why wallow in *that much* dejection and abuse?"

"T'ain't healthy," Martin frowned. "That's for sure."

Finally he closed the book, put it back. After a moment, looking around the room, he asked her where she managed to paint.

"Where?—Right here," she shrugged, indicating the same space.

Martin looked around. "So where's your easel and all that? Your canvasses?"

"Packed up and put away."

"Any chance I can see some of them?"

"My paintings?"

"Yeah," he grinned. "Your paintings."

Lola appeared undecided, but at last, standing up, said, "Well ... *all right*. Wait here." And uneasily left the room in the direction of the kitchen.

Martin could hear her rustling a bead curtain, open and close a cupboard. Some cutlery clattered to the floor. "Shit!" he heard her cry.

Lola finally returned clutching a knotted garbage bag in her right hand. In her left hand she was holding a bottle and a corkscrew. Handing him the wine, she insisted, "Before you look, you gotta open this."

"Sounds cool to me," Martin grinned and, accepting the bottle, put it between his knees, applying the corkscrew.

Lola joined him on the couch and unknotted the garbage bag, taking a nervous look inside. "These are *early* ones. But I still like 'em."

"I'm sure they're good," he said, grimacing as he pulled out the cork, then peeled away the remaining pewter wrapping.

Lola lunged for the bottle: "Me first!" Taking a long pull, then passing it back: "*Ahora tú.*"

"*Gracias.*" Obliging her, some wine dribbled from his lip.

"And now the art!" she announced, digging into the sack and yanking them out. Kicking the empty plastic bag away with her foot. "*Tah-dah!*"

His eyes widened in regarding the work: two canvasses— both portraying, in startling hyper-realistic detail, night-marish scenes of intense psychopathic violence.

In the first, entitled "Pig Party," several NYPD officers

were shown gruesomely dismembered, the amputated limbs of one cop brutally wedged up his own obscenely stretched rectum. In the other, untitled, a white-haired girl in pigtails sat dreamily on a curb, site of a traffic accident, munching human entrails like raw link sausages. In her lap, like a grinning moon, a severed head. Carved on the forehead was a tiny cross and, just above it, the word, *"Lolita."*

Both canvasses were slathered in blood *red* from top to bottom.

"These are my least hostile paintings," she informed him.

"'That right." He took another slug of wine, wrinkling his nose.

"So," she nudged, "whaddaya say?"

Martin continued to regard them with a dazed expression. A minute skirted by. At last, he thought to remark, "Sure ain't *'new age'*—I'll say that!"

30.

Twenty minutes later, Lola and Martin were both on the carpet, the empty bottle between them.

"Let me ask you another one," he said.

They were side-by-side, flat on their backs, Lola gamely answering each far-flung, drunken question.

"Did you say you believed in *God*?"

Squinting: *"Who?"*

"You know, in some 'higher power'?"

Lola paused. "Nah."

"Then, what, do you believe in fate?"

Again she thought about it, finally wagging her head. "Nuh-uh." She clicked the jewelry in her mouth. "I think things just happen. Without reason. One person is born. Another vanishes. No one knows why. Or has any real say."

"But, don't people *initiate* things sometimes?"

"What do ya mean?"

"I mean, here I placed a personal ad and you answered it."

She shrugged, rubbing a nipple ring through her top. "Yeah. So."

Martin slid the empty bottle away, moving closer. "So, I'm just saying, it *was* through some *active* effort on *our* part that we connected at just this time."

"What are you getting at, exactly?"

He shrugged. "I guess I was just thinking it does seem like a lucky break."

"Oh sure," said Lola. "I believe in luck."

"And I guess," he said. "'Guess, I'm trying to say"—he forced a laugh—"I'm glad you answered my ad."

Lola rolled on the floor to face him. "You're not about to tell me you're 'hooked,' or anything like that?"

"Huh?"

"In *love*."

He forced another laugh. "All I'm saying is, I'm glad we met."

"Oh. All right." She turned away.

He prodded her. "Aren't *you* glad?"

"Uh." She took a moment. "Can you repeat the question?"

Martin laughed. Lola finally smiled.

"Hard," he teased. "You're *hard*. I'm totally convinced."

"That's right," she said proudly. "I'd sooner be a bitch

than a doormat."

He sat up. "That right, that how it is? You're not *interested* in me, at all?"

Smiling faintly, she looked him in the eye. "I didn't say *that*," she replied. "Who said *that*?"

They remained gazing at each other.

Finally Martin leaned in. Lola met him: they kissed softly, then more passionately. At last, as Lola tipped her head and parted her lips, Martin tasted her heated jewelry.

His tongue mingling with hers, Martin's fingers trailed down her spine, slowly between her buttocks, slipping at last between her thighs—Lola letting out a moan. Embracing each other now, still kissing and groping, they playfully rolled on the floor—once—with her landing on top. Then, unable to resist, Martin awkwardly tried to unbutton her denims. At which point, Lola's expression fell and she stiffened, pulling back.

He froze, beneath her. "What."

She sighed. Not saying anything. Her face impassive.

"What is it?" he asked.

"Um," she frowned and tried to laugh. "It's kinda embarrassing."

"What is?"

"I got my ... you know."

He shook his head, waiting.

"My 'little friend.'"

He looked at her, forcing a smile. "So? Can't we work around it?"

"No—I know. Just..." She shrugged again, red-faced. "I'm not sure I *feel* like it now, that's the thing."

Martin looked at her in amazement. "You seemed interested a minute ago."

"I was. A minute ago."

"So?" He wasn't getting it.

"So, we better not. I mean, not now," Lola said. "Anyway, my mom should be coming home soon."

"*What?*"

"I live with my *mother*, remember?"

"*And?*"

"She may be coming home soon.—Are you *deaf?*"

Apart from disbelief, Martin felt a sinking disappointment. He took a deep breath. "What," he asked. "You want I should go then?"

She thought about it, still looking embarrassed.

"Maybe."

31.

At the door, hiding his displeasure, he asked her, "So, what comes after this?"

"What do you mean?"

Martin sighed. "What, y'know ... what comes next?"

"Let's take it easy."

"Okay, fine." Then, in the next breath: "What are you doing this weekend?"

"Don't know. Painting, I guess."

"Even Saturday night?"

"Actually, Saturday, I'm going to a party."

"Oh?"

"Yeah, with Mina. You met Mina, remember?"

He tried not to appear jealous. "The stripper. Yeah."

"Well, she's not *just* a stripper," said Lola. "She's my friend."

"Okay, yeah."

"It's just some party," she said consolingly.

"Uh-hmm."

"We can go out some other time."

Martin shrugged, trying to feign indifference. Then countered: "What makes you think *I* want to?"

Lola smiled. "*I* think you want to."

He shrugged again, irritated. She was right, of course. Could she read him *that* easily?

She reiterated, "We'll go out some other time."

"Yeah," Martin sighed. "Whatever."

"Whatever," she laughed.

"I just said that."

Lola laughed again. Finally Martin cracked a smile.

With that, she leaned forward to offer him a final kiss. This time, his tongue invading her mouth, he managed to draw her stud between his teeth:

"—Promise?"

Startled, she nearly gagged, "*Yeh!*"

He let go.

32.

```
Japantrack - Air Export Operations
MAIN OPERATIONAL ROUTINES

(1) Consolidation Manifesting
(2) Shipper's Export Declaration
(3) Direct Airline/Masterbill Entry
(4) Shipment Booking Entry
(5) Housebill Entry & Update
(6) Consolidation Pre-scheduling
```

At last, Martin hit (6), which brought him to the next screen.

Picking up the phone, he arranged the usual booking with JAL, then hit (5), the bulk of his daily work. Facing the stack of invoices on his desk, he began with the *Shipper's Address*, then *Company Consigned*, continuing to *Airport of Departure* and *First Carrier*. On and on, down the face of the template.

Hitting *Return* again, a second screen appeared, and Martin hastily filled in the requested information (weight, "airfreight" charge, reference and license numbers, transport and customs fees), completing the form at the bottom, by adding his own name, humble company position ("Export Assistant") and the date.

Finally, he punched "Post & P", and the dot matrix printer behind him began loudly scraping and sputtering, jamming almost immediately.

Realigning the paper, Martin tried again. It lodged and crumpled. He leveled it strategically. And this time, at long last, a completed House Air Waybill emerged (in a twin, multi-layered form) from the crusty, outmoded, mostly unreliable machine.

And, straightening the pile of sixty or so invoices left on his desk, he thought then, *'Makes one down ...* his gaze landing on the sticker over his monitor (placed by some distant, long forgotten export assistant):

"ANY IDIOT CAN FACE A CRISIS –
IT'S THIS DAY-TO-DAY LIVING
THAT WEARS YOU OUT."

33.

"How about the second one? The one with the beeper?" Nikki asked. They were on the phone.

"Amaris?"

"That her name?"

"Paged her yesterday, early. And she rang me back."

"So you talked?"

"Yeah. A good long time. At first she said she was up to something that afternoon and couldn't meet me. Then agreed to meet, anyway."

"Where?"

"Nik, she made a *weird* suggestion. You'd *never* guess...."

34.

Wandering down a winding asphalt path, Martin stopped to ask a caretaker for directions. At last, beyond a mammoth willow tree down a hill, he spotted her: a stark angel dressed in black.

Approaching her, feeling more than a bit anxious, he called out, "Amaris?"

She faced him.

Lustrous, shoulder-length hair with bleached highlights and indigo tips. Dark, blue-tinged shades. Liver-colored lipstick in contrast to a powdered face.

She removed her sunglasses, smiling and squinting in the light. He saw that she was *Amer*asian. "You showed!"

"I said I would." He extended a hand.

She grabbed it, shook it. "So, at last we meet," she said.

"Yep. Call it fate, call it persistence."

"I prefer *fate*," she grinned.

Pulling him closer, she suddenly—*firmly*—kissed him on the mouth.

Amaris laughed at his reaction—then apologized and gently wiped his lips. "It's just—I like to get it over with," she smiled. "You know, that 'first-kiss' business."

"Right." Wiping off the lipstick traces with his fingers.

"It's so annoying," she said, helping him.

"Uh-huh...."

"Actually," she teased, "if you don't mind my saying it, you don't look so *bad* in that color." And removing a slim tube from her box purse, suggested, "Want a full application?"

"I'll pass. *Thanks.*"

Amaris opened the lipstick and, without the aid of a mirror, deftly re-applied a coat. "Suit yourself." And laughed.

Poised, comfortable with herself. He liked her already.

Martin smiled. "Prefer men who primp, is that it?"

"So long as *I'm* with them," she confided, laughing again. Then, putting her glasses back on: "Hope you don't mind."

"What."

"These," she indicated. "My *dayshades.* It's just, with the *light.*—I hate the sun."

"You do?"

"Well, I much prefer the moon. Being a creature of the night."

Creature of the night. "I see," he chuckled.

She appeared pleased. "A sense of humor," she grinned. "That's good."

The truth was—Martin was finding it hard *not* to laugh.

A moment later, taking in the wide manicured lawns, the thriving willows, the marble and granite slabs, he asked if she made it out here often.

"All the time," Amaris replied. "It's so peaceful."

"Oh, it's peaceful, all right."

"At least you know you won't be bothered," she added.

He looked around. "I should hope not," he said.

The twin gravesite before them consisted of a large granite headstone laid with fresh, waxy tulips.

After a while, Martin felt obliged to ask, "Relations?"

"Parents."

He felt uneasy all of a sudden.

Smiling she faced the double grave and said: "*Mommy, daddy*—meet Marty."

"I don't get it. I thought you said you *lived* with your parents?"

"—Say hello, Marty."

"Hello," Martin said.

"—I do. My adopted ones."

"Oh."

"Who are also my aunt and uncle."

"Ah. Right."

"Yeah," she went on. "They took over the reins, so to speak, after both my parents were killed. In a car accident."

"Damn," Martin said. "*Tragic.*"

She shrugged, "It happens, I guess. *Happened* ages ago."

Martin then explained about his own parents. Or the lack of them. And how he was raised by his grandparents, which, he pointed out, set up an interesting parallel between them.

She then asked about his grandparents: "Are they still alive?"

"Yep."

"See them often?"

"Nope."

"Not at all?" She seemed surprised. "Don't speak with them?"

Half ashamed, he forced a smile, "A letter, now and then. Christmas cards. That kind of thing."

With her taking the lead, they slowly began walking.

He shrugged again. "They always wanted me to have a more conventional life. Y'know, a 'professional' career. That whole bit."

"And you weren't up for that?"

Martin grinned, "Guess not." Facing her directly, he laughed. "Being a total *masochist*, I wanted a life full of perpetual *failure* and *disappointment*—so of course I chose the 'art life.'"

35.

Speaking of disappointments.

Walking along the trail, past an impressive array of black tulips, lily-of-the-valley, and yellow irises, Amaris brought up the issue of her divorce.

Martin asked if it was final.

"Still in the process. Filling out documents."

"Sounds like a drag."

"It is." She removed a pack of Dunhills from her purse. "We've been separated six months."

"Six months. And you haven't seen him since? Romantically?"

She lit up, shaking her head. "Nope."

They walked in silence for a while, then Amaris said, "It's sad. Few nights ago, I was filling out legal papers when my son trotted in, saw what I was writing, and pointed to a couple of words I'd just jotted down." She imitated a child's voice: "'*Mommy, what do these words mean?*'—I nearly cried."

"Which words?"

"'Constructive abandonment.'"

She took another drag.

Finally Martin asked, "Is it tough with a kid? Going out and all?"

Amaris shrugged, "I have family to look after him."

"Your aunt and uncle?"

"Uh-hmm. Also grandparents, on my real mother's side. Plus friends."

He asked her if she ever felt guilty, despite that.

"That's why I always carry one of these," she said, indicating her beeper.

"Oh. Right." He turned to her and smiled.

On the subject of family, Amaris told him how her uncle (and father surrogate) was actually a step-uncle and how her aunt had been married *six* times.

"You're kidding?"

She shook her head, no.

"Six times?"

She nodded, "My aunt actually had bad luck, though. Each of her husbands kept dying on her."

Finally they approached a cement bench in the shade and sat down.

It was then, regarding her self-consciously "gothic" attire—a black knit dress with black stockings and boots— that Martin could hardly suppress a laugh.

"Want to let me in on the joke?" she asked.

"That *pentagram* on your hose."

Grinning, she leaned back a bit, raising her legs so that her boots were off the ground. "Like them? Bought them on St. Marks. In a pagan shop. Bought two pair, in fact."

"Halloween sale?"

She gave him a wry look. "Ha."

He asked straight out: "You're not into magic—a 'witch,' by chance?"

"Since you're asking," she said. "*No.*" Smiling again: "But

I know people who are."

"Really?"

"It's not what you think, though. It's mostly about getting in touch with 'nature.' Fertility rites and all that. A kind of *primitivism*. Totally innocent."

"Oh yeah?"

She nodded, reaching into her bag for another cigarette. "I used to room with someone who was part of a coven, and she used to take off her clothes all the time with her other neo-pagan girlfriends, invoking nature spirits."

"Sounds awright," Martin said.

Eyeing him, Amaris smirked, lighting her smoke.

After another moment, he remembered her initial phone message and asked her, "You teach school, you said?"

"College," she said, exhaling. "Part time. In the Bronx."

"You don't look older than most of your students, I'll bet."

She grinned. "Got that right. Freaks some people out."

"The younger students can relate to you, I'm sure."

"Uh-huh. Some I even hang out with. On a social basis."

This struck him as odd. "Really?"

She nodded, privately amused.

"And that doesn't pose any problems?"

She shrugged, smiling. "I keep a short list. Any problems—I make sure to get even."

Martin said, "What, give 'em failing grades at the end of the semester or something?"

"Ain't telling."

Her pager beeped.

Reaching for it, she muttered, "*Christ.*"

"Trouble?"

She checked the number. Sighed. "Don't know. But I

guess I should get to a phone."

They left the cemetery and crossed the street to the first available pay phone. Martin stood at an awkward distance while she made the call.

Finally she hung up. Approached him.

"Sorry. It's about River, my son. Nothing catastrophic. But, I guess I need to go."

"Well, that was brief. It was nice *almost* getting to know you," he said.

Amaris smiled. "We'll do it another time, okay? Soon. Go dancing? Would you like that?"

"Why not," Martin said. "No, let me re-phrase that—*shit, yeah.*"

He then bent forward, intending to give her a friendly peck on the cheek when she suddenly leaned in, grasped him, and gave him a forceful kiss on the mouth.

Pulling back: "*All right, then!*" she laughed.

36.

Over the phone, Martin told Nikki: "I'd tramped all the way back to my car, strapped myself in, when I realized, looking up into the mirror, that I'd been wearing a *fat* coat of lipstick the whole time!"

"So she got you," tittered Nikki.

He laughed. "Yep. I looked like Marilyn Manson."

"Talked since?"

"Not yet." He admitted, "Still recovering." He laughed, again. "Anyway, whatcha' up to, tomorrow?"

She took a moment to recall, "I'm supposed to meet Mariella around two."

"What about later. At night?"

"Not sure yet."

"Maybe we can hang out?"

She thought about it, teased, "Maybe."

Then Martin laughed: "*Maybe*, yeah. Just *try* to keep it in mind."

37.

The following night, as it turned out, the eatery of choice was *Benny's*, a modest Mexican restaurant on Avenue A.

As Nikki ordered, Martin witnessed—through the plate glass window—a grubby specimen across the street swipe another man's prosthetic *arm*. (Slapstick, East Village style.)

"And you?" smiled the waitress, turning to him.

"Uh," matter-of-factly, "I'll take a whole wheat chicken Bay Burrito; brown rice and pinto beans."

Dressed down in a pair of faded Levis and a light blue mohair sweater—no make-up except for eyeliner—Nikki looked as unassumingly attractive, as radiant and beautiful as the first day they'd met.

Martin asked how things had gone that afternoon with Mariella.

She mumbled something, and Martin had to ask her to repeat it.

"Okay, I guess," she sighed.

"The 'reunion' was the main topic of conversation, I take it?"

"What else?" Cutting her veggie burrito.

Martin prodded, "*Psyched* for it, then: the big commitment?"

Quietly chewing her food, Nikki took her time. "To be honest?" she said. "I'm tired of hammering it out in my brain."

"What, feeling the pressure?"

She shrugged.

"Guess, in the end," he reminded her, "you could always move up the date. If you had to."

Wearing a lop-sided smile, Nikki looked away. Martin smiled. "You're not saying anything."

"*Oh.*" Nikki sighed. "Been over this so many times. I mean, how long has this been going on?"

Martin knew, precisely, but chose not to mention it.

They ate in silence awhile.

Then, shaking her head, she confessed, "It's just—God, sometimes … I hate her. The way she makes me feel."

"Why?"

Nikki sighed again. "I keep telling her, 'This is our *last* chance to let it hang out. Meet some people. Have some *fun.*'"

"And she says?"

"Well, two days ago she sounded all for it. Said she even *met* someone at a club. Had a blast. This morning I ask her about it and she tells me, 'Oh fuck all that—why can't we just be together?'"

"You said?"

"Marty, I told her the truth." She frowned. "I'm just … not ready."

He reminded her, "Nikki, she's a big girl, y'know. She can take care of herself."

"I know."

"She can make up her own mind. To stay involved or walk away."

"I know, I know."

"So," he shrugged, "she's made up *her* mind." He popped a nacho chip into his mouth. Crunched. "Now, you make up *yours.*"

"Easy for *you* to say," she smiled.

38.

That morning, the day Nikki and Martin first met, they had agreed to meet outside the Waverly Theatre on Third Street. And when Martin arrived there five minutes early, he discovered a woman already standing there, facing away, fitting the description she'd given him ("long straight chestnut hair, about 5'6, slender"). It was late spring and warm, so the woman wore a breezy floral print dress and a pair of laced, thin-soled sandals. The greater part of her smooth legs, he couldn't help but notice, were exposed to the sun, and he noted another detail (gaze drifting down): that above her left foot, and under the entwining straps, was a delicate, daisy-chain anklet tattoo.

She looked at the time like some young, sultry southern gal from an MTV "alternative" music video, or a dreamy nymph from a "wish-fulfillment" beer commercial (in which young, lithe beauties—the embodiment of male longing— always seemed to be just standing around, *waiting*); and at that moment, giving her the once over, Martin felt a catch in his throat, signifying—he had to admit—*lust!*

No way. It *couldn't* be her.

Her long hair loosely in a pony tail, her back to him, she stood calmly eyeing the monitor near the glass entrance, which featured film clips of movies currently showing as well as "coming attractions." Appearing lost in thought, she languidly scratched an elbow, then crossed her slender milk-white arms.

… Nah, that couldn't be her, he told himself again. For one thing, he was used to people from the personals showing up grossly late; for another, she just seemed too beautiful stand-ing there—too much like out of some damn Hollywood movie (and real life wasn't like that)!

Martin sidled up to her anyway and mumbled, "*Uh*, hello?" And when there was no response, he tapped her shoulder. "'Nikki'?"

At last she turned. And he saw her pale-green eyes for the first time.

"*Marty?*"

Martin was struck dumb.

Her eyes took on a look of concern. "Your name *is* Marty, isn't it?" she asked.

He wasn't so sure himself, now. "I *think* so," he said.

Right then Martin could hardly believe his luck.

39.

On the corner of 6th Street, ragamuffin skate punks con-gregated, soliciting funds, while up the block, a wacked-out girl with neon-green hair and yellow day-glo lipstick hawked issues of a revived journal entitled, *Fuck You: A Magazine of the Arts.*

"*Fuck you*, sir?" she cried to impassive pedestrians. "Ma'am?—*Fuck you?*"

Along the way Martin and Nikki chatted:

"What's next on the agenda?" she asked. They'd just come from a brief sojourn at a local bar, already high.

"A little movin'? Little groovin'?"

"Dancing?"

"Unless you'd suggest something better?"

"*Dancing*," she grinned, reaching for his hand. "*That's* something we haven't done together in a while."

Holding hands, swinging right on Avenue A, Martin

and Nikki rolled past the raised gate of the *Pyramid Club*, past the slouching street vendors displaying their usual wares of used books, clothes, incense and scented oils. Reaching *Alcatraz* (a head-bangers bar) and the crowded corner of St. Marks Place, they swung left. "We going where I think we're going?" Nikki asked. "Mind?" Nikki rocking hard against him, eyes narrowed in mock intensity: "Oh I *mind*, buddy.—I *mind*…."

Up St. Marks Place, across the cracked and uneven pavement, Martin and Nikki eyed the joint with the bright yellow and blue awning—their favorite drag bar/restaurant—*Stingy Lulu's*, where in the past, they'd met to share lost time together.

Nikki asked, "Remember the time that blond waiter flashed us his new tits?"

"Oh yeah," Martin laughed. "Bugged."

They passed other favorite haunts: intimate *Anseo's*, folky *Café Sin-e*. Coming up across the way was the Moroccan *Café Mogador* and the open-all-hours *Yaffa Café*. On their left, they passed the basement *St. Marks Studio Theatre*, the sidewalk billboard banked with fluttering tiny yellow flyers, declaring tonight's program: *Cannibal Cheerleaders on Crack!*

Crossing the avenue, they passed *Theatre 80*, treading over the worn cement foot-and-handprints of old actresses: Joan Crawford, Joan Blondell, Gloria Swanson, et al. (At the time Martin and Nikki first met, it was a grind house, showing scratchy, often hilariously ruined prints—double features.) Across the street was the casually decrepit *Holiday Cocktail Lounge* where, afterwards, they would go for drinks.

Nikki brought up that morning's telephone conversation

with her mom. "We're finally getting there, I think. To that place of tolerance and mutual respect." She faced Martin, eyes widening: "Oh, did I tell you. She's thinking of getting hitched, again?—*Número cinco*, can ya believe it?" *Damn*, Martin thought. Nikki laughed, "And she still wants to *rush* it!" They walked past the iron-wrought gates of the old *Club 57*—once a vital part of the East Village art scene—now, ironically, a mental health institute.

"Checked him out?" Martin asked. Nikki said, "No, not yet. She wants me down there, though. To meet him. In *Miami*." They swept by several cheerless street vendors, whose wares—displayed on ratty blankets—were being impounded by the police, until at last arriving on the busy corner of 2nd.

"So what," Martin said, "you'd be like, the maid of honor at their wedding?" "Hell *no*," laughed Nikki. "I'm not *that* far gone. I'll be there, at the reception, sure. But only as a *guest*. To show my support." Martin said, "Gotcha.'" Nikki joked: "This one should last all of *three weeks!*" They dawdled at the light, watching yellow cabs zoom by, bumping and pounding over potholes and heavy iron plates.

The street took on a carnival-like atmosphere, heightened by lights and a palpable nervous energy. Swarms of night-trippers moved in all directions, the noise level increasing, too: people laughing, shouting, crying; screeching brakes, bleating car horns, thumping woofers of sweeping car stereos: *chuga-boom! chuga-boom!, boom!-boom!-boom!, chuga-boom!…*

Crossing 2nd Avenue, pushing through sidewalk traffic, Nikki and Martin took in a dazed soul handing out psychedelic flyers, the corner Gem Spa Newsstand, and then crammed tourist stalls and brightly-lit souvenir shops.

On stoops or lolling on the sidewalk were the occasional congregations of retro-punks, existing almost as postcard images, most in leather jackets embellished with chains, metal studs, and Wite-out, or dressed in layered clothes visibly torn and held together with safety pins; some wore the perfect "hedge-hog" or Statue of Liberty cut, or the neatly ironed spectrum-colored Mohawk; others, less fashionable, wore their sheared and dyed scalps cut along the sides with giraffe and leopard skin markings. These retro-punks stood idly shooting the shit and now and then posing sourly and cadging for "y'know, man ... like cash?"

Along the way, a tipsy Martin and Nikki discussed how things *used to be*: "A *drug block* this was, I swear.... And there weren't all these stalls and crap. Things weren't so ... hyped, either." He looked around, "Things have sure changed a lot since."

"Not to mention, they even managed to outlaw all the booksellers—"

"Like the artists from Soho."

"Booksellers!" railed Nikki. "Imagine that. These days you couldn't even peddle your own poetry down here. It's *against the law*."

"Know yer rights, sistah."

"'*Rights*.'" She grinned lopsidedly. "*Uh-huh*. They went with the constitution."

In the middle of the block was the Community Center, once home of *The Dom*, a famous bar and dance hall, then site of Andy Warhols' *Exploding Plastic Inevitable*. Now a drug treatment center.

Crossing the street, Martin and Nikki stopped by a plain, unmarked steel door. Martin pulled at it—it gave—

and they slipped inside and up the long flight of stairs illuminated by blue tube light. Paying the cover, they advanced to the second floor of a space for years known as "BB's" or *Boy's Bar*, tonight hosting the bi-weekly glam revival party dubbed "Blackdoor NYC."

Inside Martin offered, "Buy ya another?"

"Shouldn't, really."

"A *short* one?"

She yielded, "All right." And they drifted across the murky, scarcely crowded room, a loud T-Rex ballad warbling over the PA.

At the bar she turned to him, "Let me get it, this time. You grab us a spot?"

"I can deal with that." And, grinning, Martin walked back across the room, finding a small table by the entrance, where he took a seat against the mirrored wall.

40.

At first glance, the joint resembled any other East Village bar, painted black and illuminated by hazy light. There was an old pool table off to one side, several TV monitors (projecting arcane commercials), and along the walls more mismatched tables and chairs.

What made the place visually exciting, though, was not the room itself or the minimal décor, but the individuals that would eventually occupy it: those oddly-obsessed and slightly-off-kilter revelers, who would put in an appearance tonight and give it an almost delirious, magical air.

All types showed up, and as Nikki brought up the Red Stripes, she and Martin watched them arrive:

There were rockabilly boys with pompadours and elephant trunk haircuts, short-cuffed vintage clothes, leather and suede creepers. And there were the out-of-wack sixties revivalists and Edie Sedgewick cultists with Twiggy-like short hair, false eyelashes, green and blue eye shadow; neo-mod girls sporting the "Cleopatra look" in micro-mini skirts and Op Art go-go boots.

Sixties revivalists also included nuevo-hippies, unwashed art degenerates mostly, wearing the occasional Afghan jacket and other yippy paraphernalia: fruit-colored granny glasses, top hats, and love beads.

The retro-futurist eighties could be seen: doomsday ethos crossed with gloss punk, *Blade Runner*-inspired artifice fused with *Liquid Sky* geometric face paints. Heavy Metal studded wristbands, plastic style, and exploding hair.

But most notably represented and re-interpreted was the era of "glam rock," the mid-seventies. Ambi-sexuality. Lip liner for men. Glitter eye shadow and blush. Camp projections. There were those glammers—heroin-thin diamond dogs—who vamped around in muddy eye make-up, wearing variations of spandex jumpsuits or flashy rock 'n' roll wear. There were razor cuts: the ever-present tousled rooster or long disheveled shag, like images culled from long-forgotten issues of *Creem* magazine. "Glam" style was glittery "show-biz" crossed with jungle-print trash esthetic: a reveling in the underbelly of sleazy club culture, vaguely illicit, diseased, and junk inspired. The androgyny and dark glamour of Ziggy Stardust, Iggy Pop, and The New York Dolls was most evident.

Neo-seventies dames, on the other hand, were more stereotypically "feminine" and retrogressive, strutting about doll-like and pouty, in tight high-water flares and platforms, satin chokers, and belly-baring baby T's. Flat, long, straight hair, parted in the middle was *de rigueur*. Thick upper eyeliner and thinly shaped eyebrows were popular, as were cherry red lipstick and bright rich nail polish. It was a glossy, "harmless" projection of early seventies Playboy bunny/baby femme appeal.

What was most peculiar and disturbing was that with some of the patrons, it was not merely a costume party—these were *not* just playful role re-interpretations: some actually *believed* that they were living in their own self-chosen, largely re-imagined eras.

As Nikki once remarked: "They all seem kinda lost in their own private little *time warps*."

And it didn't end with music sub-cults: one party regular completely believed he was Barbara Eden from the old TV show *I Dream Of Jeannie* and padded around in harem costume and curled-toed slippers, arms crossed and blinking, "Y-yyes, master!" Another mental defective seemed convinced he was the Soviet spy, Ilya Kuryakin from *The Man From U.N.C.L.E.*

. *41.*

Finishing her drink, Nikki suggested, "Let's go downstairs before it gets too crowded."

"Too late for that!" Martin laughed.

Through the jostling crowd, Martin and Nikki descended a long, brightly-lit staircase to the main floor and another bar. The wall behind the bar displayed textured junk art from the '80s: plastic dolls, piano keys, scrap metal and other debris, permanently soldered to the wall and painted flat black, existing now as a fossilized apocalyptic backdrop. If the upstairs room of *BB's* had seemed dark and forbidding on arrival, this floor was even more so. Except for sparsely hung Christmas lights and a few blinking gel-colored spots on the far end, it was completely dark. The pounding music was a louder, shag-nasty glam alternated with rare punk and funk tunes. And as Martin and Nikki made their way to the opposite end of the room, near a short wooden stage (their eyes adjusting to the light), they soon found a decent spot in which to move.

All around them, the usual partygoers, tripping or drunk, were going wild. The floor was jumping. Hands hovering and waving, arms flailing, heads rolling, bodies churning.

Taking the stage beneath a liquid projection light show, three be-wigged black girls began lip-syncing The Supremes, while a slender Japanese woman in gold bikini and platinum wig appeared behind them, working a hoola-hoop. Off to another side, a near-naked belly dancer was fluidly grinding, a pink day-glo smiley face centered on her very-pregnant belly.

Hips swaying, torsos dipping and rising, occasionally hands touching and locking—Martin and Nikki got loose, taking in the crowd around them and each other.

A young freak in turquoise feather boa and *007* glasses teetered by on what must have been eighteen-inch high, glow-in-the-dark rubber platforms.

A startled Nikki nudged Martin. "See those?—*Florescent stilts!*"

All around them revivalists were performing wicked dance moves or borrowing steps from the past: the Pogo, the Mashed Potato, the Pony, the Jerk. On the surrounding embankment, others were crowd-watching or cooling out or nodding, now and then raising their sweating cups of beer or fat glowing joints.

There was a good vibe—plenty of handshakes and smiles to go around—and everyone seemed unusually friendly.

The air filled with a kind of sweet promise, Martin and Nikki danced and danced. The music cranking, the floor vibrating under their feet, still slightly buzzed, they were lost in a timeless groove. Under the pulsating lights, they reaffirmed their connection to this time and place. And to each other. With their bodies they were able to convey what they couldn't in words: it was a perfect exchange, a faultless union. And, for a time, Martin and Nikki caught and held on to it.

Finally, at nearly four in the morning, the remaining crowd shagged out and dispersing, they gave in.

"Well, Marty," she smiled. "*That* was something."

42.

Martin and Nikki snagged the first available cab to Jackson Heights and drifted up to his studio where they hung out on his open sofa bed, eating Ben & Jerry's "Chubby Hubby" ice-cream and lazily chatting.

Sometime near sunrise, he offered her a choice: "Drive you home … or sleep over?"

Nikki took a while to decide.

At last, clearing her throat, she guiltily replied, "Maybe, tonight, I should go?"

Turning away, Martin was hardly able to conceal his disappointment.

Upon his return, Martin dumped his car keys on the sofa, finally noticing a blinking red light.

A message of hope?

Leaning over the machine, he pressed "play."

A pause, then an operator's recording:

"There appears to be a receiver off the hook, please hang up...."

43.

"So tell me," Martin said. "How was the party?"

"What party?—Oh, that. *Boring.*" It was several nights later. Lola was speaking over the phone.

"Didn't go over too well?"

"Nah," she sighed. "Two of the four people who were supposed to go cancelled. I knew they'd do that. Then, when we finally got there, it was like, totally lame. A real letdown."

"And that was it?"

"Yep. Now, aren't you glad you missed it?"

44.

The next evening, Lola was already in the lobby of the *Anthology Film Archives*, when Martin stumbled in late.

Apologizing, explaining how F train service had been held up, he asked her if she'd been waiting long.

"Just got here, myself," she owned up. "But I already grabbed a ticket."

The film they'd decided on earlier was Andy Warhol's *Trash*; and it seemed Martin hardly had time enough to pay his own admission and find a seat with Lola before the lights dimmed.

"Shit, talk about *seedy*," he chuckled. The movie was shot around the East Village circa 1970, before the closing of the legendary *Filmore East*. Yet it hardly seemed dated: dirtier maybe—but virtually the same cast of marginal types seemed to reside there still.

Trash's loosely structured story centered on "Little Joe," a heroin junkie, who—along with all the other degenerates in the film—stumbles from one listless adventure to the next, hoping to somehow "score."

Could this describe Martin's own life?

Lola sniggered through most of the movie, but especially at the closing scene, when a transvestite's half-baked scam to get on welfare as a pregnant mother blows up in his face. All the caseworker demands in exchange for a favorable report is a pair of the transvestite's silver high-heeled sandals, but he wouldn't get them. "No! They're my *only* shoes!" shrieks the transvestite. "Anyway, we're *entitled* to it…. I'm gonna have a baby … and you CAN'T HAVE MY FUCKING SHOES!" In the end, the vindictive government worker rises in a huff: " You think you're gonna get *welfare?*—You're not gonna get a *DIME!*"

"That was so ... *burlesque!*" said Lola once the film was over and they were headed up 2nd Avenue in the warm night.

"Evil, right?"

"Oh yeah," she laughed. "Totally *evil*. A *sleaze fest!*"

"Kind of like *Polyester*."

She said, "*Pink Flamingos*, more like."

"The blurb said those were the same characters—the transvestite and 'Little Joe'—that turned up in 'A Walk On the Wild Side,' that Lou Reed song."

"Oh *yeah?*" she said with some attitude.

"Just thought I'd mention it," Martin shrugged.

Lola made a pit stop at a decrepit bodega for some clove cigarettes, then they continued to 11th Street, turning right and rolling to Avenue A, where they picked out a bar next to the popular music venue, *Brownies*.

The *No-Tell Motel* was another East Village nightspot (like *Babyland*, *Max Fish* on Ludlow Street, and others) that shared a kitsch/retro esthetic. The storefront windows displayed drawn Venetian blinds and two signs propped against the glass that read: *"No-Tell Motel*, Bar & Lounge" and "Vacancy: *Yes.*"

Inside, past a doorway trimmed with bottle caps, a person swept past old strip posters, a classic jukebox, large soda cap signs, and other assorted trash Americana to join the crush at the dimly lit bar. One old sign by the mirror read, for no apparent reason, "Audrey's Diner," another, "God Bless America!"

In the back was a lounge area comprised of zebra-striped floor, Salvation Army sofas, thrift store lamps, and about a dozen tacky black velvet portraits. Contributing to the self-consciously warped ambience was a suspended TV monitor that flashed loops of Super-8 smut, featuring "erotic" dances by the cheerful '50s pin-up icon, Betty Page.

After buying drinks from the heavily pierced barmaid, Martin and Lola pressed to the rear, past a mounted rabbit's head with antlers, and a passageway tiled with campy, obscure album covers from the '50s and '60s.

A weeknight, they had no problem finding seats.

Lola leaned back on the leatherette couch near Martin, after taking the third or fourth sip of her drink. "… God," she said. "I don't mean to go all 'touchy-feely' on you."

Consciously or not, she was steering the conversation to a more intimate level.

"No, go ahead," he insisted, smiling. "Tell me."

"About my last *real* relationship?"

"Why not."

She appeared embarrassed. "What would you like to know about it?"

Martin took a swallow of his drink. Laughed. "Was it terrible?"

"When it ended. Sure."

"Ended badly?"

"Don't they always?"

"What happened in this case?"

"We dumped each other. Sort of." Lola grew quiet. "No. Actually, he dumped *me*."

Her expression changed, grew harder: "Not that I'm keeping a score card or anything. But I've dumped more guys than've dumped me."

"I don't doubt that."

She took a moment, sighed. "We were going out. Treating each other ... ah, badly; just being petty and mean. Finally, one bad night, we split without speaking, I called him up, I said, 'Well, what's the story? Is it over, or what?'"

"What'd he say?"

Lola frowned. "That's just it. He wouldn't say *anything*. I kept asking him, 'Well, what is it? Yes or no?' But he wouldn't say anything. I could hear him sucking on a cigarette. I could hear the TV. 'Say something, you *asshole!*' I yelled and nearly burst out crying. Finally, he goes, 'I don't think it makes any sense.' '*What?*' I say. 'Us,' he goes. 'Being together.' 'What do you mean?' I ask, waiting for him to go on. Of course he doesn't. He was quiet again— that silence was killing me. Finally he goes, 'I'll make it real clear, okay: I *don't* want to see you anymore.' And I felt my heart beat ninety miles a minute. 'But *why?*' I just wanted him to talk. He wouldn't, though. The blood was in my ears, pounding. Finally he mumbles, 'Look, I don't wanna chitchat.' 'All right. Okay,' I say, 'I'll call you next week.' A few days pass and I call, and he still wasn't talking. Finally I ask, 'Do you feel the same way?' He goes, 'Yup.' That's all: '*Yup.*' I say—'Fine. Fine,' and hang up."

"Never heard from him after that?"

She swallowed. "Nope." Shook her head: "*Nothing.* Like … like I never mattered to him. Never existed. And all that passed between us was like a joke, ha ha…. *Dumped* over the phone. That's so cold, so shitty. I swear I could never do that to anyone in my life."

"How long ago was this?"

"Last October. The 27th, to be morbidly exact."

"I can see you're over him."

"No, I am." She remained a bit down. "I mean, I ran into him a few weeks ago—we go to the same school. Even though we met through an ad. He was in the cafeteria with his scamp buddies. And, at one point, we just happened to catch each other's eyes. And stare. And I tell you, it was like the *purest* form of *hate* I ever felt!"

"So you won't ever see him, again."

She turned to him, glaring. "What, are you *kidding?*"

Martin finished his drink. And she continued, "I wouldn't see him again if he came crawling on bloody knees."

"Excellent," Martin said.

She bridled, "*God* —how I fucking hate him!…"

45.

"He was into all this *weird* stuff," she went on. "'Atrocity memorabilia,' some people call it."

They were on their way to *CBGB*, up 3rd Street, Lola still compulsively rattling on about her ex-boyfriend—somewhat to Martin's dismay now.

"'Atrocity memorabilia'?"

"All kinds of depraved and macabre shit," she explained. "Crime scene photographs, skull casts, tombstone rubbings of famous serial killers, swatches—you name it."

"Swatches?"

"*Swastikas.*"

He sighed. "Oh."

Just then they were tracking past the emblazoned steel door of the New York Hell's Angels H.Q.

"Yeah. He even collected artwork by convicted killers and insane people—the famous ones, of course. Like paintings done in prison. He had one by that pig, what's his name, the former clown … John Wayne Gacy."

"The child molester?" He turned to her.

She nodded. "Killed over thirty kids and buried them in his basement."

Martin frowned. "And he still appealed to you, this guy?"

"Okay," she granted. "It was 'unconventional,' maybe. But in a way I could see where it was coming from."

"You *could?*"

Lola nodded again. "It's this … dark *fantasy* with a lot of guys. '*Staring into the abyss.*' Really—it's just compensating for feeling insecure or *invisible* or whatever. And I can understand that. I mean, everyone wants to leave their mark, right? But most people *can't.*"

What was he supposed to say to that?

She kept on, "So one way of dealing with it—I read this

somewhere—of dealing with this sense of 'powerlessness,' or of feeling insignificant is to *identify* with 'someone or something stronger and more powerful.'"

"Shit, you sound like a sociologist."

She laughed. "Well, it's true. It has to do with *empowerment* or whatever. Like with the Nazi stuff, the *Oi!* skinhead music. Even gangsta rap and all that macho posturing. Where do you think all that crap comes from?"

"Haven't a clue."

"Young boys feeling insecure or *impotent*. It's so basic! It's *way* easier to identify with some kick-ass *sadist*, than to commiserate with a *victim*. Compassion is complex, hate easy."

Martin was impressed. "That's quite an analysis you got goin' there."

Lola remained pensive.

"Anyway," she finally confessed. "The prick was a lot younger than me."

"Oh yeah. He was?"

"Well, only a *year*. But he seemed way younger."

"Was he from here, originally? The Village?"

She looked suddenly amused. "Texas. Some backwater town."

"So, why's *that* funny?"

She shrugged, grinning. "Just that, in the beginning, when I first met him, he was like this typical 'white boy,' freezer stocked with TV dinners. Only ate Wonder Bread without the crust and processed chicken." She took a couple of steps. "After a while, boy *that* sure changed!"

Martin remarked, "Downtown everyone morphs. Must be the air down here."

"Sometimes, it gets to be too much," she said.

"How so?"

She explained, "Well, think about it: everyone turns up in this place to 're-invent' themselves, y'know? So you have all these people 'fronting,' changing get-ups, changing names. Changing sex. Makes it hard to tell who's who and what's what."

"That might get old," Martin said.

"It does. It gets really *annoying*. Everything is so fucking *transitory*, you start to wonder if *anyone* or *anything* is real." Again she grew reflective: "And, personally, I'm tired of all the fakers and fuck-ups and users. 'Specially the *users*."

Martin told her that was one reason he didn't move down here himself—that and the ridiculous rents. "I mean I'm afraid I might grow bored with it all," he said. "Then, I'd have nothing left, nothing to look forward to."

"Now *that's* pathetic," Lola teased him.

"Glad you think so." Martin laughed. "At least *now* you know the *truth!*"

46.

CBGB was part of a strip mall. The *CBGB* "Pizza Boutique" was to the left, and to the right, was *CB's 313 Gallery*.

The club's rough exterior was white-washed cement stucco, covered with primitive spray-painted graffiti and encrusted with decades of urban grime and soot, windows boarded up and textured with a collage of torn posters and handbills.

Martin graciously opened the pockmarked wooden door. "After you," he offered.

"Piss on that," she laughed. "—After *you*."

Finally, nearly knocking heads, they both squeezed in together.

Just inside, flat as a rug, lay the world-weary CBGB mascot, a black-and-white Afghan—so fatigued it tried to eat a nearby slice of pizza without so much as raising its head.

"Too many drugs," smiled Lola.

They coughed up the green, had their wrists stamped and walked in.

Seven bands were on the bill. They'd missed all but the last two: *King Missile* and *Tribe 8*.

"'Tribe 8,'" he asked. "That some riot girl band?"

Lola more accurately defined it: "*'Post riot girl dyke.'*"

CBGB hardly ever changed. A former derelict bar, it maintained a coarse, ultra-squalid ambience. Intensely dark, of course, every available spot was covered with old posters, flyers, and dusty band stickers.

On the far end, the main floor was oddly narrow and claustrophobic, walls covered with dense graffiti or scraped bare of plaster. As always, the place seemed in a state of decay and deconstruction.

No band was on stage, only a soundman setting up gear. And just then Patti Smith's cover of "My Generation" played over the PA.

"This spot won't be a problem for you?" Martin asked. They'd angled themselves to the extreme left of the jutting stage and against the wall, beside a huge monitor.

"It's perfect. Why?"

"Just asking." In years past, it was *here* in this same spot where he would prop himself when he went to the club alone, burnt-out after another thankless day at work, a night of empty wandering—right here where he'd hang back with amusement, catching the self-destructive antics of some raucous post-punk band, members of which (in a desperate attempt at comedy) would sometimes hurl themselves off-stage or drive themselves headlong into nearby speaker cabs or the bare-brick wall in his direction. Splat!

"*Oh no!*" Lola shrieked, facing the dressing room cubicles and two guys apparently on their way back from the bathroom.

Martin turned to look.

She burst out laughing. "You'll *die!* Just wait. I'll introduce you."

The two seemed engaged in a frivolous argument. As in a slapstick routine, one kept swinging back wildly, trying to swat the other.

As they came up, Lola shouted, "Hey!"

They looked in her direction. And Martin had to turn away to keep from laughing.

"Thought you guys were in Portland!"

"We was," explained one. "We left. That place is beat."

"Yeah. *Beat,*" echoed the other.

"Jeremy. Justin. This is my uh, friend. Marty."

The two awkwardly nodded hello.

"These are the *Dukowski* brothers," she informed him.

"Nice to meet ya," Martin nodded, trying hard to keep a straight face.

"As you can see," said Lola. "They were hatched from the same *egg*."

Martin saw it was true. About twenty-years old, identical twins—and *both* crossed-eyed!

"Yeah," said Justin (or was it Jeremy?), "we're, uh, practically related."

"I'd sooner be related to a *chimpanzee!*" cracked the other.

Martin chuckled.

"So. Whatcha' here for?" she asked, as other patrons irritably pushed by.

"Me?" confessed one. "I'm here to watch a goddamn band."

"Yeah," said the other. *"He's* here to watch a goddamn band. *I'm* here to mosh!"

"'*Mosh*,'" scoffed the first. "Like you know about 'moshing!'"

"'*Ey*," countered the other. "I was moshin' before *you* were born!"

The first wore a look of contempt. "Asscrack, do you even *know* what you're talkin' about?"

"—'Ey!" hollered a voice behind them. "Quit blockin' the aisle!" Musicians were trying to haul equipment to the stage.

"Now see whatchoo' started?" sneered the first. He eyed his brother menacingly. "We'll square this, later!"

But no sooner did the first twin turn his back, than the other soundly cracked him across the back of the head. Wheeling abruptly, the first retaliated by going for a classic eye-poke.

"Will you two PECKERHEADS just get goin'!" boomed someone else from the blocked passageway.

Pointing at his brother, the first threatened, *"Later* for you, wingnut!"

"*Ooo*, I'm shakin' all over," smirked the other.

They both moved, unclogging the aisle. And, finally, Lola and Martin turned to each other and laughed.

47.

The band *King Missile* took the stage, cranked up, their first song, "Jesus Was Way Cool!" and soon, Martin noticed, the Dukowski twins appeared front and center, going at it full tilt, recklessly crashing into each other and those around them in "the pit."

"C'mon *get it up!*" yowled one brother.

"'Dat's right —*yeah!* Time ta get *stoo-pid!*" bawled the other.

"Like you need *practice!*" slinged the first.

"*Eat it!*" he barked, slamming his brother—"Fuckin' *squash* you!"—the two stumbling and falling, then completely vanishing into a crowd that appeared to be getting swiftly energized by the bottom-heavy rock onstage and the smoldering, freewheeling anarchic atmosphere—almost as good, Martin thought, as in *the old days!*

Lola announced at this point, in his ear, "*Shit*—I gotta go downstairs, use the restroom!"

"Good luck!"

"May take a while!"

And, eyes lighting up, he saw his chance.

When the Dukowski twins next resurfaced in the mosh pit, they discovered they had company.

"Look who came to join us!"

"*Who?*"

"Him, *ding-a-ling!*" bellowed the first, "That guy!" then barreling into Martin, instantly dropping him through the bustling mob, the two then piling directly on top. From the hardwood floor, Martin looked for a way out but all he could see was a flurry of shifting legs and flying steel-toed boots.

"*Aah,* what's yer name, again?" rasped the closest twin. From the bottom of the pile, Martin grunted it. "Nice ta meetcha', then," replied the twin, extending a hand. Martin tried but couldn't manage to shake it. "Yeah," groaned the other from somewhere higher up—"nice ta make ya like, 'acquaintanceship.'" "*Aaah*," creaked his brother, "dummy up, porky!"

Soon all three were being helped to their feet, and Martin, unhurt, felt an odd twang of nostalgia: he'd forgotten what it was like to share in this kind of boyish camaraderie and excitement.

Before Martin could think of anything else, he was again being tossed through the riotous crowd: roughly bucked in one direction, bounced in another. In the center of the pit, meanwhile—hooting and howling—the Dukowski twins were back at it, lurching and bugging one way for a while, then circle slamming the opposite way the next. Throughout it all, feeling helplessly foolish and out-of-control, Martin couldn't help *laughing*. Even as a blunt weight—a broad twenty-something body—came crashing down from god-knows-where to take him down, along with three or four mindless others.

Hitting the floor, Martin realized it was soaked with spilt beer.

"Jesus!" cried a young female voice. "It fucking *reeks* down here!"

"Hey," shouted someone else. "A goddamn boot just went up my *ass!*"

"My friggin' clodhopper!—Was that you?"

More clasping hands reached down to pull them up. But again, before Martin could regain his balance, he was swept back into the mindless, rolling crowd. "Heads up!" someone shouted from behind him. And a heavy combat boot came flying at him. Just in time, he ducked.

KLOCK!—And Martin saw that the boot had hit someone directly in front of him. A flurry of hands reached down to give that fellow a lift; the red-faced sport rose slowly, shaking his head, grinning—apparently all right.

"Piss off!" he snarled at those showing excessive concern.

Other audience members had begun stage diving, meanwhile. And, as the band continued to loudly thrash it out, the incited mob was literally bouncing off the walls. "Anarchy!-anarchy!-anarchy!" one galoot kept wailing. Amid the chaos, Martin was helping to pass along an anonymous body surfer, when suddenly—surrealistically—this person's entire *leg* came off in his hands while the rest of the body continued to be smoothly passed along to the stage.— *The fuck!* Martin thought; before realizing he was holding a prosthetic limb. "*Gimme that!*" growled a no-neck lummox beside him and, snatching it away while letting out a war whoop, swung it loosely around like a giant chicken-wing before slinging it unto the stage where it crashed between the drummer and startled lead guitarist.

Martin had wondered about the twins whereabouts when suddenly one of them appeared tottering high on the edge of the stage, ready to do a full dive. "Here I go!" he bellowed. "*Catch me!*"And leapt only to have the crowd below split apart to watch him fall on his face.

The other twin resurfaced next to Martin, chortling: "*Putz!* Serves 'im right!"

Then nudging Martin: "*Up* and *at 'em*, Jim!" With a mischievous gleam, the twin extended his clasped hands, palms up: offering him a "boost" over the crowd.

Martin debated it for an instant, before putting a hand on the twin's shoulder and the tip of his boot in his hands. Then, like in a dream, *up* he went! *Hoisted*, on his back, over the crammed, heaving audience. Like floating *weightless* on an ocean. Like being sixteen again! In motion, Martin took in the dark moving shapes around him, the rippling laughing faces and flailing arms, absorbing the furious energy, surrendering to it, feeling himself being swept as on a raging tide, time speeding up now—faster and faster—until *boom!* He blacked out.

In the next moment, coming to his senses, Martin realized he was onstage at CBGB, in front of the screaming audience, the band's bass guitarist glaring down at him. Touching his forehead, Martin felt the start of a big knot.

Shaking off his grogginess, he got up and prepared to "dive."

"*JUMP! JUMP!*" screamed the blur of grotesques below.

All pumped up, Martin stood poised on the edge of the stage—only to choke.

That is, till spotting the bass guitarist charging at him, wielding his instrument like an ax. Adrenaline pumping, Martin leapt, managing a near-somersault. He felt himself fall back—arms stretched wide, body tensed—caught by a ready audience, who effortlessly buoyed and passed him back over the throng, until he was finally dropped, after fifteen or twenty heads.

As Martin staggered to his feet, the final blow came from a grinning cro-magnon who cheerfully yanked him up: "Aah, you're all right!"—then plowed into him, knocking him across the aisle.

After that, he was a little slow in rising.

Miraculously, the helping hand this time belonged to Lola.

"God," she exclaimed. "*There* you are!"

"I was looking all over for you!" he lied. His shirt was torn at the shoulder, his hair wildly disarranged.

Seeing the bump on his forehead, she broke up laughing.

"Sure you were!"

48.

When the next band, Tribe 8, mounted the stage, the Dukowski twins were nowhere to be found—in fact, nearly half the entire male audience had mysteriously vanished. When Martin asked Lola for a possible explanation, she replied, "Oh, you'll find out why!"

Amused by the band's compelling lead singer, Martin liked *Tribe 8* at once. As with most punk-inspired bands, performance and attitude were everything; the point was to be abrasive, rude, reckless. And this front-woman *was*. She wore purple locks, a bandolier with holstered bowie knife around her waist and, sticking out of her shorts, a giant prosthetic penis. (It was the night for prosthetics.)

Although she insisted on no stagediving—and threatened to mutilate anyone who tried—she fearlessly dove herself, blasting stilted lyrics while propped on the bobbing heads and shoulders of cooperative fans. Other times, she'd drop to the stage and slither across it, belly-heavy, reptile-like, strangling her words in some kind of hell-bent agony.

Apart from abusing and insulting the agitated crowd, other tasteless antics included mooning the audience, pouring water and beer on them (when she was unable to produce sufficient spit), performing simulated oral and anal sex on female attendant groupies, kicking a sound man who appeared briefly on stage to secure some loose wires and then someone else who tried to help that person off.

But the crowning moment, the *climax* came at the end of the last dissolute song, when her face glistening with sweat, she peered out into the audience, scowling: "Do I see any *dicks?* Any *dicks* left in the house, tonight?" At which point, she ominously unsheathed the bowie knife and, with her other hand, rigidly held out the spit-slathered member.

"Do it. Do it!" crowed a she-devil from the audience.

The lead singer brought the blade down near the base of the phallus.

"*Ice* it, girl!" "Slice away!" others shrieked.

Then, supremely smug, she followed through, hacking with the edge of the knife—until at last the almighty "oppressor" and symbol of "patriarchal evil" was ritualistically *unmanned*, to wild applause and cheers.

"—There ya go!" "*Hoo-hoo*, girl!" "Way ta go!…"

Concluding the show, the front-woman triumphantly held the now pitiful realistic-looking phallus over her head like a matador waving the ear of a bull, dedicating the kill to the avenging feminist spirit of the audience.

And, as other band members began to drop their instruments and stalk off stage—one or two of them flipping the bird at the uncontrolled crowd—the lead singer tossed what was left of the prop to the back of the room.

"Good night!" she exclaimed, exhausted and satisfied now. "And, sweet mother*fuckin' dreams!*"

"Well, that sure was *cathartic*," Lola remarked.

Martin looked at her.

49.

Outside *CB's*, young women were tossing around the severed penis, playing a friendly game of "catch." Martin searched for the Dukowski twins, wanting to thank them for a fun time. But they appeared nowhere in sight.

"Oh, they'll turn up some other time," Lola assured him. "Sooner or later they always pop up."

50.

Walking up the Bowery, ears ringing, the Empire State Building looming in the distance like a brightly lit syringe, they arrived on the busy corner of St. Marks Place, amid lollygagging neo-punks.

Lola surprised him by saying: "You don't have to walk me the rest of the way."

Startled, he turned to her. "Whatcha' talking about? I don't mind."

"No ... *really*," she insisted, trying to be "diplomatic."

Confused, Martin nevertheless decided not to argue. "Pissed at me for slam-dancing?"

"Nah," she said, vaguely distracted. "Just, I wanna be alone, I think."

Okay. Martin shrugged.

He offered her a friendly kiss, which she accepted with surprising warmth, gently cupping his jaw with a hand and closing her eyes.

At last she murmured, "Bye."

"See you later," he smiled, already facing away.

"—Oh, and Marty?"

He stopped, turning back.

"Take care of *that*," she said, pointing to the lump on his head.

Eyes rolling up in that direction: "Oh. Right."

51.

"More office forms, bro. Take it or leave it."

Martin was at work the next day with a big band-aid on his head, looking disgusted. "This new guy, man!"

"Like it or not, we still gotta do it. Follow up. I got kids to feed, you got rent to pay, am I right?"

"We need to mention that?"

After a moment, Chaz went on, "Speaking of which, bro. Lately he's been getting on my case about you."

This caught him unexpectedly. *"Me?"*

"'At's right," frowned Chaz. "And not for nothing, but I'm getting a little tired of hearin' it, too."

Facing the wall map of Japan, Martin sighed.

"Be a little careful, that's all I'm saying. Ease up on the lateness an' that shit. And *fake* some interest. I'm saying this for your sake. The old boy is due in from Japan. After that, *who knows* what changes may be goin' down. Meantime, in this 'transitional period,' we may hafta' put up with a little *bull*-shit."

"I'd say we've seen plenty, already."

"And, maybe, we ain't seen *nothing* yet. Keep in mind, bro, keep in mind—things ain't never so bad that they can't get worse."

After that uncharacteristic, unsettling sermon from Chaz, Martin got down to some grunt work in the warehouse: re-taping and labeling cartons, banding and preparing skids for that evening's TYO consolidation….

Some time past one o'clock, Martin heard a knock on the door and went to answer it. As he expected, it was a delivery, and the trucker handed him a slip, asking, "Where de' otha' fellah?"

Martin replied, *"Lunch."* Tugging on his work gloves, he inspected the pro. "All stacked on skids, I hope?"

"I only drive it, ye' know. Don't load it."

Martin dragged the heavy draw-chain to open the warehouse gate. The tractor-trailer was backed in on a perfect line, both wing doors opened and tied back.

"—Shit, no!" Martin felt his legs go numb. From ceiling to floor, as far as he could see, the truck was crammed with tall, bulky cartons. Not a single skid in sight!

Martin burst into the warehouse office, got on the intercom.

"*Moshi-moshi!*" answered Tani, the Japanese secretary.

"Listen, uh, this is Marty, downstairs? I'm alone with a tractor-trailer and a shipment of a hundred and sixty-two *loose* cartons that weigh"—he checked the figure—"*two thousand six hundred and thirty-two pounds!*"

There was a pause while she put him on hold.

Martin tapped his fingers, waiting.

"Marteee," she returned. "Martee-san, everyone away! You must take! Sorry!"

"*I* 'must take,' huh?" And Martin came very close to breaking on her: the words *fuckee you!* right on the tip of his tongue. "Unbelievable!" And slammed the phone.

"Well, hoss," he sighed, turning back to the trucker. "Looks like it's just you and me."

"Weeze' about ta' get fucked, a-gin'?"

All he could say: "Hope ya had yer *Wheaties*, this morning." And: "Pass the K-Y."

52.

That night at home, too exhausted to move, he lay on the couch, watching a cult video, *Carnival of Lost Souls*. Bootleg, of course.

Yep, he thought, sipping his forty. Carnival of lost souls. That about summed up his world.

The phone rang. And for a moment he considered

answering it. At last, he let it ring, muting the TV.

"Hi, Marty. This is Amaris," began the voice. "I'm on a broken pay phone right now, so I'll have to make it quick: I was wondering if you'd wanna meet up, tomorrow? Maybe even do a little dancing, like we said last time? There's this little thing happening at the *Pyramid Club*, called 'Necropolis.' A kind of *goth* theme party. Might be fun. And I was wondering—*"click-click!* She was momentarily disconnected. "—*Please deposit an additional five cents*," interrupted a recording. "—Anyway," she returned, "*page me*, let me know what you think!—*Click!*" That ended her message.

He'd call her back later. If he could ever get up.

53.

That night, Martin did page her. But after a half an hour with no call back and, feeling woozy and bored, he decided to dial the *Voice* Personals. With no new messages in his box, he stayed on the line, this time to "browse."

"Please choose from the following categories," the prerecorded operator went on.

"'One' for 'Men seeking women.'

"'Two' for 'Men seeking men.'

"'Three' for 'Women seeking men.'"

Martin pressed "3."

Beep! "… Hi, er. This is a straight female looking for a straight male? I don't know—they kinda screwed up my ad in this newspaper? I was kinda hoping they would put 'SF,' y'know, in big bold letters, but they didn't? Uh, anyway, if you're an 'MF' please leave a number? And a name or something? Okay, bye—no *wait!* Did I say 'MF'? I meant '*SM!*' Oh, for shit's sake! Now I'll have to do this whole stupid message over!—"*click!*

Martin continued to browse:

Beep! "… Hi. My name is Kim. Just to add a little more to my ad, I have long brown hair with blonde highlights. Blue eyes. I'm about five-*nine*, full-figured…. Absolutely no drugs, no beards, no mustaches. No bald guys or midgets…. And don't forget to leave a name, *first* and *last*, and number with the *area code*. *And* a business phone!…."

Beep! "… Hello. My name is Dorothy. I'm rather quiet. (long pause) I am a professional woman and would like to meet a professional man. (long pause) I hate sports, I really do. But that's the way it is. I like swimming. Aqua-aerobics. But that's as far as it goes. (another long pause) I've recently been in therapy for nine years because I came from a dysfunctional family—(line cut off)"

Beep! "… Hiiii! You have reached *Vanilla* and *Caramel!* We're so glad you've chosen our ad! So we'll briefly describe ourselves":

Another young female voice: "—*Hi!* I'm *Vanilla!* I'm twenty-four years old, five-*five*, a hundred and twenty pounds, attractive, with long shoulder-length blond hair and a most radiant smile! I like long walks on the beach, great conversation, romantic candlelit dinners, and quiet moments!

First voice, again: "—And, *Hi!* I'm *Caramel!* I have caramel colored skin with dark brown hair below my shoulders. I'm twenty-five years old, five-*two*, a hundred twenty-five pounds, with beautiful eyes and a dazzling smile! I'm a future Botanist, who likes traveling and visiting museums. I enjoy talking, horseback riding, and love to laugh!"

Both voices (in unison): "—We're beautiful, energetic, and sincere! We're seeking two attractive, physically fit, sweet and honest men, twenty-four to thirty-five years old, who will treat us like ladies! Don't be shy to leave long messages!...."

Beep! Click! (a hang up)

Beep! "... Hello! (a male voice cleared his throat) We're an attractive, middle-aged Asian *couple*. And what we're looking for, basically, is a special gentleman to join us in having a bit of fun.... Give us a physical description of yourself, maybe your penis size, what your preferences and limits are, any kinks you might be into—that kind of *thing*. And we'll give you a jingle. Sound *agreeable?*..."

Beep! "... Hi. I'm Liz. My extension number is 3567. Please don't respond to my ad if you SMOKE or do DRUGS or are extremely OVERWEIGHT—or are MARRIED. I'm just *not* interested.... (sighing wearily) Bye...."

Beep!...

Beep!...

Beep!...

54.

The next night, the *Pyramid Club* spun music that was full of dirge-like incantations, guttural groans, and slow desolate howls of infernal agony. Through faux cobwebs, smoke machines huffed and hissed while masked red and blue gel-colored spots cast the appropriate somber, sepulchral-like glow.

Amaris was dressed appropriately for the evening, wearing a long inky skirt, mesh top with a black bra, and studded dog collar.

After Martin commented favorably on her top, Amaris moved in close, asking, "Know how a person makes one of these?"

He shook his head.

"It's real easy," she explained. "Take a regular pair of fishnet stockings, cut out the crotch. Then pull it over your head."

"Oh, I get it," he said, taking a closer look. "Then poke out holes for your fingers?"

"Right."

"*Tri-cky*." He glanced up as several black, spectral faces floated by in the darkness.

Then she asked him, "Do you believe in *vampires*?"

What did she say?

"In vampires," she repeated. "Do you believe in them?"

Martin wasn't sure what she was talking about. "You mean, like in the movies?"

"No," she said in all seriousness. "In real life."

Martin almost laughed, but in keeping with the mood of the evening put forth, "You know, I'm *not sure*...."

This answer seemed to please her.

He asked her, "Why? Do you?"

"Do I?"

"—Believe in vampires?"

Amaris confided, "Well actually ... I do."

"You do?"

She nodded. "In fact, I know one."

"You *know* one?"

Again she nodded. "Sounds a bit strange. But it's true."

"How can you tell?"

"—That she's a vampire?" Finishing his sentence. "She *showed* me."

"How'd she do that?"

At first she seemed reluctant to tell him. Then, prodded, she confessed: "I met her in the ladies room of a club. Saw her, and to be perfectly honest, felt drawn to her. Don't know why. Anyway, she was feeling a bit 'anemic,' she said, in need of some 'ruby red,' and asked if I could spare some."

Martin narrowly looked at her. "And what did you say?"

"I told her, 'depends on how much.' And she replied, 'Oh, only a *few drops*.'"

A beat. His eyes went wide "—So you *gave it* to her?"

"Well I was already a little toasted by then so I said, 'Why not.'"

"You let her *suck your blood?*" Martin was horrified.

"Just for a little while," she said.

"But … how?" he wanted more details now. "How'd she do it? With fangs? She pierce your neck?"

Amaris burst out laughing. "No, nothing like that. We both pulled into a stall—where two women were already doing it—and she took out a surgical needle. Then she took my finger and just stuck the pin into it. And I let her suck on it a while."

"She just sucked on your finger?"

Amaris grinned. "Uh-huh. And every now and then, her eyes kept rolling up at me. And I got a little turned on, actually. Because she was really *pretty*."

Perversely Martin felt himself getting a little turned on, too. "And that's it? That's all that happened between you?"

"That's all. Afterwards you could say we *bonded*."

"Really? You still get together?"

"Now and then," said Amaris. "At clubs."

"Is she here? Tonight?" he said, excited.

She scanned the floor. "Don't see her."

"And when you bump into her," he persisted. "You let

her, *y'know*—"

"*Feed?*"

He nodded, grimacing.

Amaris raised an eyebrow. Laughed, "Not telling."

Nodding, Martin fell quiet, lost in the bizarre, erotic possibilities.

Fuck, he thought. *Fuck me.*

55.

Much later, drifting from the back room to the bar, where they both ordered drinks, Amaris and Martin sat half-watching the monitor movie, *Nosferatu*. She had lit a cigarette.

"So tell me," she asked. "How'd you make out with the ad?"

He put down his glass. "Okay, I guess."

"Get many responses?"

He shrugged. "A few."

"Only a few?"

"With a guy," Martin pointed out, "it's different."

"How's that?"

He then explained how a "women seeking men" ad usually pulled down dozens of replies, whereas the reverse ad bagged maybe two or three. At best.

"Is that as many as you got?"

"Just recently."

"Had many dates then?"

He replied, "Some."

"And how'd they go?" She seemed unthreatened.

Again Martin shrugged, not wanting to give too much away.

"Too early to tell?"

He nodded. "I'd say so. Yeah."

Amaris took a drag. "It's not like in the movies, right? Where strangers meet and everything happens *slam-bang*."

"Nah," he smiled. "Never that way. Or else—it's over just as quick."

"Yeah," she sighed, exhaling smoke.

He took a sip of his drink. "What about you? Tried other ads?"

"A few," she admitted.

"Oh yeah?" He tried to sound disinterested. "How'd they go?"

Amaris flicked ash into a nearby tray, frowning. "Mostly? They *sucked*."

He felt somehow relieved. "How's that?"

"Huh?" She turned to him.

"I mean, *why* did they suck?"

"Oh." She sighed again. "I don't know…. One guy was too old. Another was too uptight. Another seemed—I don't know—too emotionally *unstable*." She took another drag, squinting a bit, "Maybe, it's just me. Maybe I'm really not ready to get involved right now. So I keep finding fault. Making excuses."

Martin asked, "Has it been hard, making the adjustment? Not being married?"

She thought about it, saying finally, "The security is gone, that's for sure. Can't tell you the last time I've had a solid night's sleep. At the same time, it's also been liberating." She smiled. "It's a relief not always having to answer to somebody."

"You can do as you please now?"

"Kinda. Except that I have a baby son to think about."

"Not a drag, being a mom?"

"Not really," she smiled. "You get used to it: another fact of life." She leaned back a bit. "Come to think of it, without him, I think I'd be pretty *lost*. I mean, that's what's great about kids. I know it's cliché and all, but it's true. They give you a purpose; a reason to get up in the morning."

Martin took another sip. "See," he said, "I wouldn't know anything about that."

56.

She asked him, "Where'd you say you live, again?" They were headed south on Avenue A, after leaving the club.

"The Heights," he told her.

"Brooklyn?"

"Queens," he laughed. "Do I look rich to you?"

"I'm parked just around the corner," she said.

"Oh yeah?" he smiled. Adding: "Would you mind swinging by?"

Walking ahead, she grinned. "Of course not."

57.

As her Honda Civic warmed up, Amaris claimed she had something she wanted to give him. "Oh yeah?"

"Here you go," she said, gently dropping it in his lap. It was in a brown paper bag.

Martin carefully reached inside, removed the present, letting out: "You're really *into* this stuff, huh?"

She laughed. "You might say I have a closet interest."

"Well, thanks," he said politely, turning the volume over to scan the back. *"The best vampire compendium ever!"*—Stephen Rice, author of *Vampire A-Go-Go*

"Wait," Amaris said. "Let me inscribe it." She took back the book, removing an antique fountain pen from her purse.

When she was done, the first page read:

To one of the few,
I hope you will regard this volume kindly.
May it prove useful in exploring your own vampire nature.
A kindred soul,

A.

58.

"Excuse the mess and all."

Once in his apartment, the first thing Amaris noticed was the titanic stack of rejection letters piled in the corner.

"What on earth is *that?*"

"Mount Everest—no, just some junk." He shrugged. "Care for another drink?"

She declined.

"Not even a short one? Another white Russian?"

"Well," she wavered. "But go easy on the alcohol, okay?"

"Yeah right." He went to mix it.

59.

Amaris was regarding two small-framed photographs on his bookcase when he re-appeared with the tall drinks.

"Who's this?" she asked, indicating the one on the left.

"Actually, my mom." He handed her a glass.

"Deceased?"

He nodded, taking a swallow.

"She looks ... *young,* here." She examined the photo closely.

"How did she?—I mean?—"

"Wish I could tell you myself," Martin said.

"You don't know?"

"One day ... she just left."

"'Left'?"

"Vanished."

Amaris paused uncomfortably. "And you never got an explanation?"

"Not really. She was *ill*." He tapped his head. "I mean, up here."

"Oh, I'm sorry," Amaris said. "Maybe"—she forced a smile—"I shoudn't've brought it up."

Martin shook it off.

Allowing a long moment to pass, she then inquired of the other photograph.

"Which?"

"Here." She pointed.

In the photo, the woman was dressed in thigh-high boots and a billowy silk top. The occasion was the Halloween parade in the Village. Martin said, "That's my *bud*, Nikki."

"'Bud'?"

"My pal. My best friend," he said.

"'Best friend,' huh?"

"Yeah," he smiled. "Why?—What's up?"

She smiled back, narrowing her eyes. "Just makes me a little suspicious."

"'Suspicious'? Why?"

"I don't know," she shrugged, grinning. She turned to the photo again. Intently appraising it: "Quite the *babe*, actually."

"*Oh*, I get it," chuckled Martin. "Because she's *good*

looking."

"Yeah," said Amaris. "*Of course.*"

60.

A drink or two later, they sat cross-legged on the hardwood floor, randomly going through bootleg videos, all of which, coincidentally, were Nikki's: *Edie in Ciao Manhattan, The Attack Of The Fifty-Foot Woman, Faster Pussycat! Kill! Kill!...*

"I guess you really have to be drunk to appreciate some of these," Martin said.

Fellini's, *The Clowns* was playing on his VCR.

"Ever see *Satyricon?*" Amaris asked.

"No," he admitted. "But I've read the book by Petronius."

"Like it?"

"Yeah," he admitted. "One of my favorites."

"Name some others," she insisted.

"Other books?" Leaning back, he tried to recall: "*Basketball Diaries, The Lotus Crew* by Stewart Meyer, *A Fan's Notes* by Frederick Exley—"

"Oh, I hate that last book," she said.

"Why?"

"That misogynist asshole!"

The next moment had a dreamlike quality.

Martin wasn't sure at what point it happened, but as they sat near each other, debating books, personal likes and dislikes ("male" vs. "female" writers), they began to gaze at each other expectantly, to drop their defenses, finally to exchange gropes and short, playful kisses.

Soon they were French-kissing and laughing in earnest, teasing each other mercilessly, Amaris aggressively unbuckling his pants, as Martin dug under her fishnet top to unlatch the black bra.

"Hurry up, you sexist prick," she told him.

Martin was startled. "Hang on a second," he demanded.

"Second, my *fucking* ass!"

Martin unfolded his sofa, and, fueled by alcohol, they proceeded to engage in a kind of heady, rough sex that involved some quasi-wrestling and light bondage. Using her mesh top, Amaris insisted on tying his wrists while she got on top and fucked him.

He maintained: "Frederick Exley rules!"

"Just shut up!" she gasped, inserting him inside her. "Hold still!" Closing her eyes, after an adjustment or two, she then tried to focus on her own amplifying sensations as she slowly undulated, rolling her hips—the straining and contracting of her movements now creating almost unbearable pleasure for him. Martin, for his part, held back. "*Proves zip!*" he asserted, straining against his binds, trying hard not to come. "Hold still," she kept insisting, when he began to grind against her. "I like my *bottoms* to hold still," she wickedly told him.

Now and then, as she rode him, he would see her grinning down at him, her eyes hard with a kind of fierce determination. "Don't come," she implored, squeezing him harder now. "—Don't come." "*I won't*," Martin grimaced, trying to slow his breathing, let his mind drift—away from this sexual assault. "Now repeat after me," she said, antagonizing him. "—Edith Wharton, Willa Cather, Jane Austen, Isak Dinesen!" "Isak Dinesen was a *man!*" "Wrong, fucking wrong!" she laughed. "Now repeat: '*Women's literature* rules! *Women's literature…*'" And she was soon redoubling her efforts.

"So tell me, do you—do you—*like* it?" What could he answer? She was persuasive. "—*Yeah*." "And my tits? Like 'em?" "*Yeah!*" "Then show me!" And leaning forward, she brought a jutting breast to within inches of his mouth. And as Martin awkwardly raised his head and proceeded to wetly suck it, she insisted: "*Harder. So I can feel it. Bite—bite it!*" And Martin took her hard nipple, slick with his saliva, between his teeth and lightly bit down. "No! *Harder!*" she cried. He did so, clamping down hard. And she finally shrieked.

Gasping for breath, his cock painfully hard, the room spinning, he could sustain only so much more of this, before he felt a sensation like molten lead build up in his groin, and—rearing—"*Fuck, not yet!*" came, groaning hoarsely: "*Uuuhhh!...*" He felt himself shoot up into her— balls scalding—felt her constrict around him, melting him.

Amaris held him inside her, still straining to squeeze out a full orgasm but too late: he was already numb, losing it. As she mercifully untied his wrists and slid off, he felt the need to whisper, "Sorry." "That's okay," she said kindly. "It felt good, anyway, you *asshole*."

After she untied him, Martin discreetly reached for some tissues, dispensed with the soggy condom. They hugged and kissed a while, Martin finally feeling her skin which was warm and sticky now, her softly protruding belly, and round ass—*full and sexy*—Amaris later nuzzling his chest a long time and lightly biting his neck.

At last, in the early hours of the morning, they fell apart, naked under the sheets, hands touching, and in a haze drifted off to sleep.

Sometime later, he heard her rise to go to the bathroom, heard the water flush. After which he again descended into a deep preternatural sleep.

61.

Sunlight slashing through the shades, Martin awoke again, turning with a stiff neck to realize he was still alone.

Bleary, yet vaguely concerned, he rose and headed for the bathroom where he flicked on the light and with a jolt realized there was a message across the medicine cabinet mirror written in black lipstick.—*The fuck!*...

Marty,
Had to go.
Nice.
See you soon.

A

This was *bizarre*.

Stranger still, in regarding his own reflection, he raised his chin to notice two conspicuous marks that weren't present the night before. Of all places—on his *neck*!

—Could they be? Was it—*possible?!*..

His eyes widened, focusing in on the marks.

"*Ohhhh—Fuuuuuuuuuuuuuuuuuuck MEEEE!*..."

Wait. He took another look, leaning in—sobered instantly. Blinked.

—*Aw, no*, he dimly realized. *Just acne.*

62.

"We got fucked, bro."

Martin remarked, "Oh really."

"That's right," Chaz asserted. "*I* got fucked, *you* got fucked, we *all* got fucked. Reamed right up our bungholes: *cheated!*"

Martin was, of course, back at work, seated on his side of the warehouse office, when Chaz returned from a meeting with Haizu, the bossman upstairs. The meeting this time concerned budgeting and their former branch head, a man known as "Henry" Tanaka, who under mysterious circumstances had been recalled to Japan and summarily replaced.

"How'd he do it? How'd he fuck us?" Chaz was directly facing Martin. "By skimmin'. Big part of the money meant for us—that is, 'export,' the hump was pocketing. Money for a motorized gate, jumpers, even a new loading plate. Money for you and me, bro. We got fucked outta all of that. When the boy upstairs showed me the budget, the way it was *supposed* to break down, I bugged…." His voice trailed off as he wagged his head.

"This just comes out now? I mean, no one was watching *before?*"

"I'm telling you, bro. Ya got middle-management in Japan wearing rose-tinted glasses, not willing to target one of their own. But you wanna hear the *best* part, what the man's punishment amounted to?"

"What."

"A 'window seat.'"

Martin squinted.

"A muthafuckin' *window seat!*" he guffawed. "His punishment! Some dicked position in the company. And this is supposed to make him feel mortally *ashamed*, or some shit."

Martin cracked up. "That's pretty good." He thought about

it. "Fucking guy must have a fat account in Switzerland by now."

"Wouldn't surprise me. And who could blame him," laughed Chaz. "*Damn.*" Then, sitting back and blowing a heavy sigh, he faced the JAL office clock, which already read past noon.

Shifting gears, he asked Martin, "What's the call, bro? Taking lunch?"

"You go first."

Sure enough, no sooner did Chaz exit the door than Martin turned to the phone.

All morning long, despite the usual levity, something had been bugging him: preying on his mind. And it was only now—alone in the office with the JAL clock ticking— that Martin grasped what it was: he was ailing, feeling oddly *hollow. No other way to describe it.* The source of this unease might have been that he was still slightly hung-over from the night before. But he began to suspect another reason, largely sentimental: that he hadn't spoken to Nikki in *days* and—*Dios!*—he missed her, missed his *bud.*

He was afraid to admit it: an ad date—his life—didn't seem *real* unless he shared it with her first.

Martin phoned her at work, caught her voice mail, quickly thought of an excuse for why he might be calling: "Hey, stranger. *What's up?* Listen, uh—since the 'reunion thing' between you and Mariella isn't so far away, I was wondering if we couldn't get together some time soon. Maybe even tonight? Grab some Thai, a film?—The new Wong Kar-Wai movie playing at *The Angelika*?"

He paused as if he had more to add—something intimate and heartfelt—but froze. "*Anyway,*" he said. "Let me know."

63.

That same evening, before opening his mailbox in the Heights, bag of lo mein in hand, Martin mused on how swiftly his day had gone. Every day should be as painless, he thought.

He reached inside the box to withdraw a single envelope. A bill? Another rejection letter? Notice from the IRS?

Martin opened it. Of all things, it was a personalized advertisement from a cemetery—coincidently, the same cemetery he passed on the Brooklyn-Queens Expressway each morning ... where his attention would linger, amid the stark, carved angels and shaded tombstones ... until he realized he was again at work, already in the parking lot....

"Above-ground burial at affordable prices," read the cheerful notice. "**Martin Sierra**, discover the savings and peace of mind available to almost everyone!"

64.

Later, after dinner, Martin was mindlessly sacked out on his couch, pouring himself a Red Stripe, watching TV.

On the wall near his television was a recent concept "word poster" he'd made using stencils and the copier machine at work:

AND
JUST
FEEL...

RI
DI
CULOUS.

At last, he decided to ring Nikki at home since she hadn't returned his call.

But her machine clicked on: "Hi, this is Nikki...."

"Hey, Nik. *Me.* Just wondering if we were on, for tonight. Give me a ring when you get the chance. I'll be here. Hanging out."

"Fuck *meeeeee....*"

It was becoming his anthem.

He was there, all right. *All* night. What else did he have to do—except cry out in boredom?

Five hours—and a full six-pack of Red Stripe—later, Martin was still in front of his TV. He'd killed the time watching "reality television," then two colossally dumb sci-fi movies: *Invisible Invaders* and *The Angry Red Planet.*

Yes, yes. His enjoyment of them was supposed to be *purely* ironic.

He was supposed to laugh at the cheesy production values and clueless direction of *every* scene. Not laugh *out loud*, of course, but *inwardly*—to himself. How *kitsch!*

Sitting there, he still felt like an asshole.

At midnight, feeling a burning humiliation, he dialed her number, again. This time when the recording began, he simply hung up.

That night, in bed, for the first time ever, Martin vividly imagined her with Mariella. And he was filled with such sudden, painful jealousy that he could hardly sleep....

The notion rolled over and over in his mind, forming a poem:

Come,
Come away
To permit
Your own
Dank tongue
To remain
A soft-bodied
Portion—
To remain
A retracted
Mollusk,
A tied,
Visceral mass
Nestled slickly
Within
The mantle
Of your mouth.
Take away!

Your thick, wet
(Membranous),
Labial palps
From her own
Clean,
Child-warm
Skin:

She *don't* need ya!

65.

The next day at work, Martin called Lola, in part to suggest a retrospective on East Village art happening at *The New Museum*.

She seemed reluctant, as usual, so he had to work on her a while. Finally she came around. Agreeing to meet him, "Well, okay. For an hour."

Next, Martin asked that since he'd seen her artwork, would it be okay if he brought along some of his?

There was a confused silence on her end.

"You know, like *poems* and stuff," he explained.

"Oh."

"I don't *have* to bring them, of course," he said, embarrassed. "Just thought you might wanna take a look."

"All right," she murmured. "So. Bring them."

Martin was already having second thoughts. "Well, okay. Guess I'll meet you there?"

"But, remember," she said again. "Only for an *hour*."

"Right."

"I have a lot of things to do."

Martin frowned. "Yeah, I know."*And I guess I don't...*

66.

"Get a load of this shit!" Martin said.

"Yeah, great," said Lola. "Can you *lower* your voice?"

The retrospective at The New Museum entitled, "Punk and No Wave: East Village art of the '80s," centered predictably on three famous artists of the era, all of whom emerged from the local club scene: Keith Haring, Kenny Scharf, and Jean-Michel Basquiat. Fortunately, other lesser known—but equally talented artists—were also featured. As was an "eclectic" variety of art: graffiti, stencils, copy collage, documentary photography, video, and several conceptual installations.

From the start, Lola appeared on edge.

He asked if she'd ever been here before.

"To this museum? Sure," she replied. "Lots of times. With my ... y'know."

He rolled his eyes. "Your 'ex'?"

"Uh, well. Yeah.... Also, my mom, believe it or not."

He was surprised. "No shit." Smiling: "How is she, anyway?"

"Who?"

"Your *madrecita*."

"Fine," she said.

Like talking to a nine year old.

"Look at that one there," Martin said, pointing to a painting. It had a tuft of pink faux fur growing from it.

"Where?"

"Right in front you."

Lola blinked at it as if she couldn't see it, then regarded it sourly.

Addressing her mood finally, he delicately asked, "Lola—you okay?"

"Huh? *Why?*" She looked at him narrowly.

"It's just, you seem a little..."

"What?"

"*Distracted.*"

She shrugged sullenly, eyeing another painting or two, but offered no explanation.

He persisted, "Don't tell me it's your mom."

"Huh?"

"Have another falling out with her?" he asked.

At first she wouldn't answer, but finally managed, "Hey, just leave *Broomhilda* out of it, okay?..."

Tentatively, they both entered a partitioned and topped black light installation: the interior, from floor to ceiling, was covered with fluorescent colors and trippy day-glo cartoons. Bright objects and plastic toys were suspended from the ceiling.

After a long silence, he tried a few weak comments about Kenny Scharf's obsession with plastic dinosaurs and the Jetsons. Then Martin said, "I never asked you, Lola—but, since that guy, your last boyfriend, did you go out after that? See anyone else?"

"What made you bring that up?" She turned to him, startled.

Martin shrugged, moving along.

Again she took a while to reply. Finally saying, "No. Not really."

"No one steady?"

"Nuh-uh." At the moment, she seemed distracted by a particular visual arrangement. "I mean, there was this one guy, but I don't know—he seemed kind of a simp."

"A 'simp'?"

"Just how he talked," she said wearily. "How he'd phrase these *questions*."

Turning paranoid: "Shit—like *how?*"

"I dunno." She sighed. He waited for her to elaborate but she let it hang.

They finally exited the installation, which might've been fun at another time.

Lola continued, "He still writes me, y'know. Sends me cards."

"That guy? Yeah?"

She nodded.

"And you write back?"

"No."

"Why not?"

"He's a *pest*…. I figure if I just ignore him long enough, he'll forget about me."

They paused before some other paintings.

"When was the last time he wrote you?"

"The other day."

"And when was the last time you actually saw him?"

"I don't know—four, five months ago." Lola moved up to a canvas as if to better examine it. "I just tossed his letter in the garbage. Didn't bother to even open it."

"No?" he had to ask. "Why not?"

"Wasn't up to it."

"Sounds like he's a little hung up on you," Martin said.

Lola narrowed her eyes, stepping away from the painting. "Yeah, well. Some people need to get a *life*."

The next group featured the acrylic work of David Wojnarowicz.

She seemed attracted to one composition, studying it a

131

while. Then, without turning to him, Lola blurted out: "Did I ever mention that my mom was *nuts?*"

"More than a few times."

"No," and suddenly her eyes looked heavy and pained. "I mean, did I ever tell you she was diagnosed a schizo-phrenic?"

"*What*—no." He felt a pang of dread. He stared at her, waiting for her to tell him she was kidding, that it was just a joke.

She looked back at him wearily, then quickly away.

"It's true." She issued a deprecating little laugh. "Last night, she tried to pull a knife on me."

"What?" He was stunned.

"Don't make a big deal of it," she told him.

"Are you fuckin' kidding?"

"Will you *lower* your voice!"

Gathering his senses, but no less intensely, he whispered, "Shit—listen—you've *got* to get out of there!"

She remained unmoved, silently regarding an earlier painting.

"Hey—Lola—you listening?" He took her by the arm, forcefully.

She angrily pulled away. "Don't do that!"

He felt shaken. "*Fuck*—sorry," he finally managed.

She continued to examine the artwork as if nothing were wrong, nothing out of the ordinary. "Anyway," she finally said, "it's not as easy as all that." Then, more softly, with-drawing: "You don't understand."

He stared at her sadly. "But I do."

Lola looked resigned. "Just forget it. Forget that I brought it up. Let's talk about something else, please?"

"Like what?"

"I don't know. Anything."

Martin tried to continue the conversation about her mother. He plied her with questions, but she was unwilling, obstinate. Out of politeness, somewhat desperately now, he changed the subject, asking about her work.

"Huh?"

"Your canvases, how are they coming along?"

"Don't ask," she murmured.

"—Huh?"

"*Don't ask.*" Her face crumpling.

Unsettled, Martin fell silent. They proceeded with the exhibit. The next group of paintings by Martin Wong and Richard Hambleton seemed to drive her into deeper gloom.

Finally, Martin felt drained. Utterly exhausted. Hard-pressed to think of anything to say.

He suggested getting out of there, maybe going for a drink somewhere.

Lola paused. "Actually," she frowned. "Would you be 'upset' if I just went home?"

"You mean, now?"

She nodded.

"Not feeling well?" He gave her the out.

"Actually ... *no.*"

67.

On the corner of Houston, Lola and Martin stood awkwardly facing each other. About to go their separate ways.

Lola reminded him, "Got your poems, right here." She held up the manila envelope.

"Uh-huh." He felt like an idiot. *Poems.* "Can I walk you home?"

She forced a smile. "No. I'd rather be alone. Thanks."

Martin nodded, looking at her intensely.

"Well," she said. "Take it easy."

"Right. You, too." He leaned over to give her a kiss on the lips. She hardly responded. "*Ciao!*" Then off she went. He watched her walk away, combat boots scraping the pavement.

Bewildered, he started in the opposite direction. '*The fuck happened there?...*

68.

From a pay phone down the street, Martin decided to check his answering machine for messages.

No calls. Nothing.

Martin leafed through his wallet, finally extracting a slip of paper and dialing.

"*Hi*," began the message. "This is *Amaris*. You've reached my pager. Following the beep you can key in a phone number or, if you like, leave a brief voice message...."

Feeling a swell of self-loathing, he began, "*Hey!* This is Marty. Just wondering whatcha' up to, Amaris. Kinda hoping to hook up. If you get this message soon, and you're not too busy, ring me back. I'll be checking in with my machine, tonight. Maybe we can set something up, okay?"

He hooked the receiver, feeling vaguely ridiculous.

All right, *guilty.*

Eyeing his watch he was surprised to find it was still early.

"*Emptiness*,"
she said.

"All emptiness
is open to me...."

The remainder of the night, as it turned out, Martin spent wandering the Village, a vague desperation—all too familiar—creeping into his bones.

He started with the bookstores: *The Strand, Gandhi's, St. Marks.* Then progressed to the bars: *Mona's, Max Fish, Ace bar.* A pint in each. Between stops, to keep the buzz on, he'd enter a convenience store to cop a cheap ice-cold one.

Long ago, I dreamt
I fell through
the clouds...

From another pay phone, in a somewhat righteous drunken state, he even tried calling Lola with the idea of "straightening her out." After the fourth ring, her machine clicked on: "Hi. This is you-know-who. We're not home right now. But after the last beep, leave your name and number, and we'll get back to you"—a girlish giggle—"*maybe.*"

Beep, beep, beep, beep, beep, beep, beep, beep, beep—Beeeep!
He slammed the phone.

How well—
how well
and easily
I kept falling.

Around 10:00 he checked his answering machine for messages a second time. The third and final time he checked it was two.

It was 3:00 A.M. when he arrived at home; 3:20 by the

time he got into bed.

He lay there, wide awake.

Nearly
A quarter to four:

Outside,
The wind,
Dense as an ocean,
Swells and surges
And rattles
My storm window.

In the basement,
The furnace
Stops and starts,
Rumbling, faintly.

And, again,
Tonight...
I feel
I will be unable
To sleep.

69.

```
Japantrack - Air Export Operations
MAIN OPERATIONAL ROUTINES
```

Numbly gazing at the computer screen, he tapped (6) *Consolidation Pre-Scheduling*, which brought up the next screen. Thus, with the tedium of the worst porno movie, another work day unspooled.

"Yo, *Robert Frost!*"

Martin snapped out of it, turning to Chaz where he sat at his desk.

"Do me a solid, bro. Book the consol?..."

70.

In the Heights, Martin cruised, looking for parking. He drove up 78th Street, past the tightly-parked cars lining both curbs. Red light at 37th Avenue, he stopped. He signaled left. Waited. On 37th Avenue, he stopped again, another red light. Waited.

On the north side of 79th Street, Martin pulled alongside a Chevy Celebrity apparently ready to pull out. Martin gestured to the driver: "Leaving?"

The woman, an attractive thirtyish Latina, rolled down her window and shouted: "*No!*"

71.

Martin checked his mailbox. Three rejection letters. Two bills past due.

Upstairs, at last. He went straight to his answering machine. Nope, no messages.

He sat down on the floor near his phone. Lola's number was on a crumpled slip of paper nearby, and he dialed it.

"—¡*Quien es, entonces!*" replied an older woman's hostile voice, not Lola's.

Martin panicked and hung up.

Lying back on the floor, he rationalized: *I'll call later...*

After fixing himself a drink, Martin tried Nikki's number. But again got her machine.

"*¡Miérda!*" he shouted.

Then he tried Lola again.

This time neither she nor her mother answered the phone. After the fourth ring, the machine clicked on: "...after the last beep leave your name and number, and we'll get back to you...."

Martin left her a plain message.

He confessed, "Lola, I just need to *talk*, okay?..."

72.

Martin was in bed, nearly falling out, when his phone rang.

He jumped on it, startled "—*Hello?*"

A voice sounding like Nikki's answered, "Hello?"

"*HELLO?*" he repeated.

"*Marty?*" Sounding like she was at a pay phone, outside.

"Yeah?"

"You sounded *different* just now," she said.

At that moment Martin realized who it was.

"Oh ... hi." His voice sank.

"Try not to sound so enthusiastic!" laughed Amaris.

Martin felt vaguely annoyed. "No, it's not that. I just dozed off." Finally he asked, "Where are you?"

"In the Village. St. Marks."

"Oh yeah? By yourself?"

"Yeah, by myself." She paused to let some traffic noise go by. "Wanna come down? Meet me?"

Snapping to life: "Right now, y'mean? Tonight?"

"If you're up for it."

Anything to get out of his depressing studio. "Shit, just

name the place!"

73.

They met at *Dojo*, an inexpensive, laid-back health food restaurant on St. Marks Place, where they were quietly seated in the back.

Amaris was dressed in her usual goth finery and was a little drunk. In T-shirt and jeans, Martin felt embarrassingly self-conscious and sober.

There was a long, awkward silence as they both sat facing each other. Evidently, the fact that they'd slept together didn't make them any less strangers.

Sweating it until the food arrived, Martin finally asked, "So, tell me, how goes the 'teaching life'?"

Amaris smiled at the question.

"All right, I guess. Frustrating, of course. But that's to be expected."

He asked about her students. "Still hanging out with them?"

She laughed. "I told you I was doing that?"

Martin nodded, taking a bite of his shrimp tempura.

"It's true." She grinned. "Now and then we even go dancing."

"You mentioned that to me."

She chuckled, admitting, "One of my students has even developed a crush on me, I think."

"Oh yeah?"

"Yeah. His name is Martin. Like you. Not very bright, though." She awkwardly bit into a Chinese noodle. "One evening ... a few weeks ago, we were together ... late at night. We were inside a playground, dropping a little *e*," she paused to swallow, "when one thing led to another and…" she made a gesture with her head.

"And what," Martin said.

"We … y'know…"

"Y'know—what?"

"Did it."

"'Did it'?"

Smirking: "*That.*"

He stared at her blankly. "That a fact."

She nodded, blushing through her powdered face. "Right there in the sandbox. Of all places. After we were through, I looked back and saw I left a perfect imprint of my ass. Cheeks like twin basketballs pressed in the sand."

She conveyed these last earthy details with a kind of relish.

Trying to conceal his surprise and mild embarrassment, he said, "*Jesus*, Amaris."

"*What.*"

"Lucky you weren't caught."

"You're telling me," she laughed. "The police kept driving by. Right in the middle, we kept seeing these swirling lights—or at least I *think* it was the police. Maybe it was the drugs."

He blinked. "No, I mean … you being his teacher and all."

She assured Martin, "He's 'legal.'"

"—I know. But…"

Amaris admitted, "We've been together *lots* of times."

Martin was taken aback. "Have you?"

"Why not?" she maintained, holding his gaze.

He remained stunned.

"It wasn't *in* the classroom, for Christ's sake." She put down her glass, looking up righteously. "'S'matter of fact, it's happened *a lot*."

Martin said, *"How's that?"*

"Wha." She laughed lewdly.

He asked, "How do you mean, 'a lot'?"

Shrugging her shoulders, she finally confessed, "I've gotten together with more than one of my students."

His eyes wide: "You have?"

Why was she telling him this?

She stared back at him. "What, it isn't like *incest*, y'know."

His morbid curiosity flaring, he finally asked, "How do you manage that? I mean, 'it'?"

"What do you mean?"

"I mean, where do you go?"

"Anywhere. Where does *anyone* manage to do it?"

"How many?" he couldn't help but ask. "How many students have you slept with?"

She took a moment before answering him. "You want a 'body count'?"

He felt embarrassed. "Never mind. That was fucked— *intrusive*. None of my business, I know."

She took another sip of her drink, "It's okay. Ask anything you like." She laughed, "I may not *tell you*—but *ask* anything."

Martin managed to laugh finally.

"There were a few others. Five or six."

Martin stopped laughing.

She grew more sober. "But, actually, all this is pretty recent."

"Is that so?"

She nodded.

He thought about it, reaching for his glass of water. "Since when?"

"Since ... half a year ago."

He took a sip. "Since your separation, y'mean?"

"Uh-hmm," she took a tiny bite of food. "Before all this ... I have to admit I lived like a nun."

"Meaning?"

"No sex."

"So then," he quietly suggested, "you're kinda making up for it? Making up for lost time or something?"

She laughed painfully. "Maybe." She grew pensive. "— Yeah." Putting down her fork: "See, up till that point, my separation, I thought ... there was something wrong with *me*."

"How's that?"

"I mean—" She'd lowered her voice, glancing sideways. "Sexually."

Martin asked her to explain.

"I married young. And for most of my married life, I never ... really *felt* much."

"That might be a common complaint," said Martin semi-facetiously.

"No. I mean, well ... there was this real lack of passion in our sex life."

"Oh."

"I just couldn't understand it." She went on, "Then, one day, about seven months ago, I made a surprise discovery.... One afternoon, I came home early to find..." Her voice trailed off.

"What."

She paused, forced a laugh "—It's such a cliché."

"What is?"

She took a breath, starting up again. "One afternoon I came home early to find ... *two* people under the covers."

"Oh *shit*—don't tell me."

"That's right."

"Oh *no*."

"My *best friend*, no less."

"Oh man—*heavy*."

"—Best friend since *high school*."

"*Damn!*—It *is* a cliché!"

"I know."

"You must've been ... devastated."

"I'll say. Especially since my best friend's male."

"—Wha?"

"You heard me," said Amaris. "*Male*." She sighed, "So, as it turned out, you see, our 'problem' had less to do with me, than with Alex. My husband."

"He was *gay*," Martin said flatly. "*Is* gay, I mean."

"Anyway," she nodded, "holding another man's cock, he caved. Started sobbing. Told me everything. What he'd been hiding."

"Damn." Martin blew a sigh. "Life is full of surprises."

"I'm telling you," she said. "Later ... I felt so *dumb*."

Martin looked at her.

Amaris reached for her mixed drink. "Actually—if you want to know the truth—Alex was the one who first took up the ads. Right after our separation. Told me later."

Of course, Martin couldn't resist asking: "And how'd it go with him? How'd he make out?"

"He met someone, got laid, fell in love—then got *dumped* right away!" Amaris burst out laughing. "That's the *world*.... Anyway, that's how I got into them. I thought, let's see what these ads are about." She paused again. "For a while I even tried to meet other women."

"Really?"

Amaris nodded, smiling, "I began to experiment. Like my ex. I wanted to see where *I* was at sexually."

"So, what did you discover?"

She shrugged. "That I'm basically 'straight.' That some days I like being a 'top,' other days a 'bottom.' That I like a little 'kink,' now and then." She smirked. "At this point, you might even say, I've tried it all. Men, women. Threesomes."

"And," Martin asked, still trying hard not to seem surprised, "all in all, what was it like?"

She shrugged. "*Fun.*"

Right then, Amaris's pager sounded. Casually pressing a button, she glanced at the number, then ignored it.

Placing his bunched-up napkin beside his plate, leaning back, Martin let a long moment go by.

Then he said, "You know, my best friend Nikki is *bi*."

Amaris thought for a moment. "Is she the one—the 'looker'—you showed me a picture of in your apartment?"

He smiled, nodding.

"She's 'bi'?"

Again he nodded.

Amaris looked at him curiously. "So you've seen each other, then? Romantically, I mean?"

Oops: an unexpected question.

Martin hesitated, unsure of what to tell her. He ended up saying, "We're good friends, y'know."

"Oh, I know," said Amaris. "She's your *best friend*, isn't she?"

"That's right."

Amaris looked amused. "Lovers can't start out as *friends*, is that what you're saying?"

He paused. "I'm not saying that at all."

"Okay. So what about this Nikki?" she pressed, grinning archly.

He admitted, smiling, "*Of course*, I'm attracted to her."

"Yes, *and?*"

"And—*what?*"

"So, nothing's ever come of it? No physical intimacy?"

"Oh—don't know if I should say it—I mean, there have been … certain episodes. 'Slip-ups,' you might call them."

"Yeah?" She grinned, interested.

"One occasion that went down recently."

Leaning in, she seemed eager to hear about it.

He smiled remembering it. Took his time in recounting it: "Well, most recently it happened after we'd been out together. Dancing. At a little club on Avenue B." He laughed. "We'd left the place, just got into the back of a cab, all warm and cozy. When halfway on our ride to the station, we started playing around, touching a bit. We do care for each other, after all."

She helped the story along: "You started to touch *and?*"

"We started to touch. To caress each other a little bit. And gradually our touching became a little more than just 'affectionate.'" Martin was smiling. "Before long, before we both even knew it, we were kissing. Really '*kissing*.' Not at all as 'friends' at this point, but something more. And I gotta tell you, it was nice. I mean, *sweet*."

"The clothes come off?" she rushed.

"We were in the back of a taxi, for Chrissake. No, first thing I did was ask the driver to take us both to Jackson Heights. But Nikki insisted we go to her place."

"What happened when you got there?"

"I'm getting to that part. Once there, we paid the driver and went in. We hardly made it past the door. I can't tell you what was going through my mind then. It was like this overwhelming *rush*. But I tried to hold back, go slow. Then, the next thing I knew, there I was. All over her. My hands were lifting her top. She pulled off my shirt, then my belt. After a moment, it was her satin bra—helping to slip off the smooth straps, her body glowing in the half-light, exposed and beautiful." He looked down: "*God.*"

"What happened then?" Amaris was riveted.

He smiled. "Don't know if I should tell you the rest."

Amaris playfully reached for an appetizer fork, raising it: "I'll stab!"

"It gets kinda … *intimate.*"

"But you *did it?*" She wanted to know.

"What do you think?"

Starved for graphic details, Amaris looked disappointed. "How was it, at least? Tell me that."

"Speaking for myself?" he said, a bit flushed. "A *dream.*"

"And then?"

"And then. We woke up." He heaved a sigh. "The phone rang. It was her girlfriend."

"And that was it?"

"Just about. I knew Nikki felt badly, like she usually did. Right then, we both knew it wasn't right. Because she was still 'involved,' after all."

"So after the call what happened?"

Martin shrugged. "Nikki looked a bit depressed after she hung up. When she came back, I just handed her her clothes, slipped my own shirt back on. We both knew I couldn't sleep over that night. I ended up calling another cab," he softly smiled. "But we still ended up holding each other a bit. I mean, it was still nice, being together—if just for that moment."

Amaris said, "That's sweet, your relationship with her."

"The truth is, I realize now, we kinda need each other — corny and old-fashioned as it sounds." He let out, "Really, I don't know what I'd *do* if she ever went away for good."

Amaris looked at him intensely. Suddenly Martin felt self-conscious. He forced a smile. "Maybe I've said too much."

"Well, I *asked*."

"And I blabbed," he said.

At this point, they ran out of things to say. And both of them, suddenly embarrassed, sat quietly finishing their food.

In time the waitress mercifully appeared asking if there would be anything else. Sighing, Amaris looked to Martin. He shook his head. Nope: nothing more for him. "Nothing more for me, either," said Amaris. "Just the check, please."

Absently removing a lipstick from her purse, she happened to glance at the time. "God, it's getting late!"

Martin eyed his own watch; it read, *2:13 A.M.*

Snapping back to reality, he thought, *Christ! And work tomorrow...*

74.

Late again.—*Uh-oh...*

Martin dumped his knapsack into the bottom drawer of his office desk.

The red light on his phone was already blinking. He pressed the button, the Japanese secretary, Tani, crying out: "Maartee-san?"

"Yes?"

"Boss want to see you! Upstairs!"

Sighing and closing his eyes, Martin leaned back in his chair.

"Tell him," he replied. "Tell him, I'll be up. In a while."

Instead, alone with the phone, he tried phoning Nikki at work. Again, her voice mail. But this time he left her a message:

"Hey, Nik. Just thinking about ya. Don't know. When you get a chance, ring me back. Just ... ring me back."

He hung up.

About to open the office door to go upstairs, his hand on the brushed chrome knob, Martin froze.

Suddenly, he felt a catch in his throat.

It was that uneasy feeling, again: that hollow morbid sense he was experiencing a lot more of lately—that bleak sort of dawning—underscoring all at once that something was wrong. Missing.

Something.

Comforted again by the sight of the phone, he thought, *Fuck it*... He sat back at his desk. Dialed his favorite number.

Again, the red light on his phone blinked with Tani crying out: "Maartee-san?"

He ignored it. Put a finger in his other ear.

"—Hello and thank you for calling *The Voice Personals* line!"

He poked a digit, skipping ahead.

"Thank you," continued the message. "Please enter your four number extension."

He entered it.

"Now your five digit security code."

Martin did so. Waited. Was about to hang up:

"You have," the recorded operator informed him, "*zero*

messages!..."

The sky is barren.

Long ago, I dreamt
I fell through
the clouds...
I fell easily and
kept falling.
My arms extended,
my eyes open,
I descended
through the clouds
without a whisper,
without a sound
(as in a flickering
silent picture
show).

75.

He was expecting *this*, maybe?

Beep! "Hi, Martin. My name is Nikki. You don't know me, but you answered my personal ad, wrote me a nice letter. I'll leave you my phone number and maybe we can talk?..."

76.

Later that day, back at home, he'd just finished locking his front door when the phone rang.

Expecting Nikki, he pounced on it.

"—Hello?"

"Hi."

For a moment he was uncertain.

At last, she spoke: "Whatcha' up to?"

"Nothing." Still he wasn't sure.

"This is Lola."

An awkward pause. "Oh."

"Am I … interrupting?"

"No," he admitted. "No. I just got in."

"Oh. Good." She paused.

"So," Martin said. "What's this about? About getting together or something?"

She sounded uneasy. "Um…. Not exactly."

Sitting down. "Oh?"

She shifted gears, sounding nervous, "I, uh, looked over your poems and stuff. Read them."

"Yeah?" He perked up. "Whadja' think?"

She said earnestly, "Did you say there were people who *didn't* like the way you write?"

Martin put it bluntly: "Lots."

She said, "I find that hard to believe. I mean, you write *well*. So focused and clear."

"Yeah?" He chuckled. "Tell it to the fuckin' editors."

"You're really good," she insisted.

"Thanks," he said. The compliment actually left him light-headed.

A moment later, she added awkwardly, "But, your writing, um … is not why I called."

Still a bit giddy: "No?"

"Nuh-uh." She paused. "There's something more. Something that's been on my mind to tell you. That's been bugging me."

"Yeah?" He leaned back.

"Um, well ... remember that party I went to that time?"
He drew a blank

"With Mina, remember?"

"Okay," he said.

"I think I left out an important detail."

"How's that?"

"Well, when we were both leaving the party, Mina and me." She took a moment, adjusting the phone. "We, uh, were leaving ... going downstairs, when I happened to bump into ... *him*."

"Who."

"'Dre.'"

"Who's that?"

"My ex-boyfriend. Yeah, that's his new name. Used to be 'James.'"

"Oh."

"Yeah, I kinda bumped into him," she said weakly.

"—And?"

Lola mumbled, "Well, I bumped into him. We fell to talking a little. A *lot*."—correcting herself. "Coupla' days later, he called my house." She cleared her throat, buying time. "Anyway, to make a long story short, we've decided ... we've decided to give it another try. Get back together."

Martin went blank. It was a moment before he was able to gather his thoughts. At last saying, "But *wait*—this is the *same* guy you told me about? That you *wouldn't* go out with again, if he came 'crawling on bloody knees'?"

She took a moment. "Well. I guess I feel differently now."

"*Well*"—he nearly shouted—"did you feel differently, *then?*"

She hesitated. "I don't know."

"You don't *know*?" Martin was seething.

"No."

A protracted silence followed.

Lola finally urged, "Say something."

"What am I supposed to say?"

She murmured, "I don't know."

More silence. Eyes closed, his mind was already floating off.

Lola tried, "Really, I meant to tell you before. I mean, at the museum. But ... I dunno, I guess I chickened out."

In a daze, he recapped: "So, the two of you just 'bumped' into each other? And now you're getting back together, just like that?"

"Uh ... yeah."

"What a coincidence, though," he said sarcastically. "The two of you. Just 'meeting up' like that."

Lola let out a guilty sigh on her end. "Listen, Marty, you have to understand ... this has nothing to do with you."

He forced a dry laugh. "Oh, I think it has a *little* to do with me."

"You know what I mean."

"So," Martin ventured at last. "That's it, then?"

"I don't know. I guess."

Another extended gap followed, during which they both quietly held the line.

"Hey," she offered. "For what it's worth. You seemed pretty decent. A good guy."

Growing impatient: *"Yeah."*

"What else can I say?" Her voice growing faint.

Right then—out of the stillness—another thought seized his mind, highjacked his mood. The next time he spoke, his voice was tender. "Lola?"

"Yeah?"

He wasn't quite sure how to put it. It stuck in his throat. "This ... you know, this ... has nothing to do with your home life or anything?"

"What do you mean?"

"Your not seeing me, I mean." Reiterating: "*Esto todo, no tiene nada qué ver con tú mama, ¿verdad?*"

Lola fell silent. Finally she managed to get out, her voice low and even: "What the *fuck* is this?"

"Huh?"

"What kind of fuckin' *inquisition* is this?"

"Whaddaya mean? We were just talking, that's all."

"You know," she snapped, "you got a *big ego*. Anyone tell you that?"

"Hah?"

"—The whole *fucking* world revolves around you, is that what you think? You're *irreplaceable, lo qué piensas?*"

"Calm the fuck down."

"Fuck *you!*" She slammed the phone.

Martin remained motionless, listening to the silence on her end and his own solitary breathing, then the dial tone, his eyes tracing the cracks across the ceiling. A recorded message came on, which sounded familiar enough: "*There appears to be a receiver off the hook, please hang up....*"

77.

Inamorata

You smile softly
at me;

Your kisses burst

like blown leaves.

* * * *

In your eyes is
the fragrance
of Spring flowers.

2:30 A.M., sitting on the edge of his sofa, shit-faced drunk, Martin was seized by the sudden overwhelming desire to *purge*—clean out his studio apartment.

Draining his last *forty*, he stuffed two thirty-gallon garbage bags full of torn, twisted paper.

Martin started with the mountain of rejection letters and envelopes that had built up in the far corner, tearing them into smaller and smaller pieces. From there, in a disgusted rage, he proceeded to attack his own work, removing original poetry and fresh copies from his knapsack and drawers and shredding them, too.

In the end, he managed to destroy everything personal he could find. And, tying off the tops of the bags, he felt, much to his surprise, an almost unbearable sense of satisfaction and relief.

78.

The next day at work, depressed and hung-over, Martin rested his head on his folded arms.

"So she dumped you, bro?"

He had confided in Chaz, giving him the lowdown on his most recent dates, not leaving out any embarrassing details.

"—Bro, she dumped you? That it?"

"First she complimented my writing," he said. "*Then* she dumped me."

"But what about that second one? The vampire lady. Contestant number two?"

"Amaris?"

"Yeah."

"Y'mean," raising his head and turning around, "after all I told you about her, you *still* think I should pursue it?"

"I say, go for it, brother!"

79.

Martin tried paging Amaris all that day at work, and as it happened, just before quitting time, she finally called him back. They spoke briefly, if somewhat awkwardly, arranging a get-together that evening. "Dinner," he offered. "Some dancing or whatever. We'll have ourselves a *night*."

"*Uh-huh*," she said, sounding less than enthusiastic.

"What's wrong?"

Sounding slightly put off, she murmured, "I don't know. I guess, I'd rather not get into it."

"Well, tell me about it tonight."

"Sure," she said. "*Tonight*."

Ringing Nikki at her job after that, again he got her voice mail.

He mustered: "Hey, Nik. *Me*. Tried calling again last night. I know you're probably hung up with other things. The Mariella situation. Have a lot on your mind, right now." He hesitated, unsure of what else to add. "I don't know... I'm here."

He hooked the receiver, frowning at his own idiocy:

"'I'm *here.*'"

80.

Somewhat overdressed for the occasion, Martin waited for Amaris at *Stingy Lulu's*.

Amid its campy quasi-50s layout, he sat distracted at a formica-topped table for two, when a waitress, a towering transsexual in high-heels appeared before him.

Martin had only to glance up *once* to recognize her: the front person of the band *Useless-Nameless*, this evening looking abysmally depressed.

"We ready to order, sir?" She tried to sound peppy, but it came off flat.

Martin forced a smile. "Uh, no. Actually, I'm waiting for someone."

"Get you anything to drink?"

"I'm gonna try and stay sober, I think."

Twenty minutes later, staring his paper place mat, which showed "Drink Mix Recipes"—*Gin Ricky*, *Manhattan*, *Pink Lady*, *Singapore Sling*—Martin was starting to feel edgy.

"Are we about ready to order, now?" asked the waitress.

"*Uh* ... not yet."

Way later:

"—Your friend still hasn't shown?"

Struggling to maintain his composure, Martin shook his head.

"Believe me," said the transsexual. "*I* know the feeling."

At last:

His table littered with appetizer plates, empty glasses, Martin finished another drink, looking a bit disheveled.

His waitress: "Bring ya another *screwdriver*?"

61.

After squaring the tab at *Stingy Lulu's*, Martin wandered along Avenue A angrily looking for an available payphone. Outside the *Pyramid Club*, he found a graffiti-splattered mini-booth housing two.

Picking up the receiver on the right, Martin loaded one nickel and two dimes, punched his home number, and immediately got—*zilch*. In a burst of static, he lost his call, along with his change.

Martin hung up and tried again, first listening for an adequate dial tone. Again after depositing the coins another burst of static followed, then *click-click*—nothing. No call, no returned money. "Shit."

And now he realized he was also out of change. *Great....*

At the bodega across the street, Martin was obliged to buy a quarter bag of *Cheez Doodles* to break a dollar.

Back again, moments later, the phone on the left was occupied.

The creep was a ratty, dreadlocked boho-type who held a battered instrument case between his legs while he spoke. Quietly crunching his bag of *Doodles*, Martin tried not to eavesdrop but of course heard every word:

"... No, I *won't* be comin' over.—*What*?... No, nuh-uh. That's *not* what I said. Huh? Like what?... Yeah, when?... Yeah? Yeah?... *No*, that's *not* what I fuckin' said!... No, that was *you*. You and your *cunty* friends!... Yeah? When?..." On and on it went, until he concluded: "*Uh-huh.... Yeah?*—Fine wit *me*, babe!... Yeah? Oh yeah?—That's how you wannit'?

You wannit' that way?—*Fine*. Fuck *you*, then!... No, fuck *YOU!*"

The guy slammed the phone, abruptly scooping up his case and stalking away. "Fuckin' bitch," he muttered.

At least Martin knew the phone was working.

Wiping his orange fingers, he deposited the coins, punching his home number for messages: an apology from Amaris, an explanation—something. He waited while his phone rang once, twice, three times—there it was—*zip!* No messages.

His heart sank as he numbly hung up the receiver.

After a moment Martin found her number in his wallet and dialed.

"*Hi,*" began her message. "This is *Amaris.* You've reached my pager. Following the beep you can key in a phone number or, if you like, leave a brief voice message...."

Beep! Forcing a chuckle, he started, "Hey, Amaris, just wondering what happened. Can't imagine you would stand me up or anything." Narrowing his eyes, he looked at the scratched number on the dial. "Listen, I'm at a pay phone. *555-2588.* I'll hang here another five minutes. Buzz me back at least, let me know what's happening."

He stood by the booth and waited.

Fifteen minutes, no call back. Still like a dunce he waited.

A smarmy A&R type wearing a tailored pin-stripe suit finally stepped up asking to use the phone. Martin pointed to the other one, trying to be sly.

"That one's always broken," said the suit.

Martin stepped back. The jackass made his call, raving about a recent trip to Martha's Vineyard for five or ten minutes, then smugly turned in Martin's direction and abruptly walked away without even hanging up.

Asshole, Martin thought.

Just as Martin hung up the receiver and went back to waiting, the phone rang!

He anxiously picked it up: "H-hello?"

The recorded operator's voice came on: "*Please deposit another twenty-five cents!...*"

82.

Later, back at his miserable studio apartment, Martin again checked his answering machine. Was the machine working? Yes.

Any calls? No.

Then, not knowing what else to do, wanting to page her again, picking up the phone—he wearily thought, *fuck it...*

He slammed the receiver.

With that Martin went to the bathroom, relieved himself, washed his hands, his face—grabbed some money, his car keys, and rushed out the door.

Forfeiting his treasured, hard-to-find parking spot just near the building, Martin warmed up his Horizon—and turned toward the expressway.

83.

Bayside: Northern Queens.

Nikki's apartment was located on the second floor of a semi-attached home, and after Martin rang her doorbell a few times and got no response, he began to knock on the door.

Just then her downstairs neighbor appeared—an elderly widow who Martin had met before—"Oh, your friend isn't in."

"She isn't?"

The neighbor shook her head.

He tried to smile: "Any idea where she might be?"

"I saw her leave with a suitcase and some things."

Martin was startled. "Was this, today? This afternoon, maybe?"

"No, dear. Three or four days ago."

As Martin stood there, dazed, evidently dissatisfied, the neighbor quietly reiterated: "She just *left*...."

84.

At the first available pay phone, Martin thought to do the unmentionable: call the "other woman."

Mariella's number was on an old slip of paper marked "emergency only" which he quickly tore from his wallet.

He punched the digits. A pause, then: "Beep-*beep-BEEP!*"—in ascending tones. A recorded message followed: "The number you have reached, *555-0113*, has been *disconnected*...."

"¡*Miérda!*"

Hoping he misdialed, he tried the number again. But got the same result.

He couldn't believe it. "*Mutha'-fuck!*" he shouted and slammed the phone—hands shaking.

He stood there frozen for nearly ten minutes.

Then he numbly retrieved the quarter from the slot.

His gaze drifting upward along a telephone pole, Martin noticed a parks department's sign posted with an arrow.

With that, he took off, heading in the general direction of a place he knew not far away.

85.

The place was "Oakland Lake." And Oakland Lake, of course, was the park he had often visited with Nikki. It was also the refuge he would escape to alone, in his pre-Nikki school days.

It had been years since he'd approached the park from the west end. Now, instead of the wide tear in the chain-link fence he remembered, there was an actual entrance with stairs in the center of the block.

He crossed into the park.

Inside, the sloping hills surrounding the lake were shadowed with grass and vegetation. The pin oaks loomed dark and full. The sky was cloudless and surprisingly clear, filled with a spread of stars and a huge, luminous moon.

Leaving the trail at one point and taking to the trees (over crackling weeds), Martin eventually made his way up the hill to the quiet, half-buried rocks and tree stumps he'd sought out during his college years, often to rest and contemplate his future.

In the dark, he had to feel his way around. He could hear mice and other creatures scuttling through the grass.

Seated for a while, gazing at the still lake, his view partly obscured by the trees, he inevitably dwelled again on those days, the high hopes he'd had for himself. From that vantage point, that vantage point in his life—anything seemed possible; the world had seemed like an open horizon, a wedding banquet freshly laid—he'd seen no reason he couldn't succeed in it—romantically, artistically.

"*Idiotez. Fantasías,*" his grandfather would grouse, reproving his impractical ambitions. And although Martin would insist of his work, his writing: "*¡Es muy importante!*"—precisely how it was important in the world, he was unable to articulate, then as now.

"A *waste* of time!" his grandfather would argue. "*Vas a tirar la vida*—you'll throw away your life—for *what?*"

He recalled how his grandfather once asked him in Spanish what greater importance "art" had over working in a factory, say—or in preparing for a "responsible" career?

Martin rolled his eyes, annoyed that the old man could be so mundane.

How could he ever explain? Explain what was *inside* him?

His grandfather's ideal, of course, involved *traditional* values—abysmally *conventional* values. Based on the superficial, the material. Working selflessly to maintain a nuclear family, a "stable" life, an "appearance." *Not* to be a loner, a drifter. Above all was "*decencia*."

Even with evidence contrary to the fact.

But Martin had turned his back on all that, turned his back on his family, too—what family he had left. In fact, he'd considered his grandparents to be hollow relics of a bygone era. Philistines. *Soulless tyrants who only sought to squash your dreams.* As far as he was still concerned? *fuck materialism, fuck having a family, fuck a "stable" life,* and fuck "*security*." His own mother would've understood that!

"¡*Vas a tirar la vida!*" his grandfather would protest. "You'll throw away your life. *Just like your mother!*"

His face then pressed against hers, his lips kissing her. *Smack!* Affectionately kissing her. *Smack! Smack!* Anna, his mother, cringing. His voice laughing; light laughter passing between them, cascading, ringing like bells....

"Emptiness,"
she said.
"All emptiness
is open to me..."

The Sky Is Barren.
 Dreams Are Useless.
Dissolution Rules.

86.

Martin remained on that slope, lost in a tangle of charged memories and daydreams until midnight, at which point, with some reluctance, he rose stiffly from his spot and carefully descended, clinging to deep-rooted weeds and tree branches on the way down. Once again on the asphalt trail surrounding the lake, Martin decided to walk around the park once, and did. Taking his time.

Past a raging chorus of crickets back at the west end entrance, he wearily ascended the wide stairs in the dark and straggled back to his parked *Horizon*.

After cranking the old bomb—these days it took a full five minutes to warm up—Martin made a broken U-turn on the block and drove up the street, slowing to a near crawl outside of Nikki's place.

Nothing: the lights were out—there was no sign of her. Martin felt sick at heart.

87.

That night, morbidly depressed, Martin tossed and turned in bed, shifting from one awkward position to the next.

Demons and dark thoughts tortured him until daybreak.

In one half-dream, he saw his body being buried in a mass grave at Potter's Field, in another he was naked and smeared with shit outside of Barnes and Noble on Astor Place, utterly invisible to pedestrians. Even to a passing nun—who as it turned out was his youthful first-grade teacher, Sister Rita Marie.

"Can't you see me, Sister!" Martin shouted.

No sound would leave his mouth.

The world would go on without him, like he never existed.

"Things just happen," Lola had said. "Without reason. One person is born. Another vanishes. No one knows why. Or has any real say…."

At around 6:00 A.M.—bleaching light seeping through his blinds—Martin gave up the pretense of trying to sleep and readied himself for work. On autopilot, he showered, shaved and made lunch. With what he had left in his refrigerator, he fixed a semi-decent breakfast. Maybe after work he'd go grocery shopping.

'Least, I still have a job, he thought. And what's more, he said aloud, "For once I'll be early!"

88.

At work that morning, oddly enough, Martin almost felt content.

He picked up the ringing phone: "'Ey, Marty here—*Japan World! Howarya'*?"

"*Ah*," said the truck dispatcher, "no sense in complainin', y'know."

"I hear ya, yeah." Then shifting gears: "Got any freight for me?"

"Yep."

Martin noticed the blinking red light on his telephone. "Hang on," he said, hitting "hold," then the flashing button.

"Martin-san!" his boss said. "Come up to my office, please."

Martin replied, "I'm busy, now. Is it like, *really* important?"

"*Eh?* Yes, '*important!*' Come up, okay?"—*Click!*

89.

Up in the main office the mood had dimmed. Suddenly, there was a pall in the air.

"Kim-san," the new temp, whom Martin was told avoided work at any cost, now had his head buried in an old ledger. Others were somberly pouring over files and standard import documents, as if these papers had suddenly taken on an inordinate importance. Even Tani, the Japanese woman who ran the office, remained absorbed in what appeared to be yesterday's mail. Everyone seemed preoccupied, too preoccupied to even look up and take notice of his presence.

Martin joked aloud, "What, we having a *funeral*, this morning?"

No reply.

90.

Martin took a seat in the carpeted office.

The room was tastefully decorated, walls newly painted lily white. Hung with museum posters. The obligatory golf clubs were propped in a corner. On the man's desk was a framed portrait of his family: wife, three smiling children. Also a signed baseball and a globe of the world with the names in Japanese.

Haizu sat behind the desk, wearing an uneasy smile, dressed in a tailored olive suit with a silk, gray tie.

Martin? Basically he wore the same things he wore yesterday—and the day before that. A ratty T-shirt and a pair of old jeans.

"Your eyes are red," was the first thing Haizu said to him, trying to break the ice.

Martin shrugged, "Guess I didn't get much sleep last night."

"Out late?"

"No. Just one of those nights. Couldn't sleep."

"Bad dreams?"

"You said it."

An uncomfortable pause followed. Nodding feebly, eyes averted, Haizu seemed unsure of how to proceed. He heaved a sigh.

Martin had a sinking feeling: he could tell that this was not going to be just another empty discussion on employee/customer relations.

Opting for the sympathy angle, Haizu quietly began by noting his "difficult position" as head of the "troubled" New York branch. In a roundabout way, he enumerated the many problems he currently faced, the challenging decisions he was forced to make, and at length expounded on the unfortunate losses of company revenue in recent years. (Delicately skirting any mention of Tanaka now and his flagrant role in it.) Next, came his long-winded explanation of the obvious "necessity" for the company at this point in its "illustrious history" of having to trim its roster, or—to use a more direct "American term"—of having to "downsize." (The word pronounced with absolute, practiced clarity.)

Martin's gaze fell to the plush beige carpeting, newly installed—he felt his insides softening. Felt himself float away: out of body, out of mind.

"So you see," Haizu was saying. "Facing these difficult circumstances, the company can no longer *afford*—"

Losing patience, Martin cut in, "You saying I'm *fired?*— That it?"

Eyes wide, Haizu looked startled—as if Martin had kicked the chair from under him. Recovering, still a bit flushed, he painfully admitted, "Yes."

Martin nodded curtly, "That's all I wanna know." He took a deep breath, a final glance at the surrounding walls.

Without saying another word, without looking at his former boss, without hardly feeling his own legs beneath him, Martin moved with deliberate grace to the door, opened it, and walked from the room.

Passing through the wider office, all eyes now trained on him, Martin's final word was to the point:

"*Sayonara.*"

91.

Downstairs in the warehouse office, as he emptied his desk—what was it he was feeling? Anger? Hostility? Bitterness?

No. Strangely, he felt none of that.

At this point, it seemed he felt … nothing. He was oddly detached from it all. It was as if the whole scene had happened to someone else, some other unfortunate, and he was just another disinterested bystander.

"Bro, it wasn't *my* idea—you know that." Chaz stood nearby watching him pack his things.

Martin was sorting through folders he'd had in a bottom drawer.

"I tried to talk to him," insisted Chaz. "Tried to get him to change his mind."

Martin found an old *Beck* tape. Held it up. "This yours or mine?"

Chaz squinted. "Must be yours." He went on, "Like I said, I tried to talk to him. Over and over. Man wouldn't listen."

In short order, Martin blankly began to cop some office supplies—fit them into his knapsack: a few new pencils, some BiC pens, several "stick it" pads.

Chaz said quietly, "What can I say, bro? This company's *fucked*."

"So you knew for a while?"

Chaz frowned.

"Yeah, well." Martin zipped up his knapsack. He could tell Chaz felt awful about it. Guilty. "Fuck it, y'know. Just … fuck it."

"Bro…."

Martin sighed, closing the drawers. "Nothing, man—don't even say it."

Chaz was still frowning. "I don't know *what* to say. All these years a' workin' together…."

Chaz had reached into his own desk for something. A dusky-green bottle. "Guess I been savin' this." It was cognac: *Remy-Martin*. "No time like the present, right?" He cracked the seal.

Setting up plastic cups on the copier machine, he poured out two generous shots. "Take home what's left, bro. For tonight."

For the first time since getting fired, Martin felt a real sadness. He was afraid if he thought about it too long he might lose it.

Chaz raised his cup, "Here's to"—he looked at the flag a moment: no—he scanned the rest of the office: nothing there worth toasting to.—Finally: "Here's to gettin' drunk!"

They drank.

92.

And that was that….

Incredible how quickly things turned. All this time, it seemed, Martin had just been mindlessly adrift, never considering how things might change—or how to change them—and just like that his life was turned on its head, just like that he was out of a job.

Chaz stood in the open dock as Martin finished warming up his car.

He called out, "Bro, if you ever need anything!…"

Martin had no hard feelings. The truth was, the man had covered for him long enough. And if he hadn't considered it before, he thought it now: Chaz was a decent guy; there was no denying it.

Right there—*that* was the last image he had of him: the man standing tall, framed in the opened dock—Chaz, like a sentinel from another era, his hair flecked white, a vague look of regret on his face.

Just before Martin fully backed out of the lot, Chaz raised a hand—a final good-bye.

Martin vaguely waved back.

"And that's that...."

93.

At long last, back in Jackson Heights, Martin remained in a stupor for hours.

Slumped on his open sofa bed, taking occasional pulls from the *Remy-Martin*, he watched but didn't watch a pointless talk show—*Ricki?* Or was it *Jenny Jones?* Who cared?—replaying the day in his mind. He marveled at the speed with which things had happened: saw himself in Haizu's office, then emptying drawers into a box. *Unbelievable.*

He put down the cognac since it was making his head spin, flicked off the tube, rose and stood in the room. Not quite sure what to do with himself.

Pausing before his bookcase, he blankly pulled out two poetry books: *Selected Poems*—Mark Strand, Delmore Schwartz—then, eyed the framed photograph of Nikki.

On the other side, of course, was the picture of his mother.

Disregarding the books, he scooped it up now, quietly examining the old photo in the light:

His mother: *the poetess....*

Not a bad looking woman, he thought objectively. *I'd date her*. This was the period in her life when she had cut her hair short. She had Martin's features—or he had hers—except that her face was softer, rounder. Her nose was smaller than his, too—pretty—and her lips fuller, frowning slightly in the shot. What else could the photograph tell him?—what meaning could be extracted? *Speak up, sucia. Don't just look at me*. Then he saw it. Right then, looking carefully into her eyes, Martin believed he could recognize her disillusionment and pain.

Allowing his mind to drift, he thought of his mother, then: thought of them both together, cherishing what frail memories he had of her....

Like once being called to the kitchen table and a wordless dinner of *bacalao* and potatoes, a meal he truly hated—his mother intensely scribbling some corrections on a recent poem, her fist crinkling the top of the page. Bored, Martin repeatedly asking aloud if he could take a ride down the dumbwaiter, afterwards—the dumbwaiter which he realized had long been sealed and painted over because of the roaches, yet which remained (for all its imagined potential for adventure) a source of endless boyish curiosity for him.

Not hearing his request the third time because of her impenetrable gloom, he repeated it yet again, this time screaming it.

"*¡Pero que!*" his mother hollered back. "*¡Eres idiota!?*"

He recalled how five minutes later, unable to bear the silence any longer, he then impishly picked up his *bacalao* and with a look of disdain casually winged it across the room where it fell—*flop!*—behind the refrigerator and stayed: roach food. To his chagrin his mother not even noticing!

"*¡Estoy ABU-RRIDO!* (—I'm *bo-red!*)" he moaned aloud. With his fork then launching bits of boiled potato at his mom as she continued to write and ignore him.

"*¡Pero, qué té pasa, hoy!* (—What's wrong with you, today!)" she scowled, at one point springing from her end of the table to chase him, Martin cackling and calling her *cabra*, a goat—and snatching her pages of poetry. "*¡Miérda!*"—his mom shrieking, tearing after him, "*¡Demonio!* (—Devil!) *¡Cuando té cojo!* (—When I catch you!)"

In all honesty, Martin preferring a spanking, a sound beating to being treated like a non-entity, to being invisible and perpetually ignored....

Now Martin reached to the top shelf of his bookcase, moving some papers, locating a ragged manila envelope. Taking it across the room, he leaned back against the windowsill.

Suddenly he had a yearning to look at more photographs.

There weren't many in his possession, maybe a dozen. Reaching into the envelope, he pulled them out, started through them:

First photo—showed Martin as a toddler before a frosted birthday cake with two candles. On each side of him (present in body but not in mind) his well-meaning, dutiful grandparents.

Second—a Polaroid. Showed preschooler-Martin, seated on a faded carpet, blankly facing the camera. A skinny silver Christmas tree behind him. Again in the background, like unsmiling ghosts, his grandparents.

Third—Martin, wearing a clip-on tie, standing stiffly in front of his parochial school. Shading his eyes from the bleaching sunlight, next to his tired grandfather.

Fourth—a large, creased school picture. Third grade. Small for his age, Martin front left, in shirt and tie, shoulders slumped, eyes closed.

Fifth—age nine, Martin beside a fragile Spanish woman. (Of the few pictures taken together, this would be their last.) Wearing a floral print dress and cork platform shoes, his mother, Anna, is crouched near him, smiling vaguely.

This photograph was dog-eared and cracked.

There were more but he couldn't go on.

He tucked them away, sat unmoving, felt the sun on his neck. Closed his eyes a moment.

What next?

Feeling a need to cry without any tears rising to the surface, Martin could no longer resist the urge to try Nikki's number again, so he dropped to the floor and called.

On the fourth ring, her machine clicked on.

There was no point.

He hung up the phone.

With that, he spiritlessly got to his feet, put the manila envelope back in its place, and went quietly to his open bed to take a nap.

God, he was tired.

94.

He dreamt he was lost in a deep, circuitous East Village dive, like a long sewer. No matter which way he turned, he encountered the same dank, mist-shrouded passageways.

Open-mouthed, Martin felt himself suddenly stumbling. Trying to escape. Heart tight in his chest, he was swaying, breathing heavily—almost about to fall—when he heard a distant alarm: *ringing, ringing....*

Martin had no idea what time it was.

He was in total darkness, uncradling the phone:

"Hello?"

The voice said, "Hi!"

Martin snapped on the nearby clip-light.

"Marty? Are you there?"

He remained silent for nearly a minute.

"I'm here."

"I just got in," Nikki informed him.

Was he still dreaming?

"From where?" he asked.

"Florida," she told him. "*Miami*."

Still trying to get his bearings, he rubbed his eyes: "*Where?*"

"'*Mom's house*,'" she finally explained.

"*Nik*," he spoke up, "you just leave without telling me?"

"Don't be angry." She exhaled. "I just needed to take a break."

He sat up stiffly. "You just leave for a whole week *without* telling me?"

"Marty, it was *four* days."

"'Four days'?" He paused to think. Was it possible?

"I left Monday and today is Friday," she pointed out.

Martin thought about it another moment, vaguely counting the days on his fingers, suddenly embarrassed.

"I guess I wasn't thinking straight," she said. "You know that desperate feeling, that feeling of wanting to lose yourself, sometimes?"

His spirits were starting to lift finally. "I know that feeling."

"Well, it was like that—*everything* had taken a bizarre turn."

"I know," he said, almost laughing. "Believe me, I *know* the feeling."

He was almost afraid to ask the next question.

"Nik, what about ... *you know?*—"

"The 'reunion'?" she finished his sentence. "Postponed, Marty."

"—How's that?"

"Postponed," she repeated. "Postponed *indefinitely*."

Martin was startled. Asking finally: "Meaning?"

"Off. *Over*, Marty." She said it like it was old news.

"So." He sat up all the way. Shook his head. "—Simple as that, that's it, then?"

"Yep."

Martin still had trouble believing it.

Nikki explained, "She's gone. Had enough, she said. Packed off to San Diego with a friend."

"She went *west* and you went *south*," Martin said.

"Something like that."

Martin asked, "So—what brought this on?"

"Listen, Marty. Wasn't gonna bring this up. Thought maybe it was corny or something. But I want to, now…." She took a deep breath. "I had this *dream*. About you. About us.—Don't laugh." She settled into it: "It started where we were both in this jungle. Floating on giant lily pads. At first we were enjoying it, just drifting along on this river, taking it as it came—laughing. But, then, things changed. The current began to pick up, get rougher and faster—more wild. And at one point you were dragged away. It made me *so sad*. Because I couldn't reach you. And soon it got so I couldn't even see you anymore. And soon you were gone. Forever." She confessed, "I actually woke up crying…."

Martin felt a tightness in his chest.

They both let a long moment pass.

"Marty?"

"Yeah?"

She laughed on her end.

"What?" Martin whispered.

"Can't we talk about it?"

At last he had to smile. "Right now, y'mean?—Tonight?"

"Why not?"

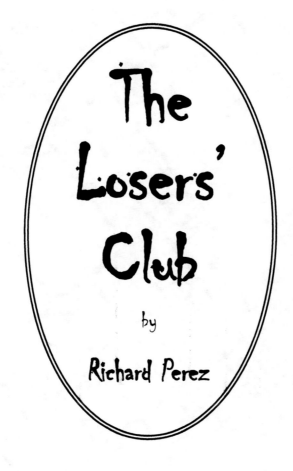

The Losers' Club

by

Richard Perez

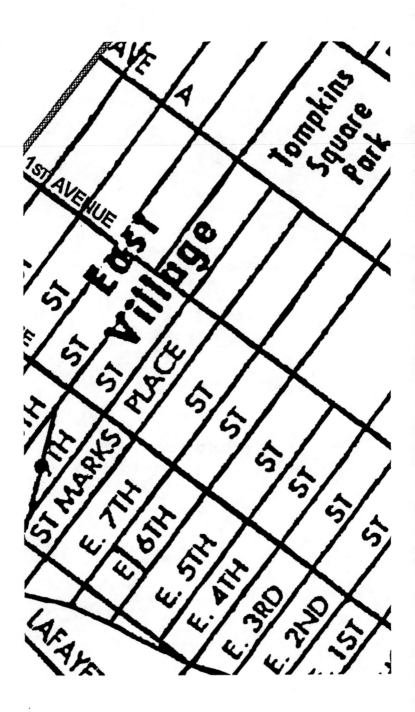

Recipient of numerous writing awards, Richard Perez was,
among other things, managing editor at Angel Sun Press.
He currently lives and writes in Galicia, Spain.
Viya!

Who will save the world?

Some of the classic works of 20th century fiction got their start in Paris: Hemingway's *In Our Time*, Joyce's *Ulysses*, Miller's *Tropic of Capricorn*, and Nabokov's *Lolita*.

Now—with Gallimard presenting the French translation—Ludlow Press is proud to issue *WILL@epicqwest.com* in its premier, long-awaited English edition.

In vividly compressed comic form, *WILL@epicqwest.com* takes the reader on a contemporary quest that is as cyberspatially and pharmaceutically fantastic as anything Ulysses encountered on his trek home from Troy.

In a daring cross between Voltaire's Candide and Stanley Kubrick's Dr. Strangelove, *WILL@epicqwest.com* follows the post-post modern exploits of our hero, WILL, a medicated college student on his heroic quest to uncover the truth behind a new virus that threatens to wipe-out all of humanity: IS (Information Sickness).

Helping him in his calling are a whole lot of psychotropic drugs—his faithful companion and always-handy, chatty laptop, Spunk®—and his virology lab partner and centerfold, wish-fulfillment fantasy ultra-babe, Naomi.

With all of contemporary existence muffled by feel-good medications, deconstructionist double-talk, fat free food, and a never-ending faith in the wisdom of the marketplace, who are you gonna call to save the world? Try:

WILL@epicqwest.com

Tom Grimes is the author of the novels *A Stone of The Heart*, *Season's End*, and *City of God*, the plays *Spec* and *New World*, and the fiction anthology, *The Workshop: Seven Decades From The Iowa Writers Workshop*. His work has been named a New York Times Notable Book of the Year, a New & Noteworthy Paperback, and an Editor's Choice pick; it has won three Los Angeles Dramalogue Awards, been awarded a James Michener Fellowship, and has been selected for the Barnes & Noble Discover series. He now directs the MFA Program in Creative Writing at Southwest Texas State University.

WILL@epicqwest.com
(a medicated memoir)

Tom Grimes

"Eerie and brilliant ... Tom Grimes is our new visionary."
—Chris Offutt

"Grimes's voice speaks to the spirit and his vision stretches the mind."
—Boston Globe

"Transcendent in its own right for its breathtaking set pieces, its dissection of media marketing run brilliantly amok, its elegiac depiction of the sad, last fruits of class warfare. Grimes's deft probing of philosophy is leavened by a talent for quick, biting humor ... [and] his talent for the breathtaking phrase, the arresting word, brings exhilaration to page after page."
—Philadelphia Inquirer

"Grimes is a natural ... renders the afflictions of adolescence in both unique and universal terms."
—The New York Times Book Review

"Grimes shows an eye for evoking ... a tormented family on the short end of the American dream ... while making believable a capacity for compassion and forgiveness."
—The Chicago Tribune

"All is not Platonic ... here. Pynchon seems a closer model."
—Seattle Post-Intelligencer

"Pungent with the lunatic language of consumer-driven tabloid America ... Grimes makes a quantum leap into Delillo land."
—Kirkus Reviews

"[His work] ... is so well written that you want there to be more: more pages, more unexpected allusions, more pleasing insights.... One can only hope that there is more Tom Grimes in the offing."
—West Coast Review of Books

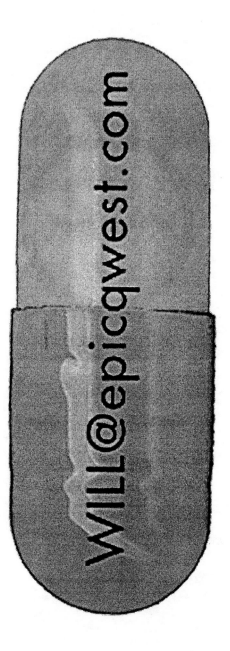

Ludlow Press Books

For *individual* copies and info, log on:
LudlowPress.Com
or
write:
Ludlow Press
P.O. Box 2612
New York, NY 10009-9998

....

The Losers' Club
ISBN 0-9713415-9-1

WILL@epicqwest.com
ISBN 0-9713415-7-5

....

Distributed to the Trade by **Biblio** (a division of NBN)
To place an order and/or contact
Customer Service:
Phone (toll free): 1-800-462-6420
FAX (toll free): 1-800-338-4550
Email: custserv@nbnbooks.com

"A non-faddy diet that offers incredible health benefits and weight loss. Aidan and Glen show how everyone can reap the benefits of the Sirtfood Diet through eating delicious food. I'm a huge fan!"
—**Lorraine Pascale, TV chef and food writer**

"A revelation to my diet. With the help of Aidan and Glen, introducing Sirtfoods has allowed me to attain a body composition and well-being previously unimaginable."
—**David Haye, champion heavyweight boxer**

"People keep asking me my secret to looking great. The answer is Aidan and Glen's Sirtfood Diet. Since following it, I feel unstoppable."
—**Jodie Kidd, model and TV personality**

"Working with Aidan and Glen has revolutionized my nutritional approach beyond anything I have experienced in the past. Their knowledge and Sirtfood Diet is unrivaled, and was key for getting me into top shape and feeling and performing at my best for the 2015 Rugby World Cup."
—**James Haskell, international England rugby star**

"I'm healthier, more alert, and in top physical condition. Sirtfoods are key to me reaching new peaks in performance to face the upcoming challenges in making British America's Cup history."
—**Sir Ben Ainslie, four-time Olympic gold medalist**

THE

SIRT
FOOD
DIET

Aidan Goggins and Glen Matten

Gallery Books
New York London Toronto Sydney New Delhi

G

Gallery Books
An Imprint of Simon & Schuster, Inc.
1230 Avenue of the Americas
New York, NY 10020

Copyright © 2016 by Aidan Goggins and Glen Matten
Originally published in Great Britain in 2016 by Yellow Kite, an imprint of
Hodder & Stoughton

First Gallery Books trade paperback edition March 2018

GALLERY BOOKS and colophon are trademarks of Simon & Schuster, Inc.

For information about special discounts for bulk purchases, please contact Simon &
Schuster Special Sales at 1-866-506-1949 or business@simonandschuster.com.

The Simon & Schuster Speakers Bureau can bring authors to your live event. For more
information or to book an event, contact the Simon & Schuster Speakers Bureau at
1-866-248-3049 or visit our website at www.simonspeakers.com.

Interior design by Renato Stanisic

Manufactured in the United States of America

10 9 8 7 6 5 4 3 2

Library of Congress Cataloging-in-Publication Data is available.

ISBN 978-1-5011-6377-7 (hc)
ISBN 978-1-5011-6379-1 (pbk)
ISBN 978-1-5011-6378-4 (ebook)

We would like to thank public health expert Dr. Padhraig Ryan of the University of Dublin for his invaluable input to the design of the study and analysis and reporting of outcomes.

Contents

Foreword

N utrition plays a key fundamental role in the success or failure of our daily battles with the bulge, from how we fuel
our bodies and the food choices we make to the portion
sizes we serve. It all seems like stereo instructions or rocket science,
but what if I told you there was an easier way to lose weight and
be healthy?

I've always been the anti-diet trainer. I detest the word *diet*, as it
carries negative connotations for so many people. Most of my clients
despise the word too. It makes them feel like they've been given a
life sentence to eat only boring and uninspiring meals that will have
them falling off the wagon within a week! So why jump at the
opportunity to write the foreword for *The Sirtfood Diet*? Why have
I introduced it to my clients to follow? My answer is quite simple:
It is different from every other diet that has come before it. It is a
whole new way of eating that brings fantastic benefits for everyone.

I've worked in the health and fitness industry for over twenty years and have seen fad diets come and go. In order to give my clients a proper insight into these "Hollywood-driven" diets, I tried them all. I wanted to get a better understanding of how they worked. I wanted to know things like: What were their effects on the body? What kind of results were achievable? Did the promises they made only have short-term success with long-term failure? In my opinion, diets that promote weight loss at the cost of your well-being or force you to deprive yourself of the foods you enjoy eating should be avoided at all costs. Those types of meal plans will only set you up for failure. My clients have no time for them. Some are high-profile individuals who are constantly under the scrutiny of the media spotlight. How they look is given more importance and attention than if they are happy and healthy. From grueling careers and performance schedules to busy daily life, nutrition should not have a negative impact on any facet of life. It should only complement and enhance it.

I've worked closely with Aidan and Glen for a number of years now. The breadth of their knowledge is simply unrivaled, and I have seen up close the numerous lives they've changed. How with equal authority and effect they can devise the nutrition for an elite athlete to become a world champion and reverse someone's disease where conventional medicine had not worked. They have an irresistible passion for spreading the message of scientifically backed, accurate nutrition, about how our modern-day health woes can be corrected with the food we eat. If we could just get the right messages out from under all the nutrition noise, we could possibly reverse and stop the obesity and ill health that plague us.

No matter who the client is, I always work in conjunction with

Aidan and Glen to formulate their nutritional plan. The Sirtfood Diet is used as the foundation for the menu creation. The reason being is simple: there is no one who will not benefit from following it. Big boosts in energy, mood, and well-being, while slashing the risk of chronic disease. Who could ask for anything more?! My clients love the fact that they can spend less time in the gym with shorter, more effective workouts, while eating their favorite delicious foods. The added bonus effect: in order to fuel all these amazing metabolic processes, our body turns to our fat stores. As a result, we see dramatic weight loss even if that is not our driving force for following it. These are all benefits I have encountered firsthand, with myself and my clients, and each time the results were awe inspiring.

What's also fantastic about the Sirtfood Diet is that it is a diet for food lovers. So many weight-loss and healthy-eating messages are divorced from real life. You can't expect people to eat the way you prescribe for the long term if it means living in dietary hardship. The Sirtfood Diet turns all this on its head. The benefits are all from eating delicious-tasting food and not from what you are *not* eating. The more great-tasting food you eat, the more benefits you see. It's why my clients love it!

It also encourages us to rekindle that lost relationship of enjoying mealtimes. Depending on what your daily life entails, whether it's working on a movie set, being on a concert world tour, or running a busy household, the company you keep bonds you as a family. Meals are an event where everyone gets together to enjoy each other's company. With the Sirtfood Diet, this can easily be done. Eating freely and without guilt. Knowing the foods you are eating are nourishing your well-being. The recipes are practical and simple to follow, while always producing delectable meals. There's real satisfaction in seeing empty plates and everyone content at the end of a meal.

The word *diet* in the title of this book may almost be a disservice. This is not a diet in the traditional sense but a way of eating for life. It's for everyone who wants to put their body into a healthier state and feel their best while still enjoying life and their food. It's for people who want to see big differences from little changes and for those who want weight loss that lasts without spending hours in the gym or starving themselves.

I've experienced firsthand these astounding benefits, and so have my clients. We've gone from saying we would never go on a diet to never eating any other way. Now it's your chance to experience and enjoy it too!

Warmest wishes,

Pete Geracimo

Celebrity trainer to Adele, Pippa Middleton,
Bryan Singer, Jimmy Barnes, and Kim Catrell

THE
SIRT
FOOD
DIET

Introduction

Laurenne felt her world crumble when she heard the word come out of her doctor's mouth. This year, 2014, was meant to be her year. At just fifty-one she had given up work a few months earlier and was excitedly planning her next life adventures. In what could have graced a Hollywood romance script, she had just been reunited with her early-life sweetheart, Rannoch, after being apart for thirty years. They would soon marry. Then she was told she had breast cancer. . . . Fortunately, the treatment was a success, but the side effects of the chemotherapy took their toll.

Over the years Laurenne had always struggled with her weight and tried every diet trend going, only to regain the weight plus more each time. But now she simply didn't feel good. She felt "uncomfortable, heavy, and lethargic." She fell into a pattern of comfort eating, and the simplest of activities that she used to enjoy, such as going out for a walk, felt like having to complete a marathon. Within just a matter of months Laurenne had gained 20 pounds. The doctor then informed her that she would be on anticancer medication for the next ten years. It was the popular drug called tamoxifen, well known for causing weight gain and lethargy. She faced the prospect of swallowing a tablet every day to stave off cancer but at the expense of her vitality and feeling good about herself.

Still, Laurenne was determined not to let it beat her. Her now-husband, Rannoch, the rock by her side, was a diet skeptic. But having read about a new weight-loss diet based upon the power of eating natural plant foods that boasted tremendous well-being benefits, he felt there was nothing to lose. Together, they embarked upon the Sirtfood Diet. Within the first six weeks, Laurenne lost 20 pounds. Rannoch himself had lost 12 pounds despite not carrying much excess weight to begin with. This was a major breakthrough for Laurenne, but even more profound was the transformation in how she felt. Her energy levels soared and her zest for life returned. The need to comfort-eat disappeared and junk food lost its appeal. She was back to her normal activities again, and with each passing day she felt better and better. In Laurenne's words, "It is one of the best things we have ever done, it's the best we have both felt in years. This is not a diet in the usual sense, but a way of eating for life. I don't feel the side effects of the medication now, and I never have to worry about 'dieting' again."

Of the hundreds of millions of people who will follow popularized diets this year, less than 1 percent will achieve permanent weight loss.[1] Not only do they fail to make a difference in the battle of the bulge, but they do nothing to curb the tsunami of chronic disease that has engulfed modern society.

We may be living longer but we are not living healthier. Staggeringly, over the course of a mere ten years, the amount of time we spend in ill health has doubled from 20 to 40 percent. It means we now spend almost thirty-two years of our lives in poor health. Just look at the stats. Right now, one in ten has diabetes and another three are on the verge of getting it. Two out of every five people will be diagnosed with cancer at some stage in their lives. If you see three women over the age of fifty, one of them is going to have an osteoporotic fracture. And in the average time it takes you to read a single page of this book, a new case of Alzheimer's will develop and someone will die of heart disease—and that's in the United States alone.

For these reasons, "dieting" has never been our thing. That is, until we discovered Sirtfoods, a revolutionary new—and easy—way to eat your way to weight loss and amazing health.

WHAT ARE SIRTFOODS?

When we cut back on calories, it creates a shortage of energy that activates what is known as the "skinny gene." This triggers a raft of positive changes. It puts the body into a kind of survival mode where it stops storing fat and normal growth processes are put on hold. Instead, the body turns its attention to burning up its stores of fat and switching on powerful housekeeping genes that repair and rejuvenate our cells, effectively giving them a spring cleaning. The upshot is weight loss and improved resistance to disease.

But, as many dieters know, cutting calories comes at a cost. In the short term, the reduction in energy intake provokes hunger, irritability, fatigue, and muscle loss. Longer-term calorie restriction causes our metabolism to stagnate. This is the downfall of all calorie-restrictive diets and paves the way for the weight to come piling back on. It is for these reasons that 99 percent of dieters are doomed to fail in the long run.

All of this led us to ask a big question: is it somehow possible to activate our skinny gene with all the great benefits that brings without needing to stick to intense calorie restriction with all those drawbacks?

Enter Sirtfoods, a newly discovered group of wonder foods. Sirtfoods are particularly rich in special nutrients that, when we consume them, are able to activate the same skinny genes in our bodies that calorie restriction does. These genes are known as sirtuins. They first came to light in a landmark study in 2003 when researchers discovered that resveratrol, a compound found in red grape skin and red wine, dramatically increased the life span of yeast.[2] Incredibly, resveratrol had the same effect on longevity as calorie restriction, but this was achieved without reducing energy intake. Since then studies have shown that resveratrol can extend life in worms, flies, fish, and even honeybees.[3] And from mice to humans, early-stage studies show resveratrol protects against the adverse effects of high-calorie, high-fat, and high-sugar diets; promotes healthy aging by delaying age-related diseases; and increases fitness.[4] In essence it has been shown to mimic the effects of calorie restriction and exercise.

With its rich resveratrol content, red wine was hailed as the original Sirtfood, explaining the health benefits linked to its consumption, and even why people who drink red wine gain less weight.[5] However, this is only the beginning of the Sirtfood story. With the discovery of resveratrol, the world of health research was on the cusp of something big, and the pharmaceutical industry wasted no time jumping on board. Researchers began screening thousands of different chemicals for their ability to activate our sirtuin genes. This revealed a number of natural plant compounds, not just resveratrol, with significant sirtuin-activating properties. It was also discovered that a given food could contain a whole spectrum of these plant compounds, which could work in concert to both aid absorption and maximize that food's sirtuin-activating effect. This had been one of the big puzzles around resveratrol. The scientists experimenting with resveratrol often needed to use far higher doses than we know provide a benefit when consumed as part of red wine. However, as well as resveratrol, red wine contains an array of other natural plant compounds, including high amounts of piceatannol as well as quercetin, myricetin, and epicatechin, each of which was shown to independently activate our sirtuin genes and, more important, to work in coordination.

The problem for the pharmaceutical industry is that they can't market a group of nutrients or foods as the next big blockbuster drug. So instead they invested hundreds of millions of dollars to develop and conduct trials of synthetic compounds in the hopes of uncovering a Shangri-la pill. Right now multiple studies of sirtuin-activating drugs are under way for a multitude of chronic diseases, as well as the first-ever FDA-approved trial to investigate whether a medicine can slow aging.

As tantalizing as that may seem, if history has taught us anything, it's that we should not hold out much hope for this pharmaceutical ambrosia. Time and time again the pharmaceutical and health industries have tried to emulate the benefits of foods and diets through isolated drugs and nutrients. And time and time again it's come up short. Why wait ten-plus years for the licensing of these so-called wonder drugs, and the inevitable side effects they bring, when right now we have all the incredible benefits available at our fingertips through the food we eat?

So while the pharmaceutical industry relentlessly pursues a drug-like magic bullet, we have to retrain our focus on diet. For at the same time those efforts were under way, the landscape of nutritional research was also shifting, raising some big questions of its own. Red wine to one side, were there other foods with high levels of these special nutrients capable of activating our sirtuin genes? And if so, what were their effects on triggering fat loss and fighting disease?

NOT ALL FRUITS AND VEGETABLES ARE CREATED EQUAL

Since 1986 two of the largest nutritional studies in US history have been undertaken concurrently by researchers at Harvard University: the Health Professionals Follow-Up Study, examining men's dietary habits and health, and the Nurses' Health Study, investigating the same for females. Drawing on this vast wealth of data, researchers explored the link between the dietary habits of more than 124,000 people and changes in body weight over a twenty-four-year period ending in 2011.[6]

They found something remarkable. As part of a standard American diet, consuming certain plant foods staved off weight gain, yet consuming others had no effect at all. What was the difference between them? It all boiled down to whether the foods were rich in certain types of natural plant chemicals known as polyphenols. We nearly all tend to put on weight as we age, but consuming higher amounts of polyphenols had notable impact in preventing this. When examined in greater detail, only certain types of polyphenols stood out as being effective for keeping people slim, the researchers found. Among those effective were the same groups of natural plant chemicals that the pharmaceutical industry was furiously trying to turn into a wonder pill for their ability to turn on our sirtuin genes.

The conclusion was profound: not all plant foods (including fruits and vegetables) are equal when it comes to controlling our weight. Instead, we need to start investigating plant foods for their polyphenol content, and then in turn investigate the ability of those polyphenols to switch on our "skinny" sirtuin genes. This is a radical idea that runs counter to the prevailing dogma of our times. It is time to let go of the generic, blanket advice that tells us to eat two cups of fruit and two and a half cups of vegetables a day as part of a balanced diet. We need only look around us to see how little impact that has had.

With this shift in judging how plant foods are good for us, something else became apparent. The many foods that supposed health experts warned us away from, such as chocolate, coffee, and tea, are in fact so rich in sirtuin-activating polyphenols that they trump most fruits and vegetables out there. How many times do we grimace as we swallow our vegetables because we're told that's the right thing to do, only to feel guilty if we even look at that after-dinner chocolate treat? The ultimate irony is that cocoa is one of the best foods we could possibly be eating. Its consumption has now been proven to activate sirtuin genes, with multiple benefits for controlling body weight by burning fat, reducing appetite, and improving muscle function.[7] And that's before we take account of its multitude of other health benefits, more of which to come later.

In total we have identified twenty foods rich in polyphenols that have been shown to activate our sirtuin genes, and together these form the basis of the Sirtfood Diet. While the story started with red wine as the original Sirtfood, we now know these other nineteen foods either match or trump it for their sirtuin-activating polyphenol content. As well as cocoa, these include other well-known and much-enjoyed foods such as extra virgin olive oil, red onions, garlic, parsley, chilies, kale, strawberries, walnuts, capers, tofu, green tea, and even coffee. While each food has impressive health credentials of its own, as we are about to see, the real magic happens when we combine these foods to make a whole diet.

A COMMON LINK AMONG THE WORLD'S HEALTHIEST DIETS

As we researched further, we discovered that the best sources of Sirtfoods were found in the diets of those boasting the lowest rates of disease and obesity in the world—from the Kuna American Indians, who appear immune to high blood pressure and show remarkably low rates of obesity, diabetes, cancer, and early death,

thanks to a fantastically rich intake of the Sirtfood cocoa; to Okinawa, Japan, where a buffet of Sirtfoods, svelte figures, and long
life all go hand in hand; to India, where the voracious appetite for
all things spicy, especially the Sirtfood turmeric, has left cancer in
its wake.

But it is the diet that is the envy of the rest of the Western world,
a traditional Mediterranean diet, where the benefits of Sirtfoods
truly stand out. Here obesity simply does not prevail and chronic
disease is the exception, not the norm. Extra virgin olive oil, wild
leafy greens, nuts, berries, red wine, dates, and herbs are all potent
Sirtfoods, and all feature prominently in the native Mediterranean
diet. The scientific world has been left in awe in light of the most
recent consensus that following a Mediterranean diet is more effective than counting calories for weight loss, and more effective than
pharmaceutical drugs for stopping disease.[8]

This brings us to PREDIMED, a game-changing study of the
Mediterranean diet, published in 2013. It was conducted on almost
7,400 individuals at high risk of cardiovascular disease, and the results were so good that the trial was actually stopped early—after just
five years.[9] The premise of PREDIMED was beautifully simple. It
asked what the difference would be between a Mediterranean-style
diet supplemented with either extra virgin olive oil or nuts (especially walnuts) and a more conventional modern-day diet. And
what a difference it was. The change in diet reduced the incidence
of cardiovascular disease by around 30 percent, a result drug com-
panies can only dream of. Upon further follow-up, it was found
that there was also a 30 percent fall in diabetes, along with significant drops in inflammation, improvements in memory and brain

health, and a massive 40 percent reduction in obesity, with notable fat loss especially around the stomach area.

Yet initially researchers were unable to explain what produced these dramatic benefits. Neither the amounts of calories, fats, and sugars eaten—the typical measures used to assess the food we eat—nor physical activity levels differed between the groups to explain the findings. There had to be something else going on.

Then the eureka moment struck. Both extra virgin olive oil and walnuts stand out for their exceptional content of sirtuin-activating polyphenols. Essentially, by adding these in significant amounts to a normal Mediterranean diet, what the researchers had unwittingly created was a superrich Sirtfood diet, and they found that it delivered breathtaking results.

So researchers analyzing PREDIMED came up with a clever hypothesis. If it is the polyphenols that ultimately matter, they mused, then those who ate the most of them would experience their cumulative benefits by living the longest. So they ran the stats, and the results were staggering. Over just five years, those who consumed the highest levels of polyphenols had 37 percent fewer deaths compared to those who ate the least.[10] Intriguingly, this is double the reduction in mortality that treatment with the most commonly prescribed blockbuster statin drugs is found to bring. Finally we had the explanation for the mind-blowing benefits this study observed, and it was more powerful than any drug in existence.

The researchers also noted something else of importance. While many studies have previously found that individual Sirtfoods confer impressive health benefits, they were never profound enough to actually extend life. PREDIMED was the first of its kind. The difference was that it looked at a pattern of foods rather than a single food. Different foods provide different sirtuin-activating polyphenols, which work in harmony to produce a much more powerful outcome than any single food can. This left us with an irrepressible conclusion. True health is not reaped through one single nutrient or even one "wonder food." What you need is a whole diet filled with a combination of Sirtfoods all working in synergy. And this is what led to the creation of the Sirtfood Diet.

THE SIRTFOOD PILOT STUDY

Bit by bit, we had pieced together all the observations from traditional cultures and findings from major scientific studies, culminating in PREDIMED, one of the best studies of diet ever conducted. But even the findings of PREDIMED, like many health breakthroughs, came through chance. It never set out to design and test a diet of Sirtfoods. It was only later that science discovered that this was effectively what PREDIMED had done. This meant there were still many Sirtfoods the diet hadn't included that could have increased its immense benefits even further.

Additionally, all the research to date had established the benefits for long-term weight management and reducing disease. But we still didn't know how quickly those benefits for body weight and well-being could be realized. We all want to protect our future health, but don't we want to look and feel good in the here and now too?

To answer these questions, we needed a purposefully conducted Sirtfood Diet intervention that included all twenty of the most powerful Sirtfoods for which we could gather earlier measurements of the results. So we embarked on a pilot study of our own.

Nestled in the heart of London, England, is KX, one of Europe's most sought-after health and fitness centers. What makes KX the perfect place to test the effects of the Sirtfood Diet is that it has its own restaurant, which gave us the opportunity not just to design the diet, but to bring it to life and test it on the fitness center's members.

Our remit was clear. For seven days in a row, members would follow our carefully constructed Sirtfood Diet and we would meticulously track their progress from beginning to end, not just measuring their weight, but also monitoring changes in their body composition, which meant checking how the diet affected the levels of fat and muscle in the body. Later, we added metabolic measures, to see the effects of the diet on levels of sugar (glucose) and fats (like triglycerides and cholesterol) in the blood.

The first three days were the most intense, with food intake restricted to 1,000 calories per day. In effect, this is like a mild fast, which is important because the lower energy intake turns down growth signals in the body and encourages it to start clearing old debris out of cells (a process known as autophagy) and kick-start fat burning. But unlike popular fasting diets, this fast was mild and short-lived, making it much more sustainable, as proven by the study's exceptionally high 97.5 percent adherence rate. Plus, we wanted to investigate the differences that adding Sirtfoods made to the normal downfalls experienced with fasting diets. And as we were soon to find out, they were dramatic.

Our primary goal was to make a big difference to the fat-burning effects of this mild calorie restriction by packing the diet full of Sirtfoods. This was achieved by basing the daily diet on three Sirtfood-rich green juices and one Sirtfood-rich meal.

For the final four days of our program at KX, calories were increased to 1,500 per day. Effectively this was only a very mild calorie deficit, but enough to keep growth signals turned down and fat-burning signals turned up. Importantly, that 1,500-calorie diet was jam-packed with Sirtfoods, consisting of two Sirtfood-rich green juices and two Sirtfood-rich meals per day.

THE REMARKABLE RESULTS

The Sirtfood Diet was tested by forty and completed by thirty-nine members at KX. Of these thirty-nine, two in the trial were obese, fifteen were overweight, and twenty-two had a normal/healthy body mass index (BMI). The study had a fairly even gender split, with twenty-one women and eighteen men. Being members of a health club, before they started they were more likely to exercise and be aware of healthy eating than the general population.

A trick of many diets is to use a heavily overweight and un-healthy sample of people to show the benefits, as at first they lose weight the quickest and most dramatically, essentially fluffing up the diet results. Our logic was the opposite: if we obtained good results with this relatively healthy group, it would set the minimum benchmark of what was achievable.

The results far exceeded our already high expectations. Results were consistent and astounding: an average 7 pounds of weight loss in seven days after accounting for muscle gain.

As if that weren't admirable enough, we saw something else even more impressive, which was the *type* of weight loss. Typically, when people lose weight, they will lose some fat but they will also lose some muscle—this is par for the course when it comes to dieting. We were stunned to find the opposite. Our participants either maintained their muscle or actually gained muscle. As we will find out later in the book, this is an infinitely more favorable type of weight loss, and a unique feature of the Sirtfood Diet.

No participant failed to see improvements in body composition. And remember, all of this was achieved without dietary hardship or grueling exercise regimens.

Here's what we found:

- Participants achieved dramatic and rapid results, losing an average of 7 pounds in seven days.
- Weight loss was most noticeable around the abdominal area.
- Rather than being lost, muscle mass was either maintained or increased.
- Participants rarely felt hungry.
- Participants felt an increased sense of vitality and well-being.
- Participants reported looking better and healthier.

CASE STUDY

Laura, a twenty-nine-year-old TV sports reporter, was worried about her diet and health. For years it had appeared she could pretty much eat what she wanted and get away with it, but now this habit was starting to catch up with her, and the extra pounds were becoming visible. The problem was that, for as long as she could remember, Laura was a self-confessed sugar addict, to the extent of carrying around a bottle of syrup to pour onto her meals and into drinks, even her coffee. She'd tried diets previously, but inevitably the growing cravings for sweet things led to their quick cessation. With a new reporting season about to start and keen to lose some weight in advance, Laura tried the Sirtfood Diet.

After three weeks, Laura contacted us to update us on the diet. "I feel amazing," she gushed. "My memory, my energy, my skin, my happiness . . . I can't get over how much it's changed. I don't obsess about food anymore, no more sugar cravings, and have a much smaller, more appropriate appetite. It's helped my job so much; I used to get brain fog and think it's normal. Now it's gone. I remember my lines so much better, and feel so much more confident presenting. I can't praise the diet enough."

And the weight loss? "Oh, yeah," she responded, "I'm down over ten pounds, but let me tell you more about how clearheaded I feel."

A DIET IN THE REAL WORLD

It's one thing to get great results following a diet in a controlled environment where all the food is expertly made and provided, and nutrition experts are on hand to answer any queries. It's something else altogether when people are left to fend for themselves with nothing more to assist them than can be found in the pages of this very book.

But it was these reports that really blew our minds. A diet that can so powerfully promote fat loss and improve body composition while turbocharging energy levels and well-being has many useful applications. Before long, hundreds of testimonials had poured in. From sporting superstars who were world champions and Olympic gold medalists to TV personalities and models to the biggest names in showbiz, not only were they following it and sticking to it, but they were raving about it.

Readers were smashing the 7 pounds in seven days weight loss we'd seen in our trial, proving our hypothesis that our already fit and healthy study population was underestimating the benefits. The maximum weight loss we have seen to date was with a reporter and diet cynic who set out to independently test the program's merits. Instead of bad-mouthing it, he lost 14 pounds in the first week. Safe to say he now joins the cohorts of converts. Away from the scales, others reported equally impressive results through inches lost around the waist. And best of all, the weight was staying off, with the results only getting better over the months.

As fantastic as all this feedback was, for us as nutritional medicine consultants who specialize in reversing and preventing disease, there was something that inspired us even more: the personal stories that, just like Laurenne's at the start of this chapter, were nothing short of life-changing.

There was Robert, who had suffered depression for years. He lost 10 pounds in just two weeks but was far more delighted with the lifting of his depressed mood, so much so that he was "loving life" once more. Melanie was in terrible pain with lupus. Five weeks in, she was down 11.5 pounds, but much more important, her aches and pains had vanished. In fact, she had no lupus symptoms at all. Feeling amazing, she no longer had to go to her specialist; there was nothing to treat. And Linda, who was down an incredible 50 pounds after three months, reversed her worsening diabetes and had the energy once more to enjoy life again. This is just a taste of the many inspirational stories that have come in. Heart disease has reversed. Menopause symptoms have ceased. Irritable bowel conditions have disappeared. For the first time in years people were sleeping well again. One perplexed ophthalmologist even contacted us with the news that after just a week on the Sirtfood Diet, her patient's chronic sclera discoloration had totally reversed and was now perfect white again. She even sent photos for proof.

HOW THE SIRTFOOD DIET WILL WORK FOR YOU

The sheer breadth of benefits that people have experienced has been a revelation, all achieved by simply basing their diet on accessible and affordable foods that most people already enjoy eating. And that is all the Sirtfood Diet requires. It's about reaping the benefits of everyday foods that we were always meant to eat, but in the right quantities and the right combinations to give us the body composition and well-being we all so dearly want, and that can ultimately change our lives.

It doesn't require you to perform severe calorie restriction, nor does it demand grueling exercise regimens (although, of course, staying generally active is a good thing). And the only piece of equipment you'll need is a juicer. Plus, unlike every other diet out there that focuses on what you should be excluding, the Sirtfood Diet focuses on what you should be including.

To sum it all up, the Sirtfood Diet will help you:

- lose weight by burning fat, not muscle
- burn fat, especially from the stomach area, to fuel better health
- prime your body for long-term weight-loss success
- look and feel better and have more energy
- avoid enduring severe calorie restriction or extreme hunger
- be free of grueling exercise regimens
- live a longer, healthier, disease-free life

1

The Science of Sirtuins

What makes the Sirtfood Diet so powerful is its ability to switch on an ancient family of genes that exists in each of us. The name for this family of genes is *sirtuin*. Sirtuins are special because they orchestrate processes deep within our cells that influence such important things as our ability to burn fat, our susceptibility—or not—to disease, and ultimately even our life span. So profound is the effect of sirtuins that they are now referred to as "master metabolic regulators."[1] In essence, exactly what anyone wanting to shed some pounds and live a long and healthy life would want to be in charge of.

OF MICE AND MEN

Understandably, sirtuins have become the subject of intense scientific research in recent years. The first sirtuin was discovered back in 1984 in yeast, and interest really took off over the course of the next three decades when it was revealed that sirtuin activation increases life span, first in yeast, and then all the way up to mice.[2] Why the excitement? Because from yeast to humans and everything in between, the fundamental principles of cellular metabolism are nearly identical. If you can manipulate something as tiny as a budding yeast and see a benefit, then repeat it in higher organisms such as mice, the potential exists for the same benefits to be realized in humans.

AN APPETITE FOR FASTING?

Which brings us nicely to fasting. The lifelong restriction of food intake has consistently been shown to extend the life expectancy of lower organisms and mammals.[3] This remarkable finding is the basis for the practice of caloric restriction among some people, where daily calorie intake is reduced by about 20 to 30 percent, as well as its popularized offshoot, intermittent fasting, which has become a successful weight-loss diet, made famous by the likes of the 5:2 diet, or Fast Diet. While we still await proof of increased life span for humans from these practices, there is proof of benefits for what we might term "health span"—chronic diseases drop and fat starts to melt away.[4]

But let's be honest, no matter how big the benefits, fasting week in, week out, is a grueling business that most of us aren't willing to sign up for. Even if we do, most of us can't stick to it. On top of this there are drawbacks to fasting, especially when we follow it long-term. In the introduction we mentioned the side effects of hunger, irritability, fatigue, muscle loss, and metabolism slowdown. But in addition, ongoing fasting regimens could put us at risk of malnutrition, affecting our well-being due to a lowered intake of essential nutrients. Fasting regimens are also wholly unsuitable for large proportions of the population such as children, women during pregnancy, and very possibly the elderly. While there are clearly established benefits to fasting, it's not the magic bullet we would like it to be. It had us asking, is this really the way nature intended for us to be thin *and* healthy? Surely there's a better way. . . .

Our breakthrough came when we discovered that the profound benefits from caloric restriction and fasting were mediated through activation of our ancient sirtuin genes.[5] To better understand this, it might be helpful to think about sirtuins as the guardians at the crossroads between energy status and longevity. What they do there is respond to stresses.

When energy is in short supply, exactly as we see in caloric restriction, there is an increase in stress on our cells. This is sensed by the sirtuins, which then get switched on and broadcast a constellation of powerful signals that radically alter the way cells behave. Sirtuins ramp up our metabolism, increase the efficiency of our muscles, switch on fat burning, reduce inflammation, and repair any damage in our cells. In effect, sirtuins make us fitter, leaner, and healthier.

In humans, there are seven different sirtuins (SIRT1 to SIRT7). Of these, SIRT1 and SIRT3 are the two most important sirtuins involved in energy balance. While SIRT1 is found throughout the body, SIRT3 is predominantly found in our mitochondria—the energy powerhouses of our cells. Together their activation gives us the many benefits we are looking to achieve.

A ZEAL FOR EXERCISE?

It's not just caloric restriction and fasting that activate sirtuins; exercise does too.[6] Just like in fasting, sirtuins orchestrate the profound benefits of exercise. But while we are encouraged to engage in regular moderate exercise for its multitude of benefits, it is not the means through which we are meant to focus our weight-loss efforts. Research shows that the human body has evolved ways to naturally adjust and reduce the amount of energy we expend when we exercise,[7] meaning that in order for exercise to be an effective weight-loss intervention, we need to commit substantial time and strenuous effort. That grueling exercise regimens are the way nature intended us to maintain a healthy weight is even more dubious in light of research now suggesting that too much exercise can be harmful—weakening our immune systems, damaging the heart, and contributing to early death.[8,9]

Enter Sirtfoods

So far we have discovered that if we want to lose weight and be healthy, the key is to activate our sirtuin genes. Up until now the two known ways to achieve this have been fasting and exercise. Alas, the amounts needed for successful weight loss come with their drawbacks, and for most of us are simply incompatible with how we live life in the twenty-first century. Fortunately, there is a newly discovered, groundbreaking means of activating our sirtuin genes in the best possible way: Sirtfoods. As we will soon learn, these are the wonder foods particularly rich in specific natural plant chemicals that have the power to speak to our sirtuin genes, switching them on. In essence they mimic the effects of fasting and exercise and in doing so bring remarkable benefits of burning fat, building muscle, and boosting health, which were previously unattainable.

Summary

- Each of us possesses an ancient family of genes called sirtuins.
- Sirtuins are master metabolic regulators that control our ability to burn fat and stay healthy.
- Sirtuins act as energy sensors within our cells, and get activated when a shortage of energy is detected.
- Fasting and exercise both activate our sirtuin genes, but can be hard to stick to and even have drawbacks.
- There is a new groundbreaking way to activate our sirtuin genes: Sirtfoods.
- By eating a diet rich in Sirtfoods, you can mimic the effects of fasting and exercise, and achieve the body you want.

2

....

Fighting Fat

One of the dramatic findings from our pilot study of the Sirtfood Diet was not just the amount of weight the participants lost, which was impressive enough—it was the *type* of weight loss that really got us excited. What grabbed our attention was the fact that many people were losing weight without losing any muscle. In fact, it was not uncommon to see people gain muscle. This left us with an inescapable conclusion: fat was just melting away.

Normally, achieving significant fat loss requires a considerable sacrifice, either severely cutting back on calories or engaging in superhuman levels of exercise, or both. But contrary to that, our participants either maintained or reduced their exercise levels, and didn't even report feeling particularly hungry. In fact, some even struggled to eat all the food that was provided for them.

How is this even possible? It's only when we understand what happens to our fat cells when sirtuin activity is increased that we can begin to make sense of these remarkable findings.

LEAN GENES

Mice that have been genetically engineered to have high levels of *SIRT1*, the sirtuin gene that drives fat loss, are leaner and more metabolically active,[1] whereas mice lacking *SIRT1* are fatter and have more metabolic disease.[2] When we look at humans, levels of *SIRT1* have been found to be markedly lower in the body fat of obese people than their healthy-weight counterparts.[3,4] In contrast, people with increased *SIRT1* gene activity are leaner and more resistant to weight gain.[5]

Stack all that up and you start to get a sense of just how important sirtuins are for determining whether we stay lean or get fat, and why by increasing sirtuin activity you can achieve such amazing results. This is because through sirtuins we get benefits on multiple levels, starting at the very root of it all: the genes that control weight gain.

To better understand this, we need to delve deeper into what happens in our cells that causes us to gain weight.

CASE STUDY

Kate is a housewife in her mid-thirties and mother to two young children. With a body fat measurement of more than 25 percent, she was classed as "acceptable" in terms of the amount of fat stored in her body, but was unhappy that she was still carrying those extra few pregnancy pounds around the middle. Despite being quite active—exercising in the gym when she could and being constantly on her feet with two energy-filled children to look after—her weight did not shift. Diet-wise she had always tried to eat quite healthily, and stated that, if anything, she ate too little instead of too much, with it not being uncommon for her to skip a meal to ensure the children were looked after.

The ease and convenience of the Sirtfood Diet made it perfect for her to try it out, and she achieved fantastic results. By the end of a week Kate was down 6 pounds 8 ounces on the scales and had gained 1 pound in muscle for a net fat loss of 7 pounds 8 ounces. Her body fat was now 22 percent, putting her in the "fit" range that she so desired.

FAT BUSTING

We're going to explain this in terms of a Hollywood drug-ring film. The flooding of the streets with drugs is the flooding of our body with fat. The drug pushers on the street corners are the equivalent of the reactions in our body that peddle weight gain. But in reality, they are only the low-level thugs. Behind it all is the true villain masterminding the whole operation, directing every deal the peddlers make. In our film, this villain is called PPAR-γ (peroxisome proliferator-activated receptor-γ). PPAR-γ orchestrates the fat-gain process by switching on the genes that are needed to start synthesizing and storing fat.[6] To stop the proliferation of fat, you must cut the supply. Stop PPAR-γ, and you effectively stop fat gain.

Enter our hero, *SIRT1*, who rises up to bring down the villain. With the villain securely locked up, there is no one to pull the strings and the whole fat-gain organization crumbles. With the activity of PPAR-γ halted, *SIRT1* moves its attentions to "cleaning the streets." Not only is this done by shutting down the production and storage of fat, as we've seen, but it actually changes our metabolism so we start ridding the body of excess fat.[7] Just like every good crime-fighting hero, *SIRT1* has a sidekick, a key regulator in our cells known as PGC-1α. This powerfully stimulates the creation of what are known as mitochondria. These are the tiny energy factories that exist within each of our cells—they power the body. The more mitochondria we have, the more energy we can produce. But not only does PGC-1α promote more mitochondria, it also encourages them to burn fat as the fuel of choice to make the energy. So on the one hand fat storage is blocked, and on the other fat burning is increased.

CASE STUDY

Linda is a night-shift worker in her fifties. Significantly overweight for many years, like many she had tried all the latest diets, but without success. Then two years ago the inevitable happened: Linda was diagnosed with type 2 diabetes. She was put on the popular diabetes drug metformin, yet her blood sugar levels continued to deteriorate to the point where she was on the brink of needing treatment with insulin as well. Desperate to not succumb to a lifetime of multiple daily injections, Linda ordered *The Sirtfood Diet* after hearing how others had lost so much weight on it.

In just one week, Linda lost a breathtaking 13 pounds. Twelve weeks in, her weight had dropped by a staggering 50 pounds, reflected in her BMI, which was now down by an incredible seven points. All the more remarkable was the fact that this was achieved with no exercise whatsoever, just the power of Sirtfoods. As for forgoing all the things that Linda loved? Nothing could be further from the truth, as she was more than happy to point out, "I look forward to my chocolate and red wine—Pinot Noir is gorgeous. It's just being sensible with the bad stuff and wolfing down the good."

Even better news was to come at her six-month diabetic checkup: incredibly, her blood sugar levels were now normal. Linda had not only halted the deterioration of her disease, she had reversed it. With Sirtfoods now firmly established as part of her everyday life, and with her energy levels skyrocketing, Linda is now ready to embark on some exercise too, paving the way for further weight loss and a future free from diabetes.

WAT or BAT?

So far we've looked at the effects of *SIRT1* on fat loss on a well-known type of fat called white adipose tissue (WAT). This is the type of fat associated with weight gain. It specializes in storage and expansion, is horribly stubborn, and secretes a host of inflammatory chemicals that resist fat burning and encourage further fat accumulation, making us overweight and obese. This is why weight gain often starts slowly but can snowball so quickly.

But there is another intriguing angle to the sirtuin story, involving a lesser-known type of fat, brown adipose tissue (BAT), which behaves very differently. In complete contrast to white adipose tissue, BAT is beneficial to us and wants to get used up. Brown adipose tissue actually helps us expend energy and has evolved in mammals to allow them to dissipate large amounts of energy in the form of heat. This is known as a thermogenic effect and is critical to small mammals to help them survive in cold temperatures. In humans, babies also possess significant amounts of brown adipose tissue, although it decreases soon after birth, leaving smaller amounts in adults.

Here is where *SIRT1* activation does something truly amazing. It switches on genes in our white adipose tissue so that it morphs and takes on the properties of brown adipose tissue in what is called a "browning effect."[8] That means our fat stores start to behave in an altogether different way—instead of storing energy, they start to mobilize it for disposal.

As we can see, sirtuin activation has potent direct action on fat cells, encouraging fat to melt away. But it doesn't end there. Sirtuins also positively influence the most relevant hormones involved in weight control. Sirtuin activation improves insulin activity.[9] This helps to reduce insulin resistance—the inability of our cells to respond properly to insulin—which is heavily implicated in weight gain. *SIRT1* also enhances the release and activity of our thyroid hormones,[10] which share many overlapping roles in boosting our metabolism and ultimately the rate at which we burn fat.

CASE STUDY

Gary is a busy entrepreneur in his mid-forties. His hectic schedule had left him feeling run-down and exhausted, and his weight had gradually crept up to just over 200 pounds, classing him as overweight even for his tall 6-foot-2 frame. With a family history of metabolic disease, Gary wanted to do something to ensure that wasn't his future fate. But despite fitting in exercise around his work commitments and trying to eat well as best he could, his weight was inexorably creeping up.

After seven days of the Sirtfood Diet, Gary had lost 7 pounds 8 ounces. While he was still classified as overweight, this was the springboard he needed to make longer-term changes. Over the next eighteen months Gary repeated the seven-day Phase 1 of the Sirtfood Diet two more times, and in between consciously chose to incorporate more Sirtfoods into his dietary patterns. It was "a reboot into a different eating behavior," as he described it. At last measurements, Gary had reached and maintained his target weight of 172 pounds. His body fat percentage had been slashed from an overweight 24 to a fit 14 percent. And better news was to come in the form of a very substantial reduction in his measured visceral fat levels (the fat that we can't see stored around the liver), which is the number one driver of metabolic disease.

APPETITE CONTROL

There was one thing we couldn't wrap our heads around in our pilot study: despite a reduction in calories, participants didn't really get hungry. In fact, some individuals struggled to eat all the food provided.

One of the big advantages of the Sirtfood Diet is that we can achieve great benefits without the need for long-term calorie restriction. The very first week of the diet is the hyper-success phase, where we combine moderate fasting with an abundance of powerful Sirtfoods for a double blow to fat. And as with all fasting regimens, we expected some reports of hunger here. But we got absolutely none!

As we trawled through research, we found the answer. It's all due to the body's foremost appetite-regulating hormone, leptin, nicknamed the "satiety hormone." When we eat, leptin increases, signaling to a part of the brain called the hypothalamus that inhibits hunger. Conversely, when we fast, leptin signaling to the brain decreases, making us feel hungry.

So important is leptin in regulating appetite that early hopes were that it could be administered as a "magic bullet" to treat obesity. But that dream was shattered with the realization that the metabolic dysfunction that occurs in obesity actually causes leptin to stop working properly. In obesity, not only is the amount of leptin that can get into the brain reduced but the hypothalamus also becomes desensitized to its actions. This is known as leptin resistance: the leptin is there but no longer works properly. Thus for many overweight individuals, even though they eat enough, the brain continues to think they are underfed and signals for them to continue to seek out food.

The upshot of this is that while the level of leptin in the blood is important for regulating appetite, what is far more important is how much of it reaches the brain and is able to have an effect on the hypothalamus. This is where Sirtfoods shine.

New evidence shows that the nutrients found in Sirtfoods have unique benefits for reversing leptin resistance.[11,12] This is through both increasing the transport of leptin to the brain and increasing the sensitivity of the hypothalamus to leptin's actions. So back to our original question: why don't people feel hungry on the Sirtfood Diet? Despite a drop in leptin levels in the blood during the mild fast, which would normally increase hunger, adding Sirtfoods into the diet causes leptin signaling to become more efficient, resulting in improved appetite regulation.

As we will see later, Sirtfoods also have powerful effects on our taste centers, meaning we get much more pleasure and satisfaction from our food and do not therefore fall into the trap of overeating to feel satisfied.

Even for the most dedicated dieters, sirtuins are likely to be a brand-new concept. Yet targeting sirtuins, the master regulators of our metabolism, is the cornerstone of any successful weight-loss diet. Tragically, the very nature of our modern society, with abundant food and sedentary lifestyles, creates a perfect storm for switching off our sirtuin activity, and we see the fallout of this all around us.

The good news is that now we know what sirtuins are, how they control fat storage and promote fat burning, and most important, how to switch them on. And with this revolutionary breakthrough, finally the answer to effective and sustained weight loss is yours for the taking.

SUMMARY

- Fat melts away on the Sirtfood Diet. This is because sirtuins have the power to determine whether we stay lean or get fat.
- Activating *SIRT1* inhibits PPAR-γ, blocking the production and storage of fat.
- Activating *SIRT1* also turns on PGC-1α, which makes more energy factories in our cells and increases fat burning.
- Activating *SIRT1* even gets our fat cells that specialize in energy storage to behave differently and start disposing of energy.
- You are unlikely to feel hungry on the Sirtfood Diet because it helps to regulate appetite in the brain.

3

....

Masters of Muscle

A striking finding from our pilot trial that really got us intrigued was that the muscle mass of the participants didn't drop; in fact, it increased, on average by just over 1 pound. While it was common to see weight loss of 7 pounds on the scales, we also saw something fascinating occurring. For almost two-thirds of our participants, the losses on the scales initially appeared more disappointing than this, albeit still very impressive, with a weight loss of just over 5 pounds. But when body composition tests were performed, we were amazed. Muscle mass was not just maintained in these participants, it had increased. The average muscle gain for this group was almost 2 pounds, giving what is called a "muscle gain adjusted weight loss" of 7 pounds.

This was completely unexpected and in stark contrast to what typically happens on weight-loss diets, where people lose some fat but they also lose muscle. It's the classic trade-off for any diet that limits calories: you kiss muscle good-bye as well as fat. This is not at all surprising when you consider that when we deprive the body of energy, cells shift from growth mode to survival mode and will use the protein from muscle for fuel.

WHAT'S SO GOOD ABOUT MAINTAINING MUSCLE?

So what's the big deal? you might ask. Firstly, it means you'll look much better. Stripping away fat, but retaining muscle, leads to a more desirable lean, toned, and athletic physique. And even more important, you'll stay looking good. Skeletal muscle is the major factor that accounts for our body's daily energy expenditure. This means the more muscle you have, the more energy you burn, even when resting. This really helps to support further weight loss and increases the likelihood of success in the long term. As we now know, with typical dieting, weight loss comes from both fat loss and muscle loss, and with that we see a marked decline in the metabolic rate. This primes the body for weight regain when more normal eating habits are resumed. But by keeping hold of your muscle mass with Sirtfoods, you burn more fat with a minimal drop in metabolic rate. This provides the perfect foundation for long-term weight-loss success.

Additionally, muscle mass and function is a predictor of well-being and healthy aging, and maintaining muscle prevents the development of chronic diseases such as diabetes and osteoporosis, as well as keeping us mobile into older age. Importantly, it also appears to keep us happier, with scientists suggesting that the way sirtuins maintain muscle even has benefits for stress-related disorders, including reducing depression.[1]

All in all, losing weight while protecting muscle is a biggie and an infinitely more favorable outcome. It's a unique feature of the Sirtfood Diet, and to better understand this, we need to get back to sirtuins and their powerful effects on muscle.

SIRTUINS AND MUSCLE MASS

There is a family of genes in the body that act as guardians of our muscle and halt its breakdown when under stress: the sirtuins.[2] *SIRT1* is a potent inhibitor of muscle breakdown. As long as *SIRT1* is activated, even when we are fasting, muscle breakdown is prevented and we continue to burn fat for fuel.

But the benefits of *SIRT1* don't end with preserving muscle mass. Sirtuins actually work to increase our skeletal muscle mass.[3–5] To explain how this phenomenon works, we need to venture into the exciting world of stem cells. Our muscle contains a special type of stem cell, called a satellite cell, which controls its growth and regeneration. Satellite cells just sit there quietly most of the time, but they are activated when muscle gets damaged or stressed. This is how our muscles get bigger through activities like weight training. *SIRT1* is essential for activating satellite cells, and without its activity muscles are significantly smaller because they no longer have the capacity to develop or regenerate properly.[6] However, by increasing *SIRT1* activity, we give a boost to our satellite cells, which encourages muscle growth and recovery.

SIRTFOODS VERSUS FASTING

This leads us to a big question: if sirtuin activation increases muscle mass, then why do we lose muscle when we fast? After all, fasting activates our sirtuin genes as well. And herein lies one of the massive drawbacks of fasting.

Bear with us while we delve into how this works. Not all skeletal muscle is created equal. We have two main types, conveniently called type-1 and type-2. Type-1 muscle is used for longer-duration activities, whereas type-2 muscle is used for short bursts of more intense activity. And here's where it gets intriguing: fasting increases *SIRT1* activity *only* in type-1 muscle fibers, not in type-2.[7] So type-1 muscle fiber size is maintained and even noticeably increases when we fast.[8] Sadly, in complete contrast to what happens in type-1 fibers during fasting, *SIRT1* rapidly declines in type-2 fibers. This means fat burning slows down, and instead muscle starts to break down to provide fuel.

So fasting is a double-edged sword for muscles, with our type-2 fibers taking a hit. Type-2 fibers are what comprise the bulk of our muscle definition. So even though our type-1 fiber mass increases, we still see an overall significant loss of muscle with fasting. If we could stop the breakdown, it would not only make us look good aesthetically but also help promote further fat loss. And the way to do this is to combat the drop in *SIRT1* in type-2 muscle fiber brought about by fasting.

In an elegant mice study, researchers at Harvard Medical School put this to the test, and showed that by stimulating *SIRT1* activity in type-2 fibers during fasting, the signals for muscle breakdown were switched off and muscle loss didn't occur.[9]

The researchers then went one step further and tested the effects of increased *SIRT1* activity on muscle when the mice were fed rather than fasted, and discovered that it triggered very rapid muscle growth. Within just a week, muscle fibers with increased levels of *SIRT1* activity showed an astounding 20 percent increase in weight.[10]

These findings are very similar to the outcome of our Sirtfood Diet trial, though our study was milder in effect. By increasing *SIRT1* activity through eating a diet rich in Sirtfoods, the majority of participants had no muscle loss—and for many, with it only being a moderate fast, muscle mass actually increased.

CASE STUDY

David "the Hayemaker" Haye is a former world heavyweight boxing champion. After being out of the ring for three years with a career-threatening shoulder injury, he is now successfully on the comeback to reclaim the title of world champion.

David has earned a reputation as one of the most gifted boxers in the world, but in the heavyweight category he often faced opponents who carried 20 to 40 pounds more muscle than he did. Plus, having been out of action for so long with an injury meant that he was carrying about 20 pounds more body fat than an elite boxing champion in this category should.

What was important to him for his return to the ring was to increase muscle mass while losing fat. An avid proponent of plant-based diets, he wholeheartedly adopted the Sirtfood approach, and the results quickly followed. In David's own words: "Sirtfoods have been a revelation to my diet. Introducing Sirtfoods has allowed me to attain a body composition and well-being previously unimaginable, paving the way for my return to the ring and regaining my title as heavyweight champion of the world. I have always endorsed the virtues of eating plants, and the discovery of Sirtfoods shows just how powerful they are and why we should eat more of them. If anyone asks me my number one tip for getting in great shape, my answer is to start eating a Sirtfood-rich diet."

KEEPING MUSCLES YOUNG

And it's not just muscle size. The prolific effects of *SIRT1* on muscle extend to how it functions too. As muscle ages, its ability to activate *SIRT1* declines. This makes it less responsive to the benefits of exercise and more prone to damage from free radicals and inflammation, which results in what is known as oxidative stress. Muscles gradually wither, get weaker, and fatigue more easily. But if we can increase activation of *SIRT1*, we can stop the age-related decline.[11-13]

Indeed, by activating *SIRT1* to stop the loss of muscle mass and function we normally see with aging, we see multiple related health benefits, including the halting of bone loss and prevention of increased chronic systemic inflammation (known as inflammaging), as well as improvements in mobility and overall quality of life. Unsurprisingly, then, the latest research shows that the higher the polyphenol content (and thus sirtuin-activating nutrients) in the diets of older people, the greater the protection they experience against physical performance decline with age.[14]

Don't be fooled into thinking these benefits only apply to the elderly; far from it. By the age of twenty-five, the effects of aging can begin and muscle slowly erodes, with 10 percent of muscle lost by age forty (even though overall weight tends to increase) and a 40 percent loss by age seventy. Yet evidence is growing that this can all be prevented and reversed by stimulating our sirtuin genes.

Muscle loss, growth, and function: sirtuin activity plays a pivotal role in it all. Stack it up, and it's no wonder that in a recent review in the prestigious medical journal *Nature*, sirtuins were described as master regulators of muscle growth, with increasing sirtuin activation cited as one of the promising emerging avenues for combating muscle loss, and thus increasing quality of life as well as reducing disease and deaths.[15]

Viewed in the context of the powerful effects our sirtuin genes can have on muscles, the shock results of our pilot trial no longer seemed so shocking. We began to realize it was possible to fuel weight loss while feeding our muscles, all through a Sirtfood-rich diet.

But that's just the start. In the next chapter we will see the benefits of Sirtfoods extend so much further, to all aspects of health and quality of life.

SUMMARY

- Despite losing weight, we found, people following the Sirtfood Diet either maintained or even gained muscle. This is because sirtuins are master regulators of muscle.

- By activating sirtuins, it is possible both to prevent muscle breakdown and to promote muscle regeneration.

- Activating *SIRT1* can also help to prevent the gradual loss of muscle that we see with aging.

- Not only will activating your sirtuin genes make you look leaner, it will help you stay healthier and function better as you age.

4

·······

Well-Being Wonders

D espite all the amazing advances in modern medicine, society is getting fatter and sicker—70 percent of all deaths are due to chronic disease, a truly shocking statistic. Radical change is needed, and fast.

Yet, as we have seen, we can begin to change all of this. By activating our ancient sirtuin genes we can burn fat and build a leaner and stronger body. And with sirtuins at the hub of our metabolism, master programmers of our biology, their importance extends far beyond body composition alone, to every facet of our well-being.

SIRTUINS AND THE 70 PERCENT

Think of a disease that you associate with getting old and the chances are a lack of sirtuin activity in the body is involved. For example, sirtuin activation is great for heart health, protecting the muscle cells in the heart and generally helping the heart muscle function better.[1] It also improves how our arteries work, helps us handle cholesterol more efficiently, and protects against the clogging up of our arteries known as atherosclerosis.[2]

How about diabetes? Sirtuin activation increases the amount of insulin that can be secreted and helps it work more effectively in the body.[3] As it happens, one of the most popular antidiabetic drugs, metformin, relies on *SIRT1* for its beneficial effect. Indeed, one pharmaceutical company is currently investigating adding natural sirtuin activators to metformin treatment for diabetics, with results from animal studies showing a staggering 83 percent reduction in the dose of metformin needed for the same effects.[4]

When it comes to the brain, sirtuins are involved again, with sirtuin activity found to be lower in Alzheimer's patients. In contrast, sirtuin activation improves communication signals in the brain, enhances cognitive function, and reduces brain inflammation. This stops the buildup of amyloid-β production and tau protein aggregation, two of the main damaging things we see occurring in the brains of Alzheimer's patients.[5,6]

Bones are next. Osteoblasts are a special type of cell in our bones responsible for building new bone. The more osteoblasts we have, the stronger our bones. Sirtuin activation not only promotes the production of osteoblast cells, but also increases their survival.[7] This makes sirtuin activation essential for lifelong bone health.

Cancer has been a more controversial area for sirtuin research, and while recent research shows that sirtuin activation helps to suppress cancer tumors, scientists are only just beginning to unravel this complex field.[8] While there is much more to learn on this particular topic, those cultures that eat the most Sirtfoods have the lowest cancer rates, as we will soon see.

Heart disease, diabetes, dementia, osteoporosis, and very probably cancer: it's an impressive list of diseases that can be prevented by activating sirtuins. It may come as no surprise to find out that cultures already eating plenty of Sirtfoods as part of their traditional diets experience a longevity and well-being most of us could barely imagine, which you'll hear more on very soon.

That leaves us with an exciting conclusion: simply by adding the world's most potent Sirtfoods to your diet, and making that a lifelong habit, you too can experience this level of well-being—and more—all while getting the physique you want.

CASE STUDY

David Carr is a professional sailor who is competing in the prestigious 2017 America's Cup campaign. David trains like a top athlete, and his diet could only be regarded as healthy, including taking supplements. Yet in his own words, he was "always the fat athlete," and it irked him that he ate better and trained harder than many of the athletes around him, yet they were leaner. Despite all his exercise and good diet, he also showed risk factors for metabolic disease with high levels of blood sugar, cholesterol, and other fats in his blood.

With a Sirtfood-rich diet, including a Sirtfood drink each morning, as the cornerstone of his nutritional plan, David experienced tremendous results. Within six months he was down from 229 pounds to his target weight of 205 pounds, an incredible 24-pound weight loss. His body fat percentage had dropped by half to 7 percent, marking him as elite. And in his own words, "Every time I do something aerobic I set a personal best and I am stronger than ever." Not only did he now look like a top athlete, something else was evident: he also looked so much healthier. And his blood tests backed it up. Tests showed that David experienced:

- a 45 percent reduction in "bad" LDL cholesterol
- a 29 percent increase in "good" HDL cholesterol
- an 80 percent drop in triglycerides (fats in the blood)
- a decrease in blood sugar levels that took him back down to normal from the brink of prediabetes

By basing his nutritional plan on Sirtfoods, David can not only compete at his best, but has completely reversed his future risk of heart disease and diabetes.

SUMMARY

- Despite all the advances in modern medicine, as a society we're getting fatter and sicker.

- Seventy percent of all deaths are due to chronic disease, with low sirtuin activity implicated in the vast majority.

- By activating sirtuins, you can prevent or forestall the major chronic diseases of the Western world.

- By packing your diet full of Sirtfoods, you too can enjoy the same level of well-being as the healthiest and longest-living populations on the planet.

5

....

Sirtfoods

So far we have discovered that sirtuins are an ancient family of genes with the power to help us burn fat, build muscle, and keep us superhealthy. It is well established that sirtuins can be switched on through caloric restriction, fasting, and exercise, but there is another revolutionary way to achieve this: food. We refer to the foods most powerful at activating sirtuins as Sirtfoods.

BEYOND ANTIOXIDANTS

To really understand the benefits of Sirtfoods requires us to think very differently about foods like fruits and vegetables, and the reasons they are good for us. There's absolutely no doubt that they are, with stacks of research testifying that diets rich in fruits, vegetables, and plant foods generally slash the risk of many chronic diseases, including the biggest killers, heart disease and cancer. This has been put down to their rich content of nutrients, such as vitamins, minerals, and, of course, antioxidants, probably the biggest health buzzword of the last decade. But we're here to tell a very different story.

The reason Sirtfoods are so good for you has nothing to do with those nutrients we all know so well and hear so much about. Sure, they are all valuable things that you need to get from your diet, but there's something altogether different, and very special, going on with Sirtfoods. In fact, what if we threw that whole way of thinking on its head and said that the reason Sirtfoods are good for you is *not* because they nourish the body with essential nutrients, or provide antioxidants to mop up the damaging effects of free radicals, but quite the opposite: because they are full of weak toxins? In a world where almost every touted "superfood" is aggressively marketed on the basis of its antioxidant content, this might sound crazy. But it's a revolutionary idea, and one worth coming to grips with.

WHAT DOESN'T KILL YOU MAKES YOU STRONGER

Let's get back to the established ways of activating sirtuins for a moment: fasting and exercise. As we've seen, research has repeatedly shown that dietary energy restriction has dramatic benefits for weight loss, health, and very possibly longevity. Then there's exercise, with its innumerable benefits for both body and mind, borne out by the finding that regular exercise dramatically slashes mortality rates.[1] But what is the one thing they have in common?

The answer is: stress. Both fasting and exercise cause a mild stress on the body that encourages it to adapt by becoming fitter, more efficient, and more resilient. It's the body's response to these mildly stressful stimuli—its adaptation—that makes us fitter, healthier, and leaner in the long run. And as we now know, these highly beneficial adaptations are orchestrated by sirtuins, which are switched on in the face of these stressors, and ignite a host of favorable changes in the body.

The technical term for adaptation to these stresses is hormesis. It's the idea that you get a beneficial effect from being exposed to a low dose of a substance or stress that is otherwise toxic or lethal if given at higher doses. Or, if you prefer, "what doesn't kill you makes you stronger." And that's exactly how fasting and exercise work. Starvation is lethal, and excessive exercise is detrimental to health. These extreme forms of stress are clearly harmful, but as long as fasting and exercise remain moderate and manageable stresses, they have highly beneficial effects.

ENTER POLYPHENOLS

Now, this is where things get truly fascinating. All living organisms experience hormesis, but what has been greatly underappreciated until now is that this also includes plants.[2] While we typically wouldn't think of plants as being the same as other living organisms, let alone humans, we actually share similar responses in terms of how we react, on a chemical level, to our environment.

As mind-blowing as that sounds, it makes perfect sense if we think about it in evolutionary terms, because all living things evolved to experience and cope with common environmental stresses such as dehydration, sunlight, nutrient deprivation, and attack by pathogens.

If that is difficult to wrap your head around, get ready for the truly astonishing bit. Plant stress responses are actually more sophisticated than our own.[3] Think about it: if we are hungry and thirsty, we can go in search of food and drink; too hot, we find shade; under attack, we can flee. In complete contrast, plants are stationary, and as such, they must endure all the extremes of these physiological stresses and threats. In consequence, over the last billion years they have developed a highly sophisticated stress-response system that humbles anything we can boast. The way they do this is by producing a vast collection of natural plant chemicals—called polyphenols—that allow them to successfully adapt to their environment and survive. When we consume these plants, we also consume these polyphenol nutrients. Their effect is profound: they activate our own innate stress-response pathways. We're talking here about exactly the same pathways that fasting and exercise switch on: the sirtuins.

Piggybacking on a plant's stress-response system in this way, for our own benefit, is known as xenohormesis.[4,5] And the implications are game-changing. Let the plants do the hard work so we don't have to. Indeed, these natural plant compounds are now referred to as caloric restriction mimetics due to their ability to turn on the same positive changes in our cells, such as fat burning, that would be seen during fasting.[6,7] And by providing us with more advanced signaling compounds than we produce ourselves, they trigger outcomes superior to anything we can achieve through fasting or exercise alone.

> *Due to a greater need to adapt to survive in their environment, foods grown in the wild, or even organically, are better for us than intensively farmed produce since they produce higher levels of polyphenols.*

SIRTFOODS

While all plants have these stress-response systems, only certain ones have developed to produce noteworthy amounts of sirtuin-activating polyphenols. We call these plants Sirtfoods. Their discovery means that instead of austere fasting regimens or arduous exercise programs, there is now a revolutionary new way to activate your sirtuin genes: eating a diet abundant in Sirtfoods. Best of all, this one involves putting (Sirt)foods onto your plate, not taking them off!

It's so beautifully simple and so easy it seems like there must be a catch. But there isn't. This is how nature intended us to eat, rather than the stomach rumbling or calorie counting of modern dieting. Many of you who have experienced these hellish diets, where initial weight loss is fleeting before the body rebels and the weight comes piling back on, will understandably shudder at the thought of another false promise, another book boasting the dreaded "d" word. But remember this: the modern approach to diet is only 150 years old; Sirtfoods were developed by nature more than a billion years ago.

And with that, you're probably itching to know what specific foods count as Sirtfoods. So without further ado, here are the top twenty Sirtfoods.

SIRTFOOD	MAJOR SIRTUIN-ACTIVATING NUTRIENTS
1 arugula	quercetin, kaempferol
2 buckwheat	rutin
3 capers	kaempferol, quercetin
4 celery, including its leaves	apigenin, luteolin
5 chilies	luteolin, myricetin
6 cocoa	epicatechin
7 coffee	caffeic acid
8 extra virgin olive oil	oleuropein, hydroxytyrosol
9 garlic	ajoene, myricetin
10 green tea (especially matcha)	epigallocatechin gallate (EGCG)
11 kale	kaempferol, quercetin
12 Medjool dates	gallic acid, caffeic acid
13 parsley	apigenin, myricetin
14 red endive	luteolin
15 red onion	quercetin
16 red wine	resveratrol, piceatannol
17 soy	daidzein, formononetin
18 strawberries	fisetin
19 turmeric	curcumin
20 walnuts	gallic acid

References for table:[8-35]

Summary

- We need to radically rethink the idea that fruits, vegetables, and plant foods are good for us simply because they contain vitamins and antioxidants.

- They are good for us because they contain natural chemicals that place a mild stress on our cells, just as fasting and exercise do.

- Plants, because they are stationary, have developed a highly sophisticated stress-response system and produce polyphenols to help them adapt to the challenges of their environment.

- When we eat these plants, their polyphenols activate our stress-response pathways—our sirtuin genes—mimicking the effects of caloric restriction and exercise.

- The foods with the most powerful sirtuin-activating effects are called Sirtfoods.

Sirtfoods Around the World

Sirtfoods may be a recent nutritional discovery, but it is clear that different cultures have been experiencing their benefits throughout history. As we become more familiar with the top twenty Sirtfoods in chapter 8, we will see how many have been revered since early civilization for their medicinal properties and were often considered sacred foods for their ability to confer vigor and well-being.

In fact, it now appears that written records of such benefits of Sirtfoods go way back to being the subject of the very first clinical trial ever recorded. Documented more than 2,200 years ago, we find it in the Book of Daniel in the Bible. What was perceived to be the best available food of the day was prescribed to keep the young men healthy and fit so they could later enter the king's service. Yet seemingly, when this was challenged by Daniel, a diet of only plants produced a superior outcome in just a matter of days: "Daniel made up his mind not to let himself become ritually unclean by eating the rich food and drinking the wine of the royal court. . . . So Daniel went to the guard . . . Test us for ten days, he said. Give us vegetables [plants] to eat and water to drink. Then compare us with the young men who are eating the food of the royal court, and base your decision on how we look. He agreed to let them try it for ten days. When the time was up, it was seen that they were better in appearance and fatter in flesh [muscular] than all those who had been eating the royal food. So from then on the guard let them continue to eat vegetables instead of what the king provided."

Such benefits, especially increased muscle mass, would never normally be expected from a diet of just plants. That is, of course, unless those plants happened to be extremely rich Sirtfood sources. With records showing that the common plants consumed back then were similar to the Sirtfood-rich traditional Mediterranean diet, and the results strikingly similar to our own pilot trial, one can't but wonder whether the Daniel trial is the stuff of fable, or have we unwittingly had the answer to achieving the body and health we've always desired for more than two millennia?

ENTER THE BLUE ZONE

While our health is ailing, there are regions around the world, dubbed Blue Zones, where the intake of Sirtfoods is much, much higher than the amount we consume in a typical Western diet. Indeed, for the cultures eating Sirtfood-rich diets, the benefits seem more like the stuff of legend. In fact, not only do we see people living longer in Blue Zones than in countries where a typical Western diet is the norm, but much more important is how they retain youthful vitality in old age. In the Blue Zones, there are incredibly low rates of Alzheimer's, cancer, diabetes, heart disease, and osteoporosis. Go there and you will see people aged ninety or older walking, dancing, and working. They are not active in the pursuit to lose weight; there's no need—there are no gyms. Instead they retain the vigor and energy of youth into old age. You will see them on motorcycles or riding bicycles in the street. Get chatting to them and you might hear them boast about how great their sex life still is! And it is no surprise that they also happen to be the slimmest populations in the world.

I SHOULD COCOA

To better understand this incredible phenomenon, let's begin our journey with a trip to the San Blas Islands of Panama, the indigenous home of the Kuna American Indians, who appear immune to high blood pressure and show remarkably low rates of obesity, diabetes, cancer, and early death. At the turn of the twenty-first century, a research team unearthed the Kuna's secret when they found that their major source of fluid was a beverage made from locally grown cocoa. This cocoa is fantastically rich in a specific group of polyphenols called flavanols, especially epicatechin, which qualifies it as a Sirtfood.

But how could we know that the robust health of the Kuna was attributable to their high intake of cocoa flavanols? The researchers found that when the Kuna Indians migrated to Panama City and switched to consuming intensively processed commercial cocoa (which is stripped of its flavanols and thus no longer a Sirtfood), the health benefits vanished.[1]

The case of the Kuna is but one piece in a growing body of evidence that flavanol-rich cocoa has extraordinary health benefits. In clinical studies, flavanol-rich cocoa has been found to improve blood pressure, blood flow, blood sugar control, and cholesterol measures.[2,3] Reviews suggest that cocoa also has positive effects in diabetes[4] and cancer.[5] Consumption has been shown to enhance memory performance, proffering a valuable dietary option in the search for the brain's fountain of youth.[6] And despite the oft-repeated warnings that chocolate is bad for you, we now know that cocoa improves oral hygiene and protects teeth from plaque and cavities.[7]

SPICE FOR LIFE

Turmeric, known as "Indian solid gold," has been used in Ayurvedic medicine for more than 4,000 years for its wound-healing and anti-inflammatory properties. We now know these healing effects are due to the fact that it contains curcumin, a major sirtuin-activating nutrient, which makes it a Sirtfood.

Turmeric is a prevalent spice in traditional Indian cooking and is believed to contribute to the fact that cancer rates in India are significantly lower than in Western countries. Yet interestingly, the cancer rate for Indians increases by 50 to 75 percent when they move from India to the US or UK and abandon their traditional diet.[8] While this might be due to a number of different lifestyle factors, scientific evidence now indicates that curcumin has potent anticancer properties.

In addition to its anticancer claims, there is mounting evidence of other sirtuin-activating health benefits. In recent studies, a special form of curcumin that was made to be more easily absorbed was shown to improve cholesterol levels, improve blood sugar control, and reduce inflammation in the body.[9] It has been investigated for osteoarthritis of the knee and shown to be as effective as commonly taken painkillers.[10] Researchers are now uncovering its many mechanisms for preventing weight gain and helping to treat obesity.[11] And in patients with early type 2 diabetes, just eating a gram of turmeric a day improved their working memory.[12]

GREEN LIVING

Green tea is another tantalizing Sirtfood offering. Green tea consumption is thought to have begun more than 4,700 years ago when the Chinese emperor Shen Nung ("Divine Healer") produced a pleasant, refreshing beverage with green tea leaves by serendipity. It was only much later that the beverage developed its reputation for medicinal and healing prowess.

Asia's high intake of green tea has been cited as a key reason for the "Asian paradox." Despite an extremely high prevalence of cigarette smoking, Asia, and especially Japan, boasts some of the lowest rates of cardiovascular disease and lung cancer in the world. A high intake of green tea is linked with much lower rates of coronary heart disease and a reduced risk of many common cancers, such as those affecting the prostate, stomach, lung, and breast. It is little wonder therefore that green tea consumption is linked to substantially fewer early deaths.

Green tea also has a thermogenic effect, which means it increases the amount of energy the body burns off, aiding fat loss while maintaining muscle. Combine green tea with a diet abundant in leafy greens, soy, herbs, and spices (turmeric use is especially prevalent), to create a smorgasbord of Sirtfoods, and we have a diet very similar to that found in Okinawa—"the land of the immortals." Okinawa might be the poorest province in Japan, yet it holds the record for longevity and the greatest number of centenarians in the world. So astounding is their quality of life, researchers assumed it must be because of superior genes. But along came the Westernization of its diet, and with it burgeoning rates of obesity and crippling diseases that younger generations are now experiencing for the first time, firmly putting any idea of superior genes to rest.

A MEDITERRANEAN PRESCRIPTION

For a true bounty of Sirtfood combinations, we need to travel to the Mediterranean. This is where we find the coming together of a host of potent Sirtfoods, namely extra virgin olive oil, nuts, berries, green leafy vegetables, herbs and spices, and, of course, wine. Eating this type of diet is linked to a 9 percent reduction in death from all causes, with substantial reductions in cardiovascular disease and degenerative brain diseases like Alzheimer's, as well as cancer.[13] And as we saw in our introduction, the landmark PREDIMED trial, carried out in Spain, found that a Mediterranean-style diet supplemented with either extra virgin olive oil or nuts (especially walnuts) slashed the incidence of cardiovascular disease and diabetes.

Researchers also did something very interesting in a substudy of PREDIMED. They examined the genetic profile for

PPAR-γ—which, if you remember, is the obesity villain we came across earlier. While some of us are quite resistant to its actions, others are not so fortunate, and can really get clobbered by it. This means you might eat the same as someone else but be much more susceptible to weight gain. However, it doesn't need to be that way with Sirtfoods. In those who followed the Sirtfood-rich Mediterranean diet, the negative effects of this gene were reversed.[14] Incredibly, despite no drop in calories, the diet richer in Sirtfoods was linked to a 40 percent drop in the risk of obesity, especially weight stored around the tummy.[15] Forget low fat and forget obsessing over calories: those who follow a traditional Mediterranean diet will always be slimmer than the general population.

So there we have it. The cultures around the world whose members are healthiest and slimmest and live the longest lives have something in common: they eat the highest amount of Sirtfoods. They stay lean and slim without so much as counting a calorie or going on a diet. That leaves us to do just one thing, which is to piece together all of the most potent Sirtfoods on the planet to create a diet the likes of which has never been seen before—in essence, a diet to drive a health and weight-loss revolution.

Summary

- While obesity and chronic disease are rampant in the Western world, there are Blue Zones that are virtually immune to these problems.
- One thing that people living in Blue Zones have in common is a diet very rich in Sirtfoods.
- Classic examples include the Kuna American Indians with

their penchant for cocoa, the turmeric-infused diet of India, the Japanese predilection for green tea, and the extra virgin olive oil at the heart of the traditional Mediterranean diet.

- The Sirtfood Diet brings together all these great foods—and more—into a world-beating diet for health and weight loss.

Building a Diet That Works

With the Sirtfood Diet, we have done something very special. We've taken the most potent Sirtfoods on the planet and have woven them into a brand-new way of eating, the likes of which has never been seen before. We have selected the "best of the best" from the healthiest diets ever known and from them created a world-beating diet.

The good news is, you don't have to suddenly adopt the traditional diet of an Okinawan or be able to cook like an Italian mamma. That's not only completely unrealistic, but totally unnecessary on the Sirtfood Diet. Indeed, one thing that may strike you from the list of Sirtfoods (see page 54) is their familiarity. While you may not currently be eating all the foods on the list, you most likely are consuming some. So why are you not already losing weight?

The answer is found when we examine the different elements that the most cutting-edge nutritional science shows are needed for building a diet that works. It's about eating Sirtfoods in the right *quantity*, *variety*, and *form*. It's about complementing Sirtfood dishes with generous servings of protein, and then eating your meals at the best time of day. And it's about the freedom to eat the authentically tasty foods that you enjoy in the amounts you like.

Hitting Your Quota

Right now, most people simply don't consume nearly enough Sirtfoods to elicit a potent fat-burning and health-boosting effect. When researchers looked at consumption of five key sirtuin-activating nutrients (quercetin, myricetin, kaempferol, luteolin, and apigenin) in the US diet, they found individual daily intakes to be a miserly 13 milligrams per day.[1] In contrast, the average Japanese intake was five times higher.[2] Compare that with our Sirtfood Diet trial, where individuals were consuming hundreds of milligrams of sirtuin-activating nutrients every day.

What we are talking about is a total diet revolution where we increase our daily intake of sirtuin-activating nutrients by as much as fiftyfold. While this may sound daunting or impractical, it really isn't. By taking all our top Sirtfoods and putting them together in a way that is totally compatible with your busy life, you too can easily and effectively reach the level of intake needed to reap all the benefits.

The Power of Synergy

We believe it is better to consume a wide range of these wonder nutrients in the form of natural whole foods, where they coexist alongside the hundreds of other natural bioactive plant chemicals that act synergistically to boost our health. We think it is better to work with nature, rather than against it. It's for this reason that time and time again supplements of isolated nutrients fail to show lasting benefit, yet the very same nutrient when provided in the form of a whole food does.

Take, for example, the classic sirtuin-activating nutrient resveratrol. In supplement form, it is poorly absorbed; but in its natural food matrix of red wine, its bioavailability (how much the body can use) is at least six times higher.[3,4] Add to this the fact that red wine contains not just one but a whole range of sirtuin-activating polyphenols that act together to bring health benefits, including piceatannol, quercetin, myricetin, and epicatechin. Or we might switch our attention to curcumin from turmeric. Curcumin is well established to be the key sirtuin-activating nutrient in turmeric, yet research shows that whole turmeric has better PPAR-γ activity for fighting fat loss and is more effective at inhibiting cancer and reducing blood sugar levels than curcumin in isolation.[5] It's not difficult to see why isolating a single nutrient is nowhere near as effective as consuming it in its whole food form.

But what makes a dietary approach really special is when we begin to combine multiple Sirtfoods. For example, by adding in quercetin-rich Sirtfoods, we enhance the bioavailability of resveratrol-containing foods even further. Not only this, but their actions complement each other. Both are fat busters, but there are nuances in how each of them achieves this. Resveratrol is very effective at helping to destroy existing fat cells, whereas quercetin excels in preventing new fat cell formation.[6] In combination they target fat from both sides, resulting in a greater impact on fat loss than if we just ate large amounts of a single food.

And this is a pattern we see over and over again. Foods rich in the sirtuin activator apigenin improve the absorption of quercetin from food, and enhance its activity.[7] In turn, quercetin has been shown to synergize with the activity of epigallocatechin gallate (EGCG).[8] And EGCG has been shown to work synergistically with curcumin.[9] And so it goes on. Not only are individual whole foods more potent than isolated nutrients, but by combining Sirtfoods we tap into a whole tapestry of health benefits that nature has weaved—so intricate, so refined, it is impossible to try to trump it.

Juicing and Food: Get the Best of Both Worlds

Both juices and whole foods are integral to the Sirtfood Diet. Here, we are talking about juices specifically made using a juicer—blenders and smoothie makers (such as the NutriBullet) won't work. For many, this will seem counterintuitive, on the basis that when something is juiced the fiber is removed. But for leafy greens this is exactly what we want.

The fiber from food contains what are called non-extractable polyphenols (or NEPPs). These are polyphenols, including sirtuin activators, that are attached to the fibrous part of the food and are only released when broken down by our friendly gut bacteria. By removing the fiber, we don't get the NEPPs and lose out on their goodness. But importantly, the NEPP content varies dramatically depending on the type of plant. The NEPP content of foods like fruit, cereals, and nuts is significant, and these should be eaten whole (in strawberries, NEPPs provide more than 50 percent of the polyphenols!). But for leafy vegetables, the active ingredients in the Sirtfood juice, they are far lower despite a large bulk of fiber.

So when it comes to leafy greens, we get maximum bang for our buck by juicing them and removing the low-nutrient fiber, meaning we can use much greater volumes and achieve a superconcentrated hit of sirtuin-activating polyphenols.

There is also another advantage to removing the fiber. Leafy greens contain a type of fiber called insoluble fiber, which has a scrubbing action in the digestive system. But when we eat too much of it, just like if we overscrub something, it can irritate and damage our gut lining. That means leafy green–packed smoothies will be fiber overload for many people, potentially aggravating or even causing IBS (irritable bowel syndrome) and hindering our absorption of nutrients.

Having some of your Sirtfoods in juice form can also have big advantages when it comes to absorbing their goodness. For example, one of the ingredients we include in the green juice is matcha green tea. When we consume the sirtuin activator EGCG, found in high levels in green tea, in drink form without food, its absorption is more than 65 percent higher.[10] We also find it interesting to note that when we ran blood tests on our own clients, switching from smoothies to green juices brought about dramatic increases in their levels of other essential nutrients such as magnesium and folic acid.

The crux of it all is that to really get those sirtuin genes firing for dramatic weight loss and health, we need to build a diet that combines both juices and whole foods for maximum benefit.

The Power of Protein

It's plants that put the Sirt into the Sirtfood Diet, but to reap maximum benefit, Sirtfood meals should always be rich in protein. A building block of dietary protein called leucine has been shown to have additional benefits in stimulating *SIRT1* to increase fat burning and improve blood sugar control.[11]

But leucine also has another role, and this is where its synergistic relationship with Sirtfoods really shines. Leucine potently stimulates anabolism (building things) in our cells, particularly in muscle, which demands a lot of energy and means our energy factories (called mitochondria) have to work overtime. This creates a need in our cells for the activity of Sirtfoods. As you may recall, one of the effects of Sirtfoods is to stimulate more mitochondria to be made, improve how efficient they are, and get them burning fat as fuel. Thus our bodies need them to meet this extra energy demand. The upshot is that by combining Sirtfoods with dietary protein, we see a synergistic effect that boosts sirtuin activation and ultimately gets you burning fat to fuel muscle growth and better health.[12] This is why the meals in the book are designed to give a generous serving of protein.

Oily fish are an exceptionally good protein choice to complement the action of Sirtfoods, as they are rich in omega-3 fatty acids in addition to their protein content. You will undoubtedly have heard lots about the health benefits of oily fish and specifically omega-3 fish oils. And now recent research is suggesting that the benefits of omega-3 fats may come through enhancing how our sirtuin genes work.[13]

There have been concerns raised about the negative effects of protein-rich diets on health in recent years, and without Sirtfoods to counterbalance the protein, we can begin to understand why. Leucine can be a double-edged sword. As we've seen, we need Sirtfoods to help our cells meet the metabolic demand that leucine places on them. But without them, our mitochondria can become dysfunctional, and instead of improving health, high leucine levels can actually promote obesity and insulin resistance. Sirtfoods help to keep the effects of leucine not just in check but powerfully working in our favor. Think of leucine as pressing your foot on the accelerator of weight loss and well-being, with Sirtfoods the machinery that ensures the cell meets the increased demand. Without the Sirtfoods, the engine blows. . . .

Getting back to concerns about the health effects of protein-rich diets, Sirtfoods are the missing piece of the puzzle. The US diet is typically protein-rich, but lacking Sirtfoods to counterbalance it. This makes it vital that Sirtfoods become an integral part of how Americans eat.

Eat Early

When it comes to eating, our philosophy is the earlier the better, ideally finishing eating for the day by 7 p.m. This is for two reasons. First, to reap the natural satiating effect of Sirtfoods. There's a lot more benefit to eating a meal that will keep you feeling full, satisfied, and energized as you go about your day than spending the whole day feeling hungry only to eat and stay full as you sleep through the night.

But there is a second compelling reason, which is to keep eating habits in tune with your internal body clock. We all have a built-in body clock, called our circadian rhythm, that regulates many of our natural body functions according to the time of day. Among other things, it influences how the body handles the food we eat. Our clocks work in synchrony, primarily following the cues of the light-dark cycle of the sun. As a diurnal species, we're designed to be active in the daytime rather than at night. Consequently, our body clock gears us up to handle food most efficiently during the day, when it is light and we are expected to be active, and less so when it is dark, where we are instead primed for rest and sleep.

The problem is that many of us have "work clocks" and "social clocks" that are not in sync with the powering down of the sun. After dark is sometimes the only chance some of us get to eat. To a degree, we can train our body clock to sync to different schedules, such as "evening chronotypes" who prefer or have to be active, eat, and sleep later in the day. However, living misaligned from the external light-dark cycle comes at a cost. Studies find that evening chronotype individuals have increased susceptibility to fat gain, muscle loss, and metabolic problems, as well as often suffering from poor sleep. This is exactly what we see among night-shift workers, who have higher rates of obesity and metabolic disease, which is at least partly due to the effects of their late eating patterns.[14,15]

The upshot is that you're better off eating earlier in the day when possible, ideally by 7 p.m. But what if this is just not feasible? The good news is that sirtuins play a key role in body clock synchronization. In fact, research has found that the polyphenols in Sirtfoods are capable of modulating our body clocks and positively adjusting circadian rhythm.[16] That means if you simply cannot avoid eating later, the inclusion of Sirtfoods with your meal will minimize the detrimental effects. Indeed, one of the recurrent pieces of feedback we hear from followers of the Sirtfood Diet is just how much their sleep quality has improved, suggesting potent effects on harmonizing their circadian rhythm.

Go Big on Taste

A fundamental problem with conventional dieting is that it typically makes for a miserable dining experience. It drains every last drop of pleasure from food, leaving us feeling dissatisfied. But for us, it's essential that you maintain the joy of food in the pursuit of a healthy weight. That's why we were delighted when we realized that Sirtfoods, as well as the foods that enhance their action such as protein and omega-3 food sources, are primed to satisfy our desire for taste. It's the ultimate win-win: the Sirtfood Diet boosts our health *and* tastes great.

Let's take a step back to see how this works. Our taste buds determine how tasty we find our food, and how satisfied we are from eating it. This is done through seven major taste receptors. Over countless generations, humans have evolved to seek out the tastes that stimulate these receptors in order to achieve maximum nourishment from our diet. The better a food stimulates these taste receptors, the more satisfaction we get from a meal. And in the Sirtfood Diet we have the ultimate menu for happy taste buds, because it offers maximum stimulation across all taste receptors. To summarize these tastes and the foods you'll be eating on the diet that satisfy them: the seven major taste sensations are sweet (strawberries, dates); salty (celery, fish); sour (strawberries); bitter (cocoa, kale, endive, extra virgin olive oil, green tea); pungent (chilies, garlic, extra virgin olive oil); astringent (green tea, red wine); and umami (soy, fish, meat).

Crucially, what we have discovered is that the greater the sirtuin-activating properties of a food, the more powerfully it stimulates those taste centers, and the more gratification we get from the food we eat. Importantly, it also means that we satisfy our appetite quicker, and our desire to eat more is reduced accordingly. This is a key reason why those who follow a Sirtfood-rich diet are pleasantly fuller more quickly.

For example, natural cocoa has a striking, appealing bitter taste, but remove the sirtuin-activating flavanols with aggressive industrial food-processing techniques and we are left with mass-produced, bland, and characterless cocoa that is used to make highly sugared chocolate confectionary. By this point, the health benefits have vanished.

The same principle applies to olive oil. Consumed in its minimally processed form—extra virgin—it has a powerful and distinct flavor, with an invigorating kick that can be felt at the back of the throat. Yet refined and processed olive oil loses all character, is mild and bland, and carries no such kick. Similarly, hot chilies boast much greater sirtuin-activating credentials than the milder varieties, and wild strawberries are much tastier than farmed ones due to a richer content of sirtuin-activating nutrients.

Not only this, we also find that individual Sirtfoods can trigger multiple taste receptors: green tea is both bitter and astringent, and strawberries have a combination of sweet and sour flavors.

Initially, some palates will not be accustomed to certain of these flavors—so much of our modern food is devoid of both nutrients and true taste—but you will be amazed how quickly you acquire a love for them. After all, humans evolved to seek out a diet rich in Sirtfoods, alongside healthful protein and omega-3 fatty acids, to satisfy the basic desires of our appetite and, in turn, our health. This evolutionary process occurred over millennia, without us knowing the reasons, yet it ensured we got maximum benefit from consuming these foods.

Embrace Eating

Let's try an experiment. We just want you to do one really simple thing for us: don't think of a white bear. . . .

What did you just think of? A white bear, of course. Why? Because we told you not to. Don't tell us you are still thinking about it!

This was the trailblazing experiment performed by psychology professor Daniel Wegner in 1987, which showed that forced suppression of thoughts causes a paradoxical and counterproductive escalation in how often we actually think about what we are trying to suppress.[17] So instead of blocking it from our thoughts, the effort produces a preoccupation with the suppressed thought.

And as you've probably guessed, this phenomenon is not applicable just to white bears. The exact same thing happens when we make villains of and restrict foods for weight loss. Studies show we actually think about them more often, increasing temptation.

It eats away at us until we eat it! And with the diet broken and the escalated thinking about the "forbidden" foods we endured, we are now much more likely to binge.

Scientists have now explained what is happening here. We all have a deep need to be autonomous. When we feel controlled, such as going on a strict diet, it creates a negative environment that makes us feel uneasy. We feel captives of this negativity and rebel to break out of it. We rebel by doing what we were told we should not, and doing it a lot more than we would have in the first place. It happens to all of us, even the most self-controlled. It's not a matter of if, but when. Scientists now believe this is a critical reason why we can maintain diets and even see results in the initial stages but fail to see long-term success.

So does this mean there is no point in even attempting to change our eating habits? Are we just destined for failure? No, it means that when we make a change, in order to succeed we need to make it our own positive, desired decision. We now know the way to achieve this is not through dietary *exclusion* but through dietary *inclusion*. Rather than focusing your energy on the negatives of what you should not be eating, instead you focus on the positives of what you should be eating. By doing this, you avoid the psychological backlash. And this is the beauty of the Sirtfood Diet. It's about what you put into your diet, not what you take out. It's about the *quality* of your food, not the *quantity*. And it's about you wanting to do it because you feel satisfied by eating great-tasting foods with the added knowledge that each bite provides a bounty of benefits.

Most diets are a means to an end. They're about hanging in there, trying to keep sight of the "thin ideal." But ultimately that rarely comes before the diet fails, and even if it is achieved, it's rarely sustained. The Sirtfood Diet is different. It is all about the journey. Phase 1, which does restrict calories, is kept purposely short and sweet to ensure it is finished with motivating results before any negative backlash. Then the focus is solely on Sirtfoods. And the motivation for eating Sirtfoods is driven not just by an end result of weight loss. Instead it is as much if not more about the appreciation and enjoyment of real food for a healthy and fit lifestyle.

What's more, once you are reaping the unique benefits of Sirtfoods, from satisfying your appetite to increasing your quality of life, you will find that your habits and tastes change. With the Sirtfood Diet, foods that would previously have set off the cascade of negative reactions if you were told you could not eat them will lose their appeal and their hold over you will diminish. They become a minor part of your diet, and all achieved without a single sighting of a white bear.

Summary

- The Sirtfood Diet takes the most potent Sirtfoods on the planet and brings them together in a simple and practical way of eating.
- To achieve optimal results for weight loss and health, it is necessary to eat Sirtfoods in the right quantity, combination, and forms to reap the synergistic benefits of their sirtuin-activating compounds.
- We further enhance this by including other healthy ingredients, such as leucine-rich protein foods and oily fish, to make the effects of the Sirtfood Diet even more powerful.

- When we eat is also important, and eating earlier in the day helps to keep us in tune with our built-in body clock.
- Unlike our modern diets, Sirtfoods satisfy all our taste receptors, which means we get more gratification from our food and feel content more quickly.
- The Sirtfood Diet is a diet of inclusion—not exclusion, making it the only type of diet that can deliver long-term weight-loss success.

Top Twenty Sirtfoods

N ow that you know all about Sirtfoods, why they are so powerful and what it takes to create an effective diet that delivers lasting outcomes, it's time to get started. In the next chapter, day one of the Sirtfood Diet begins. So this is the perfect time to familiarize yourself with each of the top twenty Sirtfoods that will soon become staples of your everyday diet.

Arugula

Arugula (also known as rocket, rucola, rugula, and roquette) certainly has a colorful history in US food culture. A pungent green salad leaf with a distinctive peppery taste, it quickly ascended from humble roots as the base of many peasant dishes in the Mediterranean to become a symbol of food snobbery in the United States, even leading to the coining of the term *arugulance* (the coming together of *arugula* with *arrogance*)!

But long before it was a salad leaf wielded in a class war, arugula was revered by the ancient Greeks and Romans for its medicinal properties. Commonly used as a diuretic and digestive aid, it gained its true fame from its reputation for having potent aphrodisiac properties, so much so that growth of arugula was banned in monasteries in the Middle Ages, and the famous Roman poet Virgil wrote that "the rocket excites the sexual desire of drowsy people." What definitely excites us about arugula, though, is its bumper levels of the sirtuin-activating nutrients kaempferol and quercetin. In addition to powerful sirtuin-activating properties, a combination of kaempferol and quercetin is being investigated as a cosmetic ingredient because together they moisturize and enhance collagen synthesis in the skin. With those credentials, it's time to drop any elitist tag and make this the leaf of choice for salad bases, where it pairs perfectly with an extra virgin olive oil dressing, combining to make a potent Sirtfood double act.

Buckwheat

Buckwheat was one of the earliest crops to be domesticated in Japan, and the story goes that when Buddhist monks made long trips into the mountains, all they would bring was a cooking pot and a bag of buckwheat for food. So nutritious is buckwheat that this was all they needed, and it nourished them for weeks. We are big buckwheat fans too. Firstly, because it is one of the best-known sources of a sirtuin activator called rutin. But also because it has benefits as a cover crop, improving soil quality and suppressing weed growth, making it a fantastic crop for ecological and sustainable farming.

One reason that buckwheat is head and shoulders above other more common grains is probably that it is not a grain at all—it's actually a fruit seed related to rhubarb. It would be more apt to refer to it as a "pseudo-grain." Having one of the highest protein contents of any grain, as well as being a Sirtfood powerhouse, makes it an unrivaled alternative to more commonly used grains. Plus, it is as versatile as any grain going and, being naturally gluten-free, is a great choice for those who are gluten intolerant.

Capers

In case you're not so familiar with capers, we're talking about those salty, dark green, pelletlike things that you may have only had occasion to see on top of a pizza. Yet they are surely one of the most underrated and overlooked foods out there. Intriguingly, they're actually the flower buds of the caper bush, which grows abundantly in the Mediterranean, before being handpicked and preserved. Studies now reveal that capers have important antimicrobial, antidiabetic, anti-inflammatory, immunomodulatory, and antiviral properties, and they have a rich history of being used as a medicine in the Mediterranean and North Africa. Hardly surprising when we discover that they are crammed full of sirtuin-activating nutrients.

We think it's about time these tiny morsels, so often overshadowed by the other heavy hitters from the Mediterranean diet, had their share of glory. Flavor-wise it's a case of big things coming in small packages, as they sure do pack a punch. But if you're not familiar with using them, don't feel intimidated. We'll soon have you up to speed and falling head over heels for these diminutive nutrient superstars, which when combined with the right ingredients provide a beautifully distinctive and inimitable sour/salty flavor to round off a dish in style.

Celery

Celery has been around and revered for millennia—with leaves found adorning the remains of the Egyptian pharaoh Tutankhamun, who died around 1323 BCE. Early strains were very bitter, and celery was usually regarded as a medicinal plant especially for cleansing and detoxing to prevent illness. That's particularly interesting in light of the fact that liver, kidney, and gut health are among the multitude of promising benefits that science is now demonstrating. It was domesticated as a vegetable in the seventeenth century, and selective breeding diminished its strong bitter flavor in favor of sweeter varieties, thus establishing its place as a traditional salad vegetable.

When it comes to celery, it is important to note that there are two types: blanched/yellow and Pascal/green. Blanching is a technique that was developed to reduce celery's characteristic bitter taste, which was perceived to be too strong. This involves shading the celery from sunlight prior to harvesting, resulting in a paler color and milder flavor. What a travesty that is, for as well as dumbing down the flavor, blanching dumbs down celery's sirtuin-activating properties. Luckily the tide is changing and people are demanding real and distinct flavor and are turning back to the more vivid green variety. Green celery is the type we recommend that you use in both the green juices and meals, with the most nutritious parts being the hearts and the leaves.

Chilies

For thousands of years, the chili has been an integral part of gastronomic experience around the world. On one level, it is baffling that we would be so enamored of it. Its pungent heat, triggered by a substance in chilies called capsaicin, is designed as a plant defense mechanism to cause pain and dissuade predators from feasting on it, yet we relish it. There is something almost mystical about the food and our infatuation with it.

Incredibly, one study showed that eating chilies together even increases cooperation between individuals.[1] And, from a health perspective, we know that their seductive heat is fantastic for activating our sirtuins and boosting our metabolism. The chili's culinary applications are endless too, making it an easy way to give any dish a hefty Sirtfood boost.

While we appreciate that not everyone is a fan of hot or spicy food, we hope we can entice you to consider adding chilies in small amounts, especially in light of recent research showing that those who eat spicy foods three or more times a week have a 14 percent lower death rate compared to those who eat them less than once a week.[2]

As a general rule, the hotter the chili, the better its Sirtfood credentials, but be sensible and stick with what is suited to your own tastes. Serrano peppers are a great start—while packing heat, they are tolerable for most people; and for more experienced heat-seekers, we recommend seeking out Thai chilies for maximum sirtuin-activating benefits. These can be more difficult to find in grocery stores but can often be found in Asian specialty markets. Opt for peppers with deep colors, avoiding those that look wrinkled and soft.

Cocoa

We saw the impressive health benefits of cocoa on pages 59–60, so it's no surprise to learn that for ancient civilizations such as the Aztecs and Mayans, cocoa was considered a sacred food and usually reserved for the elite and the warriors, being served at feasts to gain loyalty and obligation. Indeed, the cocoa bean was held in such high regard that it was even used as a form of currency. Back then it was usually served as a frothy drink. But what could be a more delicious way of getting our dietary cocoa quota than through chocolate?

Alas, the diluted, refined, and highly sweetened milk chocolate we commonly munch doesn't count here. To earn its Sirtfood badge, we are talking about chocolate with 85 percent cocoa solids. But even then, cocoa percentage aside, not all chocolate is created equal. Chocolate is often treated with an alkalizing agent (known as Dutch process) to reduce its acidity and give it a darker color. Sadly, this process massively diminishes its sirtuin-activating flavanols, thus seriously compromising its health-promoting qualities. Fortunately, and unlike in many other countries, food labeling regulations in the United States require that alkalized cocoa must be declared as such and labeled "processed with alkali." We recommend avoiding these products, even if they boast a higher cocoa percentage, and instead opting for those that have not undergone Dutch processing to reap the true benefits of cocoa.

Coffee

What's all this about coffee as a Sirtfood? we hear you say. We can assure you it's not a typo. Gone are the days when our enjoyment of coffee needed to be tempered by a twinge of guilt. The research is unequivocal: coffee is a bona fide health food. In fact, it is a veritable treasure trove of fantastic sirtuin-activating nutrients. And with more than half of Americans drinking coffee every day (to the tune of a staggering $40 billion a year!), coffee boasts the accolade of being the number one source of polyphenols in the American diet. The ultimate irony being that the one thing that so many health "experts" chastised us for doing was actually the best thing we were doing each day for our health. This is why coffee drinkers have significantly less diabetes,[3] as well as lower rates of certain cancers[4] and neurodegenerative disease.[5] As for that ultimate irony, instead of being a toxin, coffee actually protects our livers and makes them healthier![6] And contrary to the popular belief that coffee dehydrates the body, it is now well established not to be the case, with coffee (and also tea) contributing perfectly well to the fluid intake of habitual coffee drinkers. So while we appreciate that coffee is not for everyone, and some people can be very sensitive to the effects of caffeine, for those who enjoy a cup of joe, it's happy days.

Extra Virgin Olive Oil

Olive oil is the most renowned food of the traditional Mediterranean diet. The olive tree, also known as the "immortal tree," is among the oldest-known cultivated trees in the world. And its oil has been revered ever since people started to squeeze olives in stone mortars to collect it, almost 7,000 years ago. Hippocrates cited it as a cure-all; a couple of millennia later, modern science now unequivocally affirms its wonderful health benefits. There is now a wealth of scientific data showing that regular consumption of olive oil is powerfully cardioprotective, as well as playing a role in reducing the risk of major diseases of the modern world such as diabetes, certain cancers, and osteoporosis, and being associated with increased longevity.

When it comes to olive oil, the key is to buy extra virgin in order to reap full Sirtfood goodness. Virgin olive oil is obtained from the fruit solely by mechanical means under conditions that do not lead to the deterioration of the oil, so you can be assured of the quality and polyphenol content. "Extra virgin" refers to the first pressing of the fruit ("virgin" is the second pressing); it has the greatest taste, quality, and Sirtfood credentials, and thus is the one we strongly recommend you use.

Garlic

For thousands of years garlic has been considered one of nature's wonder foods, with healing and rejuvenating powers. Egyptians fed garlic to pyramid crews to boost their immunity and ward off various maladies, as well as to improve their performance through its ability to prevent fatigue. Garlic is a powerful natural antibiotic and antifungal often used to help treat stomach ulcers. It can stimulate the lymphatic system to "detox" by expediting the removal of waste products from the body. And as well as being investigated for fat loss, it also packs a potent heart health punch, lowering cholesterol by about 10 percent and blood pressure by 5 to 7 percent, as well as reducing the stickiness of the blood and blood sugar levels.[7] And if you are worried about that off-putting garlic odor, take note. When women were asked to assess a selection of men's body odors, those men who consumed four or more cloves of garlic a day were judged to have a much more attractive and pleasant smell.[8] Researchers believe it is because it is perceived as signaling better health. And, of course, there are always mints for fresher breath!

There is a trick to getting maximum benefit from eating garlic. The Sirtfood nutrients in garlic are complemented by another key nutrient in it called allicin, which gives off garlic's characteristic aroma. But allicin only forms in garlic after physical "injury" to the bulb. And its formation is stopped when exposed to heat (cooking) or low pH (stomach acid). So when preparing garlic, chop, mince, or crush, and then allow it to sit for around ten minutes to allow the allicin to form before cooking or eating it.

Green Tea (Especially Matcha)

Green tea, the toast of the Orient, and ever more popular in the West, will be familiar to many. As will the increasing awareness of its health benefits, linking green tea consumption with less cancer, heart disease, diabetes, and osteoporosis. The reason green tea is believed to be so good for us is primarily due to its rich content of a group of powerful plant compounds called catechins, the star of the show being a particular type of sirtuin-activating catechin known as epigallocatechin gallate (EGCG).

But what's all the fuss about matcha? We like to think of matcha as normal green tea on steroids. It is a special powdered green tea that is prepared by dissolving it directly in water, in contrast to common green tea, which is prepared as an infusion. The upshot of consuming matcha is that it contains dramatically greater levels of the sirtuin-activating compound EGCG compared with other types of green tea. If you're looking for further endorsement, Zen priests describe matcha as the "ultimate mental and medical remedy [which] has the ability to make one's life more full and complete."

Kale

We are cynics at heart, so we are always skeptical of what's driving the latest superfood publicity craze. Is it science or is it vested interests? Few foods have exploded on the health scene in recent years as dramatically as kale. Described as the "lean, green brassica queen" (referring to its family of cruciferous vegetables), it has become the chic vegetable all health enthusiasts and foodies are gunning for. There is even a National Kale Day each October. But you don't have to wait until then to show your kale pride: there are T-shirts too, with trendy slogans such as "Powered by Kale" and "Highway to Kale." For us, that's enough to set the alarm bells ringing.

Filled with suspicions, we did the research, and we have to

admit that our conclusion is that kale does actually deserve its plaudits (although we still don't recommend the T-shirts!). The reason we are pro-kale is that it boasts bumper amounts of the sirtuin-activating nutrients quercetin and kaempferol, making it a must-include in the Sirtfood Diet and the base of our Sirtfood green juice. What's so refreshing about kale is that, unlike the usual exotic, difficult-to-source, and exorbitantly priced so-called superfoods, kale is available everywhere, locally grown, and very affordable.

Medjool Dates

The inclusion of Medjool dates in a list of foods that stimulate weight loss and promotes health may come as a surprise—especially when we tell you that Medjool dates contain a staggering 66 percent sugar. Sugar possesses no sirtuin-activating properties whatsoever; rather, it has well-established links to obesity, heart disease, and diabetes—quite the opposite of what we are looking to achieve. But processed and refined sugar is very different from sugar carried in a vehicle provided by nature that is balanced with sirtuin-activating polyphenols: the Medjool date.

In complete contrast to normal sugar, Medjool dates, eaten in moderation, actually have no real noticeable blood-sugar-raising effects.[9] On the contrary, eating them is linked to having less diabetes and heart disease. They have been a staple food around the world for centuries, and in recent years there has been an explosion of scientific interest in dates, which sees them emerging as a potential medicine for a number of diseases.[10,11] Herein lies the uniqueness and power of the Sirtfood Diet: it refutes the dogma and allows you to indulge in sweet things in moderation without feeling guilty.

Parsley

Parsley is a culinary conundrum. It appears so often in recipes, yet so often it's the token green guy. At best we serve a few sprigs chopped up and tossed on a meal as an afterthought, at worst a solitary sprig purely for decorative purposes. Either way, it's often still languishing there on the plate long after we've finished eating. This culinary typecasting stems from its traditional use in ancient Rome as a garnish to eat after meals to refresh breath, instead of being part of the meal itself. And what a shame, because parsley is a fantastic food packing a vibrant and refreshing taste that's filled with character.

Taste aside, what makes parsley really special is that it is an excellent source of the sirtuin-activating nutrient apigenin, a real boon given that it is rarely found in significant quantities in other foods. Fascinatingly, apigenin binds to the benzodiazepine receptors in our brains, helping us to relax and aiding sleep. Stack it all up, and it's time we appreciated parsley not as a ubiquitous food confetti but as a food in its own right in order to reap the wonderful health benefits it can bring.

Red Endive

As far as vegetables go, endive is a relatively new kid on the block. Story has it that endive was discovered by accident by a Belgian farmer in 1830. The farmer stored chicory roots, then used as a type of coffee substitute, in his cellar, only to forget about them. Upon his return he discovered that they had sprouted white leaves, which upon tasting he found to be tender, crunchy, and rather delicious. Now endive is grown all over the world, including the United States, and earns its Sirtfood badge thanks to its impressive content of the sirtuin activator luteolin. And in addition to the established sirtuin-activating benefits, luteolin consumption has become a promising therapy approach for improving sociability in autistic children.

For those new to endive, it has a crisp texture and a sweet flavor accompanied by a mild and pleasant bitterness. If you're ever stuck on how to increase endive in your diet, you can't lose by adding its leaves to a salad, where its welcome, tart flavor adds the perfect bite to a zesty extra virgin olive oil–based dressing. Just like onion, red is best, but the yellow variety can also be considered a Sirtfood. So while the red variety can sometimes be harder to find, you can rest assured that yellow is a perfectly suitable alternative.

Red Onions

Onions have been a dietary staple since the time of our prehistoric predecessors, being one of the earliest crops to be cultivated, some 5,000 years ago. With such a long history of use, and such potent health-giving properties, onions have been revered by many cultures that have come before us. The Egyptians held them in particular eminence as objects of worship, regarding their circle-within-a-circle structure as symbolic of eternal life. And the Greeks believed onions strengthened athletes. Before the Olympic Games, athletes would eat their way through vast amounts of onions, even drinking the juice! It's an incredible testimony to how valuable ancient dietary wisdom can be when we consider that onions earn their top twenty Sirtfood status because they are chock-full of the sirtuin-activating compound quercetin—the very compound that the world of sports science has recently begun actively researching and marketing for improving sports performance.

And why red? Simply because they have the highest quercetin content, although the standard yellow ones don't lag too far behind, and are a good inclusion too.

Red Wine

Any list of the top twenty Sirtfoods would not be complete without the inclusion of red wine, the original Sirtfood. In the early 1990s, the French paradox made headlines, with it being discovered that despite the French appearing to do everything wrong when it came to health (smoking, lack of exercise, and consumption of rich food), they had lower death rates from heart disease than countries such as the United States. Doctors suggested the reason was the copious amounts of red wine consumed. Then in 1995, Danish researchers published work to show that low-to-moderate red wine consumption reduced death rates, whereas similar alcohol levels of beer had no effect and similar alcohol intakes of hard liquors increased death rates. In 2003, of course, red wine's rich content of a bevy of sirtuin-activating nutrients was uncovered, and the rest, as they say, became history.

But there's even more to red wine's impressive résumé. Red wine appears to be able to ward off the common cold, with moderate wine drinkers having a greater than 40 percent reduction in its incidence.[12] Studies now also show benefits for oral health and in prevention of cavities.[13] With moderate consumption also shown to increase social bonding and out-of-the-box thinking, that after-work drink among colleagues to discuss work projects appears to have a founding in strong science.

Of course, moderation is key. Only small amounts are needed for benefit, and excess alcohol quickly undoes the good. The sweet spot appears to be sticking within US guidelines of up to one 5-ounce drink per day for women and up to two 5-ounce drinks per day for men. To ensure maximum sirtuin-activating bang for your buck, wines from the New York region (especially pinot noir, cabernet sauvignon, and merlot) have the highest polyphenol content of the most widely available wines.

Soy

Soy products have a long history as an integral part of the diet of many Asia-Pacific countries such as China, Japan, and the Koreas. Researchers first got turned on to soy after the observation that high soy–consuming countries had markedly lower rates of certain cancers, especially of the breast and prostate. This is thought to be due to a special group of polyphenols contained within soybeans known as isoflavones, which can favorably change how estrogens work in the body, and include the sirtuin-activators daidzein and formononetin. Consumption of soy products has also been linked to a reduction in the incidence or severity of a variety of conditions such as cardiovascular disease, menopausal symptoms, and bone loss.

Highly processed, nutrient-stripped forms of soybean are now a ubiquitous ingredient added to many processed food products. The benefits are only reaped through natural soy products such as tofu, an excellent vegan protein source, or in a fermented form such as tempeh, natto, or our favorite, miso, a traditional Japanese paste fermented with a naturally occurring fungus that results in an intense umami flavor.

Strawberries

Fruit has been increasingly vilified in recent years, getting a bad rap in the growing fervor against sugar. Fortunately for berry lovers, such a maligned reputation could not be more ill-deserved. While all berries are nutritional powerhouses, strawberries earn their top twenty Sirtfood status due to their abundance of the sirtuin activator fisetin. And studies now endorse eating strawberries regularly to promote healthy aging, staving off Alzheimer's, cancer, diabetes, heart disease, and osteoporosis. As for their sugar content, it's very low, a mere teaspoon of sugar per 3½ ounces.

Intriguingly, as well as being inherently low in sugar themselves, strawberries have pronounced effects on improving how the body handles carbohydrates. What researchers have found is that adding strawberries to carbohydrates has the effect of reducing insulin demand, in essence turning the food into a sustained energy releaser.[14] And new research is now suggesting that eating strawberries has similar effects to drug therapy in diabetes treatment. The great seventeenth-century physician William Butler wrote in praise of the strawberry: "Doubtless God could have made a better berry, but doubtless God never did." We can only agree.

Turmeric

Turmeric, a cousin of ginger, is the new kid on the block in food trends, with Google naming it the "breakout star" ingredient of 2015. Though here in the West we are only turning to it now, it has been appreciated in Asia for thousands of years for both culinary and medical reasons. Incredibly, India produces nearly the entire world's supply of turmeric, consuming 80 percent of it itself. Along with the benefits of the "golden spice" we saw on pages 60–61, turmeric is used in Asia to treat skin conditions such as acne, psoriasis, dermatitis, and rash. Before Indian weddings, a ceremony occurs where turmeric paste is applied to bride and groom as a skin beauty regimen but also to symbolize warding off evil.

One of the things that limits the effectiveness of turmeric is that its key sirtuin-activating nutrient, curcumin, is poorly absorbed by the body when we eat it. However, research shows that we can overcome this by cooking it in liquid, adding fat, and adding black pepper, all of which dramatically increase its absorption. This fits perfectly with traditional Indian cooking, where it is typically combined with ghee and black pepper in curries and other hot dishes, and proof again that science is only just catching up with the age-old wisdom of traditional ways of eating.

Walnuts

Dating all the way back to 7000 BCE, walnuts are the oldest tree food known to man, originating in ancient Persia, where they were the preserve of royalty. Fast-forward to today, and walnuts are a US success story. California leads the way, with the Central Valley of California renowned for being the prime walnut-growing region. California walnuts provide 99 percent of the commercial supply to the United States and a staggering three-quarters of walnut trade worldwide.

According to the NuVal system, which ranks foods according to how healthy they are and has been endorsed by the American College of Preventive Medicine, walnuts lead the way as the number one nut for health. But what really makes walnuts stand out for us is how they fly in the face of conventional thinking: they are high in fat and calories, yet well established for reducing weight and slashing the risk of metabolic diseases such as cardiovascular disease and diabetes. That's the power of sirtuin activation.

Less well known, but equally intriguing, is the emerging research showing walnuts to be a powerful anti-aging food. As well as preventing the decline in physical function with age, research also points to their benefits as a brain food with the potential to slow down brain aging and reduce the risk of degenerative brain disorders.

9

Phase 1: 7 Pounds in Seven Days

Welcome to Phase 1 of the Sirtfood Diet. This is the hyper-success phase, where you will take a huge step toward achieving a slimmer and leaner body. Follow our simple step-by-step instructions and make use of the delicious recipes provided for you. In addition to our standard seven-day plan, we also have a meat-free version, which is suitable for both vegetarians and vegans. Feel free to go with whichever one you prefer.

WHAT TO EXPECT

During Phase 1, you will reap the full benefits of our clinically proven method for losing 7 pounds in seven days. But remember this includes muscle gain, so don't get hung up purely with the numbers on the scales (see pages 35–36). Nor should you get into a habit of weighing yourself daily. In fact, we often see the scales creeping up in the last few days of Phase 1 due to muscle gain, while waistlines continue to shrink. That's why we want you to look at the scales, but not be ruled by them. Check out how you look in the mirror, how your clothes are fitting, or whether you need to move a notch on your belt. These are all great indicators of the more profound changes in your body composition.

Be aware of other changes too, such as in your sense of well-being, your energy levels, and how clear your skin looks. You can even get measurements of your overall cardiovascular and metabolic health performed at your local pharmacy to see changes in things like your blood pressure, blood sugar levels, and blood fats such as cholesterol and triglycerides. Remember, weight loss aside, the introduction of Sirtfoods into your diet is a huge step in making your cells fitter and more resistant to disease, setting you up for a lifetime of exceptional health.

HOW TO FOLLOW PHASE 1

To make Phase 1 as plain sailing as possible, we'll guide you through the complete seven-day plan one day at a time, including the lowdown on the Sirtfood green juice and easy-to-follow, delicious recipes every step of the way.

Phase 1 of the Sirtfood Diet is based on two distinct stages:

Days 1 to 3 are the most intensive, and during this period you can eat up to a limit of 1,000 calories each day, consisting of:

- 3 x Sirtfood green juices
- 1 x main meal

Days 4 to 7 will see your food intake increase to a limit of 1,500 calories each day, consisting of:

- 2 x Sirtfood green juices
- 2 x main meals

There are very few rules for following the diet. Ultimately it's about fitting it into your lifestyle and around day-to-day living for prolonged success. However, here are a few simple yet big-impact tips for achieving the best outcome:

1. **Get a Good Juicer:** Juicing is an indispensable part of the Sirtfood Diet, and a juicer is one of the best investments you will make for your health (to recap why, see page 68). While budget should be the determining factor, some juicers are more effective at extracting the juice from green leafy vegetables and herbs, with the Breville brand being among the best of the commonly available juicers we have tried.
2. **Preparation Is Key:** From the wealth of feedback we have had, one thing is clear: those who planned in advance were the most successful. Get familiar with the ingredients and recipes and stock up on what you need. With everything organized and ready, you'll be amazed at how easy the whole process is.
3. **Save Time:** If you are tight for time, prepare cleverly. Meals can be made the night before. Juices can be made in bulk, and kept in the fridge for up to three days (or longer in the freezer) before their levels of sirtuin-activating nutrients start to drop.

Just protect it from light, and only add in the matcha when you are ready to consume it.

4. **Eat Early:** It is better to eat earlier in the day, and meals and juices should ideally not be consumed later than 7 p.m. (to recap why, see page 71); but ultimately the diet is designed to fit with your lifestyle, and late eaters still reap great benefit.

5. **Space Out the Juices:** To enhance absorption of the green juices, they should be consumed at least an hour before or two hours after a meal and spread out throughout the day, rather than having them too close together.

6. **Eat until Satisfied:** Sirtfoods can have dramatic effects on appetite (see pages 31–33) and some people will be full before finishing their meals. Listen to your body and eat until you are satisfied instead of forcing all the food down. As the long-lived Okinawans, say, "*Hara hachi bu*," which roughly translates as "Eat until you are 80 percent full."

7. **Enjoy the Journey:** Don't get caught up on the end goal; instead stay mindful of the journey. This diet is about celebrating food in all its wonder, for its health benefits but equally for the pleasure and enjoyment it brings. Research shows that when we keep our minds focused on the path instead of the final destination, we are much more likely to succeed.

What to Drink

As well as the recommended daily servings of green juices, you can consume other fluids freely throughout Phase 1. These should be noncaloric drinks, preferably plain water, black coffee, and green tea. If your normal predilection is for black or herbal teas, feel free to include these also. Soft drinks and fruit juices are left behind. Instead, if you want to jazz things up, try adding some sliced strawberries to still or sparkling water to make your own Sirtfood-infused health drink. Keep it in the fridge for a couple of hours and you'll have a pleasantly refreshing alternative to soft drinks and juices.

One thing to be aware of is that we do not recommend sudden big changes to your normal coffee consumption. Caffeine withdrawal symptoms can make you feel lousy for a couple of days; likewise, large increases can be unpleasant for those particularly sensitive to the effects of caffeine. We also recommend that coffee be drunk black, without adding milk, because some researchers have found that the addition of milk can reduce the absorption of the beneficial sirtuin-activating nutrients.[1] The same has been found for green tea,[2] though adding some lemon juice actually increases the absorption of its sirtuin-activating nutrients.[3]

Do remember that this is the hyper-success phase, and while you should be comforted by the fact that it is for one week only, you do need to be a bit more disciplined. For this week we include alcohol, in the form of red wine, but only as a cooking ingredient.

THE SIRTFOOD GREEN JUICE

The green juice is an essential part of Phase 1 of the Sirtfood Diet. All the ingredients are powerful Sirtfoods, and in each juice you get a potent cocktail of natural compounds such as apigenin, kaempferol, luteolin, quercetin, and EGCG that work together to switch on your sirtuin genes and promote fat loss. To that we've added lemon, as its natural acidity has been shown to protect, stabilize, and increase the absorption of the drink's sirtuin-activating nutrients. We've also added a touch of apple and ginger for taste. Both of these are therefore optional. Indeed, many people find that once they are accustomed to the taste of the juice, they leave out the apple altogether.

SIRTFOOD GREEN JUICE (SERVES 1)

2 large handfuls (about 2½ ounces or 75g) kale

a large handful (1 ounce or 30g) arugula

a very small handful (about ¼ ounce or 5g) flat-leaf parsley

2 to 3 large celery stalks (5½ ounces or 150g), including leaves

½ medium green apple

½- to 1-inch (1 to 2.5 cm) piece of fresh ginger

juice of ½ lemon

½ level teaspoon matcha powder*

*Days 1 to 3 of Phase 1: added only to the first two juices of the day;
Days 4 to 7 of Phase 1: added to both juices

Note that while in our pilot trial all quantities were weighed out exactly as listed, our experience is that handful measures work extremely well. In fact, they better tailor the nutrient quantity to an individual's body size. Larger individuals tend to have larger hands and therefore get a proportionally higher amount of Sirtfood nutrients to match their body size, and vice versa for smaller people.

- Mix the greens (kale, arugula, and parsley) together, then juice them. We find that juicers can really differ in their efficiency at juicing leafy vegetables, and you may need to rejuice the remnants before moving on to the other ingredients. The goal is to end up with about 2 fluid ounces or close to ¼ cup (50ml) of juice from the greens.
- Now juice the celery, apple, and ginger.
- You can peel the lemon and put it through the juicer as well, but we find it much easier to simply squeeze the lemon by hand into the juice. By this stage, you should have around 1 cup (250ml) of juice in total, perhaps slightly more.
- It is only when the juice is made and ready to serve that you add the matcha. Pour a small amount of the juice into a glass, then add the matcha and stir vigorously with a fork or teaspoon. We only use matcha in the first two drinks of the day because it contains moderate amounts of caffeine (the same content as a normal cup of tea). For people not used to it, it may keep them awake if drunk late.
- Once the matcha is dissolved, add the remainder of the juice. Give it a final stir, then your juice is ready to drink. Feel free to top up with plain water, according to taste.

PHASE 1: YOUR SEVEN-DAY GUIDE

Please note that you need to read the recipe notes on pages 157–158 before beginning to cook.

For Days 1 to 3, take the juices at separate times of the day (e.g., first thing in the morning, midmorning, and midafternoon), and select one of the standard or vegan meal options and eat it at a time that suits you (usually eaten for lunch or dinner).

Day 1

On Day 1, you will consume:

- 3 x Sirtfood green juices (page 102)
- 1 x main meal (standard or vegan option), either:

Asian shrimp stir-fry with buckwheat noodles (page 159)
+
½ to ¾ ounce (15 to 20g) dark chocolate (85 percent cocoa solids)
or
Miso and sesame glazed tofu with ginger and chili stir-fried greens (vegan, page 161)
+
½ to ¾ ounce (15 to 20g) dark chocolate (85 percent cocoa solids)

Day 2

On Day 2, you will consume:

- 3 x Sirtfood green juices (page 102)
- 1 x main meal (standard or vegan option), either:

Turkey escalope with sage, capers, and parsley and spiced cauliflower "couscous" (page 163)

+

½ to ¾ ounce (15 to 20g) dark chocolate (85 percent cocoa solids)

or

Kale and red onion dal with buckwheat (vegan, page 165)

+

½ to ¾ ounce (15 to 20g) dark chocolate (85 percent cocoa solids)

Day 3

On Day 3, you will consume:

- 3 x Sirtfood green juices (page 102)
- 1 x main meal (standard or vegan option), either:

Aromatic chicken breast with kale and red onions and a tomato and chili salsa (page 167)

+

½ to ¾ ounce (15 to 20g) dark chocolate (85 percent cocoa solids)

or

Harissa baked tofu with cauliflower "couscous" (vegan, page 169)

+

½ to ¾ ounce (15 to 20g) dark chocolate (85 percent cocoa solids)

For Days 4 to 7, take the juices at separate times of the day (e.g., the first juice either first thing in the morning or midmorning, the second juice midafternoon); select your meals from either the standard or vegan options, and eat them at a time that suits you (usually eaten for breakfast/lunch and dinner). Also, according to your appetite, you may continue to add in ½ to ¾ ounce (15 to 20g) dark chocolate (85 percent cocoa solids) each day, at your discretion.

Day 4

On Day 4, you will consume:

- 2 x Sirtfood green juices (page 102)
- 2 x main meals (standard or vegan option), either:

MEAL 1: Sirt muesli (page 171)
MEAL 2: Pan-fried salmon fillet with caramelized endive, arugula, and celery leaf salad (page 172)
or
MEAL 1: Sirt muesli (vegan, page 171)
MEAL 2: Tuscan bean stew (vegan, page 174)

Day 5

On Day 5, you will consume:

- 2 x Sirtfood green juices (page 102)
- 2 x main meals (standard or vegan option), either:

MEAL 1: Strawberry buckwheat tabbouleh (page 175)
MEAL 2: Miso-marinated baked cod with stir-fried greens and sesame (page 176)
or
MEAL 1: Strawberry buckwheat tabbouleh (vegan, page 175)
MEAL 2: Soba (buckwheat noodles) in a miso broth with tofu, celery, and kale (vegan, page 178)

Day 6

On Day 6, you will consume:

- 2 x Sirtfood green juices (page 102)
- 2 x main meals (standard or vegan option), either:

MEAL 1: Sirt super salad (page 180)
MEAL 2: Char-grilled beef with a red wine jus, onion rings, garlic kale, and herb-roasted potatoes (page 181)
or
MEAL 1: Lentil Sirt super salad (vegan, page 180)
MEAL 2: Kidney bean mole with baked potato (vegan, page 184)

Day 7

On Day 7, you will consume:

- 2 x Sirtfood green juices (page 102)
- 2 x main meals (standard or vegan option), either:

MEAL 1: Sirtfood omelet (page 186)

MEAL 2: Baked chicken breast with walnut and parsley pesto and red onion salad (page 187)

or

MEAL 1: Waldorf salad (vegan, page 189)

MEAL 2: Roasted eggplant wedges with walnut and parsley pesto and tomato salad (vegan, page 190)

Phase 2: Maintenance

Congratulations on completing Phase 1 of the Sirtfood Diet! Already you should be seeing great results with fat loss and are not only looking slimmer and more toned, but feeling revitalized and reenergized. So, what now?

Having seen these often remarkable transformations ourselves firsthand, we know how much you'll want to not just preserve all those benefits, but see even better results. After all, Sirtfoods are designed to be eaten for life. The question is how you adapt what you have been doing in Phase 1 into your usual dietary routine. That's exactly what prompted us to create a follow-up fourteen-day maintenance plan designed to help you make the transition from Phase 1 to your more normal dietary routine and thus help sustain and further extend the benefits of the Sirtfood Diet.

WHAT TO EXPECT
During Phase 2, you will consolidate your weight-loss results and continue to steadily lose weight.

Remember that the one striking thing we have found with the Sirtfood Diet is that most or all of the weight that people lose is from fat, and that many actually put on some muscle. So we want to remind you again not to judge your progress purely by the numbers on the scale. Look in the mirror to see if you are looking leaner and more toned, see how your clothes are fitting, and lap up the compliments that you will receive from others.

Remember too that just as the weight loss will continue, the health benefits will grow. By following the fourteen-day maintenance plan, you're really starting to lay down the foundations for a future of lifelong health.

HOW TO FOLLOW PHASE 2

The key to success in this phase is to keep packing your diet full of Sirtfoods. To make it as easy as possible, we've put together a seven-day menu plan for you to follow, including delicious family-friendly recipes, with each day packed to the rafters with Sirtfoods (though see page 149 for advice regarding children). All you need to do is repeat the seven-day plan twice to complete the fourteen days of Phase 2.

On each of the fourteen days your diet will consist of:

- 3 x balanced Sirtfood-rich meals
- 1 x Sirtfood green juice
- 1 to 2 x optional Sirtfood bite snacks

Once again, there are no rigid rules for when you have to consume these. Be flexible and fit them around your day. Two simple rules of thumb are:

- Have your green juice either first thing in the morning, at least thirty minutes before breakfast, or midmorning.
- Try your best to eat your evening meal by 7 p.m.

PORTION SIZES

Our focus during Phase 2 is not on counting calories. Over the long term this is not a practical or even successful approach for the average person. Instead we're focusing on sensible portions, really well-balanced meals, and most important, filling up on Sirtfoods so you can continue to benefit from their fat-burning and health-promoting effects.

We have also constructed the meals in the plan to make them satiating, which will help you feel full for longer. That, combined with the natural appetite-regulating effects of Sirtfoods, means that you won't spend the next fourteen days feeling hungry, but instead pleasantly satisfied, well fed, and extremely well nourished.

Just as in Phase 1, remember to listen to your body and be guided by your appetite. If you prepare meals according to our instructions and find you are comfortably full before you've finished a meal, then it's perfectly fine to stop eating!

WHAT TO DRINK

You will continue to include one green juice daily throughout Phase 2. This is to keep you topped up with high levels of Sirtfoods.

Just as in Phase 1, you can consume other fluids freely throughout Phase 2. Our preferred drinks for you to include remain plain water, homemade flavored water, coffee, and green tea. If your predilection is for black or white tea, feel free to enjoy. The same applies to herbal teas. The best news is that you can enjoy the occasional glass of red wine during Phase 2. Red wine is a Sirtfood due to its content of sirtuin-activating polyphenols, especially resveratrol and piceatannol, making it by far the best choice of alcoholic beverage. But, with alcohol itself having adverse effects on our fat cells, moderation is still best, and throughout Phase 2 we recommend limiting your intake to one glass of red wine with a meal, on two or three days per week.

RETURNING TO THREE MEALS

During Phase 1 you consumed just one or two meals a day, which gave you lots of flexibility over when you ate your meals. As we now return to a more normal routine and the time-proven pattern of three meals a day, it's a good time to talk about breakfast.

Eating a good breakfast sets us up for the day, increasing our energy and concentration levels. In terms of our metabolism, eating earlier keeps our blood sugar and fat levels in check. That breakfast is a good thing is borne out by a number of studies that typically show that people who regularly eat breakfast are less likely to be overweight.

The reason for this is due to our internal body clocks (see page 72). Our bodies expect us to eat early in anticipation of when we are going to be most active and needing fuel. Yet on any given day, as many as a third of us will skip breakfast. It's a classic symptom of our busy modern lives, and the perception is that there simply isn't enough time to eat well. But as you will see, with the nifty breakfasts we have laid out for you here, nothing could be further from the truth. Whether it's the Sirtfood smoothie that can be drunk on the go, the premade Sirt muesli, or the quick and easy Sirtfood scrambled eggs/tofu, finding those extra few minutes in the morning will reap dividends not only for your day but for your longer-term weight and health.

With Sirtfoods working to supercharge our energy levels, there is even more to be gained from getting an early morning hit of them to start your day. This is achieved not just through eating a Sirtfood-rich breakfast, but especially through the inclusion of the green juice, which we recommend you have either first thing in the morning—at least thirty minutes before breakfast—or midmorning. From our own clinical experience, we do get many reports of people who drink their green juice first thing and do not feel hungry for a couple of hours afterward. If this is the effect it has on you, it is perfectly fine to wait a couple of hours before having breakfast. Just don't skip it. Alternatively, you can kick off your day with a good breakfast, then wait two or three hours before having the green juice. Be flexible and just go with whatever works for you.

SIRTFOOD BITES

When it comes to snacking, you can take it or leave it. There has been so much debate about whether eating frequent, smaller meals is best for weight loss, or whether you should just stick to three balanced meals a day. The truth is, it doesn't really matter.

The way we have constructed the maintenance menu for you ensures you will eat three well-balanced Sirtfood-rich meals per day, and you may find you really don't need a snack. But perhaps you've been busy in the office, working out, or dashing around with the kids, and need something to tide you over to the next meal. And if that "little something" is going to give you a whammy of Sirtfood nutrients and taste delicious, then it's happy days. This is why we created our "Sirtfood bites." These clever little snacks are a genuinely guilt-free treat made entirely from Sirtfoods: dates, walnuts, cocoa, extra virgin olive oil, and turmeric. For the days you need them, we recommend eating one, or a maximum of two, per day.

"SIRTIFYING" YOUR MEALS

We've seen that the only sustainable diets are ones of inclusion, not exclusion. But true success goes beyond this—the diet must be compatible with modern-day living. Whether it be the convenience to meet the demands of our hectic lives or fitting in with our role as the bon vivant at dinner parties, the way we eat should be hassle-free. You should be able to enjoy your svelte figure and radiant glow, instead of worrying about kooky food demands and restrictions.

What's so fantastic about Sirtfoods is that they are really accessible, familiar, and easy to include in your diet. Here, as you bridge the gap between Phase 1 and routine eating, you will be building foundations for a new, improved way of lifelong eating.

The key principle is what we call "Sirtifying" your meals. This is where we take familiar dishes, including many classic favorites, and with some clever swaps and simple Sirtfood inclusions we keep all the great taste but add a ton more goodness. Throughout Phase 2 you will see just how easily this is achieved.

Examples include our delicious Sirtfood smoothie for the perfect on-the-go breakfast in a time-starved world, and the simple switch from wheat to buckwheat for adding extra taste and zip to the much-loved comfort food that is pasta. Meanwhile iconic, beloved dishes such as chili con carne and curry don't even need much change, with the traditional recipes offering Sirtfood bonanzas. And who said fast food meant bad food? We combine the authentic vibrant flavors of a pizza and remove the guilt when you make it yourself. There's no need to say farewell to indulgence either, as proven by our pancakes smothered with berries and dark chocolate sauce. It's not even dessert, it's breakfast, and it's great for you. Simple changes: you continue to eat the foods you love while driving a healthy weight and well-being. And that is the dietary revolution that is Sirtfoods.

COOKING FOR MORE

To embrace this, we are now entering a "Sirtfoods for all" stage, where recipes begin to cater to more mouths than one. Whether it be for family or friends, the new dinner recipes as well as the Sirtfood-packed soup we introduce in this phase are designed with cooking for four in mind. And for those still cooking for one or two, why not take advantage of cooking batch meals for freezing to have meals ready for next week?

FOURTEEN-DAY MEAL PLAN

In addition to our standard plan, we also have a meat-free version, which is suitable for both vegetarians and vegans. Feel free to go with whichever one you prefer, or even mix and match.

Each day you will consume:

- 1 x Sirtfood green juice (page 102)
- 3 x main meals (standard or vegan options, see next page)
- 1 to 2 x optional Sirtfood bites (page 213)

Consume the juice either first thing in the morning, at least thirty minutes before breakfast, or midmorning.

	BREAKFAST
Day 8 and 15	Sirtfood smoothie (page 192)
or	Sirtfood smoothie* (page 192)
Day 9 and 16	Sirt muesli (page 171)
or	Sirt muesli* (page 171)
Day 10 and 17	Yogurt with mixed berries, chopped walnuts, and dark chocolate (page 198)
or	Soy or coconut yogurt with mixed berries, chopped walnuts, and dark chocolate* (page 198)
Day 11 and 18	Spiced scrambled eggs (page 201)
or	Mushroom and tofu scramble* (page 204)
Day 12 and 19	Sirtfood smoothie (page 192)
or	Sirtfood smoothie* (page 192)
Day 13 and 20	Buckwheat pancakes with strawberries, chocolate sauce, and crushed walnuts (page 207)
or	Soy or coconut yogurt with mixed berries, chopped walnuts, and dark chocolate* (page 198)
Day 14 and 21	Sirtfood omelet (page 186)
or	Sirt muesli* (page 171)

LUNCH	DINNER
Chicken Sirt super salad (page 180)	Asian shrimp stir-fry with buckwheat noodles (page 159)
Waldorf salad* (page 189)	Tuscan bean stew* (page 174)
Stuffed whole-wheat pita (page 193)	Butternut squash and date tagine with buckwheat (page 195)
Butter bean and miso dip with celery sticks and oatcakes* (page 197)	Butternut squash and date tagine with buckwheat* (page 195)
Tuna Sirt super salad (page 180)	Chicken and kale curry with Bombay potatoes (page 199)
Stuffed whole-wheat pita* (page 193)	Kale and red onion dal with buckwheat* (page 165)
Strawberry buckwheat tabbouleh (page 175)	Sirt chili con carne (page 202)
Strawberry buckwheat tabbouleh* (page 175)	Kidney bean mole with baked potato* (page 184)
Waldorf salad (page 189)	Smoked salmon pasta with chili and arugula (page 205)
Buckwheat pasta salad* (page 206)	Harissa baked tofu with cauliflower "couscous"* (page 169)
Tofu and shiitake mushroom soup (page 209)	Sirtfood pizza (page 210)
Tofu and shiitake mushroom soup* (page 209)	Sirtfood pizza* (page 210)
Lentil Sirt super salad (page 180)	Baked chicken breast with walnut and parsley pesto and red onion salad (page 187)
Lentil Sirt super salad* (page 180)	Miso and sesame glazed tofu with ginger and chili stir-fried greens* (page 161)

* Vegan option

Sirtfoods for Life

Congratulations, you've now finished both phases of the Sirt-food Diet! Let's just take stock of what you've achieved. You've completed the hyper-success phase, experiencing in the region of 7 pounds of weight loss, which likely includes some desirable muscle gain. You've consolidated that weight loss and further improved your body composition throughout the fourteen-day maintenance phase. Most important, you've marked the beginning of your own personal health revolution. You have taken a stand against the tide of ill health that so often strikes as we get older. Increased energy, vitality, and well-being is the future you have chosen for yourself.

By now you will be familiar with the top twenty Sirtfoods (see page 79) and have gained an appreciation of just how powerful they are. Not only that, you will also have become quite adept at including and enjoying them in your diet. It is imperative that these foods remain a prominent feature in your daily eating routine, for the continued weight loss and well-being they bring. But still, they are only twenty foods and, after all, variety is the spice of life. So what next?

In this chapter we give you the blueprint for lifelong health. It's about getting your body in perfect balance with a diet that is suitable and sustainable for all, and provides all the health-enhancing nutrients we need. It's about continuing to reap the weight-loss rewards of the Sirtfood Diet using the very best foods that nature has to offer.

BEYOND THE TOP TWENTY SIRTFOODS

We've seen why Sirtfoods are so beneficial: certain plants have sophisticated stress-response systems that produce compounds that activate sirtuins—the same fat-burning and longevity system in the body that is activated by fasting and exercise. The greater the amount of these compounds that plants produce in response to stress, the greater the benefit we obtain from eating them. Our list of the top twenty Sirtfoods is made up of the foods that really stand out by virtue of being especially packed full of these compounds, and thus the foods that have the most exceptional ability to impact body composition and well-being. Yet the sirtuin-activating effects of foods is not an all-or-nothing principle. There are many other plants out there that produce moderate levels of sirtuin-activating nutrients, and we encourage you to really expand the variety and diversity of your diet by eating these liberally too. The Sirtfood Diet is all about inclusion, and the greater the variety of foods with sirtuin-activating properties that can be incorporated into the diet, the better. Especially if that means including even more of your favorite foods to max out the pleasure and enjoyment you can reap from your meals.

Let's use the analogy of exercise. The top twenty Sirtfoods are the (much more pleasurable) equivalent of sweating it out in the gym, with Phase 1 being the "boot camp." In contrast, eating those other foods with more moderate levels of sirtuin-activating nutrients is like reaping the rewards of going out for a good walk. Compare that to the typical diet with a nourishment value equivalent to lying on the couch watching TV all day. Sure, sweating it out in the gym is good, but you'll soon get fed up with that if that's all you do. That walk should be encouraged too, especially if it means you are not choosing to lie on the couch instead.

For example, we included strawberries in our top twenty Sirtfoods because they are the most notable source of the sirtuin activator fisetin. Yet if we look more broadly at berries as a food group, we find that they have benefits for metabolic health as well as promoting healthy aging. Reviewing their nutritional composition, we find that other berries such as blackberries, black currants, blueberries, and raspberries also have notable levels of sirtuin-activating nutrients.

The same applies to nuts. Despite their calorific content, so beneficial are nuts that they actually promote weight loss and help shift inches from the waist. This is in addition to slashing the risk of chronic disease. While walnuts are our champion nut, sirtuin-activating nutrients are also found in chestnuts, pecans, pistachios, and even peanuts.

Then we switch our attention to grains. There has been a

growing aversion to grains in recent years in some quarters. Yet studies link whole-grain consumption to reduced inflammation, diabetes, heart disease, and cancer. While they don't rival the Sirtfood credentials of the pseudo-grain buckwheat, we do see the presence of significant sirtuin-activating nutrients in other whole grains. And needless to say, when whole grains are processed into refined "white" versions, their sirtuin-activating nutrient content is decimated. These refined versions are quite the toxic bunch, and are implicated in a plethora of modern-day health afflictions. We're not saying that you can never eat them, but rather that you will be much better off sticking with the whole-grain version whenever you can.

For those who want to remain gluten-free, quinoa is a good Sirtfood option. And for a great whole-grain Sirtfood snack loved by all, look no further than popcorn.

Even infamous "superfoods" get in on the act with the likes of goji berries and chia seeds having Sirtfood properties. This is most probably the unwitting reason for their observed health benefits. While it means they are indeed good for us to eat, we also know there are cheaper, more accessible, and better options out there, so don't feel compelled to jump on that particular bandwagon. We see this same pattern across many food groups. Unsurprisingly, these are usually the foods that science has established are good for us and that we should be eating more of. Below we have listed an additional forty foods that we have discovered also have Sirtfood properties. To maintain and continue your weight loss and well-being, we actively encourage you to include these foods as you really expand the repertoire of your diet.

Vegetables

- artichokes
- asparagus
- bok choy/pak choi
- broccoli
- frisée
- green beans
- shallots
- watercress
- white onions
- yellow endive

Fruits

- apples
- blackberries
- black currants
- black plums
- cranberries
- goji berries
- kumquats
- raspberries
- red grapes

Nuts and seeds

- chestnuts
- chia seeds
- peanuts

- pecan nuts
- pistachio nuts
- sunflower seeds

Grains and pseudo-grains
- popcorn
- quinoa
- whole-wheat flour

Beans
- fava beans
- white beans (e.g., cannellini or navy)

Herbs and spices
- chives
- cinnamon
- dill (fresh and dried)
- dried oregano
- dried sage
- ginger
- peppermint (fresh and dried)
- thyme (fresh and dried)

Beverages
- black tea
- white tea

PROTEIN POWER

A high-protein diet is one of the most popularized diets of recent years. The consumption of higher amounts of protein when dieting has been found to promote satiety, maintain metabolism, and reduce loss of muscle mass. But it's when Sirtfoods are combined with protein that things get taken to a whole new level.

As you may recall, protein is an essential inclusion in a Sirtfood-based diet to reap maximum benefits. Protein is made up of amino acids, and it is a specific amino acid, leucine, that powerfully complements the actions of Sirtfoods, enhancing their effects. It does this primarily by changing our cellular environment so that the sirtuin-activating nutrients from our diet work much more effectively. This means we get the best outcome from a Sirtfood-rich meal that is combined with leucine-rich protein. The best dietary sources of leucine include red meat, poultry, fish, seafood, eggs, and dairy.

Animal-Based Protein

In recent years animal products have been implicated as a contributing cause of many Western diseases, especially cancer. If that truly is the case, eating them with Sirtfoods might not seem such a bright idea. In order to lay that to rest, here's our lowdown.

One of the big concerns about dairy is that it's not just a simple food but a highly sophisticated signaling system for inducing rapid body growth in offspring. While this has a valued purpose in early life, in adult life it may not be so appropriate. Persistent and hyperactivation of the key growth signal that dairy triggers in the body (called mTOR) is now associated with aging and the development of age-related disorders such as obesity, type 2 diabetes, cancer, and neurodegenerative diseases.[1] Although the intricacies of this signaling system are a relatively new area of research and so still very much an unknown and theoretical risk, this lends validation to why people would shy away from dairy products. However, there is one thing research points to: if we add Sirtfoods to a diet containing dairy, they inhibit the inappropriate effects of mTOR on our cells, rescinding this risk, making Sirtfoods a must-include with a dairy-based diet.[2]

Overall, reviews of the link between dairy and cancer are mixed.[3-5] When we stack up all the research, in the context of a Sirtfood-rich diet, moderate dairy consumption is perfectly fine and can offer many valuable nutrients to complement Sirtfoods.

As well as being a valuable protein source, dairy is an excellent source of vitamins and minerals, such as iodine, calcium, and phosphorus. Our recommendation for adults is to consume up to three servings of dairy (but no more than about 1 quart [1 liter] of milk, or equivalent) a day.

When it comes to meat and cancer risk, poultry is perfectly okay, but red and processed meats are much more suspect. While evidence implicating them in breast and prostate cancer is pretty thin on the ground, there is legitimate concern that red and processed meat consumption plays a role in bowel cancer.[6] Processed meat, such as ham, hot dogs, and pepperoni, seems the worst culprit. While there is no need to strike it off the menu completely, it should be included in just small amounts instead of being a staple.

The good news about red meat is that research shows that cooking it with Sirtfoods rescinds its cancer risk, whether it be creating a marinade with herbs, spices, and extra virgin olive oil; cooking your beef with onions; or simply adding a nice cup of green tea to the meal or indulging in after-dinner dark chocolate. These all pack a Sirtfood punch that actually helps to neutralize red meat's harmful effects.[7-10] While we are all for having your steak and eating it, don't go overboard. Red meat intake is best kept below about 1 pound (500g) per week (cooked weight), which is roughly the equivalent of 1.5 pounds (700 to 750g) raw.

Poultry is an excellent source of protein, along with vitamins and minerals such as B vitamins, potassium, and phosphorus. Our recommendation for adults is to eat it freely.

Red meat is also an excellent source of protein, along with vitamins and minerals such as iron, zinc, and vitamin B_{12}. Our recommendation for adults is to eat up to a maximum of three servings a week.

The link between egg consumption and cancer risk has not been studied as thoroughly as meat and dairy products have, but in this regard there seems little reason for concern. Instead, what eggs have been implicated in causing is heart disease. This is because they are a major source of dietary cholesterol. Thus we are told to limit egg consumption. Interestingly, other countries, including Nepal, Thailand, and South Africa, recommend consuming eggs as often as every day for their nutritional benefits. So who is right? The evidence is convincing in siding with the latter. Daily egg consumption is not linked to any increased risk of coronary heart disease or stroke.[11] While specific genetic conditions may require reduced dietary cholesterol intake, for the general population this restriction is not relevant.

As well as being a valuable protein source, eggs are an excellent source of essential nutrients such as B vitamins, vitamin A, and carotenoids. Our recommendation for adults is to eat as desired as part of a balanced diet.

THE POWER OF THREE

The second major nutrient group that powerfully complements Sirtfoods is the omega-3 long-chain fatty acids EPA and DHA. For years omega-3s have been the cherished favorite of the nutritional health world. What we didn't know previously, which we do now, is that they also enhance the activity of a subset of sirtuin genes in the body that are directly linked to longevity. This makes them the perfect pairing with Sirtfoods.

Omega-3s have potent effects in reducing inflammation and reducing the level of fats in the blood. To that we can add additional heart-healthy effects: they make the blood less likely to clot, stabilize the electrical rhythm of the heart, and bring down blood pressure. Even the pharmaceutical industry is now turning to them as an aid in the battle against heart disease. And the litany of benefits doesn't end there. Omega-3s also affect the way we think, having been shown to improve mood as well as helping to stave off dementia.

When we talk about omega-3s we're essentially talking about eating fish, specifically the oily varieties, because no other dietary source comes close to providing the significant levels of EPA and DHA we need. And all we need in order to see the benefits is two servings of fish a week, with an emphasis on oily fish. Unfortunately, the United States is not a nation of big fish eaters, and fewer than one in five Americans achieve this. As a result, our intake of the precious EPA and DHA comes up woefully short.

Plant foods such as nuts, seeds, and green leafy vegetables also contain omega-3 but in a form called alpha-linolenic acid, which needs to be converted to EPA or DHA in the body. This conversion process is poor, which means that alpha-linolenic acid provides a negligible amount of our omega-3 needs. Even with the wonderful benefits from Sirtfoods, we should not overlook the added value that consuming sufficient levels of omega-3 fats brings. The best omega-3 fish sources are herring, sardines, salmon, trout, and mackerel, in that order. While fresh tuna is naturally high too, the majority of the omega-3 is lost in the tinned version. And for vegetarians and vegans, while plant sources should still be incorporated into the diet, a supplement of DHA-enriched microalgae (up to 300 milligrams a day) is also encouraged.

As well as being a valuable omega-3 and protein source, oily fish is an excellent source of vitamins and minerals such as vitamins A and D, B vitamins, and trace minerals including iodine and zinc. The recommendation for adults is to eat at least two servings of fish, of which one is oily fish, a week.

CAN A SIRTFOOD DIET PROVIDE IT ALL?

So far our focus has been solely on Sirtfoods and reaping their maximum benefits so that we can achieve the body we want and powerfully boost our health in the process. But is this a responsible dietary approach to be taking for the long term? After all, there is more to diet than just sirtuin-activating nutrients. What about all the vitamins, minerals, and fiber that are also essential for our well-being, and the foods we should be eating to satisfy those demands?

Intriguingly, what we find is that when we keep a strong focus on Sirtfoods, complemented by protein-rich foods and sources of omega-3, dietary needs are satisfied across the whole spectrum of essential nutrients—much more so than by any other diet, in fact. For example, we include kale because it is a potent Sirtfood, yet it is also a great source of vitamins C and K, folate, and the minerals manganese, calcium, and magnesium. As well as immune-boosting beta-carotene, kale is also a tremendous source of the carotenoids lutein and zeaxanthin, both of which are critical in eye health.

Likewise, walnuts are rich in minerals including magnesium,

copper, zinc, manganese, calcium, and iron, as well as fiber. Buckwheat is full of manganese, copper, magnesium, potassium, and fiber. Onions tick the boxes for vitamin B_6, folate, potassium, and fiber. And strawberries are excellent sources of vitamin C as well as potassium and manganese. And so it goes on.

Once you broaden your diet to include the extended Sirtfood list, as well as keeping room for all those other good foods you enjoy eating, unwittingly what you will actually end up with is a diet far richer in vitamins, minerals, and fiber than you ever had before. In effect, what Sirtfoods offer is a missing food group that changes the landscape of how we judge how good foods are for us, and how we eat a truly complete diet.

Rounding Out Plant-Based Diets

Sirtfoods are a celebration of the best plant foods on the planet. So it should come as no surprise that vegetarians, who naturally include more of them in their diet, have been shown to have lower rates of cancer, diabetes, heart disease, and obesity. Authorities such as the prestigious Academy of Nutrition and Dietetics are vociferous in their support of vegetarian diets, stating that they are healthful and nutritionally adequate, and may provide health benefits in the prevention and treatment of certain diseases.[12] Plant-based cooking is worthy of its own plaudits and deserving of a place on anyone's dinner table. Already you will have experienced this for yourself, with the inclusion of dishes such as the Butternut Squash and Date Tagine with Buckwheat (see page 195) in Phase 2 for vegetarians and carnivores alike, offering plant-based fare at its best.

However, when it comes to eating solely plant-based vegan diets, it's a different matter. As good as Sirtfoods are, the diet can come up short. Without animal protein to complement Sirtfoods, there is a risk of nutritional deficiencies.

We've already seen how essential omega-3 fatty acids are for health and how plant sources are lacking. Thus our recommendation for vegetarians and vegans is for a DHA-enriched microalgae supplement to be taken daily.

Vegetarians and especially vegans can also find themselves lacking vitamin B_{12}. We can only get vitamin B_{12} from animal products (including dairy and eggs), so eat nothing but plant foods and sooner or later you'll wind up deficient. If we become deficient in vitamin B_{12}, we put ourselves at increased risk of heart disease, anemia, neurological degeneration, depression, and dementia. If you wish to eat a strictly plant-based diet, the best way around this conundrum is to take vitamin B_{12} in the form of a supplement.

Calcium is another key nutrient vegans need to be aware of: there is a 30 percent greater incidence of fractures in vegans due to low calcium intake.[13] While it is possible to get calcium from a plant-based diet, you need to make a conscious effort. Good plant sources of calcium include green vegetables (e.g., kale, broccoli, bok choy), calcium-fortified beverages (soy milk, almond milk, rice milk), tofu set with calcium, nuts, and seeds. Even so, a moderate calcium supplement may be required.

Finally, very high rates of iodine deficiency (80 percent in vegans and 25 percent in vegetarians)[14] have been found in people eating solely plant-based diets. Iodine is vital for making thyroid hormones, which are absolutely critical in regulating metabolism. With dietary sources being fish, seafood, and milk, vegans run into trouble. Fortunately, consuming iodized salt is an effective means of boosting your iodine levels, and it is widely available in grocery stores. But for vegans not using an appreciable amount of iodized salt, a supplement is probably required. While seaweed is a very rich source of iodine, it can contain extremely high and potentially excessive levels, which is just as bad for the thyroid as getting too little, and should not be relied upon.

THE PHYSICAL ACTIVITY EFFECT

The Sirtfood Diet is about eating those foods designed by nature to promote sustained weight loss and well-being. But with the benefits you see from following the diet, it is possible to fall into the trap of thinking that there is no need to exercise. Many diet books will endorse this, saying how ineffective exercise is compared to following the correct diet for weight loss. And it's true, we cannot out-exercise a bad diet. As we saw earlier, it's not the way that was intended to drive weight loss. It's inefficient, and too much borders on being harmful. So it's true that there's no need to pound the treadmill until we are seeing stars or perform the feats of an Olympian—but what about general everyday movement?

The fact is we are far less active now than we used to be. The age of technology, for all the advances it has brought, has meant physical activity is virtually factored out of our daily lives. Unless we actually want to, we really don't have to bother with the whole business of being active. We can roll out of bed, drive to work, take the elevator, sit at a desk all day, drive home, eat, and watch TV before rolling into bed again, then do the same the next day, and the next.

Forget about weight loss for a moment and just take a look at the litany of health benefits being active is linked to. These include reduced risk of cardiovascular disease, stroke, hypertension, type 2 diabetes, osteoporosis, obesity, and cancer as well as improved mood, sleep, confidence, and sense of well-being. While a lot of the benefits of being active are driven through switching on our sirtuin genes, we should not use eating Sirtfoods as a reason not to engage in exercise. Rather we should appreciate how being active is the perfect complement to our consumption of Sirtfoods. This stimulates maximum sirtuin activation, and all the benefits that brings, exactly as nature intended.

What we are talking about here is meeting government guidelines of 150 minutes (2 hours and 30 minutes) of moderate physical activity a week. Moderate activity is the equivalent of a brisk walk. But it does not have to be restricted to this. Any sport or physical activity you enjoy is suitable. Enjoyment and exercise don't need to be mutually exclusive! And team or community sports are enriched all the more by their social aspect. It's about day-to-day things too, like taking the bike instead of the car, or getting off the bus one stop earlier, or simply parking farther away to increase the distance you have to walk. Take the stairs instead of the elevator. Go outside and do some gardening. Play with your kids in the park, or get out more with the dog. It all counts. Performed regularly, and at moderate intensity, anything that has you up and moving will activate your sirtuin genes, enhancing the benefits of the Sirtfood Diet.

Engaging in physical activity while eating a Sirtfood-rich diet gives maximum sirtuin bang for your buck. All that is needed to achieve the physical activity effect is the equivalent of a brisk 30-minute walk five times a week.

Summary

- While the top twenty Sirtfoods should remain in the center of the plate, there are many other plants with sirtuin-activating properties that should be included in our diets to make them varied and diverse.

- A diet rich in Sirtfoods complemented by the inclusion of animal products and fish provides all the benefits of sirtuin activation, as well as meeting the need for other essential nutrients.

- While vegans and vegetarians can get all the benefits from a Sirtfood-based diet, careful attention should be given to those nutrients that may be lacking and appropriate food choices or supplementation made.

- Followers of the Sirtfood Diet are encouraged to engage in moderate activity for thirty minutes five times a week to reap the many benefits of exercise for well-being and stimulate maximum sirtuin activation.

12

Sirtfoods for All

As we journeyed deeper and deeper into the wonderful world of Sirtfoods, we began to realize just how wide their application could be. We're very aware that no two people eat the same, and many health-conscious people are strongly committed to a certain way of eating, with the likes of paleo, low-carb, intermittent fasting, and gluten-free diets being especially popular. While they don't work for some, others swear by them. But just how do Sirtfoods fit in with these?

A lightbulb moment struck with the realization that every single one of these popular diets would be greatly enhanced if Sirtfoods were integrated into them. The benefits people were deriving from them—health or weight loss—could be amplified simply through the addition of Sirtfoods in sufficient quantities. In this way, Sirtfoods are universal: if there's a way of eating that really works for you, incorporating Sirtfoods into it will make your results even better.

We're both busy clinicians, and as our enthusiasm for Sirtfoods has grown, we have integrated Sirtfoods more and more strongly into the diets of the clients we work with, no matter what their preferred way of eating. Our conclusion is clear: not only are Sirtfoods compatible with all other dietary approaches, they powerfully enhance them. In fact, they should be essential ingredients in every popular diet. Overlook them and you're really missing a trick.

PALEO DIET

In a nutshell, the paleo diet promotes the idea that we should eat the foods that it is presumed our ancient ancestors were eating, before the advent of modern agriculture and more recently industrial food processing. In essence we're talking a hunter-gatherer or caveman style of diet, consisting of meats, fish and shellfish, vegetables, fruits, and nuts, while exiled to the wilderness are dairy products, cereal grains, sugar, and all processed foods.

For paleo dieters, we pose this question: what could be more paleo than eating the plant foods with which we've coevolved that switch on our ancient sirtuin genes? You will recall that both plants and animals have developed ways of coping with common environmental stresses such as dehydration, sun exposure, lack of nutrients, and attack by aggressors. Because of their sedentary nature (they can't run away!), plants have developed especially sophisticated stress-response systems, producing a complex array of polyphenols that allow them to cope with their environment. For millennia, humans have been ingesting these polyphenols, piggybacking on these sophisticated stress-response signals produced by plants and reaping huge benefits as they switch on our own sirtuin genes.

What could be more paleo than consuming the sirtuin-activating plant compounds our hunter-gatherer forebears would have thrived on? Sirtfoods are the missing piece of the paleo philosophy.

LOW-CARB DIET

Ever since Atkins, the father of low-carb diets, rose to meteoric notoriety, low-carb diets have been a major landmark on the weight-loss map. Subsequent reincarnations, such as the Dukan diet, have continued to fuel the low-carb movement. Among them, they have notched diet-book sales up to the tens of millions. While such low-carb diets can be extreme, especially in their early "assault" phases, their broad sentiments do reflect a wider shift in opinion toward an antisugar and even anticarb stance. Increasingly people are abandoning the sinking ship of the low-fat paradigm and shifting allegiances to the "carbs are the enemy" camp.

One of the beauties of the Sirtfood Diet is that it doesn't involve this territorial conflict. It's a diet of inclusion, which means that you really don't have to choose sides and exclude a whole food group from your diet in order to achieve the body you want. Nevertheless, we appreciate that many people have a preference for a lower-carb style of eating, so where do Sirtfoods fit in?

If your persuasion is toward low-carb, then we urge you not to scrimp on Sirtfoods, but to embrace them. In our clinical experience, one of the biggest traps we see people fall into when eating low-carb diets is the lack of plant-based foods they contain. Meals become heavily oriented around meats (and often processed meats), fish, eggs, cheese, and other dairy products, and plant-based foods get relegated to the bottom of the pecking order. But if it's low carb, it's all good . . . or so we're told.

Alas, the idea that plant-based foods aren't of central importance in our diets flies in the face of virtually everything we know about diet and health. A diet depleted of the vast array of beneficial compounds found in plant foods will do little to avert an avalanche of chronic diseases such as dementia, heart disease, and cancer. Yet it is perfectly possible to integrate an abundance of Sirtfoods into a carb-restricted way of eating. Just look at the top twenty list of Sirtfoods and you will discover that a vast majority of them are inherently low in carbs. We're talking about a bounty of leafy and low-carb vegetables (arugula, celery, endive, kale, onions), culinary herbs (garlic, parsley), spices (chili, turmeric), capers, walnuts, cocoa, and extra virgin olive oil, not forgetting the beverages (coffee and green tea). As for fruit, so often the target of attack on low-carb diets, even the strawberries weigh in with a mere teaspoon of carbohydrates from a generous 3½-ounce (100g) serving.

For us the bottom line is this: no low-carb diet should be a low-Sirtfood diet. Not only does incorporating Sirtfoods enhance the weight-loss benefits of a low-carb diet, but it dramatically increases its health potential.

INTERMITTENT FASTING/THE 5:2 DIET

Intermittent fasting, also known as IF, has become a huge dietary phenomenon in the last few years, epitomized by the runaway success of the 5:2 diet. This typically involves restricting calorie intake to 500 to 600 calories per day on two days per week, and eating whatever you want on the other five days.

While solid research into the benefits of intermittent fasting is still pretty limited, it does appear to be beneficial for weight loss and improving some of the risk factors for disease. But as we've seen, it's not suitable for large segments of the population, it causes undesirable muscle loss, and it's only effective if you can stick to it. And that really is the elephant in the room when it comes to intermittent fasting and why we're not overly enamored with it. In our clinical experience, the majority of people fail to stick to intermittent fasting regimens for any appreciable length of time. Hunger is an unpleasant feeling that gnaws away at you, so unsurprisingly people just don't like to feel hungry that often.

While intermittent fasting has not turned out to be a panacea, it is popular for a reason, and there will be fans who swear by its benefits. We fully respect this, of course. But why not give your fast a serious upgrade by "Sirtifying" it?

With the introduction of Sirtfoods, you will get all the benefits they bring to reduce the adverse effects of fasting, including helping to satiate hunger and preserve muscle. But there's another big bonus to their inclusion. You will remember that the benefits of fasting are mediated through the activation of our sirtuin genes, which is also exactly how Sirtfoods work. This means with Sirtfoods now present to share the fasting "burden," you can up your calorie intake to a much more manageable level while still reaping all the same benefits.

This is exactly what we have found in our clinical practice. With just the inclusion of Sirtfood-rich green juices (the same recipe used in this book) in a normal IF menu, followers have been able to increase their energy intake from a severe 500 to 600 calories on fast days to a much more manageable 800 to 1,000 calories.

So if your penchant is for intermittent fasting, you're missing a trick and making fast days unduly grueling by not embracing Sirtfoods. In fact, there's a whole other angle from which intermittent fasting diets would benefit by embracing Sirtfoods. With IF diets there's very little, if any, focus on the *quality* of the food; it's all about the calorie deficit on fast days. In fact, proponents are vociferous in endorsing the idea that you can eat whatever you want on non-fast days. Whether what you eat is good, bad, or outright terrible doesn't really seem to matter. But, as we know, the body needs a continuous supply of essential nutrients to keep everything working in tip-top shape. Can we really expect to get away with depriving the body of critical nutrition by eating whatever nutrient-stripped, processed foods we want, even if we are fasting for two days, and stave off chronic diseases like Alzheimer's or heart disease?

What if, on the other hand, you also included nutrient-dense Sirtfoods on your non-fasting days? You would no longer be burning fat and enhancing health just two days a week—it would now be seven. To us this evolution of the intermittent fasting approach is a no-brainer. It's the equivalent of upgrading a black-and-white TV to full-color HD.

GLUTEN-FREE DIET

The beauty of the Sirtfood Diet for anyone who needs to avoid gluten is that the top twenty Sirtfoods are all naturally gluten-free. Gluten is a type of protein found in wheat, rye, and barley. Some people with gluten intolerance can also be sensitive to oats (through cross-contamination). Sufferers of the autoimmune disorder celiac disease, which affects as many as 1 in 100 people in America, are hypersensitive to gluten and cannot consume it in any form, but aside from this very serious gluten intolerance, many people are increasingly experimenting with gluten-free diets and often find they feel better on them.

When people embark on gluten-free diets, which involve cutting out staples such as bread, pasta, and the myriad of other foods made from gluten-containing grains, one of the big concerns is that the diet becomes nutritionally incomplete and no longer provides the full range of nutrients and fiber needed to stay in good health. What's so great about the Sirtfood Diet is that one of our top Sirtfoods is buckwheat, a naturally gluten-free and highly nutritious pseudo-grain, which, as we have seen through the preceding chapters, is versatile enough to step in as a replacement for gluten-containing grains, whether in the form of flour, pasta, flakes, or noodles (check the package carefully to ensure that these are 100 percent buckwheat).

Of course, the best diets are the ones that are diverse and varied, not repetitive and monotonous. We saw that quinoa, another pseudo-grain, is not only gluten-free but also has noteworthy amounts of sirtuin-activating nutrients, making it the perfect backup to buckwheat. Aside from its usual guise as a grain, quinoa is increasingly available in the form of flour, flakes, and pasta from health-food stores and specialty online suppliers. With quinoa and buckwheat taking center stage, it's happy days for anyone adopting a gluten-free diet: not only do they offer a convenient alternative to other grains, but including them as staple foods adds some serious Sirtfood credentials to the average diet.

We cannot leave the topic of gluten-free diets without a word of warning about the mass of gluten-free junk food that now fills up the "free from" shelves in every supermarket. These are the highly processed, refined, sugary, gluten-free alternatives to cakes, biscuits, cookies, breakfast cereals, and so on. This has become a huge industry, but please don't fall into the trap of thinking that just because a product is gluten-free it is necessarily healthy. The majority of these foods are nutritionally empty junk, just like their gluten-containing counterparts. If you are following a gluten-free diet, we urge you to fill up on a diet rich in naturally gluten-free Sirtfoods, not gluten-free junk, and take your health and well-being to a whole new level.

SUMMARY

- Sirtfoods are not only compatible with all other dietary approaches but powerfully enhance their benefits.
- Sirtfoods are the archetypal paleo foods, containing the sirtuin-activating polyphenols that humans have evolved eating, and reaping the benefits from, over countless millennia.
- Low-carb diets that lack plant-based foods can be dramatically enhanced by the inclusion of Sirtfoods.
- Eating a diet rich in Sirtfoods means that the calorie restriction of intermittent fasting can be less severe, yet the benefits will be the same if not greater.
- The top twenty Sirtfoods are naturally gluten-free, making them a boon for anyone following a gluten-free diet.

13

Questions and Answers

Should I Exercise During Phase 1?

Regular exercise is one of the best things you can do for your health, and doing some moderate exercise will enhance the weight-loss and health benefits of Phase 1 of the diet. As a general rule, we encourage you to continue your normal level of exercise and physical activity through the first seven days of the Sirtfood Diet. However, we suggest staying within your normal comfort zone, since prolonged or overly intense exercise may simply place too much stress on the body for this period. Listen to your body. There's no need to push yourself to do more exercise during Phase 1; let the Sirtfoods do the hard work instead.

I'm Already Slim—Can I Still Follow the Diet?

We do not recommend Phase 1 of the Sirtfood Diet for anyone who is underweight. A good way to find out if you are underweight is to calculate your body mass index or BMI. As long as you know your height and weight, you can easily determine this by using one of the numerous BMI calculators online. If your BMI is 18.5 or less, we don't recommend that you embark on Phase 1 of the diet. If your BMI is between 18.5 and 20, we would still urge caution, since following the diet may mean that your BMI falls below 18.5. While many people aspire to be super-skinny, the reality is that being underweight can negatively affect many aspects of health, contributing to a lowered immune system, an elevated risk of osteoporosis (weakening of the bones), and fertility problems. While we don't recommend Phase 1 of the diet if you are underweight, we do still encourage the integration of plenty of Sirtfoods into a balanced way of eating so that all the health benefits of these foods can be reaped.

However, if you are slim but have a BMI in the healthy range (20–25), there is absolutely nothing stopping you from getting started. A majority of the participants involved in the pilot trial had BMIs in the healthy range, yet still lost impressive amounts of weight and became more toned. Importantly, many of them reported a significant improvement in energy levels, vitality, and appearance. Remember that the Sirtfood Diet is about promoting health as much as it is about losing weight.

I'm Obese—Is the Sirtfood Diet Right for Me?

Yes! Don't be put off by the fact that only a small minority of the participants who embarked on our pilot study were obese. This is because the pilot study was carried out in a health and fitness club where people are generally fitter and more health-conscious. Instead, be spurred on by the fact that the few who were obese had even better results than our healthy-weight participants. These results have been replicated by the thousands of people who have tried the diet in the real world. Based on the research into sirtuin activation, you should also stand to reap the greatest changes in your well-being. Being obese increases the risk of numerous chronic health problems, yet these are the very illnesses that Sirtfoods help to protect against.

I've Reached My Target Weight and Don't Want to Lose Any More—Do I Stop Eating Sirtfoods?

First, congratulations on your weight-loss achievement! You've had great success with Sirtfoods, but it does not end now. While we do not recommend further calorie restriction, your diet should still provide ample Sirtfoods. Many of our clients are now at their ideal body composition but continue to eat Sirtfood-rich diets. The great thing about Sirtfoods is that they are a way of life. The best way to think about them with regard to weight management is that they help bring the body to the weight and composition it was meant to be. From here they work to maintain and keep you looking and feeling great. This is ultimately the goal we desire for all Sirtfood Diet followers.

I've Finished Phase 2—Do I Stop Drinking the Morning Sirtfood Green Juice Now?

The green juice is our favorite way to get a fantastic hit of Sirtfoods to start the day, so we endorse its long-term consumption. Our Sirtfood green juice was carefully designed to include ingredients that provide a full spectrum of sirtuin-activating nutrients in potent fat-burning and well-being boosting doses. However, we are all for variety, and while we do recommend you continue with a morning juice, we fully support anyone looking to experiment with different Sirtfood juice concoctions.

I Take Medication—Is it Okay to Follow the Diet?

The Sirtfood Diet is suitable for most people, but because of its powerful effects on fat burning and health, it can alter certain disease processes and the actions of medication prescribed by your doctor. Likewise, certain medications are not suitable in a fasting state.

During the trial of the Sirtfood Diet, we assessed the suitability of each person before he or she embarked on the diet, especially those who were taking medication. Obviously we can't do that for you, so if you suffer from a significant health problem, take prescribed medications, or have other reasons to be concerned about embarking on the diet, we recommend you discuss it with your doctor first. The chances are it will be fine and actually of profound benefit for you, but it's important to check.

Can I Follow the Diet if I'm Pregnant?

We don't recommend embarking on the Sirtfood Diet if you are trying to conceive or if you are pregnant or breastfeeding. It is a powerful weight-loss diet, which makes it unsuitable. However, don't be put off eating plenty of Sirtfoods, since these are exceptionally healthy foods to include as part of a balanced and varied diet for pregnancy. You will want to avoid red wine, due to its alcohol content, and limit caffeinated items such as coffee, green tea, and cocoa so as not to exceed 200 milligrams per day of caffeine during pregnancy (one mug of instant coffee typically contains around 100 milligrams of caffeine). Recommendations are not to exceed four cups of green tea daily and to avoid matcha altogether. Other than that, you're free to reap the benefits of including Sirtfoods in your diet.

Are Sirtfoods Suitable for Children?

The Sirtfood Diet is a powerful weight-loss diet and not designed for children. However, that doesn't mean that children should miss out on the excellent health benefits offered by including more Sirtfoods in their general diet. A vast majority of Sirtfoods represent extremely healthy foods for children and help them achieve balanced and nutritious diets. Many of the recipes designed for Phase 2 of the diet were created with families in mind, including children's taste buds. The likes of the Sirtfood pizza (see page 210), the chili con carne (see page 202), and the Sirtfood bites (see page 213) are perfect child-friendly foods with a nutritional value superior to usual food offerings for children.

While the majority of Sirtfoods are extremely healthy for children to eat, we do not recommend the green juice, which is too concentrated in fat-burning Sirtfoods. We also advise against significant sources of caffeine such as coffee and green tea. You will also need to be careful with the inclusion of chilies and may opt to keep things milder for children.

Will I Get a Headache or Feel Tired During Phase 1?
Phase 1 of the Sirtfood Diet provides powerful naturally occurring food compounds in amounts that most people would not get in their normal diet, and certain people can react as they adapt to this dramatic nutritional change. This can include symptoms such as a mild headache or tiredness, although in our experience these effects are minor and short-lived.

Of course, if symptoms are severe or give you reason for concern, we recommend you seek prompt medical advice. Having said that, we have never seen anything other than occasional mild symptoms that resolve quickly, and within a few days most people find they have a renewed sense of energy, vigor, and well-being.

Should I Take Supplements?
Unless specifically prescribed for you by your doctor or other health-care professional, we do not recommend indiscriminate use of nutritional supplements. You will be ingesting a vast and synergistic array of natural-plant compounds from Sirtfoods, and it is these that will do you good. You cannot replicate these benefits

with nutritional supplements and, in fact, some nutritional supplements such as antioxidants, especially if taken at high doses, may actually interfere with the beneficial effects of Sirtfoods, which is the last thing you want.

Whenever possible, we think it is much better to get the nutrients you need from eating a balanced diet rich in Sirtfoods than from taking nutrients in pill form. Vegans will, however, have special nutritional considerations, and our specific recommendations for those following purely plant-based diets can be found on pages 131–132. Additionally, because plant proteins are lower in leucine, the amino acid that enhances the actions of Sirtfoods, we have found that vegans can benefit from supplementing their diet with a suitable vegan protein powder. This particularly applies to those engaging in high levels of exercise. This supplement should be taken at a separate time of day from the Sirtfood green juice.

How Often Can I Repeat Phases 1 and 2?

Phase 1 can be repeated again if you feel like you need a weight-loss or health boost. To ensure that there are no long-term negative effects to your metabolism from calorie restriction, you should wait at least a month before repeating. But we actually find that most people need to repeat it no more frequently than once every three months at most and continue to get amazing results. Instead, if you find you've gone off track, need some fine-tuning, or want a bit more Sirtfood intensity, we recommend repeating some or all days of the Phase 2 section as often as you like. After all, Phase 2 is all about establishing a lifelong way of eating. Remember, the beauty of the Sirtfood Diet is that it doesn't require you to feel like you are endlessly on a diet, but instead is the springboard to developing lifelong positive dietary changes that create a lighter, leaner, healthier you.

Does the Sirtfood Diet Provide Enough Fiber?

Many Sirtfoods are naturally rich in fiber. Onions, endive, and walnuts are notable sources, with buckwheat and Medjool dates really standing out, meaning that a Sirtfood-rich diet doesn't fall short in the fiber department. Even during Phase 1, when food consumption is reduced, most of us will still be consuming a fiber quantity we are used to, especially if we choose the recipes that contain buckwheat, beans, and lentils from the menu options. However, for others known to be susceptible to gut issues like constipation without higher fiber intakes, during Phase 1, especially Days 1 to 3, a suitable fiber supplement can be considered, which should be discussed with your health-care professional.

I've Read About Superfoods—Should I Be Including These in My Diet Too?

The first thing you need to know about the term *superfood* is that it is not a scientific term at all but a marketing slogan. You do not need to concern yourself with so-called superfoods because the Sirtfood Diet brings together the healthiest foods on the planet into a revolutionary new way of eating. Just as it is a mistake to rely on taking a simple vitamin pill to make us healthy, so too it is a mistake to rely on a single superfood to do the same. It is the whole diet, made up of a wide spectrum of Sirtfoods and their vast array of natural compounds, acting in synergy, that is the true secret to achieving weight loss and lifelong health.

Do I Have to Do Phase 1 for Seven Days—Can I Do Fewer?

There's nothing magical about Phase 1 being seven days. It is simply what we decided upon for our trial. We opted for that because it was long enough to get impressive results, but not so long that it became arduous. It also fits neatly into people's lives. Seven days is what was tested and what is proven to be effective. However, if for whatever reason you find that you need to cut it short by a day or two, do so by completing up to the end of Day 5 or Day 6. Don't worry, you will still reap the lion's share of the benefits.

Can I Eat Whatever I Want Once I Eat Plenty of Sirtfoods and Still See Results?

One of the key reasons the Sirtfood Diet works so well long-term is that it promotes good food instead of demonizing bad food. Diets of exclusion simply do not work long-term. It is true that processed foods that are high in sugars and fats reduce sirtuin activity in the body, and thus a high consumption will reduce the benefits of Sirtfoods. However, if you keep your focus on consuming a diet rich in Sirtfoods, in our experience you will find that you are pleasantly satisfied and will have less desire for those processed foods and end up consuming far less junk than the average person as a result. If you do occasionally find yourself indulging in these processed foods, don't worry about it—the power of Sirtfoods the rest of the time will make sure you still reap the benefits.

Can I Eat as Many Sirtfoods, Even the High-Calorie Ones, as I Like and Still Lose Weight?

Yes! Remember, calories and the drive to count them are a modern-day "advancement." Across the cultures and countless generations that have benefited from Sirtfoods, such a concept did not exist, and there simply was no need. People ate as they felt like it, and stayed slim and free of disease. Given Sirtfoods' effects on regulating metabolism and appetite, you simply do not need to worry about eating too many of them. While this is not an invitation to an all-you-can-eat challenge, feel free to eat as much Sirtfood as you like to satisfy your natural appetite. Our one exception is Medjool dates. Their inclusion showcases how high-sugar foods do not have to be bad for you when eaten in the form nature intended, and in moderation. But moderation is key to making dates a guilt-free indulgent treat. In terms of drinks, when it comes to red wine consumption, it goes without saying it should be drunk responsibly and safely within government recommendations.

Is Organic Better?

In an ideal world, we would encourage you to opt for organic produce where possible, practical, and affordable. While there is little evidence that levels of conventional vitamins and minerals differ between organic and nonorganic produce, what about the sirtuin-activating nutrients?

It is likely that organic produce carries a richer content of sirtuin-activating nutrients. Remember that the sirtuin-activating polyphenols found in plant foods are produced in response to environmental stresses, and without the intense use of pesticides, organically grown produce will have to battle that much harder to deter and ward off environmental predators. This is likely to result in higher levels of polyphenols being produced, making organic produce potentially a more powerful Sirtfood than its nonorganic equivalent. While organic is preferable, you will still get great results from the Sirtfood Diet if you opt for nonorganic produce. Organic is just the cherry on top.

14

Recipes

Some important notes about these recipes:

- The recipes specify Thai chilies (also known as bird's-eye chilies). If you have never tried them, they are notably hotter than normal chilies. If you are not used to spicy food, we suggest starting off with a milder chili, such as serrano, adapting the amount to suit your taste. As you get more accustomed to regularly including chilies in your diet, you may find that you start to enjoy hotter varieties, so please feel free to experiment.
- Miso is a delicious flavor-packed fermented soybean paste. You will find it comes in a range of colors, typically white, yellow, red, and brown. The lighter-colored miso pastes are sweeter than the dark ones, which can be quite salty. For our recipes, brown or red miso will work well, but by all means experiment and see which flavor you prefer. Red miso tends to be the saltier of these, so if you opt for this one, you might prefer to use a

little less of it. The flavor and saltiness of miso can also vary between brands, so the best bet would be to check whatever type you buy and adjust the amount you use accordingly, so it's not too overpowering. That means a little trial and error, but you'll soon get the hang of it.

- If you haven't cooked buckwheat before, it couldn't be easier. We recommend that you first thoroughly wash the buckwheat in a sieve before placing it in a pan of boiling water. Cooking times can vary, so do check the instructions on your package.

- Flat-leaf parsley would be best for all the dishes, but if you can't get hold of it, curly will do.

- Onions, garlic, and ginger are always peeled unless otherwise stated.

- Salt and pepper are not used in these recipes, but feel free to season with sea salt and black pepper to your own taste preferences. Sirtfoods offer so much flavor, you will likely find you do not need as much as you normally use. The addition of black pepper to any dish that contains turmeric is highly recommended, as it will help increase the absorption of its key sirtuin-activating nutrient, curcumin.

ASIAN SHRIMP STIR-FRY WITH
BUCKWHEAT NOODLES

SERVES 1

⅓ pound (150g) shelled raw jumbo shrimp, deveined

2 teaspoons tamari (or soy sauce, if you are not avoiding gluten)

2 teaspoons extra virgin olive oil

3 ounces (75g) soba (buckwheat noodles)

2 garlic cloves, finely chopped

1 Thai chili, finely chopped

1 teaspoon finely chopped fresh ginger

⅛ cup (20g) red onions, sliced

½ cup (45g) celery including leaves, trimmed and sliced, with leaves
set aside

½ cup (75g) green beans, chopped

¾ cup (50g) kale, roughly chopped

½ cup (100ml) chicken stock

Heat a frying pan over high heat, then cook the shrimp in 1 teaspoon of the tamari and 1 teaspoon of the oil for 2 to 3 minutes. Transfer the shrimp to a plate. Wipe the pan out with a paper towel, as you're going to use it again.

Cook the noodles in boiling water for 5 to 8 minutes or as directed on the package. Drain and set aside.

Meanwhile, fry the garlic, chili, ginger, red onion, celery (but not the leaves), green beans, and kale in the remaining tamari and oil over medium-high heat for 2 to 3 minutes. Add the stock and bring to a boil, then simmer for a minute or two, until the vegetables are cooked but still crunchy.

Add the shrimp, noodles, and celery leaves to the pan, bring back to a boil, then remove from the heat and serve.

MISO AND SESAME GLAZED TOFU WITH GINGER AND CHILI STIR-FRIED GREENS

SERVES 1

1 tablespoon mirin

3½ teaspoons (20g) miso paste

1 x 5-ounce (150g) block of firm tofu

1 stalk (40g) celery, trimmed (about ⅓ cup when sliced)

¼ cup (40g) red onion, sliced

1 small (120g) zucchini (about 1 cup when sliced)

1 Thai chili

2 garlic cloves

1 teaspoon finely chopped fresh ginger

¾ cup (50g) kale, chopped

2 teaspoons sesame seeds

¼ cup (35g) buckwheat

1 teaspoon ground turmeric

2 teaspoons extra virgin olive oil

1 teaspoon tamari (or soy sauce, if you are not avoiding gluten)

Heat the oven to 400°F (200°C). Line a small roasting pan with parchment paper.

Mix the mirin and miso together. Cut the tofu lengthways, then cut each piece diagonally in half into triangles. Cover the tofu with the miso mixture and leave to marinate while you prepare the other ingredients.

Slice the celery, red onion, and zucchini on the angle. Finely chop the chili, garlic, and ginger and set aside.

Cook the kale in a steamer for 5 minutes. Remove and set aside.

Place the tofu in the roasting pan, sprinkle the sesame seeds over the tofu, and roast in the oven for 15 to 20 minutes, until nicely caramelized.

Wash the buckwheat in a sieve, then place in a pan of boiling water along with the turmeric. Cook according to the package instructions, then drain.

Heat the oil in a frying pan; when hot add the celery, onion, zucchini, chili, garlic, and ginger and fry on high heat for 1 to 2 minutes, then reduce to medium heat for 3 to 4 minutes until the vegetables are cooked through but still crunchy. You may need to add a tablespoon of water if the vegetables start to stick to the pan. Add the kale and tamari and cook for another minute.

When the tofu is ready, serve with the greens and buckwheat.

TURKEY ESCALOPE WITH SAGE, CAPERS, AND PARSLEY AND SPICED CAULIFLOWER "COUSCOUS"

Thin cutlets are best, but if you can only find turkey breast, there are two ways to turn it into an escalope. Depending on how thick the breast is, you can either use a meat tenderizer, a hammer, or a rolling pin to pound the steak until it is around ¼ inch (5mm) thick. Or, if you feel the breast is too thick for this to work, and you have a steady hand, cut the breast in half horizontally and then pound each piece with the tenderizer.

SERVES 1

1½ cups (150g) cauliflower, roughly chopped

2 garlic cloves, finely chopped

¼ cup (40g) red onion, finely chopped

1 Thai chili, finely chopped

1 teaspoon finely chopped fresh ginger

2 tablespoons extra virgin olive oil

2 teaspoons ground turmeric

½ cup (30g) sun-dried tomatoes, finely chopped

¼ cup (10g) fresh parsley, chopped

⅓ pound (150g) turkey cutlet or steak (see above)

1 teaspoon dried sage

juice of ¼ lemon

1 tablespoon capers

To make the "couscous," place the raw cauliflower in a food processor. Pulse in 2-second bursts to finely chop the cauliflower until it resembles couscous. Alternatively, you can just use a knife and chop it very finely.

Fry the garlic, red onion, chili, and ginger in 1 teaspoon of the oil until soft but not browned. Add the turmeric and cauliflower and cook for 1 minute. Remove from heat and add the sun-dried tomatoes and half the parsley.

Coat the turkey escalope in the sage and a little oil, then use remaining oil to fry in a frying pan over medium heat for 5 to 6 minutes, turning regularly. When cooked through, add the lemon juice, remaining parsley, capers, and 1 tablespoon of water to the pan. This will create a sauce to serve with the cauliflower.

KALE AND RED ONION DAL WITH BUCKWHEAT

SERVES 1

1 teaspoon extra virgin olive oil

1 teaspoon mustard seeds

¼ cup (40g) red onion, finely chopped

2 garlic cloves, finely chopped

1 teaspoon finely chopped fresh ginger

1 Thai chili, finely chopped

1 teaspoon mild curry powder (medium or hot,
    if you prefer)

2 teaspoons ground turmeric

1¼ cups (300ml) vegetable stock or water

¼ cup (40g) red lentils, rinsed

¾ cup (50g) kale, chopped

3½ tablespoons (50ml) tinned coconut milk

⅓ cup (50g) buckwheat

Heat the oil in a medium saucepan over medium heat and add the mustard seeds. As the mustard seeds start to pop, add the onion, garlic, ginger, and chili. Cook for about 10 minutes, until soft.

Add the curry powder and 1 teaspoon of the turmeric and cook the spices for a couple of minutes. Add the stock and bring to a boil. Add the lentils to the pan and simmer for a further 25 to 30 minutes until the lentils are cooked through and you have a smooth dal.

Add the kale and coconut milk and cook for 5 minutes more.

Meanwhile, cook the buckwheat according to the package instructions with the remaining teaspoon of turmeric. Drain and serve alongside the dal.

AROMATIC CHICKEN BREAST WITH KALE AND RED ONIONS AND A TOMATO AND CHILI SALSA

SERVES 1

¼ pound (120g) skinless, boneless chicken breast

2 teaspoons ground turmeric

juice of ¼ lemon

1 tablespoon extra virgin olive oil

¾ cup (50g) kale, chopped

⅛ cup (20g) red onion, sliced

1 teaspoon chopped fresh ginger

⅓ cup (50g) buckwheat

FOR THE SALSA

1 medium tomato (130g)

1 Thai chili, finely chopped

1 tablespoon capers, finely chopped

2 tablespoons (5g) parsley, finely chopped

juice of ¼ lemon

To make the salsa, remove the eye from the tomato and chop it very finely, taking care to keep as much of the liquid as possible. Mix with the chili, capers, parsley, and lemon juice. You could put everything in a blender, but the end result is a little different.

Heat the oven to 425°F (220°C). Marinate the chicken breast in 1 teaspoon of the turmeric, the lemon juice, and a little oil. Leave for 5 to 10 minutes.

Heat an ovenproof frying pan until hot, then add the marinated chicken and cook for a minute or so on each side, until pale golden, then transfer to the oven (place on a baking tray if your pan isn't ovenproof) for 8 to 10 minutes or until cooked through. Remove from the oven, cover with foil, and leave to rest for 5 minutes before serving.

Meanwhile, cook the kale in a steamer for 5 minutes. Fry the red onions and the ginger in a little oil, until soft but not browned, then add the cooked kale and fry for another minute.

Cook the buckwheat according to the package instructions with the remaining teaspoon of turmeric. Serve alongside the chicken, vegetables, and salsa.

HARISSA BAKED TOFU WITH
CAULIFLOWER "COUSCOUS"

SERVES 1

⅜ cup (60g) red bell pepper

1 Thai chili, halved

2 garlic cloves

about 1 tablespoon extra virgin olive oil

pinch of ground cumin

pinch of ground coriander

juice of ¼ lemon

7 ounces (200g) firm tofu

1¾ cups (200g) cauliflower, roughly chopped

¼ cup (40g) red onion, finely chopped

1 teaspoon finely chopped fresh ginger

2 teaspoons ground turmeric

½ cup (30g) sun-dried tomatoes, finely chopped

½ cup (20g) parsley, chopped

Heat the oven to 400°F (200°C).

To make the harissa, slice the red pepper lengthwise around the core so you have nice flat slices, remove any seeds, then place in a roasting pan with the chili and one of the garlic cloves. Toss with a little oil and the dried cumin and coriander and roast in the oven for 15 to 20 minutes until the peppers are soft but not too browned. (Leave the oven on at this setting.) Cool, then blend in a food processor with the lemon juice until smooth.

Slice the tofu lengthways and then cut each half diagonally into triangles. Place in a small nonstick roasting pan or one lined with parchment paper, cover with the harissa, and roast in the oven for 20 minutes—the tofu should have absorbed the marinade and turned dark red.

To make the "couscous," place the raw cauliflower in a food processor. Pulse in 2-second bursts to finely chop the cauliflower until it resembles couscous. Alternatively, you can just use a knife and chop it very finely.

Mince the remaining garlic clove. Fry the garlic, red onion, and ginger in 1 teaspoon of the oil, until soft but not browned, then add the turmeric and cauliflower and cook for 1 minute.

Remove from heat and stir in the sun-dried tomatoes and parsley. Serve with the baked tofu.

SIRT MUESLI

If you want to make this in bulk or prepare it the night before, simply combine the dry ingredients and store the mixture in an airtight container. All you need to do the next day is add the strawberries and yogurt and it's good to go.

SERVES 1

¼ cup (20g) buckwheat flakes

⅔ cup (10g) buckwheat puffs

3 tablespoons (15g) coconut flakes or dried coconut

¼ cup (40g) Medjool dates, pitted and chopped

⅛ cup (15g) walnuts, chopped

1½ tablespoons (10g) cocoa nibs

⅔ cup (100g) strawberries, hulled and chopped

⅜ cup (100g) plain Greek yogurt (or vegan alternative, such as soy or coconut yogurt)

Mix all of the ingredients together (leave out the strawberries and yogurt if not serving right away).

PAN-FRIED SALMON FILLET WITH CARAMELIZED ENDIVE, ARUGULA, AND CELERY LEAF SALAD

SERVES 1

¼ cup (10g) parsley

juice of ¼ lemon

1 tablespoon capers

1 clove garlic, roughly chopped

1 tablespoon extra virgin olive oil

¼ avocado, peeled, stoned, and diced

⅔ cup (100g) cherry tomatoes, halved

⅛ cup (20g) red onion, thinly sliced

1¾ ounces (50g) arugula

2 tablespoons (5g) celery leaves

1 x 5-ounce (150g) skinless salmon fillet

2 teaspoons brown sugar

1 head of endive, about 2½ ounces (70g), halved lengthways

Heat the oven to 425°F (220°C).

For the dressing, place the parsley, lemon juice, capers, garlic, and 2 teaspoons of the oil in a food processor or blender and blend until smooth.

For the salad, mix the avocado, tomato, red onion, arugula, and celery leaves together.

Heat a frying pan over high heat. Rub the salmon in a little oil and sear it in the hot pan for a minute or so to caramelize the outside of the fish. Transfer to a baking tray and place in the oven for 5 to 6 minutes or until cooked through; reduce the cooking time by 2 minutes if you like your fish served pink inside.

Meanwhile, wipe out the frying pan and place it back on high heat. Mix the brown sugar with the remaining teaspoon of oil and brush it over the cut sides of the endive. Place the endive cut-sides down in the hot pan and cook for 2 to 3 minutes, turning regularly, until tender and nicely caramelized all over. Toss the salad in the dressing and serve with the salmon and endive.

TUSCAN BEAN STEW

1 tablespoon extra virgin olive oil

⅓ cup (50g) red onion, finely chopped

¼ cup (30g) carrot, peeled and finely chopped

⅓ cup (30g) celery, trimmed and finely chopped

2 garlic cloves, finely chopped

½ Thai chili, finely chopped (optional)

1 teaspoon herbes de Provence

⅞ cup (200ml) vegetable stock

1 x 14-ounce can (400g) chopped Italian tomatoes

1 teaspoon tomato purée

¾ cup (130g) canned mixed beans (drained weight)

¾ cup (50g) kale, roughly chopped

1 tablespoon roughly chopped parsley

¼ cup (40g) buckwheat

Place the oil in a medium saucepan over low to medium heat and gently fry the onion, carrot, celery, garlic, chili (if using), and herbs, until the onion is soft but not browned.

Add the stock, tomatoes, and tomato purée and bring to a boil. Add the beans and simmer for 30 minutes.

Add the kale and cook for another 5 to 10 minutes, until tender, then add the parsley.

Meanwhile, cook the buckwheat according to the package instructions, drain, and then serve with the stew.

STRAWBERRY BUCKWHEAT TABBOULEH

SERVES 1

⅓ cup (50g) buckwheat

1 tablespoon ground turmeric

½ cup (80g) avocado

⅜ cup (65g) tomato

⅛ cup (20g) red onion

⅛ cup (25g) Medjool dates, pitted

1 tablespoon capers

¾ cup (30g) parsley

⅔ cup (100g) strawberries, hulled

1 tablespoon extra virgin olive oil

juice of ½ lemon

1 ounce (30g) arugula

Cook the buckwheat with the turmeric according to the package instructions. Drain and set aside to cool.

Finely chop the avocado, tomato, red onion, dates, capers, and parsley and mix with the cool buckwheat. Slice the strawberries and gently mix into the salad with the oil and lemon juice. Serve on a bed of arugula.

MISO-MARINATED BAKED COD WITH STIR-FRIED GREENS AND SESAME

SERVES 1

3½ teaspoons (20g) miso

1 tablespoon mirin

1 tablespoon extra virgin olive oil

1 x 7-ounce (200g) skinless cod fillet

⅛ cup (20g) red onion, sliced

⅜ cup (40g) celery, sliced

2 garlic cloves, finely chopped

1 Thai chili, finely chopped

1 teaspoon finely chopped fresh ginger

⅜ cup (60g) green beans

¾ cup (50g) kale, roughly chopped

1 teaspoon sesame seeds

2 tablespoons (5g) parsley, roughly chopped

1 tablespoon tamari (or soy sauce, if you are not avoiding gluten)

¼ cup (40g) buckwheat

1 teaspoon ground turmeric

Mix the miso, mirin, and 1 teaspoon of the oil. Rub all over the cod and leave to marinate for 30 minutes. Heat the oven to 425°F (220°C).

Bake the cod for 10 minutes.

Meanwhile, heat a large frying pan or wok with the remaining oil. Add the onion and stir-fry for a few minutes, then add the celery, garlic, chili, ginger, green beans, and kale. Toss and fry until the kale is tender and cooked through. You may need to add a little water to the pan to aid the cooking process.

Cook the buckwheat according to the package instructions together with the turmeric.

Add the sesame seeds, parsley, and tamari to the stir-fry and serve with the buckwheat and fish.

SOBA (BUCKWHEAT NOODLES) IN A MISO BROTH WITH TOFU, CELERY, AND KALE

SERVES 1

3 ounces (75g) soba (buckwheat noodles)

1 tablespoon extra virgin olive oil

⅛ cup (20g) red onion, sliced

2 garlic cloves, finely chopped

1 teaspoon finely chopped fresh ginger

1¼ cups (300ml) vegetable stock, plus a little extra,
  if necessary

1¾ tablespoons (30g) miso paste

¾ cup (50g) kale, roughly chopped

½ cup (50g) celery, roughly chopped

1 teaspoon sesame seeds

3½ ounces (100g) firm tofu, cut into ¼- to ½-inch (0.5 to 1cm) cubes
  (about ⅜ cup)

1 teaspoon tamari (optional; or soy sauce, if you are not avoiding gluten)

Place the noodles in a pan of boiling water and cook for 5 to 8 minutes or according to the package instructions.

Heat the oil in a saucepan; add the onions, garlic, and ginger and fry over medium heat in the oil, until soft but not browned. Add the stock and miso and bring to a boil.

Add the kale and celery to the miso broth and simmer gently for 5 minutes (try not to boil the miso, as you will destroy the flavor and cause it to go grainy in texture). You may need to add a little more stock as required.

Add the cooked noodles and sesame seeds and allow to warm through, then add the tofu. Serve in a bowl drizzled with a little tamari, if desired.

SIRT SUPER SALAD

SERVES 1

1¾ ounces (50g) arugula

1¾ ounces (50g) endive leaves

3½ ounces (100g) smoked salmon slices

½ cup (80g) avocado, peeled, stoned, and sliced

½ cup (50g) celery including leaves, sliced

⅛ cup (20g) red onion, sliced

⅛ cups (15g) walnuts, chopped

1 tablespoon capers

1 large Medjool date, pitted and chopped

1 tablespoon extra virgin olive oil

juice of ¼ lemon

¼ cup (10g) parsley, chopped

Place the salad leaves on a plate or in a large bowl.

Mix all the remaining ingredients together and serve on top of the leaves.

VARIATIONS

For a **lentil** Sirt super salad, replace the smoked salmon with 1⅓ cups (100g) canned green lentils or cooked Le Puy lentils.

For a **chicken** Sirt super salad, replace the smoked salmon with a sliced cooked chicken breast.

For a **tuna** Sirt super salad, simply replace the smoked salmon with canned tuna (in water or oil, according to preference).

CHAR-GRILLED BEEF WITH A RED WINE JUS, ONION RINGS, GARLIC KALE, AND HERB-ROASTED POTATOES

SERVES 1

½ cup (100g) potatoes, peeled and cut into ¾-inch (2cm) diced pieces

1 tablespoon extra virgin olive oil

2 tablespoons (5g) parsley, finely chopped

⅓ cup (50g) red onion, sliced into rings

2 ounces (50g) kale, sliced

2 garlic cloves, finely chopped

1 x 4- to 5-ounce (120 to 150g) beef tenderloin (about 1½ inches or 3.5cm
   thick) or sirloin steak (¾ inch or 2cm thick)

3 tablespoons (40ml) red wine

⅝ cup (150ml) beef stock

1 teaspoon tomato purée

1 teaspoon corn flour, dissolved in 1 tablespoon water

Heat the oven to 425°F (220°C).

Place the potatoes in a saucepan of boiling water, bring back to a boil, and cook for 4 to 5 minutes, then drain. Place in a roasting pan with 1 teaspoon of the oil and roast in the hot oven for 35 to 45 minutes. Turn the potatoes every 10 minutes to ensure even cooking. When cooked, remove from the oven, sprinkle with the chopped parsley, and mix well.

Fry the onion in 1 teaspoon of the oil over medium heat for 5 to 7 minutes, until soft and nicely caramelized. Keep warm.

Steam the kale for 2 to 3 minutes, then drain. Fry the garlic gently in ½ teaspoon of oil for 1 minute, until soft but not browned. Add the kale and fry for 1 to 2 minutes more, until tender. Keep warm.

Heat an ovenproof frying pan over high heat until smoking. Coat the meat in ½ teaspoon of the oil and fry in the hot pan over medium-high heat according to how you like your meat done (see our guide to the cooking times on page 183). If you like your meat medium, it would be better to sear it and then transfer the pan to an oven set at 425°F (220°C) and finish the cooking that way for the prescribed times.

Remove the meat from the pan and set aside to rest. Add the wine to the hot pan to bring up any meat residue. Simmer to reduce the wine by half, until syrupy and with a concentrated flavor.

Add the stock and tomato purée to the steak pan and bring to a boil, then add the corn-flour paste to thicken your sauce, adding it a little at a time until you have your desired consistency. Stir in any of the juices from the rested steak, and serve with the roasted potatoes, kale, onion rings, and red wine sauce.

STEAK COOKING TIMES

1½-INCH-THICK (3.5CM) TENDERLOIN

- **Blue:** about 1½ minutes each side
- **Rare:** about 2¼ minutes each side
- **Medium-rare:** about 3¼ minutes each side
- **Medium:** about 4½ minutes each side

¾-INCH-THICK (2CM) SIRLOIN STEAK

- **Blue:** about 1 minute each side
- **Rare:** about 1½ minutes each side
- **Medium-rare:** about 2 minutes each side
- **Medium:** about 2¼ minutes each side

KIDNEY BEAN MOLE WITH BAKED POTATO

SERVES 1

¼ cup (40g) red onion, finely chopped

1 teaspoon finely chopped fresh ginger

2 garlic cloves, finely chopped

1 Thai chili, finely chopped

1 teaspoon extra virgin olive oil

1 teaspoon ground turmeric

1 teaspoon ground cumin

pinch of ground clove

pinch of ground cinnamon

1 medium baking potato

⅞ cup (190g) canned chopped tomatoes

1 teaspoon brown sugar

⅓ cup (50g) red bell pepper, cored, seeds removed, and roughly chopped

⅝ cup (150ml) vegetable stock

1 tablespoon cocoa powder

1 teaspoon sesame seeds

2 teaspoons peanut butter (smooth if available, but chunky is fine)

⅞ cup (150g) canned kidney beans

2 tablespoons (5g) parsley, chopped

Heat the oven to 400°F (200°C).

Fry the onion, ginger, garlic, and chili in the oil in a medium saucepan over medium heat for about 10 minutes, or until soft. Add the spices and cook for a further 1 to 2 minutes.

Place the potato on a baking tray in the hot oven and bake for 45 to 60 minutes, until soft in middle (or longer, depending on how crispy you like the outside).

Meanwhile, add the tomatoes, sugar, red pepper, stock, cocoa powder, sesame seeds, peanut butter, and kidney beans to the saucepan and simmer gently for 45 to 60 minutes.

Sprinkle with the parsley to finish. Cut the potato in half and serve the mole on top.

SIRTFOOD OMELET

SERVES 1

about 2 ounces (50g) sliced streaky bacon (or 2 rashers,
  smoked or regular, depending on your taste)

3 medium eggs

1¼ ounces (35g) red endive, thinly sliced

2 tablespoons (5g) parsley, finely chopped

1 teaspoon turmeric

1 teaspoon extra virgin olive oil

Heat a nonstick frying pan. Cut the bacon into thin strips and cook over high heat until crispy. You do not need to add any oil, there is enough fat in the bacon to cook it. Remove from the pan and place on a paper towel to drain any excess fat. Wipe the pan clean.

Whisk the eggs and mix with the endive, parsley, and turmeric. Chop the cooked bacon into cubes and stir through the eggs.

Heat the oil in the frying pan—the pan should be hot but not smoking. Add the egg mixture and, using a spatula, move it around the pan to start to cook the egg. Keep the bits of cooked egg moving and swirl the raw egg around the pan until the omelet level is even. Reduce the heat and let the omelet firm up. Ease the spatula around the edges and fold the omelet in half or roll up and serve.

BAKED CHICKEN BREAST WITH WALNUT AND PARSLEY PESTO AND RED ONION SALAD

SERVES 1

⅜ cup (15g) parsley

⅛ cup (15g) walnuts

4 teaspoons (15g) Parmesan cheese, grated

1 tablespoon extra virgin olive oil

juice of ½ lemon

3 tablespoons (50ml) water

5½ ounces (150g) skinless chicken breast

⅛ cup (20g) red onions, finely sliced

1 teaspoon red wine vinegar

1¼ ounces (35g) arugula

⅔ cup (100g) cherry tomatoes, halved

1 teaspoon balsamic vinegar

To make the pesto, place the parsley, walnuts, Parmesan, olive oil, half the lemon juice, and a little of the water in a food processor or blender and blend until you have a smooth paste. Add more water gradually until you have your preferred consistency.

Marinate the chicken breast in 1 tablespoon of the pesto and the remaining lemon juice in the fridge for 30 minutes, longer if possible.

Preheat the oven to 400°F (200°C).

Heat an ovenproof frying pan over medium-high heat. Fry the chicken in its marinade for 1 minute on either side, then transfer the pan to the oven and cook for 8 minutes, or until cooked through.

Marinate the onions in the red wine vinegar for 5 to 10 minutes. Drain the liquid.

When the chicken is cooked, remove it from the oven, spoon another tablespoon of pesto over it, and let the heat from the chicken melt the pesto. Cover with foil and leave to rest for 5 minutes before serving.

Combine the arugula, tomatoes, and onion and drizzle with the balsamic vinegar. Serve with the chicken, spooning over the remaining pesto.

WALDORF SALAD

SERVES 1

1 cup (100g) celery including leaves, roughly chopped

½ cup (50g) apple, roughly chopped

⅜ cup (50g) walnuts, roughly chopped

1 tablespoon (10g) red onion, roughly chopped

2 tablespoons (5g) parsley, chopped

1 tablespoon capers

1 tablespoon extra virgin olive oil

1 teaspoon balsamic vinegar

juice of ¼ lemon

¼ teaspoon Dijon mustard

about 2 ounces (50g) arugula

about 1½ ounces (35g) endive leaves

Mix the celery and its leaves, apple, walnuts, and onion with the parsley and capers.

In a bowl, whisk the oil, vinegar, lemon juice, and mustard to make the dressing.

Serve the celery mixture on top of the arugula and endive and drizzle with the dressing.

ROASTED EGGPLANT WEDGES WITH WALNUT AND PARSLEY PESTO AND TOMATO SALAD

SERVES 1

½ cup (20g) parsley

¾ ounces (20g) walnuts

⅛ cup (20g) Parmesan cheese (or use a vegetarian or vegan alternative), grated

1 tablespoon extra virgin olive oil

juice of ¼ lemon

3 tablespoons (50ml) water

1 small eggplant (around 5½ ounces or 150g), quartered

⅛ cup (20g) red onions, sliced

1 teaspoon (5ml) red wine vinegar

1¼ ounces (35g) arugula

⅔ cup (100g) cherry tomatoes

1 teaspoon (5ml) balsamic vinegar

Heat the oven to 400°F (200°C).

To make the pesto, place the parsley, walnuts, Parmesan, olive oil, and half the lemon juice in a food processor or blender and blend until you have a smooth paste. Add the water gradually until you have the correct consistency—it should be thick enough to stick to the eggplant.

Brush the eggplant with a little of the pesto, reserving the rest to serve. Place on a baking tray and roast for 25 to 30 minutes, until the eggplant is golden brown, soft, and moist.

Meanwhile, cover the red onion with the red wine vinegar and set aside—this will soften and sweeten the onion. Drain the vinegar before serving.

Combine the arugula, tomatoes, and drained onion and drizzle the balsamic vinegar over the salad. Serve with the hot eggplant, spooning the remaining pesto over it.

SIRTFOOD SMOOTHIE

SERVES 1

⅜ cup (100g) plain Greek yogurt (or vegan alternative,
   such as soy or coconut yogurt)

6 walnut halves

8 to 10 medium strawberries, hulled

handful of kale, stalks removed

¾ ounce (20g) dark chocolate (85 percent cocoa solids)

1 Medjool date, pitted

½ teaspoon ground turmeric

thin sliver (1 to 2mm) of Thai chili

⅞ cup (200ml) unsweetened almond milk

Blitz all the ingredients in a blender until smooth.

STUFFED WHOLE-WHEAT PITA

SERVES 1

Whole-wheat pitas are a great way to pack plenty of Sirtfoods into a quick lunch or convenient and portable packed meal. You can play around with quantities and get creative, but ultimately all you do is load the ingredients in and it's good to go.

FOR A MEAT OPTION

3 ounces (80g) cooked turkey slices, chopped

¾ ounce (20g) cheddar cheese, diced

¼ cup (35g) cucumber, diced

¼ cup (35g) red onion, chopped

1 ounce (25g) arugula, chopped

1½ to 2 tablespoons (10 to 15g) walnuts, roughly chopped

FOR THE DRESSING

1 tablespoon extra virgin olive oil

1 tablespoon balsamic vinegar

dash of lemon juice

FOR A VEGAN OPTION

2 to 3 tablespoons hummus

¼ cup (35g) cucumber, diced

¼ cup (35g) red onion, chopped

1 ounce (25g) arugula, chopped

1½ to 2 tablespoons (10 to 15g) walnuts, roughly chopped

FOR THE VEGAN DRESSING

1 tablespoon extra virgin olive oil

dash of lemon juice

BUTTERNUT SQUASH AND DATE TAGINE
WITH BUCKWHEAT

SERVES 4

3 teaspoons extra virgin olive oil

1 red onion, finely chopped

1 tablespoon finely chopped fresh ginger

4 garlic cloves, finely chopped

2 Thai chilies, finely chopped

1 tablespoon ground cumin

1 cinnamon stick

2 tablespoons ground turmeric

2 x 14-ounce cans (400g each) of chopped tomatoes

1¼ cups (300ml) vegetable stock

⅔ cup (100g) Medjool dates, pitted and chopped

1 x 14-ounce can (400g) of chickpeas, drained and rinsed

2½ cups (500g) butternut squash, peeled and cut into bite-size pieces

1¼ cups (200g) buckwheat

2 tablespoons (5g) fresh coriander, chopped

¼ cup (10g) fresh parsley, chopped

Heat the oven to 400°F (200°C).

Fry the onion, ginger, garlic, and chili in two teaspoons of the oil for 2 to 3 minutes. Add the cumin and cinnamon and 1 tablespoon of the turmeric, and cook for another 1 to 2 minutes.

Add the tomatoes, stock, dates, and chickpeas and simmer gently for 45 to 60 minutes. You may have to add a little water from time to time to achieve a thick, sticky consistency and to make sure the pan does not run dry.

Place the squash in a roasting pan, toss with the remaining oil, and roast for 30 minutes until soft and charred around the edges.

Toward the end of the tagine's cooking time, cook the buckwheat according to the package instructions with the remaining tablespoon of turmeric.

Add the roasted squash to the tagine along with the coriander and parsley and serve with the buckwheat.

BUTTER BEAN AND MISO DIP WITH CELERY STICKS AND OATCAKES

SERVES 4

2 x 14-ounce cans (400g each) of butter beans, drained and rinsed

3 tablespoons extra virgin olive oil

2 tablespoons brown miso paste

juice and grated zest of ½ unwaxed lemon

4 medium scallions, trimmed and finely chopped

1 garlic clove, crushed

¼ Thai chili, finely chopped

celery sticks, to serve

oatcakes, to serve

Simply mash the first seven ingredients together with a potato masher until you have a coarse mixture.

Serve as a dip with celery sticks and oatcakes.

YOGURT WITH MIXED BERRIES, CHOPPED WALNUTS, AND DARK CHOCOLATE

SERVES 1

about 1⅓ cups (125g) mixed berries

⅔ cup (150g) plain Greek yogurt (or vegan alternative,
    such as soy or coconut yogurt)

¼ cup (25g) walnuts, chopped

1½ tablespoons (10g) dark chocolate
    (85 percent cocoa solids), grated

Simply add your preferred berries to a bowl and top with the yogurt.
    Sprinkle with the walnuts and chocolate.

CHICKEN AND KALE CURRY WITH BOMBAY POTATOES

SERVES 4

4 x 4½- to 5½-ounce (120 to 150g) skinless, boneless chicken breasts,
cut into bite-size pieces

4 tablespoons extra virgin olive oil

3 tablespoons ground turmeric

2 red onions, sliced

2 Thai chilies, finely chopped

3 garlic cloves, finely chopped

1 tablespoon finely chopped fresh ginger

1 tablespoon mild curry powder

1 x 14-ounce (400g) can chopped tomatoes

2⅛ cups (500ml) chicken stock

⅞ cup (200ml) coconut milk

2 cardamom pods

1 cinnamon stick

1⅓ pounds (600g) russet potatoes

¼ cup (10g) parsley, chopped

2⅔ cups (175g) kale, chopped

2 tablespoons (5g) coriander, chopped

Rub the chicken pieces in 1 teaspoon of the oil and 1 tablespoon of the turmeric. Leave to marinate for 30 minutes.

Fry the chicken over high heat (there should be enough oil in the marinade to cook the chicken) for 4 to 5 minutes until nicely browned all over and cooked through, then remove from the pan and set aside.

Heat 1 tablespoon of the oil in the frying pan over medium heat and add the onion, chili, garlic, and ginger. Fry for about 10 minutes, or until soft, then add the curry powder and another tablespoon of the turmeric and cook for another 1 to 2 minutes. Add the tomatoes to the pan, then let them cook for another 2 minutes. Add the stock, coconut milk, cardamom, and cinnamon stick and leave to simmer for 45 to 60 minutes. Check the pan at regular intervals to ensure it does not run dry—you may have to add more stock.

Heat the oven to 425°F (220°C). While your curry is simmering, peel the potatoes and cut them into small chunks. Place in boiling water with the remaining tablespoon of turmeric and boil for 5 minutes. Drain well and allow to steam dry for 10 minutes. They should be white and flaky around the edges. Transfer to a roasting pan, toss with the remaining oil, and roast for 30 minutes or until golden brown and crisp. Toss through the parsley when they're ready.

When the curry has your required consistency, add the kale, cooked chicken, and coriander and cook for another 5 minutes, to ensure the chicken is cooked through, then serve with the potatoes.

SPICED SCRAMBLED EGGS

SERVES 1

1 teaspoon extra virgin olive oil

⅛ cup (20g) red onion, finely chopped

½ Thai chili, finely chopped

3 medium eggs

¼ cup (50ml) milk

1 teaspoon ground turmeric

2 tablespoons (5g) parsley, finely chopped

Heat the oil in a frying pan and fry the red onion and chili until soft but not browned.

Whisk together the eggs, milk, turmeric, and parsley. Add to the hot pan and continue cooking over low to medium heat, constantly moving the egg mixture around the pan to scramble it and stop it from sticking/burning. When you have achieved your desired consistency, serve.

SIRT CHILI CON CARNE

SERVES 4

1 red onion, finely chopped

3 garlic cloves, finely chopped

2 Thai chilies, finely chopped

1 tablespoon extra virgin olive oil

1 tablespoon ground cumin

1 tablespoon ground turmeric

1 pound (450g) lean ground beef (5 percent fat)

⅝ cup (150ml) red wine

1 red bell pepper, cored, seeds removed and cut into bite-size pieces

2 x 14-ounce (400g) cans chopped tomatoes

1 tablespoon tomato purée

1 tablespoon cocoa powder

⅞ cup (150g) canned kidney beans

1¼ cups (300ml) beef stock

2 tablespoons (5g) fresh coriander, chopped

2 tablespoons (5g) fresh parsley, chopped

1 cup (160g) buckwheat

In a large saucepan, fry the onion, garlic, and chili in the oil over medium heat for 2 to 3 minutes, then add the spices and cook for another minute or two. Add the ground beef and cook for 2 to 3 minutes over medium-high heat until the meat is nicely browned all over. Add the red wine and allow it to bubble to reduce it by half.

Add the red pepper, tomatoes, tomato purée, cocoa, kidney beans, and stock and leave to simmer for 1 hour. You may have to add a little water from time to time to achieve a thick, sticky consistency. Just before serving, stir in the chopped herbs.

Meanwhile, cook the buckwheat according to the package instructions and serve alongside the chili.

MUSHROOM AND TOFU SCRAMBLE

SERVES 1

3½ ounces (100g) extra-firm tofu

1 teaspoon ground turmeric

1 teaspoon mild curry powder

⅓ cup (20g) kale, roughly chopped

1 teaspoon extra virgin olive oil

⅛ cup (20g) red onion, thinly sliced

½ Thai chili, thinly sliced

¾ cup (50g) mushrooms, thinly sliced

2 tablespoons (5g) parsley, finely chopped

Wrap the tofu in paper towels and place something heavy on top to help it drain.

Mix the turmeric and curry powder and add a little water until you have achieved a light paste. Steam the kale for 2 to 3 minutes.

Heat the oil in a frying pan over medium heat and fry the onion, chili, and mushrooms for 2 to 3 minutes until they have started to brown and soften.

Crumble the tofu into bite-size pieces and add to the pan, pour the spice mix over the tofu, and mix thoroughly. Cook over medium heat for 2 to 3 minutes so the spices are cooked through and the tofu has started to brown. Add the kale and continue to cook over medium heat for another minute. Finally, add the parsley, mix well, and serve.

SMOKED SALMON PASTA WITH CHILI AND ARUGULA

SERVES 4

2 tablespoons extra virgin olive oil

1 red onion, finely chopped

2 garlic cloves, finely chopped

2 Thai chilies, finely chopped

1 cup (150g) cherry tomatoes, halved

½ cup (100ml) white wine

9 to 11 ounces (250 to 300g) buckwheat pasta

9 ounces (250g) smoked salmon

2 tablespoons capers

juice of ½ lemon

2 ounces (60g) arugula

¼ cup (10g) parsley, chopped

Heat 1 teaspoon of the oil in a frying pan over medium heat. Add the onion, garlic, and chili and fry until soft but not browned.

Add the tomatoes and leave to cook for a minute or two. Add the white wine and bubble to reduce by half.

Meanwhile, cook the pasta in boiling water with 1 teaspoon of the oil for 8 to 10 minutes depending on how al dente you like it, then drain.

Slice the salmon into strips and add to the pan of tomatoes along with the capers, lemon juice, arugula, and parsley. Add the pasta, mix well, and serve immediately. Drizzle any remaining oil over the top.

BUCKWHEAT PASTA SALAD

SERVES 1

2 ounces (50g) buckwheat pasta, cooked according to the
   package instructions

large handful of arugula

small handful of basil leaves

8 cherry tomatoes, halved

½ avocado, diced

10 olives

1 tablespoon extra virgin olive oil

2½ tablespoons (20g) pine nuts

Gently combine all the ingredients except the pine nuts and arrange on a plate, then scatter the pine nuts over the top.

BUCKWHEAT PANCAKES WITH STRAWBERRIES, DARK CHOCOLATE SAUCE, AND CRUSHED WALNUTS

MAKES 6 TO 8 PANCAKES, DEPENDING ON THE SIZE

FOR THE PANCAKES

1½ cups (350ml) milk

⅞ cup (150g) buckwheat flour

1 large egg

1 tablespoon extra virgin olive oil, for cooking

FOR THE CHOCOLATE SAUCE

3½ ounces (100g) dark chocolate (85 percent cocoa solids)

⅓ cup (85ml) milk

1 tablespoon double cream

1 tablespoon extra virgin olive oil

TO SERVE

2 cups (400g) strawberries, hulled and chopped

⅞ cup (100g) walnuts, chopped

To make the pancake batter, place all the ingredients apart from the olive oil in a blender and blend until you have a smooth batter. It should not be too thick or too runny. (You can store any excess batter in an airtight container for up to 5 days in your fridge. Be sure to mix well before using again.)

To make the chocolate sauce, melt the chocolate in a heatproof bowl above a pan of simmering water. Once it's melted, mix in the milk, whisking thoroughly, and then add the double cream and olive oil. You can keep the sauce warm by leaving the water in the pan simmering on very low heat until your pancakes are ready.

To make the pancakes, heat a small or medium-size heavy-bottomed frying pan until it starts to smoke, then add the olive oil.

Pour some of the batter into the center of the pan, then tip the excess batter around it until you have covered the whole surface; you may have to add a little more batter to achieve this. You will only need to cook the pancake for 1 minute or so on each side if your pan is hot enough.

Once you can see it going brown around the edges, use a spatula to loosen the pancake around its edge, then flip it over. Try to flip in one action to avoid breaking it. Cook for another minute or so on the other side, and transfer to a plate.

Place some strawberries in the center and roll up the pancake. Continue until you have made as many pancakes as required.

Spoon a generous amount of sauce over each pancake and sprinkle with some chopped walnuts.

You may find that your first efforts are too fat or fall apart, but once you find the consistency for your batter that works best for you and you perfect your technique, you'll be making them like a professional. Practice makes perfect in this case.

TOFU AND SHIITAKE MUSHROOM SOUP

SERVES 4

⅓ ounce (10g) dried wakame (seaweed)

1 quart (1 liter) vegetable stock

7 ounces (200g) shiitake mushrooms, sliced

⅓ cup (120g) miso paste

1 x 14-ounce (400g) block firm tofu, cut into small cubes

2 scallions, trimmed and sliced on the diagonal

1 Thai chili, finely chopped (optional)

Soak the wakame in warm water for 10 minutes, then drain.

Bring the stock to a boil, then add the mushrooms and simmer gently for 1 to 2 minutes.

Dissolve the miso paste in a bowl with some of the warm stock to ensure it dissolves thoroughly. Add the miso and tofu to the remaining stock, taking care not to let the soup boil as this would spoil the delicate miso flavor. Add the drained wakame, scallions, and chili, if using, and serve.

SIRTFOOD PIZZA

MAKES TWO 12-INCH (30CM) PIZZAS

FOR THE PIZZA CRUST

1 x ¼-ounce (7g) package of dried yeast

1 teaspoon brown sugar

1¼ cups (300ml) lukewarm water

1¼ cups (200g) buckwheat flour

1⅔ cups (200g) white bread flour or Tipo 00 pasta flour,

plus a little extra for rolling out

1 tablespoon extra virgin olive oil,

plus a little extra for greasing

FOR THE TOMATO SAUCE

½ red onion, finely chopped

1 garlic clove, finely chopped

1 teaspoon extra virgin olive oil

1 teaspoon dried oregano

2 tablespoons white wine

1 x 14-ounce (400g) can of chopped tomatoes

pinch of brown sugar

2 tablespoons (5g) basil leaves

OUR FAVORITE TOPPINGS

• Arugula, red onion, grated cheese (or vegan alternative), and grilled eggplant. (You may be able to buy grilled eggplant from a local deli or market. To grill your own, heat a griddle pan until it is starting to smoke, then reduce the heat to medium. Slice an eggplant crossways into thin slices no wider than ¼ inch [3 to 5mm], brush with a little extra virgin olive oil, and cook until you have achieved black grill marks on either side of the eggplant and it is nice and soft. Alternatively, you could roast the eggplant on a baking tray lined with a sheet of parchment paper at 400°F [200°C] for 15 minutes or until soft and golden brown.)

- Chili flakes, cherry tomato, goat cheese (or vegan alternative), and arugula
- Cooked chicken, arugula, red onion, olive, and grated cheese
- Cooked chorizo, red onion, steamed kale, and grated cheese

For the dough, dissolve the yeast and sugar in the water. This will help to activate the yeast. Cover with plastic wrap and leave for 10 to 15 minutes.

Sift the flours into a bowl. If you have a stand mixer, fit it with the dough hook and sift the flours into the mixer bowl.

Add the yeast mixture and oil to the flour and mix together until you have formed a dough. You may have to add a little more water if your dough is a little dry. Knead until you have a smooth, springy dough.

Transfer the dough to an oiled bowl, cover with a clean damp kitchen towel, and leave somewhere warm to rise for 45 to 60 minutes, until doubled in size.

Meanwhile, make the tomato sauce. Fry the onion and garlic in the olive oil until soft, then add the dried oregano. Add the wine and bubble to reduce it by half.

Add the tomatoes and sugar, bring back to a boil, and cook for 30 minutes until the mixture is a thick consistency. If it is too runny it will make the pizza soggy. Remove the pan from the heat. Tear the basil leaves apart with your hands and stir them into the sauce.

Start kneading the dough again to remove the air—this is called knocking back, or sometimes punching down. After a minute or so, when you have a nice smooth dough, it is ready. You can either use the dough immediately or wrap it in plastic wrap and place in the fridge for a couple of days.

Heat the oven to 450°F (230°C). Lightly dust a work surface with flour. Cut the dough in half and roll out each piece to your required thickness, then place on a pizza stone or oiled nonstick baking tray. (This quantity of dough will make two thin-crust pizzas of about 12 inches [30cm] in diameter. If you would like a deeper crust, simply use more of the dough or reduce the size of the pizza.)

Spread a thin layer of tomato sauce over the dough (you will only need about half the sauce for this quantity of dough, but freeze any left over), leaving a gap around the edge for the crust. Add the rest of your ingredients (if you're using arugula and chili flakes, add them after you've baked your pizza). Set aside for about 15 to 20 minutes before baking; the dough will start to rise again, giving a lighter base.

Bake in the oven for 10 to 12 minutes or until the cheese is golden brown. Top with arugula and chili flakes now, if using.

SIRTFOOD BITES

MAKES 15 TO 20 BITES

1 cup (120g) walnuts

1 ounce (30g) dark chocolate (85 percent cocoa solids), broken into pieces;

    or ¼ cup cocoa nibs

9 ounces (250g) Medjool dates, pitted

1 tablespoon cocoa powder

1 tablespoon ground turmeric

1 tablespoon extra virgin olive oil

the scraped seeds of 1 vanilla pod or 1 teaspoon vanilla extract

1 to 2 tablespoons water

Place the walnuts and chocolate in a food processor and process until you have a fine powder.

Add all the other ingredients except the water and blend until the mixture forms a ball. You may or may not have to add the water depending on the consistency of the mixture—you don't want it to be too sticky.

Using your hands, form the mixture into bite-size balls and refrigerate in an airtight container for at least 1 hour before eating them. You could roll some of the balls in some more cocoa or dried coconut to achieve a different finish if you like. They will keep for up to 1 week in your fridge.

Acknowledgments

We must begin by thanking the thousands of people who have now followed this diet and fed back their amazing stories of how Sirtfoods have transformed their lives. These are always our biggest motivation to spread the Sirtfood message and change how the world eats to reverse the tide of ill health and obesity.

We would like to give a special mention to Rory and Eugenie at Furniss Lawton, and Celeste and Sarah at Sterling Lord Literistic, for the belief they have shown in us and the life-changing potential of our ideas.

A special thank-you also to chef Mark McCulloch, who has the gift of taking everyday ingredients and transforming them into the stunning recipes that grace this book. Equally, we are indebted to all our willing recipe testers, who hopefully are that bit healthier for all their avid testing.

Last, but by no means least, our acknowledgments would not be complete without showing our gratitude to everyone at KX, the birthplace of the Sirtfood Diet, and in particular to Gideon, who helped nurture our original idea so that it could blossom into what it has become today.

Glossary

Antioxidant (dietary) A substance, either man-made or found naturally in food, that when consumed reduces the physical stress on the cells in our bodies.

Autophagy The process by which our cells break down and recycle waste material and debris in order to use it for fuel. Autophagy is increased during periods of cellular stress.

Blue Zones Select geographical regions of the world where people eat diets rich in Sirtfoods and live extraordinarily long, healthy, and happy lives.

Caloric restriction A dietary regimen where people purposely reduce their food intake in an attempt to lose weight, improve health, and extend life span.

Circadian rhythm Our natural body clock that runs on a 24-hour cycle and regulates the activity and efficiency of many important physiological processes, such as sleep and how we process food, according to the time of day.

DHA (Docosahexaenoic acid) One of two crucial omega-3 fatty acids (alongside EPA), primarily found in oily fish and marine plants like algae, that enhances the activity of our sirtuins and improves overall health.

EPA (Eicosapentaenoic acid) One of two crucial omega-3 fatty acids (alongside DHA), primarily found in oily fish, that enhances the activity of our sirtuins and improves overall health.

Gene Made up of DNA, the blueprint of our bodies; when activated, a gene signals our bodies to produce protein, which changes how our cells work.

Hormesis A biological phenomenon whereby exposure to something that is bad for us in high amounts is actually beneficial in small and moderate quantities. Examples include exercise and fasting.

Inflammaging A persistent low-grade inflammation that occurs with aging and increases our risk of many chronic diseases.

Intermittent fasting An umbrella term for any diet that is characterized by alternating periods of caloric restriction (fasting days) and ad lib feeding. Fasting days are usually limited to between one and three days a week and so are usually more intense than normal caloric restriction.

Leucine An essential amino acid found in dietary protein. It has a potent effect in enhancing the benefits of Sirtfoods, so a Sirtfood diet should also be protein-rich.

Master regulator A gene at the top of a hierarchy that regulates and controls other genes below it, or something that influences that gene.

Metabolism All the biochemical reactions taking place within a cell that help maintain life.

Mitochondria Tiny structures within a cell that break down nutrients and generate energy. They power the cell to carry out its functions. Muscle cells require a lot of energy, and so are particularly rich in mitochondria.

mTOR (mammalian target of rapamycin) A vital growth promoter in the body, but its activity needs to be kept in check or else disease can occur. Its activity is highly influenced by the food we eat.

Muscle gain adjusted weight loss A method for calculating weight loss where reported weight-loss results are not penalized for a desirable increase in muscle. This is a much more accurate way of reflecting changes to overall body composition than simply weight loss alone.

PGC-1α (peroxisome proliferator-activated receptor-gamma co-activator 1α) A key regulator of energy metabolism that stimulates the creation of mitochondria in our cells (see "Mitochondria").

Polyphenols A vast group of natural chemicals found in plants that are part of a plant's defenses against environmental stresses. Certain polyphenols switch on our sirtuin genes when consumed, and give rise to the many benefits of the Sirtfood Diet.

PPAR-γ (peroxisome proliferator-activated receptor-γ) A key regulator of metabolism in our cells that switches on genes involved in synthesizing and storing fat.

SIRT1 The most thoroughly researched of the sirtuin family of genes and the most important for targeting weight loss. It is activated when cells are stressed, and has numerous health and anti-aging effects.

Sirtfood A food particularly rich in specific polyphenols that, when we consume them, are able to activate our sirtuin genes.

Sirtuin An ancient family of genes that exist in all of us that are activated when our cells are put under stress. Sirtuins play an important role in health, disease prevention, and aging. In humans, there are seven different sirtuins (SIRT1 to SIRT7). Of these,

SIRT1 and SIRT3 are the two most important sirtuins involved in energy balance.

Stem cell A special type of cell that can grow into any type of cell found in the body.

Western diet The typical diet representative of industrialized, modern eating patterns, and the antithesis of the Blue Zones. A Western diet is characterized by a high consumption of processed and refined foods and a notable lack of nutrient-rich plants, especially Sirtfoods.

Xenohormesis The biological phenomenon whereby humans can piggyback on the stress responses of plants and experience a wealth of benefits by consuming the polyphenols they produce.

References

INTRODUCTION

1. Hill, A. J. "Does dieting make you fat?" *Br J Nutr* 92 Suppl 1, S15–18 (2004).

2. Howitz, K. T., et al. "Small molecule activators of sirtuins extend Saccharomyces cerevisiae lifespan." *Nature* 425, 191–96 (2003).

3. Bonkowski, M. S., and Sinclair, D. A. "Slowing ageing by design: the rise of NAD+ and sirtuin-activating compounds." *Nat Rev Mol Cell Bio*, advance online publication (2016).

4. Ibid.

5. Wang, L., Lee, I. M., Manson, J. E., Buring, J. E., and Sesso, H. D. "Alcohol consumption, weight gain, and risk of becoming overweight in middle-aged and older women." *Arch Intern Med* 170, 453–61 (2010).

6. Bertoia, M. L., et al. "Dietary flavonoid intake and weight

maintenance: three prospective cohorts of 124,086 US men and women followed for up to 24 years." *BMJ* 352:i17 (2016).

7. Rabadan-Chávez, G., et al. "Cocoa powder, cocoa extract, and epicatechin attenuate hypercaloric diet-induced obesity through enhanced β-oxidation and energy expenditure in white adipose tissue." *J Funct Foods* 20, 54–67 (2016).

8. Malhotra, A., Maruthappu, M., and Stephenson, T. "Healthy eating: an NHS priority; a sure way to improve health outcomes for NHS staff and the public." *Postgrad Med J* 90, 671–72 (2014).

9. Estruch, R., et al. "Primary prevention of cardiovascular disease with a Mediterranean diet." *N Engl J Med* 368, 1279–90 (2013).

10. Tresserra-Rimbau, Anna, et al. "Polyphenol intake and mortality risk: a re-analysis of the PREDIMED trial." *BMC Med* 12.1, 1 (2014).

CHAPTER 1: THE SCIENCE OF SIRTUINS

1. Li, X. "SIRT1 and energy metabolism." *Acta Biochim Biophys Sin* (Shanghai) 45, 51–60 (2013).

2. Morris, B. J. "Seven sirtuins for seven deadly diseases of aging." *Free Radic Biol Med* 56, 133–71 (2013).

3. Fontana, L., Partridge, L., and Longo, V. D. "Extending healthy life span—from yeast to humans." *Science* 328, 321–26 (2010).

4. Ibid.

5. Haigis, M. C., and Guarente, L. P. "Mammalian sirtuins—emerging roles in physiology, aging, and calorie restriction." *Genes Dev* 20, 2913–21 (2006).

6. Radak, Z., et al. "Redox-regulating sirtuins in aging, caloric restriction, and exercise." *Free Radic Biol Med* 58, 87–97 (2013).

7. Selinger, J. C., O'Connor, S. M., Wong, J. D., and Donelan, J. M. "Humans can continuously optimize energetic cost during walking." *Curr Biol* 25, 2452–56 (2015).

8. Schnohr, P., O'Keefe, J. H., Marott, J. L., Lange, P., and Jensen, G. B. "Dose of jogging and long-term mortality: the Copenhagen City Heart Study." *J Am Coll Cardiol* 65, 411–19 (2015).

9. Mons, U., Hahmann, H., and Brenner, H. "A reverse J-shaped association of leisure time physical activity with prognosis in patients with stable coronary heart disease: evidence from a large cohort with repeated measurements." *Heart* 100, 1043–49 (2014).

CHAPTER 2: FIGHTING FAT

1. Bordone, L., et al. "SIRT1 transgenic mice show phenotypes resembling calorie restriction." *Aging Cell* 6, 759–67 (2007).

2. Chalkiadaki, A., and Guarente, L. "High-fat diet triggers inflammation-induced cleavage of SIRT1 in adipose tissue to promote metabolic dysfunction." *Cell Metab* 16, 180–88 (2012).

3. Costa Cdos, S., et al. "SIRT1 transcription is decreased in visceral adipose tissue of morbidly obese patients with severe hepatic steatosis." *Obes Surg* 20, 633–39 (2010).

4. Pedersen, S. B., Olholm, J., Paulsen, S. K., Bennetzen, M. F., and Richelsen, B. "Low SIRT1 expression, which is upregulated by fasting, in human adipose tissue from obese women." *Int J Obes* (Lond) 32, 1250–55 (2008).

5. Zillikens, M. C., et al. "SIRT1 genetic variation is related to BMI and risk of obesity." *Diabetes* 58, 2828–34 (2009).

6. Tontonoz, P., and Spiegelman, B. M. "Fat and beyond: the diverse biology of PPARgamma." *Annu Rev Biochem* 77, 289–312 (2008).

7. Picard, F., et al. "SIRT1 promotes fat mobilization in white adipocytes by repressing PPAR-gamma." *Nature* 429, 771–76 (2004).

8. Qiang, L., et al. "Brown remodeling of white adipose tissue by SIRT1-dependent deacetylation of Ppargamma." *Cell* 150, 620–32 (2012).

9. Li, X. "SIRT1 and energy metabolism." *Acta Biochim Biophys Sin* (Shanghai) 45, 51–60 (2013).

10. Akieda-Asai, S., et al. "SIRT1 regulates thyroid-stimulating hormone release by enhancing PIP5Kgamma activity through deacetylation of specific lysine residues in mammals." *PLoS One* 5, e11755 (2010).

11. Aragonès, G., et al. "Modulation of leptin resistance by food compounds." *Mol Nut Food Res* 60, 1789–803 (2016).

12. Sasaki, T. "Age-associated weight gain, leptin, and SIRT1: a possible role for hypothalamic SIRT1 in the prevention of weight gain and aging through modulation of leptin sensitivity." *Front Endocrinol* 6, 109 (2015).

CHAPTER 3: MASTERS OF MUSCLE

1. Agudelo, L. Z., et al. "Skeletal muscle PGC-1alpha1 modulates kynurenine metabolism and mediates resilience to stress-induced depression." *Cell* 159, 33–45 (2014).

2. Sharples, A. P., et al. "Longevity and skeletal muscle mass: the role of IGF signalling, the sirtuins, dietary restriction, and protein intake." *Aging Cell* 14, 511–23 (2015).

3. Diaz-Ruiz, A., Gonzalez-Freire, M., Ferrucci, L., Bernier, M., and de Cabo, R. "SIRT1 synchs satellite cell metabolism with stem cell fate." *Cell Stem Cell* 16, 103–4 (2015).

4. Rathbone, C. R., Booth, F. W., and Lees, S. J. "SIRT1 increases skeletal muscle precursor cell proliferation." *Eur J Cell Biol* 88, 35–44 (2009).

5. Lee, D., and Goldberg, A. L. "SIRT1 protein, by blocking the activities of transcription factors FoxO1 and FoxO3, inhibits muscle atrophy and promotes muscle growth." *J Biol Chem* 288, 30515–26 (2013).

6. Ryall, J. G., et al. "The NAD(+)-dependent SIRT1 deacetylase translates a metabolic switch into regulatory epigenetics in skeletal muscle stem cells." *Cell Stem Cell* 16, 171–83 (2015).

7. Lee and Goldberg. "SIRT1 protein."

8. Sharples. "Longevity and skeletal muscle mass."

9. Lee and Goldberg. "SIRT1 protein."

10. Ibid.

11. Sharples. "Longevity and skeletal muscle mass."

12. Sousa-Victor, P., García-Prat, L., Serrano, A. L., Perdiguero, E., and Muñoz-Cánoves, P. "Muscle stem cell aging: regulation and rejuvenation." *Trends Endocrinol Metab* 26, 287–96 (2015).

13. Tonkin, J., Villarroya, F., Puri, P. L., and Vinciguerra, M. "SIRT1 signaling as potential modulator of skeletal muscle diseases." *Curr Opin Pharmacol* 12, 372–76 (2012).

14. Rabassa, M., et al. "Association between both total baseline

urinary and dietary polyphenols and substantial physical performance decline risk in older adults: a 9-year follow-up of the InCHIANTI study." *J Nutr Health Aging* 20.5, 478–84 (2016).

15. Cohen, S., Nathan, J. A., and Goldberg, A. L. "Muscle wasting in disease: molecular mechanisms and promising therapies." *Nat Rev Drug Discov* 14, 58–74 (2015).

CHAPTER 4: WELL-BEING WONDERS

1. Ma, L., and Li, Y. "SIRT1: role in cardiovascular biology." *Clin Chim Acta* 440, 8–15 (2015).

2. Ibid.

3. Milne, J. C., et al. "Small molecule activators of SIRT1 as therapeutics for the treatment of type 2 diabetes." *Nature* 450, 712–16 (2007).

4. Fu, L., et al. "Leucine amplifies the effects of metformin on insulin sensitivity and glycemic control in diet-induced obese mice." *Metabolism* 64, 845–56 (2015).

5. Wang, J., et al. "The role of SIRT1: at the crossroad between promotion of longevity and protection against Alzheimer's disease neuropathology." *Biochim Biophys Acta* 1804, 1690–94 (2010).

6. Giblin, W., Skinner, M. E., and Lombard, D. B. "Sirtuins: guardians of mammalian healthspan." *Trends Genet* 30, 271–86 (2014).

7. Iyer, S., et al. "Sirtuin1 (SIRT1) promotes cortical bone formation by preventing beta-catenin sequestration by FoxO transcription factors in osteoblast progenitors." *J Biol Chem* 289, 24069–78 (2014).

8. Wilking, M. J., and Ahmad, N. "The role of SIRT1 in cancer: the saga continues." *Am J Pathol* 185, 26–28 (2015).

CHAPTER 5: SIRTFOODS

1. Leitzmann, M. F., et al. "Physical activity recommendations and decreased risk of mortality." *Arch Intern Med* 167, 2453–60 (2007).

2. Kennedy, D. O. "Polyphenols and the human brain: plant 'secondary metabolite' ecologic roles and endogenous signaling functions drive benefits." *Adv Nutr* 5, 515–33 (2014).

3. Hooper, P. L., Hooper, P. L., Tytell, M., and Vigh, L. "Xenohormesis: health benefits from an eon of plant stress response evolution." *Cell Stress Chaperones* 15, 761–70 (2010).

4. Ibid.

5. Howitz, K. T., and Sinclair, D. A. "Xenohormesis: sensing the chemical cues of other species." *Cell* 133, 387–91 (2008).

6. Howitz, K. T., et al. "Small molecule activators of sirtuins extend Saccharomyces cerevisiae lifespan." *Nature* 425, 191–96 (2003).

7. Madeo, F., Pietrocola, F., Eisenberg, T., and Kroemer, G. "Caloric restriction mimetics: towards a molecular definition." *Nat Rev Drug Discov* 13, 727–40 (2014).

8. Bonkowski and Sinclair. "Slowing ageing by design."

9. Chung, S., et al. "Regulation of SIRT1 in cellular functions: role of polyphenols." *Arch Biochem Biophys* 501, 79–90 (2010).

10. Howitz, et al. "Small molecule activators of sirtuins."

11. Si, H., and Liu, D. "Dietary antiaging phytochemicals and mechanisms associated with prolonged survival." *J Nutr Biochem* 25, 581–91 (2014).

12. Xiao, N., et al. "Quercetin, luteolin, and epigallocatechin gallate promote glucose disposal in adipocytes with regulation of AMP-activated kinase and/or sirtuin 1 activity." *Planta Med* 80, 993–1000 (2014).

13. Pietsch, K. "Hormetins, antioxidants and prooxidants: defining quercetin-, caffeic acid- and rosmarinic acid-mediated life extension in C. elegans." *Biogerontology* 12, 329–47 (2011).

14. Vanella, L., et al. "Caffeic acid phenethyl ester regulates PPAR's levels in stem cells-derived adipocytes." *PPAR Research* 2016 (2016).

15. Escande, C., et al. "Flavonoid apigenin is an inhibitor of the NAD+ ase CD38: implications for cellular NAD+ metabolism, protein acetylation, and treatment of metabolic syndrome." *Diabetes* 4, 1084–93 (2013).

16. Rabadan-Chávez, et al. "Cocoa powder, cocoa extract, and epicatechin."

17. Duarte, D. A., et al. "Polyphenol-enriched cocoa protects the diabetic retina from glial reaction through the sirtuin pathway." *J Nutr Biochem* 26, 64–74 (2015).

18. Ramirez-Sanchez, I., et al. "(-)-Epicatechin rich cocoa mediated modulation of oxidative stress regulators in skeletal muscle of heart failure and type 2 diabetes patients." *Int J Cardiol* 168, 3982–90 (2013).

19. Ye, Q. "Epigallocatechin-3-gallate suppresses 1-methyl-4-phenyl-pyridine-induced oxidative stress in PC12 cells via the SIRT1/PGC-1α signaling pathway." *BMC Complement Altern Med* 12, 82 (2012).

20. Lee, M. S., et al. "Green tea (-)-epigallotocatechin-3-gallate

induces PGC-1α gene expression in HepG2 cells and 3T3-L1 adipocytes." *Prev Nutr Food Sci* 1, 62–67 (2016).

21. Zhang, X., et al. "Dietary luteolin activates browning and thermogenesis in mice through an AMPK/PGC1α pathway-mediated mechanism." *Int J Obes (Lond)* (2016).

22. Dong, J., et al. "Quercetin reduces obesity-associated ATM infiltration and inflammation in mice: a mechanism including AMPKα1/SIRT1." *J Lipid Res* 55, 363–74 (2014).

23. Davis, J. M. "Quercetin increases brain and muscle mitochondrial biogenesis and exercise tolerance." *Am J Physiol Regul Integr Comp Physiol* 296, 1071–77 (2009).

24. Su, K. Y., et al. "Rutin, a flavonoid and principal component of saussurea involucrata, attenuates physical fatigue in a forced swimming mouse model." *Int J Med Sci* 11, 528–37 (2014).

25. Guo, Z. "Kaempferol protects cardiomyocytes against anoxia/reoxygenation injury via mitochondrial pathway mediated by SIRT1." *Eur J Pharmacol* 761, 245–53c (2015).

26. Menendez, J. A., et al. "Xenohormetic and anti-aging activity of secoiridoid polyphenols present in extra virgin olive oil: a new family of gerosuppressant agents." *Cell Cycle* 12, 555–78 (2013).

27. Kikusato, M., et al. "Oleuropein induces mitochondrial biogenesis and decreases reactive oxygen species generation in cultured avian muscle cells, possibly via an up-regulation of peroxisome proliferator-activated receptor γ coactivator1α." *Anim Sci J* (2016).

28. Luccarini, I., et al. "The polyphenol oleuropein aglycone modulates the PARP1-SIRT1 interplay: an in vitro and in vivo study." *J Alzheimers Dis* (2016).

29. Zheng, A., et al. "Hydroxytyrosol improves mitochondrial function and reduces oxidative stress in the brain of db/db mice: role of AMP-activated protein kinase activation." *Br J Nutr* 113, 1667–76 (2015).

30. Doan, Khanh V., et al. "Gallic acid regulates body weight and glucose homeostasis through AMPK activation." *Endocrinology* 156, 157–68 (2014).

31. Rasbach, K. A., and Schnellmann, R. G. "Isoflavones promote mitochondrial biogenesis." *J Pharmacol Exp Ther* 325, 536–43 (2008).

32. Hong, K. S. "Involvement of SIRT1 in hypoxic down-regulation of c-Myc and β-catenin and hypoxic preconditioning effect of polyphenols." *Toxicol Appl Pharmacol* 259, 210–8 (2012).

33. Yadav, K. D., and Chaudhary, A. K. "Anti-obesity mechanism of Curcuma longa L.: an overview." *IJNPR- formerly NPR* 7, 99–106 (2016).

34. Lee, M. S., et al. "Reduction of body weight by dietary garlic is associated with an increase in uncoupling protein mRNA expression and activation of AMP-activated protein kinase in diet-induced obese mice." *J Nutr* 141, 1947–53 (2011).

35. Jin, T. "Fisetin up-regulates the expression of adiponectin in 3T3-L1 adipocytes via the activation of silent mating type information regulation 2 homologue 1 (SIRT1)-deacetylase and peroxisome proliferator-activated receptors (PPARs)." *J Agric Food Chem* 62, 10468–74 (2014).

CHAPTER 6: SIRTFOODS AROUND THE WORLD

1. Bayard, V., Chamorro, F., Motta, J., and Hollenberg, N. K. "Does flavanol intake influence mortality from nitric oxide–dependent processes? Ischemic heart disease, stroke, diabetes mellitus, and cancer in Panama." *Int J Med Sci* 4, 53–58 (2007).

2. Shrime, M. G., et al. "Flavonoid-rich cocoa consumption affects multiple cardiovascular risk factors in a meta-analysis of short-term studies." *J Nutr* 141, 1982–88 (2011).

3. Hooper, L., et al. "Effects of chocolate, cocoa, and flavan-3-ols on cardiovascular health: a systematic review and meta-analysis of randomized trials." *Am J Clin Nutr* 95, 740–51 (2012).

4. Duarte, D. A., et al. "Polyphenol-enriched cocoa protects the diabetic retina."

5. Martin, M. A., Goya, L., and Ramos, S. "Potential for preventive effects of cocoa and cocoa polyphenols in cancer." *Food Chem Toxicol* 56, 336–51 (2013).

6. Brickman, A. M., et al. "Enhancing dentate gyrus function with dietary flavanols improves cognition in older adults." *Nat Neurosci* 17, 1798–803 (2014).

7. Ferrazzano, G. F., et al. "Anti-cariogenic effects of polyphenols from plant stimulant beverages (cocoa, coffee, tea)." *Fitoterapia* 8, 255–62 (2009).

8. Hutchins-Wolfbrandt, A., and Mistry, A. M. "Dietary turmeric potentially reduces the risk of cancer." *Asian Pac J Cancer Prev* 12, 3169–73 (2011).

9. Panahi, Y., et al. "Antioxidant and anti-inflammatory effects of curcuminoid-piperine combination in subjects with metabolic

syndrome: a randomized controlled trial and an updated meta-analysis." *Clin Nutr* (2015).

10. Kuptniratsaikul, V., Thanakhumtorn, S., Chinswang-watanakul, P., Wattanamongkonsil, L., and Thamlikitkul, V. "Efficacy and safety of Curcuma domestica extracts in patients with knee osteoarthritis." *J Altern Complement Med* 15, 891–97 (2009).

11. Yadav and Chaudhary. "Anti-obesity mechanism of Curcuma longa L."

12. Lee, M. S., et al. "Turmeric improves post-prandial working memory in pre-diabetes independent of insulin." *Asia Pac J Clin Nutr* 23, 581–91 (2014).

13. Sofi, F., Cesari, F., Abbate, R., Gensini, G. F., and Casini, A. "Adherence to Mediterranean diet and health status: meta-analysis." *BMJ* 11, 337:a1344 (2008).

14. Razquin, C., et al. "The Mediterranean diet protects against waist circumference enlargement in 12Ala carriers for the PPARgamma gene: 2 years' follow-up of 774 subjects at high cardiovascular risk." *Br J Nutr* 102, 672–79 (2009).

15. Ibarrola-Jurado, N., et al. "Cross-sectional assessment of nut consumption and obesity, metabolic syndrome and other cardiometabolic risk factors: the PREDIMED study." *PLoS One* 8, e57367 (2013).

CHAPTER 7: BUILDING A DIET THAT WORKS

1. Hertog, M. G., et al. "Flavonoid intake and long-term risk of coronary heart disease and cancer in the seven countries study." *Arch Intern Med* 155, 381–86 (1995).

2. Ibid.

3. Biagi, M., and Bertelli, A. A. "Wine, alcohol and pills: what future for the French paradox?" *Life Sci* 131, 19–22 (2015).

4. Ortuño, J., et al. "Matrix effects on the bioavailability of resveratrol in humans." *Food Chem* 120, 1123–30 (2010).

5. Gupta, Subash C., et al. "Curcumin, a component of turmeric: from farm to pharmacy." *Biofactors* 39, 2–13 (2013).

6. Eseberri, I., Miranda, J., Lasa, A., Churruca, I., and Portillo, M. P. "Doses of quercetin in the range of serum concentrations exert delipidating effects in 3T3-L1 preadipocytes by acting on different stages of adipogenesis, but not in mature adipocytes." *Oxid Med Cell Longev* 2015, 480943 (2015).

7. Scheepens, A., Tan, K., and Paxton, J. W. "Improving the oral bioavailability of beneficial polyphenols through designed synergies." *Genes Nutr* 5, 75–87 (2010).

8. Bohn, T. "Dietary factors affecting polyphenol bioavailability." *Nutr Rev* 72, 429–52 (2014).

9. Yu, Y., et al. "Green tea catechins: a fresh flavor to anticancer therapy." *Apoptosis* 19, 1–18 (2014).

10. Bohn, "Dietary factors affecting polyphenol bioavailability."

11. Yao, K., Duan, Y., Tan, B., Hou, Y., Wu, G., and Yin, Y. "Leucine in obesity: therapeutic prospects." *Trends Pharmacol Sci* 8 (2016).

12. Bruckbauer, A., and Zemel, M. B. "Synergistic effects of polyphenols and methylxanthines with Leucine on AMPK/Sirtuin-mediated metabolism in muscle cells and adipocytes." *PLoS One* 9, e89166 (2014).

13. Feldman, J. L., Baeza, J., and Denu, J. M. "Activation of the

protein deacetylase SIRT6 by long-chain fatty acids and wide-spread deacylation by mammalian sirtuins." *J Biol Chem* 288, 31350–56 (2013).

14. Antunes, L. C., Levandovski, R., Dantas, G., Caumo, W., and Hidalgo, M. P. "Obesity and shift work: chronobiological aspects." *Nutr Res Rev* 23, 155–68 (2010).

15. Pan, A., Schernhammer, E. S., Sun, Q., and Hu, F. B. "Rotating night shift work and risk of type 2 diabetes: two prospective cohort studies in women." *PLoS Med* 8, e1001141 (2011).

16. Ribas-Latre, A., and Eckel-Mahan, K. "Interdependence of nutrient metabolism and the circadian clock system: importance for metabolic health." *Mol Metab* 5, 133–52 (2016).

17. Wegner, D. M., Schneider, D. J., Carter, S. R. 3rd, and White, T. L. "Paradoxical effects of thought suppression." *J Pers Soc Psychol* 53, 5–13 (1987).

CHAPTER 8: TOP TWENTY SIRTFOODS

1. Bastian, B., Jetten, J., and Ferris, L. J. "Pain as social glue: shared pain increases cooperation." *Psychol Sci* 25, 2079–85 (2014).

2. Lv, J., et al. "Consumption of spicy foods and total and cause specific mortality: population-based cohort study." *BMJ* 351, h3942 (2015).

3. Ding, M., Bhupathiraju, S. N., Chen, M., van Dam, R. M., and Hu, F. B. "Caffeinated and decaffeinated coffee consumption and risk of type 2 diabetes: a systematic review and a dose-response meta-analysis." *Diabetes Care* 37, 569–86 (2014).

4. Bohn, S. K., Blomhoff, R., and Paur, I. "Coffee and cancer risk,

epidemiological evidence, and molecular mechanisms." *Mol Nutr Food Res* 58, 915–30 (2014).

5. Wirdefeldt, K., Adami, H. O., Cole, P., Trichopoulos, D., and Mandel, J. "Epidemiology and etiology of Parkinson's disease: a review of the evidence." *Eur J Epidemiol* 26 Suppl 1, S1–58 (2011).

6. Masterton, G. S., and Hayes, P. C. "Coffee and the liver: a potential treatment for liver disease?" *Eur J Gastroenterol Hepatol* 22, 1277–83 (2010).

7. Hosseini, A., and Hosseinzadeh, H. "A review on the effects of Allium sativum (Garlic) in metabolic syndrome." *J Endocrinol Invest* 38, 1147–157 (2015).

8. Fialová, J., Roberts, S. C., and Havlíček, J. "Consumption of garlic positively affects hedonic perception of axillary body odour." *Appetite* 97, 8–15 (2016).

9. Alkaabi, J. M., et al. "Glycemic indices of five varieties of dates in healthy and diabetic subjects." *Nutr J* 10, 59 (2011).

10. Vayalil, P. K. "Date fruits (Phoenix dactylifera Linn): an emerging medicinal food." *Crit Rev Food Sci Nutr* 52, 249–71 (2012).

11. Baliga, M. S., Baliga, B. R. V., Kandathil, S. M., Bhat, H. P., and Vayalil, P. K. "A review of the chemistry and pharmacology of the date fruits (Phoenix dactylifera L.)." *Food Res Int* 44, 1812–22 (2011).

12. Takkouche, B., et al. "Intake of wine, beer, and spirits and the risk of clinical common cold." *Am J Epidemiol* 155, 853–58 (2002).

13. Muñoz-González, I., Thurnheer, T., Bartolomé, B., and Moreno-Arribas, M. V. "Red wine and oenological extracts

display antimicrobial effects in an oral bacteria biofilm model."
J Agric Food Chem 62, 4731–37 (2014).

14. Torronen, R., et al. "Berries reduce postprandial insulin responses to wheat and rye breads in healthy women." *J Nutr* 143, 430–36 (2013).

CHAPTER 9: PHASE 1: 7 POUNDS IN SEVEN DAYS

1. Niseteo, T., et al. "Bioactive composition and antioxidant potential of different commonly consumed coffee brews affected by their preparation technique and milk addition." *Food Chem* 134, 1870–77 (2012).

2. Hursel, R., and Westerterp-Plantenga, M. S. "Consumption of milk-protein combined with green tea modulates diet-induced thermogenesis." *Nutrients* 3, 725–33 (2011).

3. Green, R. J., Murphy, A. S., Schulz, B., Watkins, B. A., and Ferruzzi, M. G. "Common tea formulations modulate in vitro digestive recovery of green tea catechins." *Mol Nutr Food Res* 51, 1152–62 (2007).

CHAPTER 11: SIRTFOODS FOR LIFE

1. Melnik, B. C. "Milk—a nutrient system of mammalian evolution promoting mTORC1-dependent translation." *Int J Mol Sci* 16, 17048–87 (2015).

2. Liu, M., et al. "Resveratrol inhibits mTOR signaling by promoting the interaction between mTOR and DEPTOR." *J Biol Chem* 285, 36387–94 (2010).

3. Aune, D., et al. "Dairy products and colorectal cancer risk: a

systematic review and meta-analysis of cohort studies." *Ann Oncol* 23, 37–45 (2012).

4. Aune, D., et al. "Dairy products, calcium, and prostate cancer risk: a systematic review and meta-analysis of cohort studies." *Am J Clin Nutr* 101, 87–117 (2015).

5. Davoodi, H., Esmaeili, S., and Mortazavian, A. "Effects of milk and milk products consumption on cancer: a review." *Compr Rev Food Sci Food Saf* 12, 249–64 (2013).

6. Wiseman, M. "The second World Cancer Research Fund/American Institute for Cancer Research expert report. Food, nutrition, physical activity, and the prevention of cancer: a global perspective." *Proc Nutr Soc* 67, 253–56 (2008).

7. Persson, E., Graziani, G., Ferracane, R., Fogliano, V., and Skog, K. "Influence of antioxidants in virgin olive oil on the formation of heterocyclic amines in fried beefburgers." *Food Chem Toxicol* 41, 1587–97 (2003).

8. Gibis, M. "Effect of oil marinades with garlic, onion, and lemon juice on the formation of heterocyclic aromatic amines in fried beef patties." *J Agric Food Chem* 55, 10240–47 (2007).

9. Rohrmann, S., Hermann, S., and Linseisen, J. "Heterocyclic aromatic amine intake increases colorectal adenoma risk: findings from a prospective European cohort study." *Am J Clin Nutr* 89, 1418–24 (2009).

10. Nerurkar, P. V., Le Marchand, L., and Cooney, R. V. "Effects of marinating with Asian marinades or western barbecue sauce on PhIP and MeIQx formation in barbecued beef." *Nutr Cancer* 34, 147–52 (1999).

11. Rong, Y., et al. "Egg consumption and risk of coronary heart disease and stroke: dose-response meta-analysis of prospective cohort studies." *BMJ* 346, e8539 (2013).

12. Craig, W. J., Mangels, A. R., and American Dietetic Association. "Position of the American Dietetic Association: vegetarian diets." *J Am Diet Assoc* 109, 1266–82 (2009).

13. Appleby, P., Roddam, A., Allen, N., and Key, T. "Comparative fracture risk in vegetarians and nonvegetarians in EPIC-Oxford." *Eur J Clin Nutr* 61, 1400–1406 (2007).

14. Krajcovicova-Kudlackova, M., Buckova, K., Klimes, I., and Sebokova, E. "Iodine deficiency in vegetarians and vegans." *Ann Nutr Metab* 47, 183–85 (2003).

Index